W9-BUE-565

THE VOICES OF HEAVEN

BOOKS BY FREDERIK POHL

Bipohl
>*The Age of the Pussyfoot*
>*Drunkard's Walk*

Black Star Rising

The Cool War

The Heechee Saga
>*Gateway*
>*Beyond the Blue Event Horizon*
>*Heechee Rendezvous*
>*The Annals of the Heechee*
>*The Gateway Trip*

Homegoing

Mining the Oort

Narabedla Ltd.

Pohlstars

Starburst

The Way the Future Was

The World at the End of Time

Jem

Midas World

Merchant's War

The Coming of the Quantum Cats

The Space Merchants (with C. M. Kornbluth)

Man Plus

Chernobyl

The Day the Martians Came

Stopping at Slowyear

With Jack Williamson:
>*Undersea City*
>*Undersea Quest*
>*Undersea Fleet*
>*Wall Around a Star*
>*The Farthest Star*
>**Land's End*
>*The Singers of Time*

With Lester del Rey:
>*Preferred Risk*

The Best of Frederik Pohl (edited by Lester del Rey)
The Best of C. M. Kornbluth (editor)

*denotes a Tor Book

THE VOICES
OF
HEAVEN

Frederik Pohl

A Tom Doherty Associates Book

NEW YORK

This is a work of fiction. All the characters and events portrayed in this book are fictitious, and any resemblance to real people or events is purely coincidental.

THE VOICES OF HEAVEN
Copyright © 1994 by Frederik Pohl
All rights reserved, including the right to reproduce this book, or portions thereof, in any form.

Edited by James Frenkel

A Tor Book
Published by Tom Doherty Associates, Inc.
175 Fifth Avenue
New York, N.Y. 10010

Tor ® is a registered trademark of Tom Doherty Associates, Inc.

ISBN 0-312-85643-1

Printed in the United States of America

THE VOICES OF HEAVEN

1

*A*RE *you ready, Barrydihoa? Good. Do not be nervous.*

I'm not nervous. I'm concerned. I have a right to be; this is pretty important to us.

That is understood. Simply commence; we wish you to begin by describing the circumstances of your first meeting with Garoldtscharka.

Please.

Yes, of course, Barrydihoa. The correction is noted. Please.

The first time I met Captain Garold Tscharka was on his ship, *Corsair*. He was in a bad mood. The ship had just come back from the Pava colony, and it was parked in Low Lunar Orbit. The way things looked, it was going to be staying there for a while, because of the brouhaha about the interstellar colonies that was going on in the Congresses.

The reason I was there was that it was my job. I was employed by the Lederman factory as ships' fuelmaster, which meant I was in charge of the crews that defueled and refueled spaceships. It was a good job, too. I'd held it for four years at that time, having taken nearly eight years to work up to it after I left the Belt. Since the fuel was antimatter the job carried a heavy load of responsibility.

(I know you don't have any real idea of what antimatter is, but you don't really need to. Take my word for it, it's dangerous stuff. One little pod of antimatter can do more damage than any volcano you ever saw.)

Refueling spaceships was the kind of work where you really had to keep your mind on what you're doing, but it paid well. Actually, the hours were easy. Eight or ten times a lunar day—say about every four weeks of Earth time—I hopped a shuttle from the lunar surface to go up to a ship in a parking orbit. Sometimes I took a crew along with me to do the actual work. Sometimes I just made the trip by myself so I could inspect the fuel storage and make sure everything was kosher for the crew to get to work.

Naturally, nearly all the ships we serviced were interplanetary vessels, all kinds of them, everything from the little fifty-ton Space Service scouts to twelve- or fifteen-thousand-ton transports. Those were pretty routine—at least, as much as anything involving antimatter is routine. Once the ships were defueled they were safe enough to be worked on, so any repairs they needed could be done right there in lunar orbit. Then we'd fuel them up again and they'd be gone.

Captain Tscharka's ship, though, was a different kind of thing entirely. *Corsair* wasn't a short-ranger. It was a full-fledged interstellar colony-support ship, with a cruising radius of well over a dozen light-years. It was one of the very few I'd ever even seen of that long-ranging kind, much less worked on. *Corsair* was one of the half dozen dedicated transports that ferried people and goods back and forth to the colony on the planet called Pava.

At that particular moment, however, it looked as though *Corsair* might not be doing that much longer. That was what had put Tscharka in such a lousy mood. He was almost alone on the ship when I got there, with only a standby crew of two or three people left on board to keep the life-support systems going. Actually, I hadn't expected to find the captain there at all. Very few captains bother to stay on a ship in parking orbit—which was fine with me. I preferred it that way, because captains get real possessive about their ships and then they can be a major nuisance.

Which Captain Tscharka definitely was. As soon as I was aboard he came rocketing along a corridor, hand over hand, to see what I was doing. "Who're you?" he demanded.

"I'm Barry di Hoa, fuelmaster."

"What, have they changed the system again?"

"I don't know what it was last time you were here," I said, as patiently as I could. "This is the way we do it now. I'll be cleaning out your fuel supply."

He took offense at that. "It's clean already. I checked it myself."

"That's good. It'll make it easier when I check it again," I told him. He still looked as though he'd have much preferred if I wasn't there, but was quiet.

Supervising the removal of a ship's empty antimatter fuel pods is about the meanest of my jobs. You can't afford to take any shortcuts, because you don't want some tiny chunk of residual antimatter in a fuel pod when you refill it. So you want to make absolutely sure that the pods are empty before you bring them back down to the Moon for refill. That's just common sense, because everybody knows what a speck of antimatter can do if it ever touches ordinary matter, so you'd think every ship's captain would be conscientious about it. They aren't, though. So when a fuelmaster boards a returning ship he takes his life in his hands, and that was why my pay was so high.

Tscharka was still suspicious. "Are you going to do it by yourself?" he called from behind me as I started toward the main fuel store.

"I'm not going to do it at all. This is just preliminary inspection. I'll bring a crew up if I find any fuel that needs to be removed."

"You won't."

I didn't answer that.

I don't know how many of these little quirks of mammalian behavior you want me to explain to you, but, hey, you can always tell me to shut up and get on with it. The thing is, under some circumstances I think I would have liked Captain Tscharka. He was a short, dark fellow, quick and smart; a likeable person in general, you would have to say, but there was something about him that graveled me. He was one of the captains who follow you every minute of the time you're on his ship. He wasn't very courteous about it, either.

On the other hand, give the devil his due, Tscharka had left *Corsair* spotlessly clean. I appreciated that not an atom of antimatter remained in the expended pods. Every emptied pod was stripped, demagnetized, and open to prove it. "Nice job," I said, meaning it. He didn't acknowledge the compliment. There was a scowl on his face. "Captain Tscharka," I said, "am I doing something you don't like?"

The scowl stayed on his face, but his eyes were on something a long way away, and I wasn't it. A moment later he shook his head as though waking up. "What did you say?"

"I said, 'Am I doing something you don't like?' "

"Oh," he said, focusing on me. "No, I don't think so. Sorry. I was thinking of something else. Do you know they're talking about terminating Pava?"

"Well, yes," I said, because of course I did know. The debate in the Tax & Budget Congress had been going on for years. Not just about Pava, either. Delta Pavonis wasn't the only star with a planet that somebody once had thought was worth colonizing, and with the budget-cutters riding high in the Congress, all four of the extrasolar colonies were on shaky ground. Pava, as the farthest away, had just been the last to hear about it.

Evidently Tscharka had taken the news hard. He was still mad. "They say they want to use the funds to build more habitats here. That's insanity!"

I pulled myself a little farther away. "Don't blame me," I said. "Look, let me get on with the inspection. I have to get back to the surface."

Well, what I said was true, I did have to get back because I had something I wanted to do that day—that Earth day. But I had plenty of time to get my call to Earth through. Mostly I just didn't want to argue the subject of colony funding with somebody as touchy as Captain Garold Tscharka.

I've known too many people like Tscharka. Whatever their registered religious orientation may be, they all have one secular belief that they hold with great passion: that it is a sin to waste tax money on frills, except when the frill in question is one of their own.

I should concede that at that time I did personally consider the extrasolar colonies a particularly useless and ill-considered frill. I'd never seen any real reason for trying to colonize planets of other stars. I mean, why bother?

People had given all sorts of reasons for it when they started the programs, but the reasons were silly. Some said we had to have these extrasolar outposts as a matter of security, to give us some kind of Distant Early Warning in case some twelve-armed, big-brained, high-tech alien space invaders came charging out of the core of the galaxy to destroy our cities and carry off our women—or whatever. That might have seemed to be a persuasive kind of lunacy once, I mean, considering the way Colonial Americans, for instance, used to build forts all over to protect against Indian raids. But no such bloodthirsty alien invaders have ever turned up, and we've kind of got out of the habit of wars anyway, haven't we?

Then some said we'd need the colonies to give us a home for our surplus huddled masses, yearning to be free—the way Australia and the Americas were for Europe. That doesn't make any sense either. You can't make much of a dent in ten billion huddled masses when you have to cart them away fifty or a hundred at a time.

It didn't matter what they said; I thought the project made no sense at all. There was only one real reason for planting human beings in places so far away—Pava's Delta Pavonis is nearly nineteen light-years from Earth, and even the planet around Alpha Centauri B is over four—and that was just to be doing something humongous. Showing off, that is. My old chief headshrinker, Dr. Helmut Schneyman, used to say that the interstellar colonies were our Pyramids. You know? Like the old Pharaohs of Egypt. (Well, no, you don't know, but what that means is that they were showy, enormously expensive, and with no known sensible reason for existence.)

Of course, the colonists on those planets didn't agree. Not the ones who stayed there, anyway, but those weren't the ones who were heard on Earth. The colonists who stuck it out were way out *there*, and the rejects, the ones who gave up and came back home, they were *here*. You'd see a few of the returnees every time a colony-support ship came in, the people who had taken the long, slow, frozen sleep to another star, and when they got there decided it wasn't what they had really wanted at all. They almost always got interviewed on the news programs. They all said how hard life was out there and how little fun. So they were the ones the voters at home heard from . . . except when some consecrated zealot like Captain Tscharka showed up.

(You know, it's funny that I should have thought of the word "consecrated" in connection with him even then—I mean, even before I knew just how consecrated Captain Garold Tscharka really was.)

Tscharka stuck to me like a hangnail all around his ship. I do mean all around it, too, because that's where I went. A good fuelmaster doesn't stop with inspecting the fuel chambers. I looked for radioactivity everywhere, but all I found was quaintness. *Corsair* was a pretty quaint old ship. All interstellar ships are, more or less, but this one had made two round-trips to Pava—eighteen-plus light-years away. That came to a

trip-time of over twenty Earth years each way. So *Corsair* had to have
been built the better part of a hundred years ago. It was definitely the
oldest ship I'd ever been on.

The crew quarters were particularly ancient. I'd seen flatscreen vids
and optical-chip computers as a boy, back on Earth, but not in the last
twenty years or more. "So this is where you live en route," I said,
making the mistake of making conversation as I poked the radiation
scanners around.

"It's where we *work*."

I didn't argue that, though I could have—crews of interstellar ships
don't impress me, because they have damn-all work to do. Once you've
programmed the machines, they fly the ships. (There was a little bit of
snobbishness there too, I admit. When I flew a spotter ship in the Belt,
I *flew* it.) I offered, "It'd be easier if you had some new equipment. I
guess all this stuff is due for refit?"

"What for? It all works." And of course it did; the ship might have
been built a hundred years ago, but it wasn't a hundred years *old*. Most
of that time had never passed for the fittings, or for the ship, or for
Tscharka himself. "No," he said, "I'll not ask an extra penny for things
that are not needed. Pava colony is only asking for what it needs. The
Congress can't refuse us."

I nodded—not to agree, because I didn't, but only to show that I had
understood what he said. "All clean here," I reported, and we went on
to the corpsicle store. That was truly ancient. I'd never seen one like it
before, hexagonal coffins the length of a tall man, clustered like pencils
held with a rubber band. All those colonist pods were empty now, of
course, open and waiting for the poor suckers who would volunteer to
get into them, and all were radiation-clean.

And then we went to the cargo holds, and one of those was a real
surprise. It was as radiation-clean and empty as the freezers, but antimatter warning signs were plastered all over it.

I stared at the captain. "We're requisitioning two hundred extra fuel
pods," he said, sounding truculent.

Two *hundred* extra pods? Nobody needed that much antimatter; I
couldn't help asking, "What in God's name for?"

If he had been scowling at something invisible before, now the black
look was all aimed at me. "I would be grateful, di Hoa," he said
frostily, "if you would refrain from taking the Lord's name in vain
before me."

"Sorry. But hell—I mean, but really, you can't carry that many pods!"

"Not on *Corsair*, no. We'll have space for a hundred. The other hundred will follow us on *Buccaneer*."

"*Buccaneer*?"

"*Buccaneer*'s another of Pava's colony-support ships. It was still unloading when we left. I'd guess it's about two months behind us from Pava; it'll take the rest of the fuel."

Considering that the very fate of the colony was up for grabs, I admired his confidence. I didn't argue it, but I still had that big question in my mind. "It's not really my department, but what do you want with all that fuel?"

"No," he said, "it isn't your department. It is not your business at all, but I'll tell you anyway. We want the pods to fuel our short-range ships. We're going to begin a program of exploration of the other planets in our system."

Even then, that sounded improbable. I tried to be tactful. "I didn't realize the Pava colony had the resources for exploring other planets."

He gave me an amiable shrug. "I'm just the delivery boy for the message. It's the colony that voted for the ships. Oh," he said fairly, "it's not just exploration. They expect to build some tugs and use them to go out to the asteroids—Delta Pavonis doesn't have as big a belt as Sol, but there are quite a few metal-bearing ones out there—and haul them in to the orbital factory for raw materials. That makes sense, doesn't it? It certainly beats shipping bulk metals out there from Earth."

He made it all sound so plausible. Of course, it was all a lie, but I didn't know it then. Then it was just another surprise. "So you've got a fleet of short-range ships out there?"

He shook his head. "No," he said, sounding pissed off again, "we did not, not when I left. But they should be building now. By the time I get back I expect they will be completed and all set to go—as soon as they get fuel."

It sounded plausible. What you have to keep in mind about these interstellar-ship people is that by the time they get back to where they've come from, half a century or so will have passed. That elapsed time doesn't show on the people themselves, of course—Tscharka didn't look much older than I was. Well, he shouldn't have. In spite of the fact that he had been born maybe a century earlier, he wasn't older in any sense that mattered. He had spent most of the in-flight years at velocities so close to light-speed that time-dilation took over, and although the elapsed time for each trip was close to a quarter of a century, the perceived transit times were cut to not much more than a year or two—even for the ones who had to work while they were aboard and so stayed out of the freezers.

Of course, as we all know by now, there weren't really any short-range ships building out around Delta Pavonis. That was just more of the lie Tscharka and his buddies had cooked up when they had heard about the Congress debates. I don't know what his plan had been before then, but it doesn't really matter anymore anyway, does it?

By then I'd checked everything there was to check. I looked at my watch and said, "Good enough, Captain Tscharka. Let's sign off so we can both get out of here."

"Fine," he said, and led the way back to his cabin. While he was setting up the documentation on his screen a young woman appeared with capsules of coffee. She was part of the standby crew, and pretty, too, I saw at once—though maybe not as pretty as my own girl, Alma.

He introduced her as his copilot, Jillen something-or-other, and then he gave me an embarrassed grin. "Look, di Hoa, I'm sorry if I was a bastard to you. I'm kind of on edge."

"I don't blame you. I mean, if you really care about the colony."

"I do. I hope we can work it out. I'm expecting a call about the Congress." He was looking angry again. "I didn't think I'd find so many heretics on the Congress. It wasn't that way when I left."

I get uneasy around people who use words like "heretics," so I didn't answer that, and he went back to studying his screen.

The copilot had left us, and I "sat" down—you know, latched myself to a wall rest, the way you do in microgravity. I wasn't really thinking about Tscharka anymore. I was thinking about the Earth call I was going to make to wish my son a happy birthday, trying to decide what I was going to say. So I just waited for Tscharka to finish running his program, while I gazed at the wall display that showed the broad gray-brown surface of the Moon rolling under us. It was only a vidscreen, but I could recognize most of the peaks and craters. I could even pick out the narrow, bright line of the immense photovoltaic belt that girdled the Moon and gave us the power to run the accelerators that made the antimatter that fueled ships like the *Corsair*. The Lederman antimatter factory community itself—the place where I lived and worked—was out of sight below the horizon.

When the captain handed me the finished document screen, I read it over quickly; it said what it was supposed to say, namely that I certified that I had examined the *Corsair* and found its antimatter fuel stores empty, except for the small amount left to run the ship's standby systems. I signed it and thumbed it, and added my serial code; and then, just as I was holding it out to him, the captain got a call.

"Wait," he ordered, and turned eagerly to the picture on the wall. The face on the screen belonged to a middle-aged Santa Claus–looking man, fat and bearded, looking tentatively pleased with himself.

"It's not going to be as bad as we thought, Garold," the fat man said. "The Congress has agreed to give us a hearing, and we're on in a little over five hours. Will you be down to get in on it in time?"

"I'll land on the next orbit, Tuck," the captain promised, and signed off.

When he saw that I still had the screen in my hand he actually smiled. "Sorry about that. That was Reverend Tuchman. He's my chaplain."

"It sounded like good news."

"I hope so. If they give us a hearing they won't be able to turn us down. It's not," he explained, "as though we were *costing* the taxpayers much anymore. All the important money was spent long ago. The ships are all built. The colony's established. All we need is supplies."

"And a lot of antimatter," I reminded him.

He shrugged that off. "God's work must be done whatever it costs," he said. "Are you through with the screen?"

"Almost," I said, but before I handed it over I peeked at his serial code. He had piqued my curiosity, and I wanted a look at his basic data. Particularly his religious affiliation. Not many captains talked so much about God's work and traveled with a chaplain in their entourage, and not many people of any kind called other people heretics in this day and age.

My expression must have shown something, because Tscharka demanded sharply, "Is something wrong?"

"Oh, no," I said. "Not at all." And that was true, because there was nothing wrong about his being registered to the Penitential Church of the Millennium, it was just that I had never encountered a Millenarist space captain before. As it happened, I knew quite a lot about the Millenarists—more than I really wanted to, in fact—because my girl, Alma, had once been one.

* * *

I wasn't *prejudiced* against Millenarists. There were too many religions around—and some of them a lot weirder and nastier than Millenarism— for me to throw a stone at anyone's religious beliefs, especially since I didn't have any to speak of of my own. Millenarists had been around for a long time, one way or another. The current version called itself Penitential, and its adherents certainly were that. The Millenarists believed that the Bible promised the world would come to an end a thousand years after the birth of Christ and then at that Millennium the earth would open and all the dead would rise—the living too, I guess— and they'd all be singing and praising God as they headed straight for heaven's eternal joy.

It was as good a central dogma as any, if you didn't mind that actually it hadn't happened. The year 1000 A.D. had come and gone, and— oops, back to the drawing board—the Second Coming didn't come.

The Millenarists had figured that one out, though. They said the human race had been just too steeped in sin for that promised salvation, and everything that had happened after the year 1000 A.D. had simply added additional sin on top of all the sins that had gone before. That wasn't all of it. The main tenet of their belief was that, although everything was sinful, some things were less sinful than others. In their view, about the least sinful thing any Millenarist could do in this sinful world was to die and get out of it before it got any worse.

That was why you hardly ever saw an *old* Millenarist. They started out as converts—there weren't any born Millenarists, because bringing a child into the world of sin was about the most sinful thing of all— and the converts didn't usually stick around for more than ten or twenty years, tops. By the time they were around fifty they had usually taken their final step—either out of Millenarism, or out of life itself.

My girl Alma's Millenarist period was before I ever met her. She had joined up when she was just recently arrived on the Moon, and therefore naturally a little bit homesick and depressed—in other words, just the kind of person the Millenarists looked for to recruit. They did. They welcomed her, and comforted her, and took her in, and before very long Alma made her confession of faith.

That was that. She was a duly enrolled Millenarist.

When she filed her affiliation the supervisors at the Lederman factory made her sign a guarantee that she wouldn't make trouble by deciding to kill herself while on duty in a sensitive area. That's a standard precaution they take at the Lederman plant. Outside of that her life wasn't much changed. For nearly a year she went to services, until the two Millenarist circuit-riding preachers from Earth showed up one day. They were red-hots, Alma said. In the jargon of the Millenarist church, they were called "finalists." They were the ones who had passed the point of just *believing* and were getting ready to act their beliefs out. They turned up at one Sunday's services as honored guests, and when they told the congregation what they were going to do they looked (Alma said) so happy and righteous and, well, so *saved* that she thought for a moment she was going to cry.

What they were going to do was commit suicide.

The younger one said, joyously, that they couldn't escape sin—the whole world was sinning just by being alive—but by dying they could stop being *accomplices* to sin. The older one said, lovingly, that if any of the lunar congregation wanted to join them they would be glad for the company.

They were very convincing, Alma said. Still, none of the congregation volunteered to remove themselves from this vale of tears with them at that first service.

Alma didn't much want to do that, either. She said she believed at the time that they had the right idea, and she thought that that was going to be the right thing to do, someday or other. Not now, though. And yet they seemed so righteously sure of themselves that at the next Saturday's service, without having planned it, she got carried away with the sermon and the singing and all the hosannahs. "I didn't start out to volunteer for finalization," she told me. "Just all of a sudden, there I was, walking right up to the altar, while the rest of the congregation was smiling and applauding me, and I told them I was ready."

Fine, they said, beaming approval at her. Just sign here.

What she had to sign was the standard release form to say that they had not used any form of coercion on her, as indeed they hadn't unless you consider those brainwashing exercises they called sermons coercion. As soon as her consent was on the screen they said, "All right, then, let's get it done."

And so she went with them to their room. She was the only volunteer.

Alma gets sort of tongue-tied when she gets to that part of the story, but I think I can piece it together. They told her they were really yearning to die, but they couldn't indulge themselves that way because their mission wasn't complete yet. Before they could take that gladsome release for themselves they wanted to make sure any worthy person could join them, so they wouldn't actually keep her company at that moment.

They would, however, help her.

"How?" she asked.

"We'll advise you. Hanging is the best way," they said. "There are hundreds of alternatives, of course, and you can use one of them if you prefer. The reason we recommend hanging is for the church's legal protection, really, so the seculars can't trump up some charge against us. Nobody can try to prove homicide when somebody hangs herself, and you know how the heretics are."

"It made sense," she told me. "At the time."

Then they opened their trunk and handed her a coil of rope, and they showed her how to hook it to the lighting fixture, and how to climb onto the room's one straight-backed chair and kick herself off it. . . .

Of course, the important thing to remember is that these two saviors were just fresh up from Earth.

Alma wasn't. She'd been on the Moon for over a year. She should have known better. On the other hand, as she now says, she wasn't really thinking very clearly at that moment. She was in a sort of trance of exultation, and so she did as they instructed.

And then when she kicked herself loose and fell with the noose around her neck, the Moon's gentle gravity just wasn't strong enough to break her neck.

It didn't even strangle her. It came pretty close, she says, close enough to make her gag and feel as though she were going to pass out for a moment; but not so close that she didn't have time to change her mind and claw the noose off, and push her way out of the room, choking and crying and rubbing her throat and feeling like a fool, with the two finalists reproachfully calling after her; and she never, never went back to the Millenarist services again.

2

---

*Y*OU *have touched on a principal concern. As you are aware, we have difficulty in understanding why your human custom of "religions" is so important to you. Tell us more about them, your own in particular.*

You're asking me about two different things at the same time. Which one do you want answered?

Both of them. Please.

There's not much to tell about my own religion. I don't actually have one, I mean not one that I take very seriously. My parents were Western Orthodox and that's the way I was brought up, but it didn't last.

Probably my medical problems were what made me drop out, because they were hellish enough for anybody. After you spend a couple of years in the particular hell of a crazyhouse you come out of it one of two ways—either you'll believe with all your heart in anything that sounds as though it gives you some kind of hope, or you won't believe in anything at all. I went the second way. I suppose I was helped in that direction by my main therapist, Dr. Schneyman, who was unregistered himself. (He liked to quote some old guy named Benjamin Franklin, who said, "In the affairs of this world men are saved, not by faith, but by the want of it.") By the time they decided I could be allowed to go out into the world again I'd lost a lot of things. My religious belief was only one of them.

Of course, you run into a lot of practical problems if you're not registered to some recognized religious denomination—like not having anyone to vote for, for instance. So when I came to start a new life on the Moon I let myself be registered as Orthodox, meaning what they used to call "Easter Duty Orthodox." What that means is that I went to mass on the main church holidays, sometimes—if I happened to think of it at the right time and if I couldn't remember any really private recent sins that I would be embarrassed to have to confess to.

That brings us to the other part of your question, which is harder. There's no way I could name all the human religions for you. There are too many of them. There are maybe fifteen or twenty main groups, and all kinds of denominations within each group.

You could start out with the Christians, which is what I more or less was. There are two main classes of Christians: There's the Protestants, which includes the Pentecostals and the Baptists and the Fundamentalists and about forty others, most of them divided into eight or ten different sects, including the Millenarists (like Captain Tscharka) and the four or five varieties of Quakers and Old Believers and Amish and Universalists and so on. Then there's the Orthodox wing of Christianity. The Orthodox have the two big sects, Western and Roman, but there are maybe twenty littler ones there, too, like the Lifers, the True-Lifers and the patriarchates. And somewhere or other you have to put in the Christians that aren't either one or the other, like the Gnostics and Mormons and so on.

Then we get to the non-Christians, starting with the Jews—I think there are at least fifteen or twenty different varieties of those, ranging from Hassidim (including the Lubavitchers) and the Templars to the Church of Jewish Science—and to Islam, with its three major branches, Shi'ite, Suni and Reformed, and maybe half a dozen divisions of each. Then there are the Eastern religions and the African ones—I don't even remember the names of most of those, apart from Tao, Shinto and Kwanzaa and a few others like Buddhism (both Orthodox and Soka Gakkai) and Ryuho Okawa Happy Science. Most of those don't do much proselytizing, so they're pretty well confined to where they started—where, I guess, they have enough problems to keep themselves occupied. Still, they elect enough Congresspeople to be an important swing vote sometimes.

Finally we wind up with the exotics—different kinds of Rosicrucians,

Spiritualists, Scientologists, Reincarnationists, Astrologists and so on—
and the ancient revivals—Druids, Olympians, snake-handlers, Osiris
people, Wiccans, Odinists, Pyramiders, Zoroastians, Thugs and about
a million others, right down to the devotees of the Karnut Temple Rat
Cult. Of course, on the Moon some of the weirder denominations are
out of luck (due, for instance, to a local shortage of snakes or rats), and
others are hampered because it's against the law to practice some of
their commandments. (Like the ZPG-Thugs. Their mixture of Zero
Population Growth and Thuggee still has some churches in California,
but you never see them on the Moon.) They all get along, more or less.
The only sect that I remember making any real trouble in the lunar
Lederman colony were the Odinists. That happened when an opera
troupe doing *Das Rheingold* gave the role of Wotan to a Japanese singer.
The Odinists called that blasphemy and tried (unsuccessfully) to black
out the broadcast, but since there were only seven of the Odinists
altogether they couldn't work up a real riot.

(I won't even mention the secular churches that aren't really religions,
exactly. They aren't allowed to have any representatives in the Congresses, but people belong to them so they'll have places to go to
when everybody else is going to church; these are the Communals, the
Ethicals, the Rationalists, and the Humanists.)

I don't know what the total number of religious sects is. Maybe there
are a thousand or so that are large enough, and well enough organized,
to have their own official electoral constituencies, but there are thousands and thousands of splinter groups that are too small or too new to
be registered.

Most of the registered ones, even, are too small to elect their own
people to the various world commissions. The legislative commissions
are usually dominated by Christians, Muslims and Jews, although there
are almost always a sprinkling of Taoists and Buddhists in the major
legislative commissions. They are considered less dogmatic than most
of the others, so their presence is encouraged to help cool down the
steamier arguments. Some of the small ones make common cause with
others, too, so they can run what they call a "fusion" ticket. Probably
every registered sect has at least a part of an elected legislator somewhere.

(You haven't asked me just how it happened that the religions ran the
governments, but I'll tell you anyway. It wasn't always that way. They
say that in the old days people used to vote for "political parties," but
all the parties got to look pretty much alike. Whatever people said their

"political" principles were, it turned out that they were generally voting their religions and their social and ethnic backgrounds anyway—sometimes with a lot of violence. It was simpler to cut out the middleman. I wouldn't say that solved all the problems, but at least we don't have much "car bombing" or "kneecapping" or "ethnic cleansing" going on anymore. Never mind what those things were. You don't want to know.)

That's the story on the churches. It may not quite be what you were asking about, I think. Probably what you really want to know is what all these denominations believe in.

That's a much harder question. I think that the principal thing, for most of them, is that their religious beliefs are tied up in some hope of eternal life. In the Western Orthodox church, for instance, we believe— or probably I should say *they* believe—that after you die you enter a kind of world of the spirit, and if you're good it's paradise and then you just live on forever in eternal joy of one kind or another. It's pretty much the same with most of the other religions, except that in some of their heavens you don't spend eternity singing hosannahs. Maybe you just get reincarnated and have to go through the whole thing all over again. Or maybe you just abandon all your individual, personal existence entirely and join some kind of universal Soul—I'm not too clear on some of them.

On the other hand, a lot of the religions hold that there's a down side to the afterlife, too. That means that if you've been a rotten person in your lifetime—or maybe if you just ate the wrong kind of food, or didn't make the right sacrifices, or missed attending a service even— when you die you are going to pay for it because then you are going to get punished for your sins by roasting (or something) in some kind of totally agonizing hell. Forever.

I know that doesn't make a whole lot of sense to you, but we ought to be getting used to that by now. You're different from us in too many ways—especially this one, since you people have never had to worry about an afterlife at all.

3

IT is not evident that you are helping your case, Barrydihoa. In your description of these humans—Garoldtscharka, the Tuch-man, the two males who proposed suicide to the female—it is clear that their behavior is quite disturbing. Are they "crazy," in the same sense that you yourself have been?

No, of course not. With them it wasn't psychosis. It was their religion.

This distinction is unclear. You have said that in your illness you are aware of objective events but you interpret them in nonrealistic ways. Does not "religion" also involve nonrealistic belief systems?

Well, yes, but they're really two different things. I mean, personally, I don't have any doubt that Millenarism is really crazy. I guess most religious people think that all the people who happen to believe in some religion other than their own are pretty loopy. When I was ten years old in catechism class you should've heard what my old parish priest had to say about the Mormons across the street, for instance.

But that sort of thing is *accepted*, and my kind of craziness wasn't. Not by anybody. Not even by me.

That's why I was so nervous about calling my son, you see. I guess every divorced father is a little tense about his kid's birthday, but not every father has not been in the same room with his son since the boy was two years old, asleep in his bed, and the father was bending over him with a butcher knife.

You heard me, a butcher knife. The kind of thing people kill people with. I don't think I had any actual intention of hurting Matthew. I was just very, very confused.

All the same, I think it was probably pretty lucky that my wife Gina— my *then* wife Gina, who is not my wife anymore for obvious reasons— happened to look into the bedroom just then. She screamed. I didn't hurt her, either. I just threw the knife into a corner and ran out of the room, babbling.

I couldn't run far enough to keep the police from catching me and putting me away, though; and that was the last time I ever saw my son in the flesh.

So, as I say, I was a little nervous on the flight down to the Lederman landing pad. I didn't talk much to Captain Tscharka, who was full of his own thoughts anyway. When we were docked the man he called his chaplain was waiting for him, looking excited. "It's looking good, Garold," he called, waddling over toward us, and then noticed me. "Who's he?" he demanded.

Tscharka introduced us. "Our fuelmaster, Barry di Hoa. Di Hoa, this is Reverend Tuchman."

He was bigger than he had looked on the screen, at least ten centimeters taller than I was, and he gave me a quick grip that was stronger than I had expected. Then he forgot me, drawing Tscharka away and telling him that he'd reserved telecom time for their testimony at the colony hearing. If I really noticed Tuchman at all, it was only because he was obviously sixty or so and Millenarists don't usually stick around that long. Then I forgot him, too—for the moment, anyway.

Normally I would have taken the subway through the crater wall to my office in the manufacturing compound—the community where Lederman people live is outside the wall for alleged safety reasons— but I was in a hurry. I found a privacy booth and made some calls. I logged in with my reports; I left messages for my crew to tell them that they wouldn't need to decommission *Corsair*'s fuel storage because it was already clean; I put through a call to my girlfriend, Alma Vendette.

I caught her just coming out of the shower. "You shouldn't answer the phone when you aren't dressed," I told her.

She looked at me innocently. Innocent is one of Alma's best looks; it goes with her blue eyes and gentle smile. "I put a towel on, didn't I? Anyway, I knew it was you. Are we on for today?"

"Give me half an hour. Meet you in Danny's."

"Danny's in half an hour," she said, blew me a kiss, and blanked the screen.

Then I took a deep breath, checked to make sure the privacy door was closed and put through my call to Earth.

It was my ex-wife who answered the phone.

"Hello, Gina," I said, noticing that, though she had put on a little weight, she still looked good. I didn't exactly love Gina anymore, and I certainly didn't blame her for the divorce (she didn't have much choice about that, with me in the nuthouse) or for remarrying this man Gerard (who, actually, seemed to be a pretty decent guy), but there was still some little strain in talking to her.

"Hi, Barry," she answered, the usual couple of seconds later that you get on a Moon-Earth call. "How've you been?"

I told her how I'd been, while I peered past her. The room behind her wasn't one I'd ever seen before—they'd moved since Christmas—and I was pretty sure it didn't look the way it usually looked anyway. Gerard and their jointly produced three-year-old daughter, Theris, were decorating the wallpic for the occasion. Racing little dots of colored light were spelling out "Happy Birthday Matthew" and the little girl was trying to draw a birthday cake with a penlight.

"I guess you want to talk to Matthew. He's in his room getting dressed, Barry. We're going to have a party. Wait, I'll switch you over."

"Thanks," I said, but she didn't wait to hear. The screen blanked while she told him he had my call, and when it lighted up again he was peering out at me.

"Happy sixteenth birthday, Matthew," I said to my son. He was taller and skinnier, but he still had Gina's clear, brown eyes.

He said politely, "Thank you, and thanks for the check you sent me, too, friend Barry."

"Friend Barry" meant he was still a Quaker; he'd been through five or six denominations since he was twelve. It was his business; I didn't comment. I saw crossed hockey sticks hanging on the wall behind him, so I asked him if he had made the team, and he had, and I asked him how school was going, and he told me his marks, and I asked him if he'd made any decision about college, and then he surprised me.

"I don't know if I'll go. I've been thinking of going out to a colony."

"An *interstellar* colony? No more asteroid mining?" (He'd talked about that a year earlier; I had been sort of pleased that he'd decided to follow in his father's footsteps as an asteroid miner—even though his father had quit the Belt before he was born.)

"I think I want to be part of making something," he said, sounding uncomfortable about discussing that sort of thing with his father.

"But there's a good chance they'll cancel the colonies."

"No, it doesn't look that way. I don't know if you follow the debates, friend Barry—" I didn't, not very closely, anyway. "But they say the Tax and Budget hearings are leaning toward keeping the colonies going."

"Well," I said, "that'll make Captain Garold Tscharka happy," and then I had to explain that by telling him how I'd just been servicing a genuine interstellar colony ship, and what it was like. So for a good five minutes or more he sounded really interested in what his father was up to. That's a big plus, you know. One of the hard parts of talking to your sixteen-year-old son no more than two or three times a year is discovering subjects he likes to talk about.

So we had a pleasant chat, and when I finally let him go to finish dressing for his guests I felt pretty good. Even a divorced and detached father likes to think there's still *something* between him and his one and only son . . . but you wouldn't understand about that, either, would you?

I don't think I've given you any idea of how comfortable our life was on the Lederman antimatter-factory colony on the Moon. Oh, it's a little worrisome, too, of course; you never really forget that you're living in the blast area of what might someday turn out to be the biggest explosion the human race has ever seen. But the colony had churches and theaters and sporting arenas—it was astonishing to watch a basketball game in lunar gravity!—and restaurants like Danny's where I was going to meet Alma. We had everything anybody might want there, just about—as long as you didn't mind living underground.

See, we didn't live on the surface. That's not real safe. Then, when they began excavating space for living quarters, they took advantage of the fact that once, a long time ago, the Moon had had real volcanoes.

The lunar volcanoes weren't the violently explosive kind you find on some planets, like Krakatoa or Vesuvius; they were the kind that gently ooze lava over long periods of time, like Earth's volcanoes in the Hawaiian islands. And when lava flows that way, the outsides of the flowing lava river cool before the insides, so you have a sort of pipe of solidified rock on the outside, while still-molten lava is flowing inside. When the flow stops and the lava runs out, what's left is a kind of immense, empty tube.

Then those tubes get covered over with new flows from later eruptions—or, in the case of the lunar craters, by the splash of material the asteroids push out of their way when they make the craters. That impact destroys all the near-surface lava tubes in the vicinity, but the deep-down ones survive, like lengths of tunnel abandoned way underground. So the people who designed the colony simply lined them to keep the air in and built connecting passages, and, voilà!, there's your underground city.

Danny's is a big, noisy place, and at first I had trouble finding where Alma was sitting, though I didn't doubt that she would be waiting there for me.

Indeed she was, but the bad part was that she wasn't waiting alone. Rannulf Enderman was sitting at the table with her.

Rannulf Enderman was a man of about my age, and also about my size and build, or maybe just a trifle bigger. (Well, I guess we have another of those little obstacles to understanding here. You don't care about height, because yours changes so. We do care. I was 190 centimeters tall, and I liked being that way; it was an annoyance that my predecessor in Alma's affections had been just a centimeter or two taller than that.)

The fact that we looked a little bit alike didn't make us friends. We were, in fact, pretty unfriendly rivals, and what we were rivals about was Alma Vendette. Technically there should have been no rivalry, because Rannulf was history—or should have been. Alma had told me herself that they had broken up before I met her.

It bothered me very much that she didn't always treat him like history.

As I approached Rannulf looked up at me with an expression I didn't recognize: pleased with himself, a little pensive. "Hello, Barry," he said. "Nice to see you again."

I didn't think it was nice at all, but I took a grip on my feelings—the doctors kept telling me it would be prudent to do that. I said, "Hello, Rannulf," in as nearly a friendly a tone as I could manage, and bent down to kiss Alma.

Alma kissed me back, but she didn't prolong it. She had something else on her mind, and as soon as her lips were free I found out what it was. "Barry, Rannulf's gone out of his mind," she said.

"Haven't," Rannulf said, looking defensive.

"You have so. Talk sense to him, Barry, please. Tell him not to be an idiot."

I sat down next to her, gazing at Rannulf. He didn't appear to be any more idiotic than usual. "What's he done?"

"He's going to volunteer to go to Pava."

I will say for me that I did not show my pleasure at the news. I felt it, though. I just said, "Are you sure anybody at all is going there?"

"Didn't you hear? They got their reprieve, so they're going to leave with a full complement of colonists, as soon as they can get the ship ready. What do you think of that? Imagine Rannulf throwing away a career on the Moon to go and live on a *farm*."

What I thought of Rannulf's new-formed plan was that it was the best news I'd had all day. I also thought that it was a grandstand play to get Alma's sympathy—which is to say, to get Alma back. It was the oldest trick in the book, and just what I would have expected from Rannulf. "Honey," the soldier on embarkation leave tells the girl, "don't let us waste this moment, because I may be dead in a few days," and so she falls into his arms. Or, actually, his bed. I could see very clearly the gears revolving in Rannulf's head. I wished that Alma could.

"I think," I said judiciously, "that Rannulf's the only person with the right to decide what he does with his life."

"Thank you, Barry," he said. The words were friendly, but the look he gave me wasn't. "I knew you'd understand that it's what I have to do. Excuse me for a minute?"

He got up and left us, another nice thing from an unlikely source. I explained it to Alma. "He doesn't like seeing me kiss you," I said, watching him thread his way between the noisy tables.

Alma frowned at me. "Don't be silly, Barry. He just has to go to the bathroom, and don't change the subject."

"Well, what he does isn't up to me, is it?"

"Don't you think you have a responsibility to keep a friend from doing something stupid?"

"Rannulf isn't my friend."

"He's my friend, Barry."

I didn't answer that. I caught sight of a waitress in the distance and stood up to wave at her. When she gave me the kind of look that meant she'd get to me sooner or later, so relax, I did. I sat down again.

"You're looking beautiful as always," I told Alma. "What do you want to do about dinner?"

"Well, nothing. Rannulf ordered a sandwich he decided he didn't want, so I ate it. I was hungry. Barry? Don't you think he's making a mistake?"

I thought for a moment. I wasn't really thinking about whether Rannulf Enderman was making a mistake, I was thinking about Alma.

I had been thinking seriously about Alma for some time, in fact. She wasn't the first woman I'd dated in all those years on the Moon, but she was the first one in connection with whom the word "marriage" had begun to come up in my thoughts. I had not forgotten what life with Gina had been like, before everything went sour. I'd liked being married, and, now that I'd got out of the habit of waking up every morning and wondering if I were going to be crazy that day, I was beginning to think about trying it again. I had had enough of short-term lovers. I wanted something, well, permanent. I was even pretty sure that the one I wanted that permanent arrangement with was Alma Vendette—always assuming that Rannulf was really history.

But then there was the problem of children.

Matthew had not inherited the bad genes that had made me a loop; we'd checked that out as soon as the doctors diagnosed me. But that was just good luck. The genes were still there; and if Alma decided she wanted a husband who could give her a child, which I was pretty sure she might, I didn't think I qualified.

"Well?" said Alma, reminding me that she had asked me a question; but luck was with me, the waitress came up at that moment and I didn't have to answer it.

"Take a drink order for me, will you?" I said to the waitress.

She gave me an annoyed look. "I've already got your drink," she said, and put down something lime-colored with a parasol in it.

I shook my head. "Wrong. That's for the other guy," I told her; the drink looked like something Rannulf would have ordered. "What I want is whiskey and water, two centimeters of each."

I wasn't really surprised at the mistake. I had long ago discovered that strangers thought Rannulf looked a little like me; Alma seemed to go for the tall, skinny kind with rat-colored hair. When I had the waitress straightened out I thought of a subject that didn't concern Rannulf Enderman, so I told Alma about my call to Matthew.

"You're changing the subject," she said accusingly.

She let me change it, though. I had known she would, because one of the subjects Alma was always willing to talk about was my son Matthew.

You don't have to say anything. I know I'm telling you more than you really want to know.

I can't help it. I don't know any other way to try to get it all clear and I *have* to get it all clear. For both our sakes. I have to make you understand what we're like—all of us, me and Captain Tscharka and all the rest of us who were involved.

There's another thing, too. What I hope most of all is that, if I can make you understand, I'll understand it all better myself.

I wish I could tell you even more about us. I wish I could show you the whole picture of my life, of all the details of all our human lives, of who all the people were who were in Danny's that day. The couple at the next table, pretty drunk and getting drunker, gazing into each other's eyes, whispering into each other's ears, unable to keep their hands off each other; the waitress, fretfully punching out her drink tabs by the cashier station because she'd got something screwed up and couldn't figure out where the mistake was; the fourteen or fifteen Muslims sitting together in the smoking section of the bar, who didn't drink but made up for it in hashish, and the way they all together jumped to their feet at prayer time, putting down their little rugs so they could kneel toward Mecca. (Of course, Mecca wasn't exactly to the "east" on the Moon, but they all had their little wrist computers to tell them where on the Earth's surface Mecca would be at any given moment.) I wish I could explain to you why we all drank or doped; for that matter, I wish I could make you understand why that drunken couple found their fumbling explorations of each other so compelling—and why I found being with Alma so—because I know that you don't do anything like that, either.

I don't think you understand physical sexual attraction at all, you see, any more than you understand the joys of intoxication, or the force of religious belief. Some things that matter mightily to us don't matter to you at all. And that's a pity, because then you can't understand why I did some of the things I did—or, especially, why Rannulf did what he did—without realizing that the way Alma looked mattered to me quite a lot. She was quite a beautiful woman, tall and fair with a long and graceful neck and a rounded but slim body—she looked the way a Moon maiden was supposed to look, although she'd been born and grew up in west Texas until she got tired of the floods. I frequently thought that

I loved Alma, and not just for her physique. She was smart, too. I suppose that that part might make sense to you, since I know you respect intelligence. But I would be a liar if I said that her undeniable intelligence was the main attraction for me.

Human beings very often behave in the rational, sensible ways dictated by their intelligence; but the rational behaviors that our reason would direct are quite often countermanded by the nonrational yearnings of our bodies. You don't have to approve of that. You just have to accept the fact that it's true. Otherwise you can't make any sense of us at all.

Alma listened carefully to every word I had to say about what Matthew said and how Matthew looked, and how I felt about talking to Matthew, filing it all away. I knew why. I had no doubt that in her private thoughts Alma had been considering the possibility of marriage and children with me as much as I had with her. If we'd never spoken about it, it was because we both still had reservations we didn't want to discuss. When she had stored it all, she changed the subject back.

"The question is," she said, "are we going to let Rannulf throw his life away because of some romantic notion about me?"

"Is that why he's doing it?" But that was the wrong tack to take; her face clouded. "Well," I said, "it isn't up to me to stop him. Besides, that's not throwing his life away exactly, is it? I mean, Pava's about the best extrasolar colony, because it's got the best star. And a lot of people volunteer for the colonies. It's exciting. I even feel a little bit that way myself; if things were the other way around with us I might be the one who gallantly disappears into the sunset."

"You wouldn't. Besides, you aren't supposed to. Because of your health," Alma said. I didn't think it was kind of her to remind me of that, although it was certainly more or less true. That was one of the reasons I'd had to give up my career flying a spotter ship, tagging high-value asteroids for the big smelters in the Belt. I wasn't even supposed to go on any long interplanetary trips, because the doctors didn't want me to get too far from the big medical facilities on the Earth or the Moon.

She probably would have said more, but she stopped, wincing. There was a commotion from the table with the drunken lovers, only they weren't alone anymore. A man in a clerical collar was shouting at them.

"They got caught," Rannulf said from behind us. He was grinning as he sat down. "I know the preacher; he's a Nation, name is Bryce Challenor. And that's his wife drinking with the other guy."

"Oh," said Alma. It explained the shouting. If they were Carrie Nation Baptists that meant they were supposed to be dead set against drinking, among other things.

I didn't want to talk about other people's domestic disturbances, annoying though the noise they were making was. I said to Rannulf, "We've just been having a little talk about you. Alma wants me to talk you out of going to Pava."

He was pleased about that, I could see. "It's the right thing for me to do," he said, with just enough of a wistful catch in his voice to get his point across.

"Bullshit," said Alma. "The right thing for you to do is to stay here and work. There's nothing on that dumb planet but bugs and earthquakes."

He gave her a forgiving look. "Earthquakes, yes," he admitted. "But the autochtons aren't 'bugs,' dear." (I registered the "dear," as I was meant to do.) "They're highly intelligent even if they don't look a bit like human beings. And if Captain Tscharka is willing to fight so hard to keep the colony going, I think people of goodwill should give him all the help they can. Pava is a goodplace to spend your life."

"The quitters don't think so," Alma said. She was referring to the rejects, the ones who had given up and come back in *Corsair*.

Rannulf shrugged. "They just weren't motivated. I am. Pava's going to be a holy place."

"Ah," I said, the pieces fitting into place. "I didn't know you were still a Millenarist." I knew he had been once—because that was where he and Alma had first got together.

He turned the forgiving look on me, this time adding a few other ingredients like pity and noble resolve. "It's not just a religious matter, is it? It's for the glory of the human race in general."

Alma didn't say "bullshit" again this time, although it seemed to me that it was definitely the right word. She said, "There's no *life* for you on Pava, Rannulf!"

"How can you say that? It's a pity Pava is so far away, of course, but it's got a nice climate, it's got good air, it's got plenty of raw materials—"

"And it's got the earthquakes and the bugs."

He turned the forgiving look back on her and began to explain what he'd learned—what we'd all have learned, if we ever bothered to watch the documentaries—about Pava. Alma was frowning as she listened, but she was listening, though I saw her cover a small yawn.

The yawn gave me the chance I was looking for. "Honey," I said, interrupting Rannulf's catalogue of the virtues of Pava, "it's getting kind of late for you, isn't it? Why don't I take you home?"

She shook her head. "I'm worried about Rannulf."

"But," I said reasonably, "there's nothing to worry about, is there? It's his life, and it's going to be a great adventure. Matter of fact," I said, turning to Rannulf and not being entirely truthful, "I almost envy you. If I just had the chance—"

I didn't finish that particular lie, wherever it was going to go, because the trouble at the other table suddenly got a lot louder. The irate husband had begun to smash glasses, his wife screaming and trying to stop him. He was shouting, "Drink and drugs, the devil's work. Brothers, sisters, listen! I beg you to leave this place of vice for the sake of your immortal souls!"

Most of the room was laughing, but then I got personally involved. The waitress was coming through with my drinks, and one of the preacher's flailing arms caught her tray.

I was on my feet before I knew it.

I knew that it was a bad idea for me to lose my temper, but everything the doctors had told me vanished from my mind. "Goddamn it," I yelled at the furious husband, "that was my drink you just spilled!"

And when Alma put her hand on me and said, "Please, Barry," I snapped at her, too.

"Get your damn hand off me! I'm sick of these religious nuts!"

She looked strained but determined. "Remember your condition," she said, and then I caught a glimpse of Rannulf. He was looking very pleased.

That brought me back to present reality.

I took a deep breath. I closed my eyes, willing myself to be calm. When I opened them again the Security people were leading the Nation couple out of the bar. I wasn't really calm. I was still seething inside, but at least I had control of my temper once more.

"Sorry," I said. "I guess I don't really want that drink. Alma, let's get out of here."

And she came along. She hesitated. She looked doubtfully at Rannulf, who was looking nobly self-sacrificial, and for a minute I thought it could have gone either way. But then she sighed and got up, and I was the one who took her home.

Alma's rooms were three tubes and a drop away from the bar, and by the time we got there things were all right between us again. Pretty much all right, anyway. She'd chided me for my silly jealousy, and I'd apologized for it, and then we didn't talk about any subjects that involved Rannulf anymore.

Because of our schedules Alma and I didn't have much time together just then. That was the only real, tangible problem in our relationship— not counting Rannulf, I mean. It was a matter of timing. Our work shifts clashed. Basically I was coded as being on the A shift, although subject to call anytime when I was needed, while Alma was on C—you understand, "days" and "nights" on the Moon were a matter of arbitrary convenience, because the Moon's real day was so long and, mostly, because we never saw the Sun rise or set anyway.

So after we had gone to bed in Alma's rooms and finished what we had gone to bed for—as good and rewarding as though Rannulf had never been born—it was still early in my day and I was wide-awake. Alma wasn't. She had rolled comfortably away from me, her face down in the pillows so that only the barrette on the top of her head was visible, and I had my arms around her. I could feel her breathing getting more and more regular.

I thought for a bit, as I often did at such times, of how nice it would be to stay there. Not just that particular time, but on a regular basis. Nice to keep her cocooned in my arms while we slept the night away in the warm and friendly, faintly fragrant bedclothes. (Only I wasn't at all sleepy.) Nice, too, in the longer-range prospect—by which I meant (but only in my thoughts, and never aloud to Alma) the kind of long-range planning that involved getting married, and spending all our nights sleeping together, and maybe even having a baby together—

But then I began, as I usually did at that point, to think of all the reasons against.

The short-range reason against staying on, on this particular occasion, was that, although Alma had eaten a sandwich, I hadn't. I was getting hungry.

The longer-range reason was that I realized I ought to report to the clinic after that flash of red-hot adrenaline in the bar—and the reasons why that was so. Those theoretical babies could be quite a problem.

So I slid as quietly as I could out of Alma's bed—she was too sound asleep to notice—and after I had showered and dressed I went back to kiss her good night. She woke up just enough to lift her face to mine for the kiss. But what she said before she sank back was, "G'night, Rannulf." And it wasn't the first time she'd done it, either.

4

*T*HERE *is concern about the "craziness" you have sometimes exhibited. Perhaps you should give more information on this matter.*

Well, look, it gives me concern, too. Trust me on that point. But most of the time it isn't too serious, as long as I get treatment. The important thing to understand is that my problem wasn't caused by a desire to have sexual intercourse with my mother, or because I was weaned off the bottle too early. My problem wasn't Freudian at all. It was metabolic.

So I made sure, all the time I was on the Moon, that I went to see my doctor every time I thought I was behaving in even the least peculiar way; and as a matter of fact I did right after leaving Alma that night.

I hadn't made an appointment, so the doctor was busy with another patient. But she flashed me the have-a-seat sign, and I settled down to watch some news broadcasts while I waited. Wouldn't you know it? The first thing I saw was Garold Tscharka and his Santa Claus chaplain being triumphantly interviewed about the victory they had just apparently scored for Pava.

It really wasn't an issue that interested me a lot. When the Budget Congress had first announced it was going to review the question of continuing to fund the colonies I thought it was sensible of them. Those worlds were no bargains, anyway. But obviously the two Millenarists didn't agree; they were glowing with success. "A victory?" the big preacher was saying—was braying, rather; he had a big, raspy voice when he was orating, and he was taking no trouble to keep the volume down. "Certainly it's a victory, but not just for our heroic pioneers in the Pava colony. The victory is for common sense and freedom!"

"Just what have you accomplished?" the invisible interviewer asked, and it was Captain Tscharka who answered.

"They're going to leave us our ships and fill our requisitions. That's all we need. Maybe a couple of hundred years from now, when *Corsair* is getting rickety, we'll have to take up the question again. But for now the colony is safe."

Isn't that a killer? He had to be lying through his teeth, even then, but he made everybody believe him. That was the thing about Captain Garold Tscharka. He was wholly wrongheaded in almost every way I can think of—but, even now, I almost miss the man.

When the doctor let me in she looked up from her screens and said, "You again." But she was smiling when she said it.

I said, "Yes, me, Helge. I nearly blew my pod a couple of hours ago, so I thought you might want to take a look."

"Hum," she said, leaning back and looking at me. That tone and posture meant *Tell me all about it and don't leave out any details*, so I did. Helge got up and walked around. Finally, she perched in silence on the edge of her desk, kicking her heel against it, until I finished. Then she said, "All this happened hours ago?"

"Well, I would have come right in, Helge, but I had things to do." Like eat. Like Alma, but I didn't specify.

She said, "Hum," again, but this time it didn't mean anything but *Hold still* because she was running her sensors over me.

Helge's always both glad and sorry to see me. She likes me for the novelty, because I'm an interesting case, but she's also a little bit sorry when she sees me because she really can't treat me properly.

The condition I suffered from was a medical anomaly. The specific ailment I suffered from was so rare that doctors had decided long ago that it didn't exist at all, and even the words used to describe it had been expunged from the medical vocabulary. In the old-fashioned term, I had a "psychosis" that closely resembled "schizophrenia" of the type once called "manic-depressive." It wasn't something they could vaccinate against at birth. It came from my genetic heritage; my mother

THE VOICES OF HEAVEN

and my father just happened to carry some very rare recessive genes, and I was the one-in-a-billion lucky lottery winner of the chance to express them.

In itself that shouldn't have been much of a problem. Metabolic-based loopiness gets cured by changing the body's chemistry around, and that's generally easy to do. The quick and dirty way, what doctors used to do when they first figured out how the body chemistry could mess the mind up, was to deal with the symptoms. When the patient was depressed they'd give him pep-up pills, when he was hyper they'd give him tranquilizers.

Then, when they began to think about *cures*, they tried other kinds of treatments. Then they'd inject the protein or other missing chemical into the bloodstream, so that the symptoms wouldn't occur at all. The first disease they did that with, I think, wasn't a mental problem, it was something called diabetes. That kind of treatment was what they called "the needle way," and it worked. The diabetics that stuck themselves with insulin every day lived perfectly normal lives—unless they ran out of insulin.

So then the doctors began to figure out how to trick the body into making its own insulin, or whatever, as a healthy body was supposed to do in the first place. The theory was that if they could use some carrier to deliver genetically active material to the patient's system they could get the process going. Then, if the stuff they put in was tolerated by the body's system (that is, if it was not inactivated by the body's immune defenses, and if it wasn't causing anything nasty like tumors), the added genetic material would settle down and release the desired recombinant protein (or whatever) at a controllable rate indefinitely. When that happened the patient was "cured." He could forget he'd ever been sick, no needles, no worries, no nothing.

That was the right way to do it, but it didn't work for me. They couldn't find a carrier that would survive in my body.

They tried everything they could think of. For instance, one thing they could do would be simply to flood the patient's system with carriers that would just float around in the bloodstream, like bacteria or leucocytes, and do their job. When they tried it on me, though, mine didn't. The carriers were rejected, or they just stopped working. (And all through these trials, you understand, I was going loopy about half the time, depressed to the point of catatonia the rest. There's a special name for that horrid catatonic state; they call it "depressive stupor," and I never want to live through it again. So I lost patience pretty fast. I wanted to get this business finished—at least, I wanted that at such times as I was sane enough to be able to figure out what I did want.)

Then they tried carriers that would actually bond with working parts of my body, instead of just floating around unattached. They tried immature muscle cells, called myoblasts; they tried immature bone cells; they tried white blood cells, keratinocytes, fibroblasts, liver cells—they tried everything they could think of, and those wonderful strong immune defenses in my body just chewed them all up and spat them right out again. There was more they could do, they told me—when I was in one of my brief lucid periods—like try to turn down my immune defenses enough to tolerate the genes. That had some drawbacks, they admitted. For instance, I'd probably keep on catching a lot of little illnesses, everything from warts to pneumonia, but those could be treated. . . .

I said no. I said no more experimenting, please. I said I was tired of those terrible, wild mood swings, and I wanted out of the clinic.

So they sighed and went back to the quick and dirty. The needles. They made it as easy on me as they could, with time-release material so that I only needed a shot about once every three or four months . . . but I would, they said, *always* need the shots. Unless I wanted to alternate between zombie and lunatic for the rest of my life.

"You better have some blood work," Helge decided when she was through poking me. She sent me off to the medtech, who greeted me like an old friend. I didn't have to be told what to do. I had my arm stretched out for the needles before the nurses said a word. When the machine had taken its blood and finished its workup Helge called me back. "You're all right, Barry," she said, watching the colored lines on her diagnostic screen swirl around. "You didn't actually go round the bend and hurt anybody when you had that little flare-up, did you?"

I shook my head. "Well, then," she said. "I don't think that was a manic spell. I think it was just the same normal kind of spell of aggravation that I might have myself. Everybody has them. Just don't get yourself excited anymore, all right?"

That was a dismissal, but I didn't get up. "There's something else," I said.

"Hum," she said, patting a couple of strands of hair into place behind her ear. What "hum" meant this time was, *I thought so, so get on with it.*

"I've been thinking about getting married," I told her. "I think the woman I want to marry is likely to want to have children. I want to know if that's a good idea."

She looked annoyed, because she'd been all set to see the last of me and get off to her coffee break, but she looked interested, too. She frowned, trying to remember something. "Barry? Don't you have a son somewhere?"

"I do. He's sixteen."

"And he didn't inherit?"

"Thank God, no. He's been tested."

"Hum." She turned back to the screen. When it displayed my entire chart, she said, "Do you want to see where your problem is?"

"No," I said. I'd been shown those charts before.

She wasn't listening, though. "Look here," she said, moving the cursor across the screen. "That's the gene locus, in the arm of the chromosome there, do you see? That's where the little bugger is that does you in."

I wasn't even looking. "And if I have another child and this time I pass that gene on—?"

She leaned back thoughtfully. The strand of her hair had come loose again and she was twisting it around her finger. "I can only talk probabilities, Barry. You know these mental disorders aren't transmitted as classical Mendelian traits. You need both the genetic predisposition and the triggering environmental stimulus for them to appear."

"But that stimulus could happen."

"Well, sure it could. So you don't want to pass those genes along. Naturally. But there's no problem in preventing the transmission. Oh, there's a little *nuisance*, of course, but the procedure's straightforward. What I mean by 'straightforward,' " she went on kindly, "is that impregnation occurs in the normal way—I mean whatever way you and your partner consider normal. Then, as soon as she's pregnant, she comes in to see us and we flush out the fertilized ovum and examine it. The nuisance part is that she'll have to give a urine sample every morning, because we have to get that ovum as soon as we can, while it's still floating free and hasn't attached itself to the womb yet. We want to get it after the third division, when it's a cluster of eight cells. We take one of the cells and test it. That testing takes an expert, because the genes are only about a thousand base pairs apart—"

I stirred to keep her from going on forever. "Then what?"

"Then it's simple. If the gene is absent, we reimplant the rest of the cluster and pregnancy goes on normally. But if the bad gene's there, well, then we discard the cluster and you try again next month. We do it all the time—oh," she said, having switched back to my chart. "Sorry. I didn't notice you were Orthodox."

"*Western* Orthodox. And not very."

"Then you don't have a problem, Barry. Unless your fiancée—?"

"She isn't my fiancée yet. I haven't asked her."

"Well," she said, "I guess it wouldn't be your classic, romantic, on-bended-knee proposal, but when you do you'd better tell her all this stuff. You can send her to me for more information, if you want to. Some denominations don't like the idea of discarding a fertilized ovum, and then, too, some people think it's dangerous. It isn't, though. At that stage all the cells are still undifferentiated. The embryo won't notice that we've taken one to look at. You'll have a healthy baby. If your own parents had done that—"

"I know. I wouldn't have this problem. On the other hand, I wouldn't ever have been born, either, would I?"

She didn't respond to that. She mulled for a second, then said, "I should mention that there are other ways of going about it."

"Like what?"

"Complete genetic suppression. You go in for twenty-four hours, they destroy your spermatophiles—"

"Hey!"

"It doesn't hurt, Barry. And it's reversible. But that means you're sterile; then they give you an implant and you're in business again. Only the implant is tailored to suppress your bad genes." She saw the face I was making and laughed. "Men," she said. "Trust me. It doesn't affect your sex life at all."

I thought that over. "You said it only takes twenty-four hours?"

"That's all—except, of course, we don't do that here. You'd have to go to one of the big clinics on Earth."

I got up. "Thanks," I said, not meaning it, and left.

On the way out I played back some of the things Helge had said. It seemed to me that Helge was right. The only way I could find out how Alma would feel about these questions would be to ask her.

Right after that I began to wonder how I myself really felt about that other big question, the one that comes with the word "commitment."

If I asked Alma questions about how she felt about dealing with my genetic problems, there would then be only one way the conversation could go from there. That would be to propose marriage to her.

I didn't know if I was ready.

I don't know what would have happened to my life if I had got my courage together and taken that next step. My life would have been different, all right. But would it have been better?

I don't think I've succeeded even yet in giving you a very accurate idea of what our lives were like, back on the Moon. They were very different from what we have now. They were certainly a lot more comfortable.

It's true that they weren't perfect, though. When I think back to those carefree days on the Moon I have a tendency to forget that at the time I didn't think they were really carefree at all. What I remember is that the only real cares I had were the personal worries I made up for myself. Like what it meant when Alma called me by the wrong name. Like whether or not I would lose her—and whether I could somehow figure out a way to both keep her and simultaneously keep open the option to lose her, painlessly and without recrimination, if I ever decided that that was what I wanted to do.

Apart from those self-inflicted wounds—and, well, yes, apart from the faint but real worry nobody on the Moon was ever completely without, namely, that someday somebody might accidentally push the wrong button inside the crater and the whole Lederman antimatter factory would go up in a ball of plasma, of which I would myself be a tiny part—apart from that sort of thing, I mean to say, we didn't *have* any worries. The Moon was rich. We all had jobs. Anybody who didn't have one was shipped instantly back to Earth, and the jobs at Lederman were both interesting and paid well. The factory did everything possible to make our lives palatable because that was good business for them; they didn't want any disgruntled workers doing anything terminally stupid. Everything that state-of-the-art technology could provide, the lunar authorities had bought for us. They were clearing and lining additional lava tubes all the time. That meant that there were new housing units, bigger and more comfortable, appearing on the market regularly. One tube was even being half-filled with expensively manufactured water to make a swimming pool. Even the Lederman management couldn't give us solitude, of course. But we could get something close to it by taking a stroll through the farm tubes, steamy and warm with their crop racks green and sweet-smelling all around us and only a rare glimpse of a distant farm worker to disturb our privacy; Alma and I had made love two or three times in those jungly recesses. We had the best of medical care, and the best of food, and all the entertainment the networks could provide. We were spoiled rotten, in fact. I loved it.

The next day I had a date with Alma to go down to the grand concourse to watch the Taoist New Year celebration. It was kind of a personal anniversary for us—we'd met at the same event the year before. Besides, the Taoists put on a great show. They all get dressed up in red and gold, with dancing and chanting, firing off their acoustic poppers and electronic flares.

Alma loved all that kind of thing. She was flushed and happy, but something was bothering her. She kept giving me looks out of the corner of her eye until she finally said, "Barry? Have you got something on your mind?"

I leaned over to kiss her ear. "Just you," I said. That was true, it just wasn't specific. The *specific* thing on my mind was that I was wondering whether, when we got back to her room, I should start on that line of conversation that would end up with "Will you marry me?" It was a warming kind of thought, and an appropriate time to pop the question—our anniversary, after all. And then I began to wonder why I wanted to wait until we got to her room. And then I actually opened my mouth to say something—I'm not sure what, but I had the feeling it was going to be a step along that road. . . .

And then, "Watch it," she said, pulling me out of the way as three or four lion dancers pranced by. One of them lifted up the skirt of his lion suit to toss a handful of sticky poppyseed candies at us.

"Oh, great," Alma said, putting a couple in her pouch. "Rannulf loves these things."

That stopped me cold.

I hadn't wanted to think about Rannulf just then. After a moment, chewing happily, Alma gave me another of those looks. "Were you going to say something?"

"Right," I said. "I was going to say it's winding down here. Let's go back to your place." We did; and then it was easy enough to stop talking and start making love.

Yes, I know I shouldn't have been so easily put off. On the other hand, Alma could have been a little more tactful, too. Faults on both sides, I suppose.

Then we didn't have much chance to talk for a few days, because I got real busy. One of the orbiter pod-catchers began to leak propellant and had to be replaced. The catchers are where the antimatter goes to be transshipped to the customers, and they're part of a fuelmaster's responsibility—in this case, mine.

While I was busy at that, another interstellar ship, the *Jean Bart*, came in from the Alpha Draconis colony with a load of returnees. The quitters had been dropped off at the Skyhook to Earth before we ever saw them, of course. By the time the ship got to lunar orbit for defueling, the crew had had plenty of time to adjust to the fact that their colony had been almost terminated and then given a new lease on life; I wondered what they made of it, but didn't ask.

Then that second ship appeared from Pava, the one called *Buccaneer*. I didn't board it myself—another fuelmaster was servicing it—but I caught a glimpse of its captain at the landing pad, a man named Bennetton. He didn't stay on the Moon. He took right off for Earth to join Garold Tscharka at whatever Tscharka was doing while he waited for *Corsair* to be refitted.

Then I got a surprise. Two ships that serviced the Martian colonies were in orbit, and when I defueled mine I expected to be right back within a day or two for refueling—the short-run solar-system ships don't usually need repairs or anything much in the way of refitting between voyages. But its captain told me they were going to be delayed in getting fuel for a week because a big new two-hundred-pod order for antimatter fuel was coming through.

Naturally I checked it out. It was what I guessed. Captain Tscharka had got his wish, and the destination for all those extra pods was Pava.

That night Alma and I watched an operetta on the screen. Neither of us was enjoying it much. Alma seemed unusually thoughtful, and I was making up my mind about whether I wanted to discuss Tscharka, the *Corsair*, the fuel pods—and Rannulf Enderman—with her. As we were drinking a nightcap after the show she brought it up herself.

"I guess *Corsair* will be leaving soon," she said, meaning that she wanted to know if I'd heard anything.

I hadn't; it wasn't yet on my worklog. "Kept you busy making the stuff, has it?" I asked; that was Alma's job at Lederman, guiding the particle beams through the accelerator rings, and she knew better than I how much antimatter was being manufactured for what purpose.

She didn't answer the question, except with another question—a trait I've never approved of. "I wonder what they want with all that antimatter."

Well, Tscharka had told me his answer to that—true or not, I didn't know—so I repeated it for her. She didn't look impressed. "They're going to do more exploration around Delta Pavonis? What for? So they can set up more colonies? I don't see the point."

That was another trait in Alma Vendette that I hadn't entirely enjoyed in recent days. She'd seemed down. I don't mean clinically depressed— no, that was my own specialty—but more abstracted than I liked. I didn't want to think that it was because Rannulf was on his way to another star, but I took the chance of asking. "What's the matter? Is something worrying you?"

She considered. "Nothing specific, I think," she said at last. "It's just that nothing we do seems to be particularly important."

"You mean here at Lederman? But we *are* important. If we didn't make the fuel the colonies would just die."

She shrugged. That was even more displeasing; I wondered how much Millenarism was still in the back of her mind. "What I'm looking for, hon, is some kind of meaning. The way life was in the old days, when work meant something, and people got together and had babies and—listen, Barry, don't be shocked, but the other day I even thought of having the contraceptive implant taken out."

That straightened me right up. And that, at last, made her smile. In fact, she laughed out loud. "Oh, hon," she said, "don't be silly. I wasn't *serious*."

But maybe she was, I thought. And maybe that was my cue to ask the question that had been on the tip of my tongue to ask for weeks now, and maybe I would have. But I didn't get the chance, because just then the factory emergency alarms went off—beepity-beepity-*beeeeep*, over and over again, coming out of every audio point in the Lederman works and community.

When you live and work in the Lederman colony that is a sound that freezes your blood. I knew it was only a drill this time—I could be pretty sure of that, because both Alma and I were still alive—but the rules are that you have to *act* as though the drill is real, and both of us were very faithful in following those rules. We both snapped our pocket screen on and began to search our dedicated bands for data and instructions.

Any operation that's as critical as the antimatter factory at Lederman needs to keep its damage-control procedures up to speed. To make sure of that, the master controls are programmed to invent a simulated emergency at random intervals—they average fifteen or twenty a year—and when those beepers go off every one of us drops whatever he's doing and gets to work trying to deal with whatever that day's simulation had chosen to simulate.

As a fuelmaster crew chief my criticality-zone damage-control job was to make an eyeball inspection of potential danger areas. If I had been in the factory area, I would have grabbed my radiation readers and run to my first checkpoint. Since I wasn't, I simply logged on to the duty chief, Warren Bellick, and watched to make sure he was doing what I would have done.

He was. The beeping had stopped by the time he got there and the computer voice was identifying the problem. It told us that the exercise the computer had devised to entertain us this day was a (make-believe) misalignment of the particle beam, so that antimatter was being formed outside the target area. That wasn't a frighteningly big emergency, even if it had been real instead of something the computer made up to keep us on our toes. But it did mean that every operation everywhere in the complex had to be safed until it was dealt with.

Of course, the real fear we all had to live with is that sometime—anytime, maybe within the next second—there would be a *big* emergency—say, the magnetic field failing to hold an actual lump of antimatter in position, so that it somehow contacted real matter and blew . . . and thus compromised the containment shells of all the other little nuggets of antimatter, so they all blew at once.

Once in a while the computer decided to give us a really serious problem of that kind, but I never could see the point. If that happened there was *no* way we could cope with it. That was why all the workings of the factory were on the surface of the Moon, instead of deep down in old lava tubes like the residential sectors—and why the Lederman factory had been sited within the walls of a crater on the Moon's limb in the first place. The hope of the planners was that if the factory ever did blow, the walls would force most of the explosion to go straight up and out into space. "Up" from the factory crater was well away from Earth itself. Thus, a maximum accident would certainly destroy everything inside the walls. That would put a terrible crimp in space travel for lack of fuel for a long time to come, and any people who happened to be inside the crater wall at that moment would become instant plasma. So, I was pretty sure, would most of what was outside the walls, too, no matter what they said. But the accident would be only a frightful catastrophe instead of, well, the Millenarists' yearning dream of the end of the world.

Although just about everything that goes on inside the crater walls is critical, some parts are more critical than others. That makes a difference in people's working conditions. It's only the teams that do the actual insertion of antimatter into the pods that can't afford to have any distraction at all; those rooms are as sterile and concentrated as any surgical operating theater. Most of the other workers at least are allowed to play music, and some of them—in the assembly rooms for the pods themselves, for instance, or the coil-winding rooms for the magnetic containment—even are allowed to have news screens. Not that what they do isn't critical; but after they've finished their work it gets very thoroughly tested before it moves on to the next step, so mistakes can be caught. Where actual antimatter is present, there's no test. It either behaves quietly as it should. Or it doesn't, and that's all she wrote.

Since this time the "emergency" was only a practice alert the check was over in ten minutes, and the beepers were replaced with the gentle drone of the "all clear." By then Warren was already at his last stop, in the launch room. Naturally there was no antimatter there—we don't keep the stuff around; as soon as a pod is filled and ready, it's launched to one of the orbital catchers to wait for its customer—and Warren turned and grinned into the camera. "False alarm, fellows," he told us silent overseers, and blanked off.

By then Alma had been cleared, too. I suppose that I could have gone back to the subject we'd been talking about. But I didn't; and another opportunity to change my life went down the drain.

5

YOU have frequently referred to this "Lederman antimatter factory," but its exact nature and purpose are not understood, nor is it known why such an apparently dangerous establishment is tolerated. Please explain.

Well, all right, but where do I start?

Let's see. You already know that no one lives in the factory itself; when you need to get there—and you really have to need to, because nobody can get inside without a damn good reason—you take the subway through the crater rim from Lederman Town to the works inside.

I think I've also already told you that the lunar antimatter factory is the biggest single industrial complex in the solar system—in the universe, I guess, unless there's some other high-tech race out there somewhere that we just haven't found out about yet. It's big because it has to be big—you can't make antimatter in your hall bedroom. Also, there can be only one installation like the Lederman factory anywhere in the solar system. That's a law. Some people think it's a dumb law, because if we can have one antimatter factory on the Moon, what would be wrong with having a couple of spares somewhere else, even farther from civilization? Well, we probably could. There are only two reasons we don't. One is that the Moon is a good place to get the immense amounts of electrical power the factory needs—I'll tell you about that in a minute.

The other reason we don't is that the Congresses are so scared of antimatter that they damn near wanted to close Lederman itself down in the early days. But they couldn't. The human race *needs* antimatter.

Most of the antimatter we manufacture goes to fuel spaceships, but there are plenty of other customers. The habitats around Jupiter's moons and in the asteroid-mining stations need antimatter, too, for survival; they're too far from the Sun for solar power to give them all the energy they need, and we can sell antimatter to them cheaper, megawatt for megawatt, than nukes or anything else they might consider. It would be nice if we could sell to Earth, too, of course, but of course we can't. Antimatter is not allowed within a thousand kilometers of the outermost reaches of the Earth's atmosphere. For obvious reasons.

The reason we can do it so cheaply is, as I say, that we have our own solar power, which we get in copious amount, from the photovoltaic belt that goes all around the Moon.

I know you don't know what "photovoltaic power" is. Maybe you don't really need to, except that you should understand that electricity is so important to human beings that we're willing to do a lot of damaging things to get it—as you know. Photovoltaics happen to be among the least damaging. What "photovoltaic" means is a way of changing light into electricity. Any kind of light. Sunlight is the best kind of all, because there's so much of it. The way it works, when a particle of light—it's called a "photon"—strikes a photovoltaic cell it knocks an electron loose from one of the atoms in the cell. An electron is a particle of electricity, you see, and when you have enough of them knocked loose you have an electric current.

So that's what the belt around the Moon is for. It's a continuous ribbon of photovoltaic cells that goes completely around the Moon. The belt is not handicapped by a day and night sequence; it girdles the whole Moon. That means half of it is always in direct sunlight.

Why put it on the Moon? Partly to get it as far as possible from nervous neighbors, of course, but also because the Moon has no air. The energy from the Sun doesn't lose anything to Rayleigh scattering or cloudy days. (I know you don't know what Rayleigh scattering is either, but anyway.) And every point on the belt is connected to every other point by the superconductor cables that underlie the photovoltaic belt itself.

The effect is that we can tap all that power at any point. The biggest power draw is at the Lederman antimatter works, where every minute of every day we have several billion megawatts to draw on.

We draw on them pretty heavily, too. We use that power to run the giant accelerator rings that go all around the crater wall; they're a hundred kilometers in circumference. We smash particles into each other and collect the fragments, and the important part of the fragments that we get out of the rings are antimatter. Antiprotons. Which we convert and chill down to solid antihydrogen; and then we package the antihydrogen and ship it out and get rich.

Well—the owners get richest of all, of course. But the people who work there, like me, get paid pretty well, too. Hazard pay, you could call it. After all, if anything went wrong we would be the first ones to go.

The packaging of the antimatter is the hard part—well, one of the hard parts; there aren't any easy ones. Each little lump of antimatter is smaller than the meat of a walnut, but those walnuts have very large shells. The shells have to keep it away from any normal matter, you see, because if any bit of antimatter ever touches any bit of normal matter you get a hell of a big explosion. (These controlled explosions are what make our spaceships run.) So the shells are made up of magnets and vacuum pumps and motors that keep the little nugget of antimatter in suspension; and at the same time they have to be so constructed that the antimatter can be bled off to enter the combustion chambers of the spaceships in just the right measured amounts, with zero leakage at all times. The antimatter is measured in grams, but each shell masses more than six tons.

Do you get the idea that the Lederman factory was big, expensive, complicated and dangerous? Then you've got it right. It is. But it gives us power—and, you know, power is what makes our world go round. We aren't like you.

Captain Garold Tscharka wanted to know what the inside of the factory was like, too. I found that out a few days after the drill. I was getting off the shuttle after refueling a Belt transport and he was arriving from Earth, and we met at the Lederman lander pad.

We waited for the subway to Lederman Central together. "Well, di Hoa," he said genially, "I've just checked *Corsair*. We'll be loading soon."

"I heard. They must like you in the Budget Congress."

He laughed. "As long as they decided to let the colony live awhile, there wasn't any reason not to finance our supplies fully."

"Ah," I said, admiring the man's brass. I didn't know Tscharka that well at the time, or I wouldn't have been surprised at his ability to turn defeat into triumph. Later on, of course, it was different.

By then we were in the Lederman town station, and when I headed for the cars that went through the crater wall he followed me. "Listen," I said, thinking to spare him embarrassment, "you know you can't go inside the factory."

"Oh, but I can, di Hoa," he said, and proceeded to prove it. When the guards checked our IDs they didn't stop him. In fact, they pinned him with a blue badge, as good as my own.

"But nobody's allowed to enter but trained technicians," I protested.

He gave me a look of good-humored tolerance. "I know that. That's why I've been on Earth taking the course. I'm going to inspect the pods that are ready for loading, and I'm going to stay with you and your crew every minute that you're stowing them on my ship."

"You think we don't know our business?"

"*I* want to know your business too." Then he unbent enough to offer a reason—a lying one, as it turned out, but I had no way of knowing that. "When we get to the colony we're going to have to fuel the short-rangers ourselves, aren't we? I want to make sure we do it right."

It was a plausible explanation, and I let it go at that. By then we were at the main door, and when it opened for us Tscharka looked surprised. "Wait a minute, di Hoa. Aren't we going to put spacesuits on?"

"Why would we do that?"

"Don't you keep the area in vacuum? In case some air should penetrate the pods?"

"Oh, right," I said, trying not to laugh; his course obviously hadn't taught him *everything*. I shook my head. "There's no point. Even what we have on the Moon's surface isn't a perfect vacuum. There isn't a perfect enough vacuum to be allowed to contact antimatter anywhere in the universe, not even in interstellar space."

I looked at my watch. I had a little time before I had to sign off, and besides I was still in the stage of thinking that Captain Tscharka was probably a pretty decent guy, underneath it all.

So I showed him around, first to the fuel-insertion room. No fuel was being inserted at the moment, but next to it was the storage chamber where the prepared pods waited to be filled. And there they were, his first hundred pods, looking like giant steel watermelons, each one already hooked up to the power leads that would run its coolers and magnets when the antimatter was inserted.

"They're empty," he said, frowning.

"Of course they're empty. As soon as a pod is full it's out of here; we don't keep antimatter around. As soon as they start filling them for you, we'll shoot them up to the catchers so we can start loading."

"And when are you going to load?"

"When I tell them to start filling," I told him.

He didn't look as though he liked that, but he wasn't looking at me anymore. He was staring at the pods, and the expression on his face surprised me. It seemed to reflect a kind of emotion I didn't really associate with Millenarists. If I'd had to put a name to it, I would have called it . . . well . . . *love*.

He made me uncomfortable. I said, "I'll probably have the refueling order tomorrow, so you'll be leaving pretty soon."

He looked up at me, as though I'd interrupted a precious thought. "I suppose so. All the supplies are in, and the personnel list is all set. Not everybody is as hostile to the extrasolar colonies as you, di Hoa. We've had more volunteer colonists than we could carry, with all that load of antimatter."

I mentioned, "I know one of your volunteers. A man named Rannulf Enderman."

He thought for a moment, then nodded. "Enderman, yes. A deeply religious young man. You would be a happier man, di Hoa, if you had his faith."

I didn't know what to say to that. I couldn't tell whether Tscharka really believed what he said about Rannulf—"deeply religious," for God's sake!—or whether he actually remembered Rannulf at all. I took refuge in what my old shrink had told me.

"A man named Benjamin Franklin said something that makes sense to me," I said. "Franklin said, 'In the affairs of this world men are saved, not by faith, but by the lack of it.' "

I don't know what I expected from him. Maybe a thundering condemnation of Franklin's blasphemy, maybe a supercilious dismissal of his ignorance. What I got surprised me. Tscharka mulled that over for a moment, and then said, "Why, di Hoa, that is a very penetrating observation, for a secular. I must admit that this man, Franklin, is partly right."

I blinked at him for that.

"You see, in *this* world," he explained, "you really can't be saved by faith. You can't be saved at all, except by getting out of it."

6

WHAT is the meaning of the word "faith" as it is used in this context? It seems there are many meanings of the term.

Well, sure, "faith" means lots of different things. I can say I have "faith" in a person. That means I believe that person is decent, and trustworthy, and maybe even kind. Or I can have "faith" that a given action will produce a particular result; that kind of "faith" is based on prior experience.

Is either of those the kind of "faith" you and Garoldtscharka were discussing?

No, of course not. We were talking about *religious* faith. That's powerful stuff. If a person is serious about his religious faith it takes precedence over anything else. It isn't based on any kind of evidence. It's irrelevant to such things as, say, a person's character, or the things he experiences. It transcends all that real-world stuff. It shapes what you do, in ways that an outsider can't predict, and that's why Tscharka was so good at concealing his intentions.

Whatever Tscharka's intentions were, as he was getting ready to return to Pava, he didn't communicate them to me. And certainly when I first met him I might not have known how things would go in the long run even if I'd been able to read his mind. I don't know if he even had those intentions yet.

If you want me to make a guess, I'd say probably Tscharka and his chaplain, the one he called Friar Tuck, cooked their whole plan up somewhere between the time they heard that there was talk about terminating the colony—that would have been as soon as they got within two-way radio range of Earth—and when they appeared before the Budget Congress. Maybe not, though. It could have been after that. There's no way of knowing exactly.

I didn't see Tscharka again until the actual loading, at least not in person. He did show up on the vidscreen once. Alma and I switched on the screen just before going to sleep. No particular reason; just to see what was on. What was on was Tscharka and his whole group of new colonists being interviewed about their imminent departure. Some of them were looking dedicated, some happy; and there at the end of one row was old Rannulf. Looking, I thought, mostly disgruntled. I didn't say anything. Alma didn't say anything either, though I thought I heard her sigh. And when a different news story came on we turned it off and went to sleep.

We were both busy then, dealing with Tscharka's hundred pods of stored antimatter, and the sixteen additional pods he needed to run his ship as they were filled and launched. It was about as big an order as any in my experience. Handling that kind of operation takes a lot of work. As soon as each pod was filled it was shot right up into parking orbit, where one of the permanently orbiting catchers collected it.

That's the most dangerous part of the whole procedure, but this time we had no problems. The fuelmasters on the catchers were first-class, and I was supervising the surface-to-orbit launches myself. It went without incident. Then, once all the requisitioned pods were on the catcher, it was time for me to get down to my real job, and so I took a shuttle up to *Corsair*.

"You," said the young woman who greeted me at the ship's lock, "are Barry di Hoa, and you're welcome here."

I said, "Thanks, and you're—?"

"Jillen Iglesias," she reminded me. "Copilot."

"Nice to see you again," I said, remembering as she shook my hand warmly that I'd met her before. I was a little startled. I hadn't expected such a warm welcome on Captain Tscharka's *Corsair*, but then Tscharka himself wasn't there. He was asleep in his quarters, Jillen said, catching up on his rest so he'd be fresh and alert for the fueling itself, and so she would be the one to accompany me on my final inspection.

She stuck as close to me as Tscharka ever had as I made my rounds, too. The difference was that with her I didn't mind it. She was helpful rather than interfering. As we poked through the fuel and cargo compartments one more time she answered all my questions, and when I didn't have any questions to ask she kept her mouth shut.

Everything was spic-and-span. The fuel-storage sections were ready for their pods and the cargo was loaded. The most important cargo was information—recordings of all the latest songs and plays and comedians; manufacturing programs for new machines and instruments and electronic devices; a ten-year supply of journals in all the arts and sciences. None of that took up much space, but there were also bulkier items, starting with the food and supplies to get *Corsair*'s crew through their time-dilated, but still long, voyage to Delta Pavonis. For the colony itself there were ingots of scarce metals, seeds, frozen ova and sperm and, I guess, hundreds of other personal items that were none of my concern. And there were the freezer-sleep capsules, open and waiting for the colonists who would soon be filling them—including, I thought with pleasure, Rannulf Enderman.

When I had signed off I paused to look at Jillen Iglesias. "You're going back to Pava, then," I said.

"Yes, of course," she said, surprised, as though that were the most normal thing in the world. It wasn't. Most interstellar crews won't do more than a single voyage, because they get too disoriented.

"Won't you miss your friends?" I asked.

"But my friends are right here," she told me. "On this ship, and, yes, a few on Pava, too. Of course, they'll be a little elderly by the time I get back, but Pava's a wonderful planet, di Hoa. Actually, I think I might just stay there this trip—I mean if I can find someone else to take my place on *Corsair* for the voyage back. See," she said earnestly, doing her best to convince me, "the only thing Pava needs to make it just about perfect is more industry. They're bound to have that taken care of by the time I get back. Power was still kind of short when we left. They were even burning biomass to make electricity, but that's the hard way to do it—but they were starting to build a big hydroelectric plant, with a hundred-meter dam. It'll be operating by now, I'm sure. And we'll still have our orbiting factory working too, probably. I think we'll want to use some of the antimatter there to run it; solar power takes you just so far. Have you ever seen an orbiting factory? It's all computer-controlled, so we can do custom-manufacturing, short runs, building things that we need on the planet. You'd be astonished how many different little machines and devices and chips and gadgets you need to make a planet go, when you can't just call up and get them from Earth.''

I was as convinced as I wanted to be, but I was polite. I said, "And you'll need fuel for those short-range interplanetary exploration ships, too, of course.''

"I guess so. I hope so, anyway. Personally, I'm not so much using them for exploring the other planets in the system as getting some tugs to bring in raw materials from Delta Pavonis's asteroid belt—you need more than energy to make a factory go, you know." She looked wistful. "Of course," she admitted, "there are problems. The quakes can be pretty bad, sometimes."

"I imagine so," I told her. What I was thinking about was what life was going to be like for her in a place where you had constant earthquakes, and shortages of all kinds, and all the troubles that people who lived in civilization never even gave a thought to. I thought she was a brave woman. I also thought she was a fairly foolish one; but that was none of my business, after all.

Then it was time for me to drop back to the Moon, and I did.

What little free time I had in those days I tried to spend with Alma, and so I headed for her rooms. I thought she might still be sleeping, and so I let myself in quietly. She was actually in her bathroom, washing her hair. "Want to go out and get something to eat?" I called.

"Not right away," she called back, and there was the sound of water running, and a minute later she came out, toweling her hair. "I'm waiting for a call," she said. "Remember Renate beha Nard?" I did; Renate was a friend of Alma's, a big, dark woman who the last time I'd seen her had had a belly the size of a watermelon. "Well, she's delivering about now. I'll want to go see the baby when it's born."

"Ah," I said. "Uh-huh." It wasn't very articulate conversation, but that was because I didn't know exactly what I wanted to say. Then I remembered something about Renate. "She must've quit the Millenarists, too," I said, making a logical deduction from the fact that she and Alma had met at Millenarist services, and now she was having a baby.

"Right," said Alma. She finished turbaning the towel around her head and sat down to look at me. "She knew when she'd made a mistake. Being alive wasn't really a sin, and so having babies couldn't be, either."

"Absolutely," I said, to show how much I agreed with her, and then quickly changed the subject to show that I wasn't attaching any particular importance to it. "Well," I said, "if you don't want to go out, should we call up and have something sent in?"

"I'm not that hungry, actually. Are you?"

I wasn't, and the conversation began to drag. I was pleased when her phone sounded, a little less so when the face on the screen turned out not to belong to a nurse from the birthing center but to the man who seemed to me to be taking an unconscionable amount of time to get out of our lives, Rannulf Enderman.

"Hi," he said brightly to Alma. Then, when he saw my face in the background, a little less enthusiastically, "Hi to you, too, Barry. I just called up to say good-bye."

Alma looked concerned. "You're not leaving right away, are you?"

"No, but pretty soon. I just finished my course for my work on the ship. It was freezing techniques. I'm going to help tend the stiffs, freezing and thawing out."

I had known that he'd quit his job on the launch station when he volunteered for Pava; I hadn't known exactly what he'd been doing instead. I was, as a matter of fact, not sorry to hear he'd been busy; I'd had some concerns, now and then, about his having too much free time to hang around Alma. So I said, making friendly conversation, "That didn't take long, did it?"

He shrugged. "What's to learn? You put them in the freezer, then you wake them up. The cycling is automatic, anyway; all the technician has to do is stand by and make sure the machine does what it does." He went on about the course, about how the automatic systems perfused the freezees with buffers and filled them with the chemicals that slowed down ice nucleation, and I nodded encouragingly.

Alma gave me a quizzical look. "That's nice, Rannulf," she said, interrupting his discussion of how cells that lacked nucleation survived low temperatures, "but I'm going to want to kiss you good-bye. Let's have a drink together—say in a couple of hours? Fine. Let me give you a call when I'm free, all right?"

That was that. She hadn't said when *we* were free.

The call from the birthing center came a minute or two later. Renate's new offspring was a boy, it was healthy, and it was available for inspection any time. "Hey, wonderful," she said to the nurse. Then, to me, "I bet Renate's happy. What about walking me over there, Barry? We can stop and get a sandwich on the way."

"How do you know I don't want to see the baby, too?"

"Do you?"

I didn't answer that, but I thought about it for a while. And when we were eating our sandwiches I cleared my throat and took the plunge. "I really like babies, you know," I said.

"That's nice."

"I guess you do, too."

"Well, how can you help it? They're soft and smelly and helpless, and they need you. If what you're asking me is whether I want to have some of my own, yes. I definitely do. Sometime."

That was the most explicit statement Alma had ever made on the subject. I chewed for a moment, thinking. Then I said, hypothetically, "What if you married, say, someone who couldn't be a father straight-out because he carried some genetic defects?"

"Why," she said, taking the question in stride, "I'd go to the clinic and I'd talk things over with them. There are plenty of things that can be done about that. For one, there's in vitro fertilization, so they comb out the bad recessives—"

I swallowed. Alma was playing back to me just about exactly what the doctor told me, almost word for word.

She had been doing some research. Not about genetic defects in general. About *me*.

I didn't go with her to see the new baby after all, and I didn't try to get myself invited along for the farewell with Rannulf. I was making up my mind, and I wanted to do it on my own time, to be *sure*.

Isn't it funny how often taking the time to make sure a decision is right can turn out to mean you don't really have to make that decision at all?

B y the time I'd finished catching a little sleep—not as much as they had given me time off to do, but enough to get me through the job—it was time for me to go back to *Corsair* for the final loading of its operating fuel supplies. Tscharka watched me at it for a while, but there wasn't much to watch. Actually that was an easier job than dealing with the pods in the cargo hold, because there were only sixteen pods for the ship's drive. Still, it made me a little nervous simply because there was so unusually much antimatter in one place. A hundred and sixteen pods of antimatter is no small amount. It was enough to screw up a whole planet if anything went wrong, so I made damn sure nothing did.

There weren't any real problems in the fueling, except for Rannulf Enderman. I had reconciled myself, very easily, to the thought that I would never see the man again, but he showed up on the last shuttle and he wanted to see me. He chased around until he found where I was, then hailed me. "I'd like to talk to you, Barry."

I gave him a suspicious look. "What about?"

"About Alma," he said, looking somber and self-righteous. "Barry? Alma and I had a little talk. She's a good woman, you know. She wants to be a good mother. I think she ought to get married pretty soon, don't you? Her clock's ticking away, and if she's going to start a family there's no better time than now."

For one nasty, in fact unpardonable, moment I wondered just how he and Alma had said good-bye, but I got that thought out of my head pretty fast. Still, I didn't like the idea of Rannulf giving me advice on whether I should marry his ex-girl. I started to tell him I was too busy, and then I changed my mind. I don't know what made me agree—maybe just good sportsmanship, the winner gracious to the loser—but I said gruffly, "All right, I'll come see you when I'm through."

That didn't mean that I liked the man. I didn't. I especially didn't like his butting in, but what he said about Alma stuck in my mind because it was true. And besides, by then I'd actually made up my mind; as soon as I got back to the lunar surface I would find Alma and ask her to marry me.

All that was a major decision. It filled my thoughts. Rannulf's request for a talk hardly entered my mind. In fact, I might have skipped my date with Rannulf entirely, except that when I was finished I had just missed one possible drop point and had plenty of time before the next one.

So I went to the freezer chambers to look for him, and there he was.

Most of the capsules were already occupied, because all the other volunteers had already been numbed and canned and were in the process of slowly cooling to the liquid-gas temperature that would keep them fresh for their arrival on Pava. Rannulf seemed to be the last one left out. He was hanging to a wall strap with one hand as he waited for me, gazing at a screen that showed the surface of the Moon as it rolled beneath us. His expression was mournful, almost as though he were sentimentally attached to that bleak and gloomy place.

It was a little late, I thought, for Rannulf to be having second thoughts. I interrupted his reverie. "All right," I said. "What was it you wanted to tell me about Alma?"

He sighed and turned toward me. "Have a drink," he said.

"I don't much want a drink," I told him.

"Sure you do," he said, taking two bulbs from a wall rack. "Call it a farewell toast. You're off duty now, aren't you?"

I was. I did what he asked, not for any good reason, just because he'd already filled the bulbs and because I felt sorry for the poor wimp. When I had swallowed most of mine I gave him a get-on-with-it look. "I can't stay here forever," I mentioned.

"I know. I appreciate your taking the time. The thing is, Barry," he said, swallowing the last of his drink, "until you came along Alma was my girl."

"Yes?"

"So if you weren't around," he said, "she probably would be again, don't you think?"

It was around then that I realized the question wasn't entirely hypothetical, because it was around then that I began to feel so very sleepy. Too sleepy to ask him what he was talking about. Too sleepy, in fact, to do anything except go right off to sleep.

I don't know what the little rat put in my drink. I don't remember being prepped, or being lifted into the capsule, or being frozen. The first thing I remember after that was waking up to the sound of Captain Garold Tscharka's angry voice. "Damn," he said. "One more thing gone wrong. What are you doing here, di Hoa?"

When I saw him staring in bafflement down at me, and realized that what I was waking up in was a freezer-thawer capsule and a long time had passed, I got the picture fast.

It was a whole new picture, because it was a whole new life; it was a life that was no longer ever again likely to include Alma or my job or my comfortable existence as a fuelmaster on the Moon, because if I ever saw any of those things again, which I very likely would not, nearly half a century would have passed and I would no longer be involved. "Shit," I said, peering up at Captain Tscharka. "What the hell am I going to be doing on Pava?"

7

T HEN you did not voluntarily choose to come to join the human colony on Pava?

Hell, no. I was fucking *shanghaied* by that bastard Rannulf Enderman. The worst part is I should have seen it coming. He practically spelled it all out for me; I guess I just didn't think he had the guts to do anything like that. So I let him dope me and send me off to the stars so he'd have half a century or so to stay back in the plush and comfortable ease of life on the Moon—with my girl.

So I was seriously pissed when I found out I was an inadvertent volunteer to join the colony at Delta Pavonis. For that matter, so was Captain Garold Tscharka. "What's going on here?" he demanded, glaring down at me. And when I told him what Rannulf had done his face got purple. "But you're needed. I mean *he* is needed. He's supposed to help defreeze the others!" he snapped—by "he," meaning the absent Rannulf, of course. "God," he said—it wasn't meant as a swear word; his eyes were resentfully raised to the skies—"why does everything have to go wrong at once?"

I got out of there. I didn't want any more of Tscharka's bad mood; my own mood was murderous enough for two, and my body was seriously achy from its decades as a corpsicle.

When I noticed I was walking on the floor of the ship's passage instead of pulling myself along in micro-G, I realized the ship was in full deceleration mode, killing velocity to achieve a stable orbit around Pava. I climbed to the control-room level and found Jillen Iglesias talking on the radio to somebody on the surface of the planet.

She craned her neck to stare at me in astonished displeasure. "But you're what's-his-name, Barry something? The fuelmaster? What're you doing here?" she demanded.

She looked a little older and a lot more harried than the last time I had seen her, and when I told her my story, she looked even more astonished. "Well, hell," she said, grudgingly sympathetic. "That's tough. But, look, we're kind of busy, so just stay out of the way, okay?" I could see that she'd picked up a lot of habits from her captain. "I've got a little problem here," she added.

"*You*'ve got a problem?"

She thought that was worth a little smile. "Not like your problem, Barry. It's just that the captain expected that some things would have been done here while we were in transit, and they haven't happened, that's all. Please. Let me get on with it."

At least she'd said please. I did as ordered, pushing myself over to a corner of the room and staying out of the way. I didn't eavesdrop on her radio talk. I had other things on my mind.

I don't know if I can make you understand what a terrible shock it was for an average adult human male like me—set in his ways, with a place in the world and plans for the future—to find himself suddenly twenty-odd years later and eighteen-plus light-years away from everything he cared about. Well, if it happened to you it probably would be just as disorienting, I suppose. But not in the same way, because you don't care about the same things we do.

I cared a lot. The more I thought about all the things I had lost, the more I cared. I thought about my girl, Alma. I thought about my son, Matthew. (Jesus, I thought, the kid's got to be pushing forty years old by now! I've got a son older than I am! I could be a *grandfather* and not even know it.) I thought about sending them both a message. (But what could I say that they wouldn't long since have known? By the time they got it, Alma could very possibly be a grandmother herself and my teenage son Matthew would be getting along toward sixty!) Mostly I thought about Rannulf Enderman and the various kinds of things I would enjoy doing to him if I could.

Unfortunately, the bastard was clear out of my reach. There was no hope of my ever getting my hands on him again, though that didn't stop me from wishing.

Long before I had finished thinking things through, little groups of defrosted passengers began to wander into the control room, looking scared and hopeful and wanting things done for them right away. Jillen Iglesias had her hands full. All at once she was trying to stay in communication with whoever she was talking to on the surface, as long as possible before the continent rolled out from under us; and checking the elements of the orbit the ship was entering; and dealing with the very talkative newcomers. No, they couldn't have a bath just yet, no matter how grungy they felt. No, nobody was going to cook up a breakfast for them, they'd have to wait until they got down to the surface of Pava. No, they couldn't get at their baggage right away, not even to get out a camera so they could take pictures. Yes, that was Pava down below in the screens, and they could look at it for themselves if only they would for Christ's sake stay the hell out of her way.

I had a pretty good idea of what it was like to try to pilot a ship when people were bothering you, so I took a hand. "Shut up, all of you!" I yelled over the babble. "You have to let the pilot do her work, so clear out of the control room. Everybody! Wait in the passages. *Move.*" Of course I had no right to be giving orders, but they didn't know that.

I didn't have any right to stay on after I'd chased the others out, either, but Jillen didn't press the point. "Thanks," she said, and got back to her orbital solutions.

And I got around, at last, to thinking about what was next for me. Pava was my new home. Maybe I wouldn't have to stay on it very long, because I could always take the return trip on *Corsair*. (But was there any point to that?) But in any case I would certainly be spending some time there, and I began to try to contemplate what that was going to mean for me.

In the screen the planet was clear and close up, its image bigger by far than we ever saw Earth from the Moon. We were rolling along over the day side of the planet, which was mostly water, but back toward the sunset horizon I could pick out the disappearing shape of Pava's big central land mass.

What I remembered about Pava wasn't much. I was aware that Pava only had one real continent. That seemed peculiar, compared to present-day Earth, but not unprecedented. After all, Earth too (they said) had once been in the same condition, with a single giant land mass that they called Pangaea, before that big one broke up and formed all the continents you could see when you looked down from the Moon.

If Pava's one big continent had been given a name I didn't know what it was. If there were islands in that endless sea, I didn't see them. Pava wasn't quite as blue as Earth looked from space, but more of a sort of yellowish avocado green. Because the light from Delta Pavonis was a little redder than our Sun's? Because the planet of Pava had more cloud cover? I didn't know the answer to that. I tried to remember what Pava's climate was supposed to be like and drew a blank; I really hadn't paid that much attention.

Still—

Still, once my fury at Rannulf's despicable treachery began to subside, and the little chemical factories the doctors had implanted within me began to catch up with my temper, I began to discover that I was feeling a few quite different emotions. They weren't all bad. There was even a kind of tingly little excitement there. After all, this was a whole new planet! Orbiting an entirely different *star*!

Being on Pava could turn out to be quite an adventure, I thought— at least, for a limited time.

It would have been a nicer adventure with Alma along to share it, I thought, and the sensation that abruptly chilled my heart then was a lot sharper pain than I would have expected. I wondered if she missed me as much as I was missing her. . . .

It is a very curious thing that at that moment, when I was so wrapped up in my worries about the things I could do nothing about, it did not occur to me to worry about the nearer and very real problem of my personal medical history.

*C*orsair achieved Low Planetary Orbit while we were on Pava's night side. Jillen gave a satisfied grunt and grabbed for a handhold as the drive cut itself off and we were in microgravity again.

A few minutes later—we had done most of another orbit of Pava, and the buzz of chatter from the defrosted colonists outside was getting really loud again—Captain Tscharka finally pulled himself up from the freezer chambers, threading his way past the waiting and complaining colonists. He had Friar Tuck with him. The preacher was looking a little more elderly than I remembered him, with more pink scalp showing under the snow white curls at the top of his head. As soon as they were inside the control room the captain stopped short, giving Jillen Iglesias an inquiring look.

Biting her lip, she said, "It's not so good down there, Captain. Jimmy Queng says the last two ships left for Earth with full freezers. Nearly two hundred quitters gave up and went back, would you believe it? I can't think *what* went wrong with them. And he says there are still other people who are just waiting for a flight so they can go back, too—and everything's behind schedule."

Tscharka glanced at Friar Tuck and spread his hands in a what-can-you-expect gesture. All he said was, "If those people didn't have the strength to stay we're probably better off without them. Let's get on with it, Jillen. I don't want to miss the daylight. I'll take the first load down to the surface next time we hit the drop point."

"Right, Captain. Captain? I'm sorry that they've lost so much time."

He shook his head. "Lost time doesn't matter, Jillen. What troubles me is that it looks like too many of our people have lost God."

8

*T*HESE *details of your arrival are of interest, but not of direct concern.* *It is more important that you describe what you knew of Garold-* *tscharka's activities at that time.*

Well, I *am* describing all that, the best way I can. If I wasn't really paying close attention to Captain Tscharka it was because I was caught up in other concerns. As a pilot I was second-guessing everything Jillen and Tscharka did—and especially what the pilot of the shuttle that came soaring up to meet us did. I didn't relax until he'd made rendezvous without a collision. (I would have done it better, I thought. It didn't look to me as though he'd had a lot of practice, whoever he was.) And there was the job of sorting out who would go down in the first load, and the work of shifting some of the colonists' personal effects into the shuttle. How they pissed and moaned when they found out the baggage would come in random order out of the holds instead of letting each one carry his own. And, anyway, we were all in a sort of overstimulated trance. Landing on a brand-new world is a pretty emotional experience, you know. Or don't know; but you can take my word for it.

It was certainly emotional for the eight new colonists who had squeezed into the shuttle with Jillen, the captain and me for the first trip down; they were all excitedly gasping and murmuring among themselves. There was a young couple strapped in next to me for the trip— Becky and Jubal Khaim-Novello, they said their names were—and they were holding hands in trembling bliss. "Oh, Mr. di Hoa," Becky yelled to me over the racket the shuttle made, her huge brown eyes even huger with delight, "isn't it all just *wonderful*?"

I didn't answer. If it wasn't that much pure delight for me, it was because I had other things on my mind, and not all of them were abstract worries and regrets. One was the state of my stomach.

It had been a long time since I'd been down at the bottom of a gravity well any deeper than the Moon's. Even before we got there the shuttle's bouncy, twisty deceleration maneuvers shook me up pretty hard. I was concentrating on trying not to puke when we touched down. Then, after we had landed—all in one piece, wonderfully enough—I was still uncomfortable, but in a new way, because I was being squeezed by nearly normal Earth gravity.

I had known enough about Pava to expect that. It wasn't a real problem for me in the sense that I couldn't handle it; I'd unfailingly kept up my exercises the whole time I was on the Moon, on the premise that one day I'd probably go back to Earth, and so I hadn't let my muscles deteriorate the way some people do. But that didn't make the new weight feel better. It was a great discomfort to feel the way my belly sagged and the weight of my head pressed down on the unpracticed muscles of my neck.

When it was my turn to jump down from the shuttle, I staggered and nearly fell as I hit the scorched, rough ground.

I thought for a moment that my leg muscles hadn't benefited from the stress exercises as much as they were supposed to. Then I noticed that, behind me, the whole big bulk of the shuttle itself was rocking slowly on its stilty landing gear. "Hey," I said, "it's an earthquake!"

Tscharka, right behind me, laughed out loud. "That's right, di Hoa," he said. "We have earthquakes here, you know. This one's too small to worry about. Jillen? Where's the transportation to take us into Freehold?"

She waved off toward a cloud of dust rolling toward us. It turned out to be a car with very big wheels, coming along a rutted dirt trail that might have been intended to be a road. It was coming down along a hillside, which led me to notice that we were in fairly mountainous country. The shuttle landing strip had been scratched out beside one fairly straight stretch of a murky but fast-running little river. The scenery didn't look all that unEarthly. There was green stuff on the hills that looked like trees and another kind of green stuff on the ground that looked like grass—well, a little bit like grass. It was all the right color, anyway, although the stuff on the ground was spiky rather than bladed, and there were little pale blue flowers scattered across it, like dandelions on a neglected suburban lawn. The place smelled right—like vegetation growing—and the breeze was warm.

They say that Pava is the best of the extrasolar colonies, mostly because it has the best star. Alpha Centauri B is part of a binary system, and Epsilon Eridani and Alpha Draconis are variables, so the seasons on their planets can be pretty drastic. I was prepared to admit, on first impression, that Pava wasn't going to be all bad—for those who had chosen to come, anyway.

You ask what Captain Tscharka was doing. I can answer the question, but it won't be much help. What he was doing was standing off by himself, with Friar Tuck, the two of them muttering to each other about things they clearly didn't want anyone else to hear. I wasn't watching him very closely, though; I was more interested in the approach of our welcoming committee.

There was another one of those big-wheeled cars following the first one, at a reasonable distance so as to avoid at least some of the dust the wheels kicked up. The two of them rumbled up to the shuttle and four new people jumped out, shaking every hand they could reach, grinning, patting backs, even hugging. The locals had come out to meet us.

The welcomers consisted of three men and a woman. Two of the men were young, one fair, the other with a dark-haired Oriental sort of look; the third man was older and looking rather abashed. Their names? I rehearsed them three or four times—Jimmy Queng, the tall, black-haired one; Lou Baxto, the one with the pale, bristly mustache; Jacky Schottke, the elderly one who was responding with some embarrassment (or could it almost be guilt?) to Captain Tscharka's surprisingly affectionate greeting. But I forgot all the names again halfway to the town, which was out of sight on the side of a distant hill. I was too busy looking at all the sights, including the one next to me.

The sight was the driver of the lead car. I was sitting next to her, and she was worth looking at. (I don't want you to think that I had already forgotten Alma. I was working hard at trying to stop *remembering* Alma.) The person was named Theophan Sperlie, a woman maybe just a little older than myself, who not only had a pleasant, friendly face but smelled nicely of soap and mint. And she kept looking around at me in just the same way that I kept looking at her, as she gave me a running commentary on all the things we were passing.

Behind us the Khaim-Novellos and a few others were holding hands and singing in the back of the car, still wearing those fuddled grins. "Looks like those guys are happy to be on Pava, anyway," I said to Theophan Sperlie.

"We'll just have to find some way of making you happy, too, Barry," she said, and took her hand off the wheel long enough to pat my knee. It seemed I had begun to make friends on Pava very quickly.

To confirm her goodwill, Theophan Sperlie pointed out all the sights on the way in. There was the lumber camp, where they got their wood. (Well, not really *wood* like pine or oak; most of it was more like bamboo, along with some other "trees" that resembled boxwood hedges but grew ten times taller.) Off across the river there was the road that led up, she said, to the community's mostly disused iron mine. ("But if we ever get our short-range ships going properly we'll get the iron from space, and then we can close that down. People get hurt there.") Some things I saw on my own. Now and then there were things moving in the underbrush—animals, no doubt—but by the time I called Theophan Sperlie's attention to them they were gone, too fast to identify. ("Don't worry, Barry. You'll get plenty of chances to meet the local fauna!") And I saw a nice little waterfall as we passed a narrow valley— a slim stream thirty meters high and splashing prettily on the rocks at the bottom. But when I mentioned it to Theophan she cocked an eye and said, "Must be a new one. I didn't see it last time I came by. I guess a fault let go and opened up a spring."

It wasn't a long drive, but the large, orange Pava sun was getting low in the sky.

Civilization on Pava was a town called Freehold. I looked it over with care. At first sight, I wasn't that thrilled with the town—well, call it a town out of courtesy, although a population of 853 hardly even makes a village, does it? Freehold wasn't big. No part of it was much more than ten minutes from the farthest other part of it, and even so it wasn't at all densely built. There were little clusters of what Theophan Sperile said were homes—the places where the Freeholders lived, anyway; each composed of four rickety wooden structures built around a little central yard. The clusters were spaced out every hundred meters or so along the "street"—which was rutted and potholed and had never been paved; I understood why all their vehicles had those giant wheels. In the spaces between buildings were open lots, overgrown with vegetation of no kinds I had ever seen before. About all there was besides was an occasional larger structure, apparently a workplace of some kind—

and a lot of churches. I *guessed* they were churches, though some of them were tiny, from the fact that each one had a cross, star of David, crescent or other religious symbol over its door. The biggest one did have a cross, but as we passed I saw that it also displayed the omega sign of the Millenarists, and from behind me the Khaim-Novellos and the others gave a little cheer.

I should have expected that, I suppose, from what I knew about so many of the people associated with *Corsair*. I hadn't, though. What I had actually hoped—or would have hoped, if I had known that I was coming here and had given it any thought at all—was that maybe a world with a human population of less than a thousand would have simplified its religious urges.

It hadn't, though. Denominationally speaking, Freehold seemed to be even more divided than the Moon. I looked at the people in the streets as they stopped whatever they were doing to stare or wave at us, and wondered if there were quite enough of them to go around for the visible number of denominations.

We stopped in front of a shingled, flat-roofed structure that Theophan Sperlie said was the communal meeting hall, though it looked more like a roller-skating rink in some small town. Its walls didn't seem entirely straight, and the front door had a board nailed across it.

In fact, what all the buildings had in common was that they were ramshackle wooden affairs, mostly constructed out of that more-or-less bamboo and not in very good repair. A lot of them were propped up by those bamboo columns.

When Theophan saw what I was looking at, she grinned. "Blame it on the earthquakes," she said. "As I guess you know, we have a lot of them here."

"I did know, Ms. Sperlie—"

"Theo."

"I did know about the earthquakes, Theo. Sort of."

"Well, anything you don't know I'll tell you. That's my job, seismologist. The situation isn't all that bad, really. The biggest buildings are the ones that give us the most trouble when we get a serious tremor. Like our meeting hall over there. That one got its foundations shifted a while ago, and we haven't made up our minds about whether we should be repairing it or tearing the damn thing down and starting over. Fortunately it's nice weather now, so we meet outdoors mostly."

I asked the question that had been growing in my mind as we bumped along. "Does it have a men's room?"

"A what? Oh. I know what you mean. Well, Barry," she said frankly, "you see, that's one of our problems here. We haven't had much luck with sewer systems. But there's an outhouse next to just about every building, so help yourself."

In the thirty-six elapsed years of my life (not counting the time while I was both frozen and time-dilated on the ship) I had never once been anywhere that didn't have a high-tech toilet. On Earth they were mostly flush; on the Moon mostly thermal; but they always took the little contributions from my digestive system and made them disappear.

That wasn't the way it was on Pava. I didn't even know what an "outhouse" was supposed to look like until a helpful resident pointed me the right way, and then I didn't much like it. It turned out to be a little shanty built around a wooden seat with a hole in it to excrete through, and a bigger hole dug in the ground below to hold the excretions.

It smelled accordingly. I began to wonder if being on Pava was going to turn out even nastier than I had suspected.

That led me to wonder what my chances were of getting off it pretty fast. I wasn't really thinking of getting back to my unfinished business with Alma anymore. I had already written that prospect off for good; fifty years was a hell of a lot longer than I could imagine anyone waiting, not to mention what sort of condition Alma might be in after fifty years of elapsed time for her. I wasn't even thinking of getting back to my job. I was just thinking about getting *back*.

When I came back, feeling chastened, both cars were pulled up in the square, with our newcomers mingling with a bunch of the Pavan colonists. At least half of the new people, along with a lot of the ones who lived there, were clustered around Captain Tscharka. Some of the blissful smiles on the faces of the newcomers had evaporated.

It was the first chance I'd had to take a good look at my fellow passengers from *Corsair*'s deep freeze. I was not impressed. I shook hands with ten or twelve of them—and at least as many of the residents—without remembering a name. It struck me that, although the people who had lived here for a while all seemed to have reasonably useful skills, the newcomers were not the kind of prospects I would have chosen to build a new frontier. Two of them described themselves as poets, one was an actor, a couple were so young they were nothing in particular, being just out of school. The young ones, at least, I could see potentially developing into something Pava might need. The others struck me as a good sample of the kind of people who couldn't make it back home and had headed for Pava to change their luck.

I wondered if their luck was really that likely to change. It seemed a good bet to me that the would-be returnees clamoring for a freezer locker in the next ship home would include at least a few of those who had just got here . . . including, of course, myself.

Captain Garold Tscharka had detached himself from the cluster of Millenarists by then and left Friar Tuck behind to lead them in a hymn. When I looked around I saw that Tscharka was in what looked like a fairly acrimonious conversation with somebody I recognized; his name was Schottke, and he was one of the people who had come out to meet us. Then Tscharka saw me, and pointed, and Schottke came hurrying over to where I was. "Barry di Hoa? I'm Jacky Schottke—"

"We met."

"Right, at the shuttle," he said, being agreeable. He looked a little ruffled, though, and glanced apprehensively back at Tscharka now and then. "Well, Barry, we're a little short of housing here—I guess you can see that—so Garold Tscharka says you're to room with me until we can finish building some more living space. Somehow. So when your stuff comes down from the shuttle—"

"I don't have any stuff," I told him, and then had to explain that my visit hadn't been premeditated.

"Oh, hell," he said, "what a lousy deal for you! Still, you'll be all right. This isn't a bad planet. I find it pretty exciting, but then it's my work that makes it interesting, you know. What do you do?"

"Fuelmaster. Or was. I worked on the Moon, handling antimatter fuel."

"Oh." He looked pleased. "I imagine Garold is happy about that; he's brought back tons of the stuff, I hear. I'm a taxonomist, with a special interest in trophic food chains—that is, when they'll let me spare the time—though as a matter of fact I used to be—"

He stopped there, looking quickly again at Captain Tscharka. Then he finished. "I used to be something else, actually. But that was nearly fifty years ago, and I'm not that anymore. I just happened to get interested in taxonomy—you know, scientific ways of describing organisms? Seeing how they relate to each other? And fifty years is a long time, Barry, and I wanted to be here for Garold when he came back, but—well, people change."

That was about as muddled an explanation as I'd ever heard, especially since I hadn't asked him for any. The man was double-talking me, for what reason I could not guess. "Now," he said briskly, "I'm sure you're hungry, so let's eat. You can meet some of the others—if you're not too tired?"

Well, I wasn't too tired. Not exactly. What I was was confused. My life had changed too drastically in too short a time, and I was having trouble figuring out where I was going with it.

I wasn't particularly hungry, either, in spite of what Schottke had said—you don't work up much of an appetite in the deep freeze—but they'd put plates and dishes out on long trestle tables, in the shade of some of those bamboo-like trees, and I was willing to try to eat. I found a seat between Theophan and Jillen and investigated the food.

We didn't begin eating right away. Before we were allowed to start eating Captain Tscharka climbed on a bench and Reverend Tuchman pounded the table for attention. When the babble dwindled Tscharka gave us all a little speech:

"It's wonderful to be back on Pava again. In deference to our various differing beliefs I will not ask the Reverend to say a formal grace, but we all, I am sure, want to thank our God for our safe arrival and for the bounty before us. And I would like to announce that for our Millenarist brethren we will hold a special prayer meeting immediately after the meal. Thank you," he said, and sat down.

A fair number of people applauded, including most of the newcomers from *Corsair*. So, I noticed, did both Jillen and Jacky Schottke. I didn't. Tscharka hadn't said anything that I particularly agreed to.

Then we began to eat.

It doesn't really make much sense to judge a new place by its food, but I guess most of us do it. In this case, the food was not wonderful. Some of the dishes were strange, stringy vegetables that I didn't enjoy and even Jillen refused to put in her mouth. Some were assorted kinds of stew, chicken or unidentified meat, with more of those unappetizing vegetables contaminating it. There were, however, a few better choices—fresh tomatoes, lettuce and fruits, as well as a couple of reasonably decent kinds of bread.

Meeting the others didn't go particularly well. There were too many of them. The town wasn't full—much of the human population of Pava was off somewhere. Some on their routine work, others checking the damage of a recent earthquake—but there were still nearly five hundred strangers to me milling around the dining tables, and, although I tried to avoid being introduced to all of them, I only partly succeeded.

By comparison, Jillen and Theophan were old friends. But that wasn't the only reason I had chosen to sit next to Jillen. I had a question to ask her, and first chance I got I popped it.

"Jillen? When will *Corsair* go back?"

She gave me a puzzled, then sympathetic look. "That's up to the captain, I guess. What's the matter, don't you like Pava?"

I shrugged. "I haven't been here long enough to know, but I'd like to know what my options are. Maybe I should just ask the captain."

I was craning my neck to see what he was doing; he was talking with Friar Tuck, both of them scowling. Jillen pursed her lips. "Right now might not be the best time," she said. "He's had some disappointments in the last couple of hours. Some of his old friends are dead—well, Millenarists, you know? We do that sometimes." That startled me; apart from the dutiful applause she'd given Tscharka I hadn't had any idea that she was a Millenarist, too. "Oh," she said, correctly reading my expression, "I'm just kind of lukewarm, I'm afraid. But I'm still in the church, yes. I don't think Garold would have kept me on *Corsair* otherwise. Anyway, a lot of the Millenarists he expected to find have suicided and quite a few others have kind of, well, dropped out. And there haven't been that many new ones joining in. He—" She hesitated, then said it: "He didn't think the colony would have turned so *secular*. So he's, well, disappointed."

I was astonished to hear her call this community of endless churches "secular," but the rest of what she said was borne out by the evidence. Captain Tscharka was certainly looking like a disappointed man. A grumpy one, too; not the state you would hope for in someone you might have to ask for a favor. Still, since I didn't have any particular desire to be best friends with the man, his moods were not especially important to me. I was about to get up and go over to him anyway when Theophan announced, "Here comes the dessert."

And I turned around and looked.

Something was pulling a little wagon of cakes and pies toward the table, something I'd never seen before. It moved like a mink, twisting like a snake, but it did not look like any mink or snake I'd ever seen a picture of. It was big, too—more than a meter long, I thought, and then, as it extended its body to pull its little wagon, suddenly more than two meters long.

"My God," I said, "that's a damn big bug."

"Bug? Oh, no, Barry," Theophan said. "He's not a bug. He's a fifth-instar lep."

The thing dropped the little harness it was holding in its mouth and came toward us, making a sort of hissing, whispery sound. "Fifth instar," Theophan was saying, "is the last stage before they turn into the winged form and die."

She went on talking, but I wasn't listening. I was staring at the thing. It was hauling itself up to peer over the table at me, and it looked *strange*. What it looked like to me then, more than anything else, was the Caterpillar from *Alice in Wonderland*, all but the hookah. It was dappled in camouflage colors of brown, white and beige, like the meringue on a lemon pie. It had tiny hands on the end of short, double-jointed arms that were gripping the top of the table, and it had huge, faceted eyes that covered half its head, like a fly's. It had a mouth— or, anyway, a mouthpart, round and lipless—that opened and shut like the iris of a camera lens, and it was hissing at me. Its breath was vinegary and warm.

Theophan looked at me expectantly. "Say hello," she prompted me.

"Do what?"

"Say hello to him. That's St. John."

"That's who?"

She was laughing at me by then. "St. John isn't his lep name, of course, but they all oblige us by taking names we can pronounce. The leps are very polite people, mostly. St. John is talking to you."

"He is?" My conversational skills seemed to be getting more and more rudimentary.

"He wants to know what your job is going to be on Pava. Actually, I was kind of wondering that myself."

"Oh. Sorry," I said, beginning to recall more of my vocabulary. "Tell him I'm a fuelmaster, if he understands what that means—I don't suppose he speaks English."

"Barry," she said, looking disappointed in me, "he *is* speaking English. It's just that leps aren't good at voiced sounds because they don't have much of a larynx."

And, when I listened more carefully, he actually was. The sound that came out of his mouthpart was a whisper of unvoiced frequencies, as though he were whistling the sentences through teeth he didn't seem to have, but the sentences were definitely composed of English words.

It took me a while to understand what he was saying, but then that's not so surprising, is it? After all, that was the first time I had ever met any of you.

9

*I*T *is interesting that you seem embarrassed when you say we were called "bugs."*

Is that meant to be a question?

No. The question is this: Do you feel that the term "bug" is a derogatory epithet, meant to give offense to the person named, like some of the terms you humans sometimes apply to each other?

Well, I guess it is, in a way. It's not as insulting as some of the things we call each other, but it's not meant to be particularly flattering, either—although in your case I would have to say that it's sort of justified because of the way you look. I mean, the closest thing there is on Earth to your kind is the insects. Especially the moths and butterflies that they call "lepidoptera." In your case, "leps" for short.

Jacky Schottke is the reason I know as much as I do about the subject of you leps (which probably is not all that much, anyway). He did his best to explain the differences between leps and insects after we had gone to his place that night. He was talking about his work as a taxonomist, and how he was mostly self-taught out of the stored datafiles, and how he had come to specialize in the fascinating (he said) dynamics of ecological communities.

Schottke was a pretty elderly fellow, at least eighty, I judged, but he seemed so enthusiastic about his work that I made the mistake of asking him what the work was, exactly. The result was that I got a twenty-minute lecture on the interactions of Pava's living things—he referred to them as the planet's "biota." The way he organized the data he collected was, he said, in the form of *n*-dimensional food webs. That was the only rational way to do it, he said, because, after all, when you consider what effects the members of a given clutch of living organisms have on each other, your clearest road map lies in observing who eats whom. Once you had that much straightened out you could group them into what he called "trophic species" and then you could start analyzing how each species affected the others.

It was all sort of interesting, and I thought it was actually touching to see how Schottke's eyes sparkled when he talked about it. Still, an Entomology 101 lecture wasn't exactly the kind of thing I needed to hear, so I asked him specifically to tell me about you people.

He stopped in the middle of the lecture. The sparkle went out of his eyes. Then he sighed.

I could see that he was sorry to abandon the really fascinating subjects of trophic species and reciprocal predation just to give me a simple answer to a dumb question, but he was a good host. "How about a drink, Barry?" he said. I thought that was a fine idea, and so he pulled out a bottle. I looked at the label with a little surprise; it said *Moët et Chardonne*.

That made him laugh a little. "Oh, it's not champagne, I'm afraid. We reuse all our old bottles for home brew, but I think it's not bad."

He waited expectantly while I tasted it. No, it certainly wasn't champagne. Wasn't wine at all; it had been distilled and it had a healthy kick. But it went down all right, and when I acknowledged it was drinkable, he began producing pictures for me on his screen.

The leps, he said, were something like an Earthly butterfly, not counting the size—well, a *little* like butterflies—though of course butterflies didn't have lungs and circulatory systems, and certainly weren't as intelligent. Butterflies didn't have language, or laws, or settlements, or well-formed relationships. But butterflies also didn't have much consistency of shape or behavior during their lives, and neither, Schottke told me earnestly, did leps.

"I guess I knew that, Jacky—sort of. I mean, there used to be all kinds of stories about Pava and the leps when I was a kid."

He seemed pleased to hear that I was at least that well informed and went on to retrieve images for his screen and tell me the things I hadn't known.

He showed me pictures of a newly hatched, first-instar baby lep, practically nothing but mouth and digestive system. The new-hatched lep didn't look at all like St. John to me. Schottke told me that was an accurate observation. That was one of the significant morphological differences between leps and human beings, he said. A baby human does look quite a lot like an adult; but what a "one-star," or infant, lep mostly looked like, he pointed out, was a large, messy, cowflop-sized turd, and what it did in that stage, outside of eat and excrete and grow, was basically nothing.

Then the second-instar lep, a little bigger, a lot more active, began to have the intelligence, say, of a human toddler. What the picture looked like to me was a scaly sort of earthworm, though at that stage their coloring was generally bright red. At the third instar I could see the little "arms" and "hands" developing on the still-wormy torso; the fourth instar looked physically about the same, though now all the adult features were quite visible. Even the fifth looked not that much different to me, until Schottke told me that the fourth instar was full maturity, which would last unchanged for as much as thirty or forty years, and pointed out that the fifth instar was looking pretty ragged.

"You could call the five-star leps their senior citizens," he explained. "At the fifth instar they're, as you might say, retired from most activities. They're getting ready to convert to the final winged form, and their minds are beginning to suffer. Their fur gets frayed and their colors fade, and they begin to develop sexual organs—and they go on doing that for a year or so, until they molt into the final, sexual, winged, egg-laying kind."

He stopped there, thinking.

"At that point they don't have any intelligence at all left," he went on after a moment—reluctantly, I thought. "In the sixth instar they don't eat, either. They just make love, and fly around, and lay their eggs, until they die." And he stopped again.

He wasn't looking at me anymore. He was staring mournfully at the picture on the screen of the sixth-instar lep, with its giant, lacy, all-colored wings. It was a spectacularly beautiful picture, I thought, but Schottke didn't look as though he were enjoying its beauty.

He looked sadder than I had ever seen a human being look before.

I didn't know why. Not then, anyway. But I wondered if it had anything to do with his touchy worries about Captain Tscharka (I eventually discovered that it did, though not in any way I could have guessed), and so I thought it might be all right to pry a little. "Jacky?" I began. "What was it you used to be?"

He blinked and focused on me. "What?"

"You said you used to be something else before you got into taxonomy. What was it?"

"Oh." He thought for a moment, then shrugged. "I'm not ashamed of it. When I was young I thought I had the call. I was going to be a Millenarist preacher, like Friar Tuck. As a matter of fact, Tuck was the one who trained me, and not just me, either. There were half a dozen of us young ordained Millenarist ministers then, and we had a lot of people in our church—there were only about four hundred people on Pava at the time, and more than half of them Millenarists. We were all real red-hots. When Tuchman left with Captain Tscharka to make the run to Earth, we all vowed that we would carry on the faith. We knew they'd be gone for nearly half a century. It didn't worry us. We swore we'd stay consecrated, no matter how long we had to wait for their return, and we'd devote ourselves to spreading the word as long as we lived."

He swallowed, looking guilty. "We didn't, though. After he left things changed. We stopped making so many converts. When new colonists arrived a lot of them just weren't interested. We had a lot of trouble keeping the colony alive, too; this is not the easiest planet to survive on. . . . Well, things happened. A few people made the transition—you know; you call it suicide. Others just drifted away. I got interested in the goobers and the leps, and—well, you know how it is, Barry; fifty years is a long time to expect anybody to keep on burning with a white-hot flame, isn't it? I couldn't make it."

"I see," I said.

I didn't, really, of course. Do you ever really see what some other person is thinking in his secret heart? I don't think so. It wouldn't be his secret heart if you did, would it? You think you know somebody pretty well—your parish priest when you're a kid, for instance, or the recent widower who's so hopelessly, terminally devastated because his dear wife of twenty years got herself electrocuted when she fell into the hot leads for the particle accelerator. And then one day when you're not expecting anything of the kind, the priest gets caught buggering a choirboy, and the cops come and pick your friendly mourner up because his wife didn't fall, he pushed her. So what do you know, really?

Well, I knew there was something going on with Jacky Schottke, something to account for his obvious distress when he talked about the leps or his failed ministry. I just didn't know what it was, and I didn't know what questions to ask. And then, there was one other thing. I had begun to like

Jacky Schottke, enough so I didn't want to make him unhappy. And there wasn't any doubt that those subjects were painful for him.

So I just said, more or less trying to change the subject away from his private pains without being too obvious about it, "I'm a little surprised that there's such a large proportion of Millenarists here on Pava. They're kind of scarce back on Earth."

He nodded gloomily, looking at the screen again. "There was some great missionary work done here. You have to admit that Garold and Tuchman are pretty convincing people," he said. "It was hard to say no to them. It was for me, anyway. And then—"

He stopped abruptly. "Damn it. There we go again," he said.

The picture on the screen had garbled, and the room lights flickered off, then back on. I felt a little quiver in my chair, as though a heavy truck had just run past us on the road . . . although, of course, there wasn't even a road of any kind nearby, much less that heavy a truck.

"Hell," Jacky said, dismally anticipating what was going to happen next. . . .

Then the lights went all the way off. We were sitting there in the dark.

I could hear his sigh of resignation. "Sorry about that, Barry. We've obviously lost our power again. If it's any consolation, I don't think it's serious. It's probably that little tremor just now that got the transmission line. Hang on, I've got a couple of battery lights here—and I've really been a rotten host, haven't I? I haven't even shown you around the apartment yet."

I know none of this has much to do with Garold Tscharka. I can't help it. If I don't tell it all as I remember it I'll probably leave something out, and then you'll be on my case about that. Bear with me.

I also know that you people don't take much interest in houses, because you don't live in them. We do. They're important to us. They're one of the things that make us human, so when Jacky Schottke offered me the tour of his apartment I was willing to go along.

Schottke's place was on the top floor of one of the four buildings that surrounded one of those grassy squares. His was the only two-story one of the four. The apartment wasn't much, even compared with our tight living spaces on the Moon. He had four small rooms. No carpets. The furniture was an odd mixture, some of it obviously homemade, some quite new (from the factory orbiter, I supposed), some old and tattered enough to have been brought by the first settlers. It all evoked memories for me. It took me back to the place Gina and I had lived in right after we were married, before Matthew came, before—well, before everything. True, this place was only one story above ground, and the apartment Gina and I had then had been on the thirty-first floor of the high rise. But it had that same feel—scratched together, making do.

Schottke lifted his battery lamp to peer into my face. "Is something the matter?" he asked.

I shook myself. "No, I was just thinking about something." Actually, Schottke's place was quite different. It had two little bedrooms instead of the one Gina and I had shared, and each had two narrow beds that were set against a wall with a ceiling-high clothes-storage chest between them. Schottke's minute living room contained a plastic-upholstered couch, a few odd chairs and a table that bore a screen and workstation. All else the apartment had was a functionally complete but crowded bathroom and an also functionally complete but even more densely crammed kitchen.

Schottke said, "We've got a new couple moving in below us, the Khaim-Novellos. I guess they're friends of yours from the ship?"

"You don't get a chance to make friends when you're in the freezer," I told him. "Which room is mine?"

"The one on the left—I mean, if that's all right with you? They're pretty much identical. And, oh, listen, about the bathroom. There's a toilet there, but we don't use it anymore, until we figure out how to repair the sewerage system. There's something out in back."

"An outhouse, right. I've already been warned about that."

"Fine. Well, that's about it, then. God knows when they'll get the power back on, and it's late. We might as well get to bed, if that's all right with you? All right, then. Good night, Barry."

In the morning Schottke was awake before me, bright-eyed and no longer very interested in conversation. The power was back on and Schottke was in a hurry. "You'll have a lot of things you're supposed to be doing today, Barry," he said. "You'll need your shots. Then you'll have to see Jimmy Queng to get your work assignment—"

"I told you I'm a fuelmaster," I pointed out, a little surprised at the idea that I might be asked to do something different.

"Yes, but you can't *always* be shipping antimatter fuel around, can you? And when you're not busy at that you'll have to help with the colony's regular work. We all do, how else could we survive here? Me? Well, certainly, I do my share. Of course I did more when I was younger, just like everybody else. I strung lines, I cooked, I helped build the roads, I farmed for a while, I even spent three months in the mine—it's only now, when I'm getting a little past any kind of rugged outdoor work, that they let me spend most of my time on taxonomy. Come on. I guess you'll want to get cleaned up first, but then we'd better get on down to the commons. They'll have breakfast ready—and then you can get started on your chores."

By the time we arrived at the open-air dining trestles I'd learned more about Pava's housekeeping practices. There was running water in the little bathroom, at least. It didn't help with the toilet. The lid on that was lowered. Schottke had draped a cloth over the lid and then, to make sure I didn't forget, put a pot of flowers on the cloth. Still, I could wash up, as long as I didn't mind doing it in cold water, although then I had to head for the outhouse.

Incoming water, Schottke explained, was taken care of by flexible piping from the central water tower, and outgoing water was allowed to drain away in back, as long as it didn't come from the toilet. The trouble with the toilet was that they hadn't been able to arrange any underground waste pipes that didn't fracture every time there was a temblor. "And one time the town water tower itself fell over," he said gloomily. "We had real problems for a while then, but now we've got the new one pretty well braced—it's stayed up through our eight-point-one shake, which is more than a lot of the houses did."

"Grand," I said, still chewing, and got up to locate Captain Tscharka.

He wasn't hard to find, and evidently his temper had not improved overnight. As I was finishing eating Jillen came away from an interview with him, looking scalded. "Don't ask him anything now," she warned me. "He's still furious about the way the colony has backslid."

There are some things I'm good at and some things I'm not, and one of the things I'm particularly bad at is following advice I don't like. I didn't really care about how Captain Garold Tscharka felt about the religious failings of his colony. But Jillen's advice hadn't been entirely wrong, either, because by the time I got to him he was out of his seat at the breakfast table and heading rapidly toward one of the offices.

"Tscharka," I called, and finally had to trot after him and catch his arm before he stopped. He gave me a very hostile look.

"What the hell do you want?"

"Just one question, Captain. When are you going to take off for the return flight to the Moon?"

The look turned even more hostile. "Tired of the planet already? Well, don't hold your breath. *Corsair* isn't going to leave until *Buccaneer* arrives. At least."

"But I don't want to stay here. I wasn't supposed to come to Pava in the first place," I protested.

That didn't interest him. "You can file a complaint with the authorities on the Moon when you get back," he said, "assuming any of the people involved are still alive. Quit bitching, will you? It's not so bad here on Pava, di Hoa, and besides you can make yourself useful. As long as you're here you'll have to work, you know. We don't have any loafers on Pava."

I didn't take any pleasure in being reminded of that again. In fact, nothing the man said made me like him any better, but it seemed like a good idea to start lining myself up for an interesting job. "I'm a qualified pilot," I reminded him. "If there's time before I leave I guess I could take one of those exploring ships out."

He blinked at me. "What kind of ships?"

"The ships you requisitioned all that antimatter for. To explore the Delta Pavonis system."

"Oh," he said, "those." He studied me for a while, then gave me a really unfriendly scowl. "Have you seen any short-range ships in orbit? No, you haven't. There aren't any. Nobody bothered to build them."

"But—"

"But we'll probably find another use for the antimatter—maybe in the factory orbiter. If that happens you can help me transship the pods, as soon as *Buccaneer* arrives."

"But—" I began again, and never got past that "but," either, because he had pulled his arm free and was already a meter away and moving fast. I turned to Jillen. "Hell," I said.

She shrugged. "There isn't any daily shuttle service between here and Earth, you know."

I surrendered to the inevitable. "It's funny, though," I said. "Why's he going to wait until *Buccaneer* arrives to ship the fuel to the factory orbiter?"

"You'd have to ask him," she said, "and I still don't recommend doing that. Give me a hand with these dishes, will you?"

*   *   *

That was when I found what my first real job on Pava was going to be. It was kitchen police.

Well, not quite. I didn't have to do the washing up. As soon as the tables were clear I, with all the other new arrivals, was ordered—"invited" might have been a politer word, because at least they were smiling when they said it—to get out in front of the hall again for our prophylactic shots and our turn in the daily job lineup.

Shots for what? I asked the woman who was shepherding us out, name of Sharon something. Shots against native diseases, she said, and when I asked her what kind of diseases those were, she said, "How would I know? Nobody ever gets them anymore, because we all get the shots." Then she looked at me more carefully. "Do you have any special reason for asking? Like some medical problem the doctor ought to hear about?"

"Ah," I said, suddenly aware that I did. "Yes. Actually I do have—"

Nobody was letting me finish sentences that morning. "Jesus," she said in dismay, "how come they let you get here with a medical problem? Don't they give physicals anymore? Anyway, that's not my department. Ask Billygoat or his wife about it when they come to you with the shots."

When the shots came they weren't painful, of course, but there were a lot of them—two or three in each arm, a man going down the line on right arms, a woman following him and taking care of the lefts. They both looked harried and not interested in talking to their new patients. When the man began dotting my forearm with his little vaccine spray, I said, "Are you the one they call Billygoat?"

He gave me a frosty look, then a glance of suspected recognition. "Are you the one Sharon says has the medical problem?"

When I said I was, and began to tell him about my little difficulty of occasional loopiness, he looked startled, then resigned. "Oh, hell, this is all I need. I can see you're going to be a real pain in the ass," he told me. "I can't deal with that kind of thing now. You're not likely to go critical right away, are you?"

"I hope not."

"Well, don't. Come around to my office tomorrow—no, wait, better make it next week. I'm pretty busy right now. Next!"

And that was that. I didn't really have time to press the matter, because the gang boss was already whistling and gesturing at us to come over to where he was waiting.

I recognized the gang boss. He was one of the ones who had picked us up at the landing strip, the tall, black-haired fellow named Jimmy Queng. Now he was carrying a handscreen. When we were all gathered around him he stared at whatever was displayed on the screen for a second, then waved it at us for quiet.

"All right, new fellow citizens. Welcome to Pava. We're glad to have you here, we hope you'll find your new lives worthwhile, but we do need to get work done. These first assignments are all temporary, but that doesn't mean they aren't important. Everybody works here, even on the dumb, dirty jobs. *Especially* on those jobs, because they're the ones that nobody wants to do. Our biggest job is keeping ourselves alive, and that takes all of us, okay?" No one answered what evidently had already become a familiar litany for all of us, so he started right in. "Let's see, the first thing we need is about eight or nine good hands for farm work. Any of you interested in a healthy out-of-doors life?"

He waited expectantly. A moment passed, then two women and a man stepped warily forth.

"That's a start, anyway," he said. "What's the matter, does the work sound beneath you? Or just too hard? It's not so bad, you know. You'll just start out with chopping and harvesting, but it doesn't stop there. As soon as we get the new cargoes down from *Corsair* we need to do some more interesting stuff; we've got to inseminate some soil with fungus to make real trees grow, and start some new earthworm colonies to aerate the soil. And, listen, if any of you like good food, some of the fungi will make truffles—you'll be the ones who will know where to find them a couple of years from now."

This time two others began hesitantly to move up—I couldn't guess whether it was because they were truffle fanciers or because they figured some other job might be even worse. Jimmy Queng nodded. "The rest of the farm crew," he said pleasantly, "we'll just have to draft when we finish up asking for volunteers, I guess. How about building maintenance? That means carpentry, repair work, everything we need to put the town back together again every time a quake comes along. We can use about three here?"

He got his three, and he got the three more he wanted for cutting fuel for the power generator. That puzzled me, but I didn't have a chance to ask why they needed to be cutting fuel when, I was pretty sure

Tscharka had said, they were supposed to have a perfectly good hydro-electric plant in operation by now. I didn't get a chance to ask any questions at all, because he was already calling for power plant mainte-nance personnel. That sounded like skilled work, but not drudgery, and I figured I knew enough to get by from my experience as a fuelmaster. I immediately put up my hand.

Jimmy looked up at me approvingly over his glasses, but before he could accept my offer someone whispered in his ear.

"Oh, right," he said. "He's the one, eh?" He shook his head at me. "Not you, di Hoa. We've got something else for you. You're going to be doing seismology."

"I don't know thing one about seismology!" I protested.

"Then you'll never find a better time to start learning about it, will you? Anyway, the seismologist will teach you and I imagine she'll be patient. She asked for you specifically, in fact." And when I looked around somehow I wasn't surprised, and was even less displeased, to find that the seismologist in question was Theophan Sperlie.

10

AT this point we ask that you give us your assessment of Theophan-sperlie.

Oh, hell, are you still going on about that stuff? Why do you want to know? Is it going to influence you?

Every factor will be weighed by all of us, Barrydihoa, and it is your task to supply all relevant information. Omit nothing.

Well, it would help if I knew whether you wanted my personal or professional opinions about Theophan. There was a lot I liked about her. You had a different opinion, I know that, but that's how I felt. Theophan struck me as a good-natured person, and she had a sense of humor. She was reasonably pretty, too. I know it's sexist to say that. Some of the feminist sects would kick me out for heresy for even mentioning that. But she was.

She also turned out to have another trait that I appreciated very much, and she mentioned it early on: She did not belong to the Millenarist church. By then I had begun to feel a little outnumbered.

The remaining intriguing thing about Theophan was the kind of work she did for the colony. I'd never met a seismologist before. Oh, I knew that such people existed. Even on the Moon we'd hear news stories from Earth about earthquakes, but they had no apparent relevance to our own lives. Earthquakes were things that happened in New Jersey and Italy and China and all those places, not on the dead old Moon. If there was a practicing seismologist anywhere near the Lederman factory, I had never come across him.

So the first thing I said to Theophan that day was, "I appreciate the compliment but you know, don't you, that I don't know anything about seismology."

She looked up from chucking things into a backpack to study my face. Then she grinned. "I didn't expect you to. Whatever you need to know I'll teach you as we go along, if you're interested, and if we have the time. They probably won't let me have you when I'm working in my office anyway, because naturally you'll have to do regular chores. The time I really need help is when I'm in the field. That's the reason I asked for you today. A lot of what I need to do is plain donkey work, resiting strain gauges up in the hills. All that takes is a strong back and good legs. Are you willing to give it a shot?"

"I'm willing as hell, Theo," I told her, "but I've also spent the last eleven years on the Moon."

The grin vanished. "Oh, shit," she said in dismay. "I didn't think of that. Does that mean your muscles have gone all flabby?"

"Maybe not." I told her about how carefully I'd kept up the stress exercises, and I managed to lift the bigger of the backpacks when she gave it to me. So, though still looking doubtful, she requisitioned one of the big-wheeled cars and we started up the mountain.

On the way she started my beginner's-level course in Earthquakes and Volcanoes. Pava, she explained, was tectonically a very active planet. "Planets are all different, you know. They come in a lot of different shapes and sizes, and they all have their own peculiarities. The Moon doesn't have any seismic activity to speak of—well, you know that. Mars used to, look at those bitching big extinct volcanoes there, but it doesn't anymore. But even the planets that ought to be really quite a lot like the Earth aren't—Venus, for instance. That one should be an identical twin to Earth, except for its orbit being closer to the primary. It isn't. Venus certainly does have volcanoes, but what it doesn't have is any sign of plate tectonic activity at all—figure that one out if you can. Then you have a planet like Pava here. It has plenty of volcanoes in some regions, though there aren't any very active ones right near here, and it has the plate tectonics. But, as I guess you've noticed, it just has the one big continent."

"One ought to be enough for us," I said. I wasn't really listening very closely. I was looking out the windows of the car at the woods and the hillsides, wondering just what might be hiding out of sight; but I felt I ought to be taking some part in the conversation.

She picked me up on that chance remark literally. "You mean that's enough living space for the colony right now, while there's less than a thousand of us here. Sure. But Pava wouldn't ever be able to support a population as big as Earth's. The only decent parts of Pava to live on are near the coastlines. In the interior you have brutal weather, burning hot summers and miserably cold winters. That part's got a real continental climate, worse than Chicago."

She stopped the car and turned off the engine. Suddenly it was very quiet all around us, except for occasional sounds of clicking from the cooling motor. She didn't get out from behind the wheel, though. She was finishing her thought.

"That could be part of the reason," she said, gazing out at the hill before us.

"What could? For what? Did I miss something?"

"I mean, the fact that there's one big continent could account for the earthquake flux."

"All of Pava's like this, is it?"

"Well, no. Not really. There are comparatively quiet tectonic zones here and there, it's just that the original colonists didn't happen to settle in one. But there's a lot more seismicity than on Earth. The whole planet's off balance because of this continent. Here's this one big lump sticking out kilometers higher than the rest of the planet. It sets up stresses as the planet rotates."

"That makes sense," I said.

She gave me an absent, almost annoyed glance, as though I'd offered an opinion where I had no right to have one. "Or," she said thoughtfully, "it could be for a different reason. It might be that all this continental rock acts as an insulator, trapping the internal heat. Ocean crust is thinner, so the heat escapes, but it builds up under the continent. You get hot spots, and they make the strains that make the faults—maybe."

I waited a moment to see if there was going to be more. There wasn't, so I said, "Thank you, Theo. I appreciate your clearing all that up."

She laughed a little at that. "All right, I admit it's not a very exact science here and we don't know all the answers. So let's try to find a few out. This is where we park the car and walk for a while."

* * *

I had completely lost my bearings by then. When I looked around there was no sign of the town, nothing but hills and those rough Pavan approximations of trees and underbrush. Although there had been some kind of a rutted path we'd bounced along in the car (I wouldn't go so far as to call it a "road"), it was no help in trying to figure out where we were. It had forked a dozen times and I had not been paying attention.

Theo seemed to know where she was going, so we humped those packs onto our backs and started up the hill.

That put an end to conversation on my part. I was out of breath in the first ten minutes, and pretty soon even Theophan was beginning to pant a little. We weren't in jungle anymore. We were too high for that. The ferny plants were scarce now, and the bamboo-like trees were taller and sparser than they had been by the river. There was all sorts of undergrowth, green and brown and violet. There were different kinds of trees now, and I could hear insects buzzing around.

Breathing hard or not, that amazing woman kept talking, describing all the creatures that were, or might have been, in the woods around us. "You might see some jacks," she gasped. "They're more or less lizards, but they jump like rabbits; they're good eating, but we aren't going to try to catch any because I don't want to have to carry them back to the car. Dangerous? No, they're not dangerous to people. The only kind of animal that might be really dangerous are the dinowolves and the killer ants, but those are just about extinct around here—they attacked children sometimes, so we had a bounty on them for a while."

I listened, really trying to keep track of what she was saying, but I couldn't retain it all. She kept rattling off names of animals—whistling snakes, batosaurs (which I gathered flew like birds), and a dozen others—and didn't skimp on the plant kingdom, either. Those little things like Christmas trees, I found out, were actually a kind of club moss; those hollow drumlike objects were vines (she said the closest Earth relative was the strangler fig) which grew on a tree and choked it out, and then continued to grow in a sort of hollow, basketwork cylinder where the tree had been.

"The leps nest in them sometimes," she said, "or at least they lay their eggs there, if they remember to. Keeps the predators out—or used to; we've pretty well wiped out most of the predators around here. You'd think the leps'd be grateful." The "grass" was actually a ground-covering vine, like kudzu. The spiderlike webs that we had to push out of our way were webs all right, but not made by spiders; they were spun by sessile, placental mammals to catch bugs for their dinners. And the bugs—I didn't even try to keep track of the bugs.

Theophan was quite a one for lecturing. She was exceeding my capacity for taking information in, though. I almost stopped listening entirely, in fact, until I saw a big thing humping across the path in front of us and got Theophan's attention long enough to gasp: "Was that a lep?"

She stopped and stood up straight for a moment, rubbing her hip as she shook her head. "No, that one was just a goober. They do look a little like leps, I guess—if you haven't seen a lot of leps. Maybe they're related, but they're not intelligent. Actually, Barry, you really aren't likely to come across many leps as long as you're with me."

I guess that's the kind of thing you're interested in about Theophan, but that was all she said on the subject right then. I did not, at the time, know what she meant by it, and she didn't amplify it. She didn't talk anymore at all for the next few minutes of our climb. Then she stopped and looked around, and announced, "Here we are."

"Here" didn't look much different than any of the other heres we'd already climbed past. We hadn't reached the top of our mountain, just had entered a small clearing with a good view off to the west. It seemed to satisfy Theophan. She set her pack down, lifted her field glasses to her eyes and swept a distant hillside with them.

When she put them down she looked satisfied. "There's my corner reflector, right where I set it up," she said, "and here's a good outcrop of solid rock, just what we need. You can catch your breath for a minute now, Barry. What we do then," she said, pointing to the rock face, "we drill a couple of bolt holes in that, then we set up the laser rangefinder and align it to the station on that far hill. Then we're done. How are you with a hammer?"

As it turned out, not very good. We tried it that way for a while, Theophan holding the drill in place while I hammered it, but when she saw my aim wasn't that great we switched. I hit harder than she did, even with my Moon-softened muscles, but at least when she was doing it I didn't have to drop the drill and jerk my hand out of danger quite as often.

It sounded quick and easy enough when she said it. It wasn't. It took us an hour's hard work to drill the holes to bolt the instrument down, and then another half an hour to put it in place and for Theophan to sight it in.

"What we're doing here is measuring creep," she explained. "If the distance between two points changes, or if one point rises or falls, then we know something's happening in the crust. Then I plug the data into the models and see if I can figure out what the something is." She sighed. "It works pretty well—on Earth. If we had enough of these things in place maybe we could tell when the earthquakes were due as well as we used to at CalTech South. Only we don't. We don't even have enough of them to keep a decent number of plots measured on a regular basis, so I have to keep moving the instruments around." She looked up at the expression on my face, and then laughed.

"Sorry, Barry," she said. "I'm laughing at me, not you. I felt the same way when I came here. It's a real culture shock, trying to get along where everything's always *scarce*—when I was doing my post-doc we didn't bother with crap like this; we had satellite rangers that could fix any point on the surface, in three dimensions, to a millimeter. But here—" She made a face. "You can't really understand how hard it is to keep a civilization going when you don't have many people until you get here and see for yourself, can you? Listen, sit down, I've got a thermos of coffee in my bag, we can take a little break before we start back."

I was glad enough to do that. Glad enough for the coffee, too, although the first taste startled me until I realized Theophan had spiked it with a touch of their homestilled popskull.

"It's not so bad," she said, apropos of nothing—except that it startled me, because she'd been reading my thoughts. "We do have just about everything we really need here, you know. Not *enough* of everything to be comfortable, no, and some things we just don't have at all—God, I'd kill for a chocolate ice-cream soda sometimes!"

I took a swig of the coffee. "But people have been here for a hundred years. Couldn't you make ice cream by now?"

"Sure we could. We even do, sometimes—though it's not as easy as you might think, because where do we get the cows to give the milk to make it with? Goat's milk isn't the same." She pursed her lips, then added, "I don't want to give you the wrong idea. There are substitutes for most things, yes, and they do well enough. The thing is, we can't make *everything*, not in forty different flavors and five hundred different varieties and a new model of everything every year. It's better now, though. It's even better now than the way it was when my husband and I first came here on *Avenger*, eleven years ago. We were really green. We were two kid seismologist volunteers fresh out of graduate school, ready to solve all the problems of Pava." She shook her head. Then she said, "You ready for another seismology lesson?"

What I actually wanted to hear about was this husband no one had happened to mention to me before, but I let her go on.

I listened while she was talking, but I was also studying her. The funny thing was that I'd had the ghost of an idea, when I took that first swig of the spiked coffee, that just possibly maybe one idea she might have had in the back of her head when she arranged all this was that it might have been fun for the two of us to get off together in a romantic and private place for a while. The word "husband" had changed my perspective on that. It didn't mean the idea was now out of the question, but it put a somewhat different spin on a possible rendezvous. Before I let the conversation get too personal I wanted to know just who this invisible husband was and at least the important things about him—like how big he was.

She didn't seem to be heading in any very personal direction, though. What was on Theophan's mind just then was seismology, and she clearly loved her subject. "See over there?" she asked, pointing to the ridge of mountains purplish on the horizon where her "corner reflector" was mounted. "Those hills are what we call the Rockies—no particular reason, they aren't actually any rockier than any other mountains around here, just I guess some of the original colonists were from Colorado. There's a south-dipping fault along that range that's maybe forty-five kilometers long. That one is the kind we call left-stepping, same as the one in these hills we're standing on. And neither one of them is real deep—I think."

She paused to take a drink of her cooling coffee. I didn't interrupt her. It was cool and pleasant up on the hill, and I wasn't looking forward to schlepping those tools back down to the car. I wasn't really listening, either, but that didn't matter much because when she started again she was really talking mostly to herself. She couldn't really know what she was dealing with, she said, without knowing more than she did about the composition of Pava's mantle and the forces that drove it—which were not exactly the same as on Earth, of course, because after all, the tidal forces of Earth's Moon had a lot to do with churning up Earth's mantle and Pava didn't happen to have a big moon. And then she got into the chemistry of mantle rock and I must have looked as though my mind was wandering. She stopped and gave me a stare. "Are you following any of this?" she demanded.

"Not much," I admitted. "Only you're saying you don't know enough to predict earthquakes very reliably."

"Right. I don't. I won't until we get the facilities for some deep-down drilling, for instance. Which we don't have. Jesus, Barry! I'm trying to make do with surface instruments, when what we really ought to be doing is sinking some shafts a kilometer or so down, plugged with concrete. Then we could measure some shear strain—but, hell, I don't even have enough dilatometers on the surface for decent volumetric studies, much less being able to identify force vectors—"

She stopped and gave me one of those half-apologetic, half-angry looks. "Am I going too fast for you again?"

"Yes, but that's not what's on my mind. I've got a question to ask you."

"Spill it."

"Well, no offense, but *why*? I mean, you people have been living with these problems for a hundred years. Not you personally, of course. But the colony's had them all for a long time. I'd think you'd be used to them. So why do you get so excited about it now?"

She exploded. "Because we're not living all that well, idiot! Every time we get a little bit ahead along comes a quake and we're back in the soup again! We're always losing power"—I nodded, remembering the lights going out at Jacky Schottke's place—"and every time that happens we have to stop some operations. We've even lost computer data when it wasn't protected fast enough. Christ, Barry! It was a quake that cost us the *dam*. Why do you think we're burning trash to make electricity?"

"I was going to ask about that. Tscharka said you had a hydroelectric plant."

"Did have. Until a tremor collapsed it."

I said, "Oh, right, I remember that one. I guess you mean the one that hit us right when we landed—"

"Hell, Barry, I'm not talking about *that* little tremor. That was nothing. The one that took the dam out was nearly a year ago. It was the worst day of my life. That was the day when—"

She stopped there. Her lips were clamped tight, and she was staring at the rangefinder as though she hated it. She almost looked as though she wanted to cry.

Then she tossed the dregs of her coffee on the ground and stood up.

"Look, do you want to see what's left of the dam? It's not much out of the way."

"Sure."

"Then let's go. I'll tell you all about it when we get there."

So we scrambled back down to the car, and when we'd driven about half a kilometer down the hill Theophan took a sharp turn into a different goat path. She wasn't talking. Only when we hit a bigger boulder than usual and I grunted did she glance at me and relax a little. A *very* little. "Sorry about this. The road gets better past the dam," she said, the words jolting out of her.

I didn't try to answer, just held tight. I was glad for the seat harness—mostly glad—less than totally glad, maybe, because the waist belt was digging into my kidneys as I was thrown from side to side with every jolt. Theophan seemed to anticipate each dip and twist, but then she had the steering wheel to hang on to.

The other thing on my mind was that I caught another wisp of that sweet, feminine scent of hers. Whatever Earthly comforts they were missing on Pava, it seemed Theo managed to keep well stocked with perfume.

It's surprising how much smell has to do with the way the mind works. This time it started me wondering if I was blowing a good chance here. I wondered if it was time for me to put Alma out of my mind on a permanent basis. I wondered exactly what Theophan's marital condition was. I wondered just how old she was, too. The arithmetic was easy enough; say, twenty-five years to get to finish graduate school plus eleven years on Pava. About thirty-six? (Not counting the twenty-odd years in time-dilated flight.) She looked a bit older than that, I thought. Maybe plus a couple more years that I hadn't counted on. Still, however I figured it, right in the target range for me.

Besides, all that bumping around was making me horny.

I suppose that's something else you'll never understand, because you people just don't think about sex at all until you're in your sixth instar, and then I guess you just about stop thinking about anything else at all, don't you? Well, human beings are different. We think about it all our lives. What I was thinking about was partly how good it would be to take this sweet-smelling, warm-bodied woman to bed, and partly how if I did that it might easily cause more problems than it solved.

I hadn't stopped mourning the loss of Alma, but that wasn't the problem that was on my mind. There was more to it than that.

See, what I wanted was not just a quick roll in the hay. My glands certainly did want that, and they were nagging me about it pretty insistently. But human beings are more complicated than leps in that way. Our glands drive us in one direction, our reasoning facilities tell us to go another. Maybe it isn't reason; maybe it's some other glands that I'm just not as aware of, the ones that lead to having children by choice instead of as an inevitable by-product of our other urges. Anyway, besides wanting the screwing I also wanted something more permanent. Something committed, even—my failures with Alma had reformed me, I guess. Certainly something longer term.

And I did not plan to have a longer term on Pava.

I thought it was time to take my thoughts as far away from my genitals as I could. I cleared my throat. When Theophan glanced at me inquiringly, I said, "Tscharka said it was going to be a big dam. A hundred meters high, he said."

She seemed willing to break her silence, but all she said, scornfully, was, "Tscharka."

"You don't think much of him, maybe?"

"I think he's a shit. What'd he bring back for us? No new instruments for me, no equipment, no seismological programs I can use. Outside of bare necessities, about all he brought was the damned antimatter, and he's stalling about shipping that to the factory, where we might have some use for it." Having got back the habit of speech, she went on: "If you want to know what I think, I think Tscharka expected Pava would be a hundred percent Millenarist when he got back and we'd all be so full of the consciousness of sin that we wouldn't worry about earthquake prediction or getting more industry going or—or anything except praying and begging God for forgiveness for the sin of being alive. Don't talk to me about Tscharka. He makes me sick, and there are too many like him here. I'd take the next ship back if it didn't mean spending twenty-five years with him."

"You wouldn't know it if you were. Because you'd be frozen, I mean."

She gave me a sort of grin—not big, but going in the right direction. "I'd know. The son of a bitch probably molests the corpsicles along the way."

Then the grin faded. "We're getting close. This is the valley where they put the dam."

So I began to pay attention to my surroundings again. What we were seeing was a pretty river valley between the hills—broad downstream, narrowing sharply to our right, but it was obvious something big and bad had happened here. The rough track we were following abruptly became a two-lane road—unpaved, yes; partly grown over; but easily capable of handling a lot more traffic than it seemed to be getting. And that road became the top of a dam, only the dam wasn't there anymore. The road stopped three or four meters out over the valley. It began again on the far side, with another few meters going on to the other slope. In between was nothing. There had been something there once, and quite a big something. Maybe not Tscharka's hundred-meter height, but the place where the dam had spanned a throat in the valley was considerably more than a hundred meters across.

The dam itself was gone.

Downstream, to our left, there were large lumps and chunks of masonry scattered along the sides of the river as far as the eye could see. There weren't any trees there. All I could see was a little regrowth of weeds, nothing big. Where the dam had been there was hardly a trace of, say, the power plant that would have been its purpose. I looked for it. All I could find was the ruined outline of what I supposed once had been a foundation at the foot of the dam structure. The whole space had been swept clean when a couple of cubic kilometers of retained water had decided to push the dam out of its way and move on down the valley.

"Can you imagine how much work they put into building that thing?" she asked, studying the wreckage.

I easily could. "It was an earthquake that did it?" I asked, although I knew the answer.

"Oh, yes. A pretty good one, and not the first. We'd had a couple of hefty foreshocks," Theophan told me, staring out over the flood track. "We were worried about the dam, so Jake and I came up here to try to measure the strains. We had four or five other people with us, and there were about a dozen leps who had trailed along as sightseers—they always seemed to be fascinated by the dam. Naturally enough, I guess. They'd never seen anything built on that scale before. And when the shock hit, Byram Tanner and I were up here with the theodolite, and my husband Jake was right about down there at the foot of the dam with two other men and the leps. Up here it knocked me off my feet. Down there they didn't have a chance. We never even found any of their bodies."

She shook her head and smiled at me. It wasn't a happy smile. "So," she said, "now you know how we lost our hydroelectric power, and why the leps aren't too crazy about me anymore. Eight of them got killed along with Jake. Third- and fourth-instar adults, you see. And that's not counting the ones that died in their home territory when the other fault let go a little later and their nests were flooded. So that's how I happened to become a widow lady and Public Enemy Number One for the leps, all on that same one, really lousy day.''

11

THERE is no further need to discuss Theophansperlie at this time. There are other matters that need clarification.

Funny, I had an idea you'd say that. You people have a kind of a guilty conscience about Theophan, don't you?

That is inaccurate, but let us turn to the other questions. First: It is understood that the purpose of the "dam" that caused such great harm was to cause water to flow through its associated machines in order to produce "electricity."

That's right. What don't you understand?

What is not understood is why this was necessary. Why did the humans on Pava not derive their energy from this "antimatter" that you humans employ in other circumstances, instead of building this large and dangerous structure? That is the first question. The second question is more fundamental. Why do humans desire this "electricity" so much in the first place?

Look, point one: Just forget about the idea of using antimatter on Pava. It's impossible. Talk about danger, you just don't have any idea how dangerous that would be. If even the tiniest particle of antimatter got loose on the planet's surface it could cause an explosion that would make your lousy little dam-burst look like a goober's sneeze. It could conceivably kill off everything anywhere near it, yourselves included.

If you want to know why we want all this electricity—well, hell, that's just another of the differences between you and us, isn't it? You don't care to have electrical energy because you don't have the kind of machine civilization that requires it. It's not your nature. But it definitely is ours. We're a high-technology species. Electricity is pretty much the basis for civilization, as we see it. If we don't have electricity we can't run our vidscreens or our communicators or any of the other things that improve our lives. Before you knew it we'd be back to living in sod huts and cooking our food over campfires like our primitive ancestors again. Almost like you people, do you see?

I know what I'm talking about here, because in the first week or two after I arrived on Pava I got a chance to appreciate what a difference technology makes. There were so many things that Pava didn't have! We didn't have air-conditioning! For someone who'd been living in the totally, permanently climate-regulated conditions of the Moon for a large part of his adult life, that was a major shock. I had never found myself *sweating* before—at least, not outside of the stress gym. Or maybe the bed.

That was only the beginning. We didn't have automatic doors here. We didn't have sensors to turn the lights on and off for us. We didn't even have protected data storage, and that was a real surprise for me— I'd never heard of a storage system where you could *lose* some of your records when there was a power glitch.

Of course, I'd never heard of power glitches before, either.

I've already mentioned that we didn't have flush toilets, and I think that was the biggest single thing that took the fun out of the adventure for most of the new colonists who had come to Pava on *Corsair* with me. But when I happened to say something about that to Jack Schottke one night he took quick offense. "My God, Barry," he said, looking seriously insulted, "how spoiled are you, exactly? Don't I keep our outhouse clean enough for you?"

I saw that I had hurt his feelings. It wasn't true, either—the outhouse was neat as a pin, and when the lid was down on the seat it hardly even smelled bad. I said, "No, of course not, nothing like that. It's just that it's a pretty unsanitary way to do things, isn't it?"

"No such thing! You people from back home have a lot of wrong ideas. It's your flush toilets that are the ones that are unsanitary. Those things are disgusting. Think about it! You crap into a bowl, then you flush it away with water, and what happens to that filthy water? It goes into a collection pond somewhere, and it's so stinking and foul that it has to be treated with chemicals to try to kill off the stench and the germs. Then the effluent has to be discharged into something after the treatment is over, and what it's usually discharged into is a river or a lake. Then what happens to it? I'll tell you! Then somebody else farther down the stream pumps it out again and drinks it!''

"Well, by then it's safe," I said—not liking the way he put things; on the Moon, recycled water is the only water we ever get.

"Safe," he said, looking as though "safe" were a dirty word. "Safe isn't the same as *good*, is it? Maybe you're willing to drink somebody else's reprocessed piss, but I'm not. What we do here is we just dig a hole in the ground and use it until it's pretty full, then we cover it over and dig a new one next to it. The stuff is never seen again, it just gradually becomes part of the soil. Environmentally, what could be more sound?''

"Well, but doesn't it seep into the underground water?''

"What difference would that make? We don't drink well water, do we? No, we get it from a stream, way upstream, where it's perfectly pure. Take my word for it. Our system is fine. This place is as sanitary as any community on Earth. We have no infectious diseases to speak of here, and if you doubt me, just go over and ask Billygoat to show you his records.''

"Billygoat?''

"Bill Goethe. The doctor.''

"Oh, yeah, the doctor," I said, remembering—remembering a little bit late, to be sure, because it had been over a week since the doctor had told me to make an appointment. But remembering. And deciding that I'd have to take care of that particular chore real soon, the next morning in fact, because seeing this Doctor Billygoat wasn't really anything I could afford to put off forever.

When I woke up the next morning, though, I was feeling so good I wondered if I really needed to bother to talk to the doctor at all.

It wasn't just the physical kind of good. True, by then my muscles had stopped aching all the time—now it was just *some* of the time— and I didn't get out of breath in the first ten minutes of a hill climb anymore. That was all part of the feeling-goodness. But there was something else that went with it.

Surprisingly, I discovered that I was feeling good about being on Pava. I could see the distant glimmering of a possible *purpose* in being there.

It almost made me think that maybe I wouldn't take the next ship back after all, and when Schottke came bustling over to me at the breakfast table, our little tiff in the apartment forgotten, he had a receptive audience. "Barry," he said, eagerness and excitement all over him, "Jimmy Queng's getting together a search party; we need to take a launch downstream to pick up some stuff that was dropped from the factory. They're going to let me go along to collect a few specimens—want to join us?"

I forgot all about seeing Dr. Billygoat that morning. I said, "Sure."

You see, I like to work. I guess that's a human trait, too. I like to have the challenge of facing something that's hard to do, and the confidence that, if I work hard enough at it, no matter what unexpected complications turn up, I can probably get it done. And I'd never faced a tougher challenge than the planet of Pava. As long as I was there, I was going to do my best to help. I figured they needed that because, as far as I could see, there were a lot of things that they needed to have done, and maybe even more things they were doing wrong—especially by relying on the orbital factory and shipments from Earth for just about everything they needed.

I was an expert on the subject of what Pava needed by then, of course. I'd been on the planet nearly ten days.

Still, you didn't have to be much of an expert, really, to see that they couldn't rely forever on what slim handouts distant Earth was disposed to send their way. Sooner or later Pava would have to fend for itself. That meant it would have to be able to build everything it needed, in all the many varieties of all those many things, and it would have to build them out of local resources.

I didn't think the orbiting factory was a good answer to the problem, but I realized it probably would be useful for me to try to learn more about it. A nice long boat ride sounded like a good occasion to ask questions, so I let Jacky hustle me through breakfast—"It's a long trip," he kept saying, "and we have to get an early start"—and as soon as the scavenger party's car rolled up I swallowed the last of my food and climbed in.

When the man at the wheel shook my hand I realized I had met him before. He was Lou Baxto, the tall, pale guy with the scraggly pale mustache who had come out to meet the shuttle. What's more, two of the other people in the car were our downstairs neighbors, the Khaim-Novellos. The only stranger was a little man who looked like an old Irish jockey, whose name was Dabney Albright. As Baxto started the car away, all of us busy shaking hands and saying hello, I thought I heard my name called. When I looked up, there was Theophan gesturing to me from outside. She looked annoyed. But it was too late to worry about whatever it was she wanted, so I waved back and turned away and settled myself in for the bumpy run down to the river.

I could see why we had to get an early start. It was a good long trip, first in the car all the way back to the shuttle landing strip (now empty; the shuttle was busy going back and forth to unload *Corsair*'s cargo from orbit), and then boarding a kind of clumsy open-decked launch to take the river another dozen kilometers downstream. I had plenty of time to ask questions about the factory, and Baxto was willing enough to answer them.

The orbital factory had been shipped from Earth as a self-propelled vessel long before he was born, he said. It was a neatly designed (if probably by now fairly old-fashioned) piece of equipment. It was still working, and he had no doubt that it would go on working for a good long time, as long as it was supplied with raw materials and power.

But, he admitted, the orbital factory did have its problems. The worst of them was simply that the thing was, after all, in orbit. Everything it manufactured for the colony had to be paradropped or shuttled down to the surface, and that was an expensive procedure. If they used the shuttle they had to provide it with hydrogen fuel, which had to be made on the surface—Baxto pointed out the electrolysis plant that made the fuel from river water just by the landing strip. (The plant was powered by waterpower from turbines in the river, and it was so small and inconspicuous I'd taken it for some kind of storage shed.)

The parafoils were better, but they had their problems, too. The factory made them as needed (the foils themselves became useful structural materials when they were collected) and they didn't require any fuel, but the damn things were hard to control. They were likely to land anywhere within a forty-kilometer radius of Freehold, and sometimes they couldn't be found at all.

"That," Baxto said, "is where we come in. The leps have found a capsule that fell way outside the drop zone, and we're going to retrieve it."

"All of us?" I asked, looking around. We were in the boat by then. The little jockey type, Dabney Albright, was steering and Baxto was sitting in the bow with me. Behind us Jacky was talking consolingly to our downstairs neighbors, who were huddled together and looking dismayed; they were still holding hands, but that joyous flush of antici- pated wonderful adventure was gone from their faces.

"Hell, man," Baxto said, "those capsules weigh seven or eight tons each, and Schottke's not going to be much help with heavy lifting, is he? If we can salvage the whole thing that means each one of us is going to have to shift better than a ton from the drop to the boat, and again from the boat to the car when we get back. Want to try it by yourself sometime?"

I could see what he meant, and the morning didn't look like such a peaceful walk in the sun anymore. I persisted. "All right, but what about the other thing? You said there were other problems with the factory."

He looked annoyed, but he answered. The big problems with the factory were energy and raw materials. Energy came mostly from photo- voltaics, though he was hopeful that if we could juice it up with addi- tional power from some of Captain Tscharka's antimatter it could do better. The raw-material question was the tough one.

For instance, just to make the parafoils the factory needed high- strength carbon filaments, and for that the factory needed some kind of a source of carbon to process. It also needed all the other raw materials that its smelter and refiners would turn into whatever the people of Pava wanted made, and where were all those raw materials going to come from? It would be terribly uneconomic to try to shuttle them up from the surface. There was, he admitted, one obvious source. There were plenty of useful minerals aloft in Delta Pavonis's skimpy asteroid belt, but the Pavans didn't have the space tugs to bring those megaton-mass objects to Pava orbit.

"Right," I said, remembering what Captain Tscharka had told me long before. "That's what you built those short-range tugs for."

He gave me a dubious look. "The what?" And when I explained what Tscharka had said, he scowled. "Garold gets carried away some- times," he said. "Did you see any space tugs in orbit when you came in? Well, there aren't any."

I mulled that over. Tscharka hadn't seemed to me like the kind of man who got carried away, but there didn't seem to be any point in arguing it. "So what do you do for raw materials, then?" I asked, and Baxto shrugged.

They did the best they could. Even some pretty crazy things. They'd actually once taken the radical step of hijacking one of the interstellar ships to strip it down and convert it into raw materials, because they needed its metals more than they needed the ship. That worked fine for a while, but even the materials in the structure of a giant interstellar spaceship didn't last forever.

I chewed that over, and for a while we didn't talk. I was watching the scenery along the riverbanks as we cruised, but I was also wondering if maybe Baxto was thinking that it was about time to hijack another spaceship—say, Captain Tscharka's *Corsair*—and what Tscharka might think of that if the question came up.

That was kind of an amusing thought. Thinking about what Captain Tscharka might say if anybody proposed it seriously kept me entertained until I noticed that Dabney Albright had slowed the launch and we were heading into shore. Then we all stood up while he ran the launch up onto the bank and jumped out to drag it far enough out of the water so the current wouldn't pull it away.

A lep was waiting for us there on the bank. Its forepart was elevated so its bug eyes could look us over.

Baxto greeted the lep and introduced us. "This is Simon Bolivar," he said. "He'll lead us to the capsule."

I was standing right next to the thing. I sort of half extended my hand, so it was there to be available in case handshaking was a custom with you leps, or to be ignored if not. Simon Bolivar ignored it.

"I expected you earlier," he shrilled. "Come. I will show you where the object is."

The good part was that it wasn't far from the river; as we pushed through the brush toward it I was counting every step, thinking about how much work it was going to be to hand-carry seven or eight tons back to the launch. The bad part was that, when we did reach it, it was a mess. It had hit hard, the capsule had split open on impact, and it had rained.

Baxto and Albright were swearing to each other as they looked it over. Unfortunately a lot of that batch of material had been programmable chips, and they were ruined. "Tough break, but we'll salvage what we can," Baxto said finally. "Leave the spoiled chips here, but we want everything else."

"Even the capsule itself, Mr. Baxto?" Jubal Khaim-Novello ventured.

"Especially the damn capsule. That's good building material, isn't it? So if we want to get home by dark, let's start taking it apart."

If I had been in any doubt about the troubles with Pava's supply system, the next five or six hours of backbreaking labor convinced me. The system sucked. First there was the job of cutting the shell of the capsule into ragged hunks about the size of a wheelbarrow. Then there was picking up the containers of other kinds of goods that might, Baxto thought, still be worth salvaging and hauling them down to the launch. Then there was trying to carry or drag those wheelbarrow-sized, jagged-edged hunks of shell and lifting surface through those clustered vines and bushes, two or three of us sweating over each one. We didn't have real wheelbarrows, but then we couldn't have got real wheelbarrows through the brush anyway.

All those good physical feelings I'd woken up with that morning were gone long before we took our first break. I have never been more tired. I flung myself down and didn't even look up until Jacky Schottke came over with a cup of water for me.

He beamed down at me expectantly while I raised the cup to my lips. It tasted funny, quite sweet, and almost fruity. "What are you giving me?" I demanded.

"It's sap," he said proudly, showing me a thing like a beer-keg spigot. "It comes from the water tree over there—see it? With the purple fronds? If you're ever caught out in the woods without anything to drink, you just punch into one of those and you'll get all the water you want."

"All I want is to go home," I told him, but I did sit up straighter and finish the drink. Because of his age Jacky had been exempted from most of the lifting and hauling, so he'd been off in the woods with the lep, collecting biological samples for his taxonomy work. It was light labor, and he seemed fresh and eager to get on with it. I almost envied him. The lep, Simon Bolivar, was an old friend of his, he told me; they had been out on foraging trips many times before, and this time the lep had led him to a brand-new variety of edible root.

"Now," Jacky said eagerly, "I can start a new trophic tree. I'll have to see what organisms eat this root; then I can match it against the other systems, and with a little luck I'll be able to—hey," he said, stopping in the middle of a thought. "What was that?"

I'd heard it to, a female scream from the brush. When I looked around I saw that Becky Khaim-Novello was missing—gone off, I assumed, to answer a call of nature in private. She wasn't gone long, though. She came blundering through the bushes, holding up her slacks, and yelling for her husband. When he had caught her in his arms she blubbered, "Dear heaven, Jubal, has anyone got a gun? There's the biggest damn bug you ever saw out there! It was eating some other kind of animal, and I thought it was going to come after me!"

That got me on my feet. Lou Baxto gave her a disgusted look. "You're too big and tough for it to bother chasing," he said, "unless it was really starving, maybe. It was probably just a killer ant. It won't come near us—there are too many of us here."

I turned to Jacky Schottke, who was looking apologetic. "They do look a little frightening," he admitted. "They're more than a meter long, the full-grown ones."

"Maybe we ought to put out some poison bait down here," Dabney Albright said.

Jacky looked shocked at the idea. "Oh, why would we have to do that, Dabney? They hardly ever attack an adult human being—well, they *can*, but small children mostly. There aren't any children here, and we've already poisoned the ants all out anywhere near Freehold."

Lou Baxto took over. "Can we hold the debate until we're back home?" he asked reasonably. "Break's over; let's get some of this stuff on the launch."

And so we did—for another four or five hours; during which I kept my eyes open for anything that looked like it might be a killer ant.

None showed up. We finally got everything salvageable salvaged, but we didn't make it back to Freehold before dark. By the time we got there I was aching and tired and the last of that morning's good feelings were all used up.

It was a very lucky thing for Rannulf Enderman that he wasn't where I could get my hands on him that night.

12

THIS is not understood. This concept of doing purposeful harm to another is not comprehensible.

Oh, now what? Are you talking about what I said about Rannulf Enderman? You shouldn't take that kind of offhand remark so seriously. It's just something we say when we get mad. I wouldn't really have done anything *fatal* to the son of a bitch, you know.

No, this is not known. It is well established that other humans have in fact taken the lives of their conspecifics.

Well, sure, *others* have; that's one of the things about us humans. Sometimes people kill other people. I don't like it any more than you do, but it's a fact of life. But *I* haven't done that, even at my very craziest, and I'm not crazy now. I don't think I actually could—not even with Enderman, although I have to admit I would certainly have been capable of beating the pee out of him if I had the chance.

I didn't have that chance anyway. I couldn't punch Rannulf Enderman's lights out. I couldn't get back to the Moon in time to make things right with Alma. I couldn't get back to the Moon at all, in fact, until Garold Tscharka, or some other ship's captain, decided to start going that way in a ship that would give me passage. I couldn't do any of the things that I really wanted to do, and that was pretty frustrating. It made me mad.

I didn't stay mad, though. By the time I got to the breakfast tables the next morning, still achy but functioning, I had pushed all the things

I couldn't do to the back of my mind, so I could concentrate on what I
could do. Give me credit for that. I had made up my mind to quit
wasting time on frustrations and concentrate on problems that, maybe,
I could have some hope of doing something about. *Real* problems.
Pava's problems. I guess you could even say that I had talked myself
into being almost a little obsessive about it.

Theophan was eating a little green melon and talking to someone I
faintly recognized—he had come in on *Corsair* with me, I was pretty
sure. I didn't bother with him. I sat down on the other side of Theophan
and started right in with what was on my mind. "I've got a question.
If you need all those instruments for your work, why don't you get the
factory orbiter to make them for you?"

She turned away from the other guy to give me a perplexed and faintly
hostile look. "Didn't you ever hear of 'good morning'?" she asked.
"And why did you go off without checking with me yesterday?"

"I got ordered to do a different job," I said, stretching the truth a
little.

"Well, I needed you to help me on my job, Barry. I had a hard day's
work yesterday up in the hills. Since you weren't around I had to ask
Marcus to help me." The man beside her leaned forward with a small
smile, as though to acknowledge the introduction.

I remembered the rest of his name: Marcus Wendt. He was bigger
than I, but he was looking frail; I judged Theophan had worked him out
pretty hard. "Sorry about that," I said. "What I'd like to know—"

She didn't let me finish. "So how about helping me out today?" she
asked.

"Today? You want me to come out with you today? Why not Marcus?"

She was shaking her head. "Oh, no, Barry, that's out of the question.
I can't ask Marcus to do that again. Can't you see he's in pain? He
pulled a muscle yesterday; he's not as strong as you, Barry. Will you
pick me up at my place?"

I looked Marcus over without seeing any great sign of injury, but it
wasn't really my business to diagnose him. Anyway, I remembered
what I was supposed to do. "I ought to go to see the doctor this morning,
Theo."

"Really?" She frowned, then decided to make the best of it. "Well,
how long can that take? It won't hurt if we leave a little late. So, fine,

we'll work it out that way, and I'll tell Jimmy Queng you'll be going out with me so he won't put you on something else."

I didn't see any reason to argue. "All right," I said. "What about what I asked you? The factory's supposed to be able to make anything at all; why don't you have it make what you need?"

Marcus was listening in, and he gave a superior little chuckle. "Don't you think Theophan would have thought of that? Of course she did. It probably just can't be done."

I ignored him. "Can it?"

She decided to give me a straight answer. "Sure it could, if it had the raw materials to spare—I guess. But it's pushed to the limit already, just replacing the things that are needed for survival."

"There must be all the raw materials you'd need right here on Pava. It's a whole damn planet."

"But we don't have a factory down here, do we?"

"No," I said, "we don't, and that's something else I don't understand. Why haven't you people built one?"

Marcus was snickering again. He was getting harder to ignore. Theophan gave him a warning look. "Look, Barry, I know you're trying to be helpful, but you just haven't grasped the situation here. We don't have enough power to keep what we've got going, much less get into building a whole damn industrial base. You saw what happened to the dam."

"All right, then maybe the first thing we have to do is to generate more electricity. Maybe we should build a new dam in a better place?"

She shook her head impatiently. "You're really all fired up this morning, aren't you? Look, I can't talk about all this right now. Marcus is pretty well crippled up and I'd better help him back to his room. Anyway, I'm not the one in charge of that sort of thing. You want to go see Byram Tanner—see, over there? The dark-haired man with the beard? He's the power-generation expert."

So I picked up my plate and set it down at an empty place by this Byram Tanner. We shook hands when I introduced myself, and I got right to the point with him, too. "Theophan says the reason you can't build an automated factory, like the orbiter, down here on the surface is that you don't have enough power. Is that right?"

He looked surprised, but he took the question seriously. He thought for a moment. "Well, that's one of the reasons. Losing the hydroelectric plant really set us back, and we aren't really getting much of a net gain of energy from harvesting and burning biomass."

"Right. So I don't see why you're burning biomass for power in the first place," I said. "Has anybody looked to see if there's any coal around?"

Tanner gave me the same sort of faintly hostile look I'd got from Theophan—not unlike, I suppose, the look I would have given any stranger on the Moon who had started a conversation by asking me why we didn't shoot the antimatter direct to the spaceships without bothering with catchers. He didn't tell me to buzz off, though. He reflected for another moment before he answered. "There's supposed to be lignite deposits somewhere in the hills, yes. You know, brown coal? But nobody's ever bothered to try to develop it. Lignite doesn't have much more heat content than biomass, and it'd be a lot harder to dig out and transport. When they cut wood and brush they just float it down the river to the plant. To get the lignite out you'd need to have roads and trucks and all that sort of stuff. Why do you ask?"

So I told him why I was asking—as politely and tentatively as I could, because I didn't want to give the impression of the brash newcomer who thinks he's smarter than anyone who's been there, although, of course, I suppose that's pretty much what I was. Tanner was still polite about it. I was surprised to find out that he was one of those rare creatures, an expert who didn't mind dumb questions—and in fact also one of those even rarer ones, a human native Pavan. Tanner had been born right there on the planet, and he knew everything there was to know about it.

The town of Freehold, he admitted, might not have been settled in the best possible place. The original colonists had picked the site in the first place because orbital surveys had looked good. They'd shown that the locale had decent climate and good soil, as well as the river and all its branches, which would be useful for both drinking water and hydropower—though that last part hadn't worked out all that well when the dam broke. Spectroanalysis and surface geology had shown good indications of extractable minerals within a reasonable distance of the proposed site, even traces of surface hydrocarbon seepage.

That startled me. "Hydrocarbons? Are you talking about oil?"

He nodded. "Sure, there's some oil. We've drilled a couple of little wells in the marshlands downriver, but they don't produce much. What did you think we used for lubrication?"

I had never given a thought to what they used for lubrication. Then, when I pointed out that they could burn the oil to make electricity, he agreed. "We could do that, all right, if we had the furnaces and boilers and generators to build an oil-burning power plant. People have talked about it, but we don't have those things. We can't turn off the biomass plant for a year while we convert it to oil; we'd starve. So we can't use those. The generators from the dam are gone; we haven't been able to get new ones from the orbiting factory because it doesn't have enough copper or silver for the coils—the hydroplant we lost pretty well drained it."

He had hit on a subject I knew something about. "Why would the coils have to be pure metal? The lunar photovoltaic belt uses composites."

He looked at me with a little more respect. "That's true, but composites take a lot of energy to manufacture. The orbiter's running pretty close to capacity already." He thought for a minute, then brightened. "Of course, Tscharka brought back all that antimatter fuel. The factory's equipped to use either antimatter or solar power, provided it hasn't scavenged all its antimatter systems for raw materials. We could have plenty of power that way—Although I don't know how we'd hook it up. Nobody on Pava has any experience with antimatter."

"I do," I pointed out.

"Well, hell," he said, almost getting excited, "that's true. You do, don't you? You should be able to make the conversion. Maybe we could really do it!" He thought for a minute, then grinned sheepishly. He had got carried away. There was still the raw material problem, he told me. Not just for making the current-carrying cables and coils. For a building to house the generators. For the structural parts of the generators themselves. And even if they did get an oil-burning plant built and working, they'd have to get the fuel to the plant. Meaning they'd need to build a fleet of boats to carry the oil upriver—or a pipeline, maybe, though the wells weren't likely to produce enough to fill a pipeline, and then there was the problem of keeping a forty-kilometer pipeline intact in an earthquake region—

By the time we finished breakfast I thought I had Byram Tanner pretty well pegged. Every suggestion I made to him produced a first-rate explanation of why it wouldn't work.

He struck me as a perfect example of a native Pavan. He seemed to be a decent fellow, but he had an endless supply of reasons why nothing could be done.

You know, there's a funny thing there. Listening to myself now I wonder why I was so judgmental of Byram Tanner and the Pavan colonists in general. Not just judgmental, even. Maybe what you could

call, well, actually almost racist. Tanner didn't deserve that. Tanner
was really a good man, doing his best to do a damn near impossible
job. Maybe the Pavans in general didn't deserve that kind of contempt,
either . . . though I'm nowhere near as sure of that.

Maybe I was beginning to get some of those mood swings already?
I don't know. All the same, right after breakfast I headed for Dr.
Billygoat's office. People were beginning to gather for the day's work
assignments, and so were a lot of leps—it seemed there were more of
them in town almost every day, maybe because they wanted a look at
the new human arrivals? I felt I ought to do my part. I wanted to get
the visit to the doctor over so I could start doing something productive—
even if, this one morning, the most productive thing I could do was to
go out again with Theophan Sperlie.

By then I knew my way around Freehold pretty well—not that there
was that much to know, in a community of less than a thousand people.
I cut through the space between the broken-down meeting hall and the
vehicle-repair shed and found the doctor's office without trouble.

Dr. Goethe's office was also his home. He had a whole two-story
apartment of his own. His chief medical assistant, who was busy retriev-
ing data from the screen in the front room when I came in, was also his
wife, Ann. In fact, they had a one-year-old baby who was snoring
bubbles in a crib by her mother's feet while Ann Goethe worked.

Ann put her finger to her lips in the don't-wake-the-baby sign.
"Billy?" she whispered. "Oh, no, you can't see Billy right now. He's
upstairs in the lab, checking grain samples, and I don't like to bother
him there. So unless it's an emergency—? Right, then why don't you
come back right after lunch, and I'll tell him you'll be here."

That meant I had to tell Theophan that I wouldn't be going out in the
field with her at all today. I thought about skipping the doctor's visit
for one more day, but I had the uneasy feeling that I might go on putting
it off past the point when it would be purely precautionary any longer.
So I went to tell Theophan the news.

When I found her she was sitting on the edge of one of the cleared
tables, tapping her heel against the table leg as she waited. There were
half a dozen leps a few meters away, whistling softly to each other, and
when I told Theophan about my appointment with the doctor she wasn't
happy. "Oh, hell, Barry, I wanted to get out there today. Couldn't you
take care of your personal stuff after work?"

"I had to take whatever time they gave me," I said.

"For Billygoat? Don't make me laugh. You just let them walk all over you. The trouble is, it makes a problem for me. I need to take these leps along for guides and they'll work better for you than they do for me."

"Sorry about that," I said. She just shook her head. Being annoyed became her, and I wondered why I hadn't taken her up on her pretty clear come-on that first day. (Matter of fact, I still wonder about that, sometimes.)

She thought for a moment. "Well, hell, tomorrow will do, I guess," she said. "I can use a day in my office to work up some of the accumulated data." For that I was not useful, and she left me looking after her as she walked away. She looked good from the back, too.

That left me with a lot of free time. Free time was a no-no for Pava colonists. I thought for a minute about which particular kind of job I should be volunteering for—I heard a power saw in the distance, and of course the repair crews always needed all the help they could get. The little group of leps had moved toward me, eyeing me curiously, and I discovered one of them was speaking to me.

The lep was a female they called Mary Queen of Scots—I don't know why. She was a big, fifth-instar female with a bristle of reddish whiskers around her mouthpart. She humped over toward me with that inchworm stretch-and-retract movement that was the lep method of traveling, and she repeated her question two or three times before I made it out.

What she was saying was, "Does the female destroyer want us to escort you?"

I understood who she was talking about, of course. "Why do you keep on calling Theophan Sperlie a destroyer?" I asked.

The lep twisted her mouthpart—it really did look like a sneer. "We call that person what she is. Answer. Are we to take you?"

"I don't think so. I mean, no, not today; I have to do something else."

That was all the answer she wanted, it appeared. She stretched enough to raise up her head so she could look into my eyes for a moment, but all she said was, "Good-bye." Then she dropped back, twisted her body around in a U-turn and inchwormed away.

"Hey," I called after her. She didn't stop. Most of the other leps followed her, all but one. That one was a fourth-instar male, and he crawled up on the table to study me. He smelled of damp earth and greenery.

"Hello," I said, being polite. "I don't know your name, I'm sorry."

The lep didn't answer, or not in any way that mattered. He made sounds, but they weren't human sounds. That wasn't surprising; there were plenty of leps that didn't speak English, especially not the younger ones. He whistled and blew at me for a while, then he gave up. He slid himself down from the table and inchwormed over to a cart. He wiggled his head into a harness, caught the bit in his mouthpart and started down the street.

Then he paused long enough to twist around and look after me.

I got the idea. He wanted me to follow.

So I followed, and he led me to where a work team was loading foundation bricks onto the carts. I recognized a couple of them—my downstairs neighbors, the Khaim-Novellos, looking as though they hadn't planned on this kind of manual labor on Pava, and the boss of the team, the cheery, chubby Santa Claus chaplain of the interstellar ship *Corsair*. "Hello, di Hoa, I'm glad to see you," Friar Tuck greeted me. "Nice of you to come and help out. We've got to get all this stuff loaded so the leps can drag it to the new building sites."

You know, that's still the thing that puzzles me most about you leps. I mean why you were so nice to these troublesome human beings who invaded your planet and killed off so many of your food animals and cut down so many of your forests—yes, and even managed to kill some of you in the process. You seemed to put up with a lot from us—well, from everybody but Theophan Sperlie, anyway.

Understand, I'm not saying you should have done anything different. I certainly don't mean that you should have attacked our camp one night and wiped us out; I know you wouldn't do that. But you were so damn *helpful*. It was pretty obvious that the human colony on Pava would have been even worse off than it was without your volunteer labor. You did all kinds of work for us, sometimes very hard work, work that needed to be done for the survival of the colony and that there just weren't enough human hands to do. And you did it for no pay . . . well, except now and then some handouts of odds and ends of discards that even the threadbare colony on Pava didn't think were worth saving.

I couldn't figure your motivation out. It didn't occur to me that it might have been mostly pity.

I wouldn't say the Reverend Tuchman was any kind of friend of mine, but I wasn't sorry when we sat down to eat together. I was still thinking about all the things I thought the colony needed to do, and he was as good a person to bounce my ideas off as any.

For someone who hadn't seen Pava for nearly half a century he seemed pretty well informed on what was going on. He told me about the oil wells—pitiful little pumped-out things—and the fact that, yes, there was a sort of lignite mine two or three valleys away in the woods, but no one had bothered to keep it up. He explained to me about the little hydropower plant by the shuttle landing strip, and why its small electrical output couldn't be used for the town of Freehold—it was built to electrolyze hydrogen out of the river water to make shuttle fuel, and especially now, with *Corsair*'s cargo needing to be brought down from orbit, there wasn't any spare power for the town. And then he put the move on me. "I haven't had a chance to ask you, di Hoa, but what's your religious affiliation?"

The only surprise was that he hadn't done it earlier. "I'm more or less Western Orthodox," I said, "at most."

That made him smile. "What a shame," he said gently. "Of course we'd be glad to see you at our services, anytime you want to drop in."

"Not very likely," I said.

He regarded me thoughtfully, the smile still on his face. It wasn't a sneering smile. It was a smile of compassion, the kind of smile I might have given my small son Matthew—if I had been lucky enough to know my son Matthew when he was small—if Matthew had firmly declared that he didn't think the world was round.

Then, just to remind us of other problems, there was a little earth tremor right then. People looked startled; the tall trees around the dining tables swayed; some of the tea in Tuchman's cup slopped over.

I didn't let it spoil my appetite. It was only about a 4.5, I judged, and I was already getting used to them. I took the last mouthful of stew out of my bowl and began nonchalantly to chew.

Tuchman was looking at something behind me, and it turned out to be Becky Khaim-Novello. "Reverend?" she said. "I'm a little worried—"

"It's just a minor quake, Rebecca," he said soothingly.

"I don't mean that. Have you seen Jubal? He went off right after work, I thought maybe to go to the bathroom. But he never came back to eat."

"Perhaps he just wasn't hungry. There's no place for him to get lost, you know. I'm sure he'll be on hand for the afternoon work detail."

"Thank you, Reverend," she said uncertainly, and turned and went back to the serving tables for some fruit, Tuchman looking after her.

"By the way," I said, remembering, "I won't be there. I've got a doctor's appointment."

He ignored that. Earthquakes, doctor's visits and missing husbands did not distract him from his favorite subject. "Don't you believe in God at all?" he asked.

I shrugged. "Maybe I do, sometimes, in a way. But mostly I guess not."

The smile was gone now, and he was looking at me with the kind of tempered pity a driver might give a specimen of roadkill. "What a tragedy," he said. "For you, I mean."

That was all I wanted of that particular conversation. I got up, stacked my dishes, and headed toward Billygoat's office.

I don't like discussing religion, especially with religious people. I don't want to argue anybody out of something that gives him comfort, but I just can't make myself believe in the kinds of gods the sects claim, whether of divine wrath or divine love—or, as so many of them so confusingly describe it, of both at once. I mean, why would a divine being bother to throw thunderbolts of hellfire at his own creations? And a god of love is even harder to swallow, because what is there in somebody like Garold Tscharka to love?

It would be nice if there really were a god. Maybe we just don't deserve one.

Dr. Billygoat saw me right away, and he wasn't happy with me. The first thing he said, sounding accusatory, was, "I checked the datafile. You don't have any medical profile on file at all, di Hoa."

"That's because I wasn't planning to come here at all."

Of course I had to explain that. He looked surprised but not pleased. "Well," he said grudgingly, "maybe it's not entirely your fault, but Jesus, man! I wonder if you have any idea what a hell of a lot of extra work it means for me. I'll have to create a whole new medical file for you, and when am I going to have the time to do that? I've got three maternity calls and a broken leg to look at just this afternoon. You say you've got some special medical problems?"

I said, "You bet I do," but when I started to explain what they were he just looked pained.

"Save your breath. I'll have to have a profile before we get into any of that stuff, so go back and see Ann. I'll take care of you when you're through."

So I did as ordered, and his wife sighed, looked put upon, but began doing all the routine stuff—weighing me, measuring me, watching the instruments read out my respiration and pulse and blood pressure, getting me to breathe into one instrument and pee into a cup for another— while Billygoat's other patients limped or puffed up the stairs to his office. It was an hour and a half before she'd finished all the tests and had the results entered into the file and he finally let me back upstairs to tell him about my bad genes.

Then he didn't just look pained anymore, he looked seriously wounded.

"Hell," he said. "Why would anybody send someone like you out to a colony? No, don't tell me about getting kidnapped again. I just wish you'd been a little more careful."

He sighed reproachfully, as though he expected me to apologize for it. I didn't, so he began querying his database for some clue about what to do for me. That went on for quite a while.

Finally he leaned back and stared at me. He said, "Shit."

That didn't seem to me to be a useful remark. "What's the matter?" I asked.

He shook his head, meaning, *I'm the doctor so I'm the one who asks the questions around here, dammit.* "The only good thing," he said irritably, "is that you seem to be in remission right now, but I can't count on that forever, can I? I've never heard of a case like yours before. 'Bipolar affective disorder,' is that what you said they called it?"

"Among other things, yes. They also called it manic-depressive psychosis."

"Psychosis!" he said, sounding dismayed.

"Sorry to inconvenience you," I said politely.

He gave me a sharp look for that, but all he said was, "Tell me again what they did for you in the clinics."

I did, starting with the injections that kept me straight for about forty-eight hours each, and then the free-floating cells that survived for maybe a week, and then the implants that were good, usually, for five or six months before they needed to be refreshed.

He looked glum. "All right," he said. "I've got that much. How did they deliver the genetic material?"

"How would I know?"

"Come on, di Hoa! You must know something. Transposons? Fibrils? What?"

"I have no idea at all. I didn't make up the shots. I just let them give them to me."

"Oh, man. How do you expect me to treat you? Don't you think you ought to know a little more about your condition?"

"I never had to. They'd just call up my medical file and there it all was."

He gave a sort of moan. It was not reassuring. I asked him, "Can't you deal with that sort of thing?"

"The mood pills, sure. The cell implants—" He shrugged. "We're limited in what we can do about that here, especially when I don't know what's needed. And I didn't come here as a medical doctor, you know."

That got my full attention. "You *what*?"

"Hold your water, di Hoa, I didn't say I couldn't help. When I came here I was an oral surgeon—dentist, if that's what you want to call it. There were three doctors then, and another came on the next ship. But one of them died and all the others hated it here and went home. I'm what's left. Don't blame me. We were all hoping Tscharka would bring a couple of reinforcements with him on *Corsair*, but I guess he had other things on his mind."

"I can't tell you," I said, "how happy and comforted you've made me feel."

He was laughing at me—sourly, I thought. "They didn't take their equipment away with them when they took off, you know. They left all the lab stuff and the pharmaceuticals. I've got all the datafiles, too, and I know how to read them. I can deal with most of the problems I've come across here, di Hoa. I've done it. Even when they were genetically incompetent, like you. I've got two diabetics here. I keep them normo-glycemic just about perfectly with encapsulated islet allografts—they couldn't do any better at Mayo. I've got people with carcinogenous nodes that I suppress with intravascular devices wrapped in permselec-tive membranes; I've got eight or ten others with genetic problems that need the same sort of therapy, and they're all doing all right. You hear how good I've gotten at talking the lingo? It's not just the lingo. I know the techniques for dealing with most any problem that comes along, di Hoa, and when I don't know I can always look it up. Except for your problem. You see, I just don't know what the hell your problem *is*."

"Thank you very much, Doctor," I said.

"Oh, hell, di Hoa, don't be smart with me. I'll put the datasearches to work, and Nanny'll take some more blood from you, and we'll run some more tests, and we'll see what we can find. I expect we can do something. Hope so, anyway. Come back in a couple of weeks. And please, di Hoa, just do your best not to go round the bend before then.''

So, for lack of anything better to do, I went back to the apartment I shared with Jacky Schottke. That fired-up flush of enthusiasm I had woken up with was all gone. What I intended to do was to lie down and go to sleep and hope it would all go away.

It wouldn't have worked out that way, of course. I know that. But I never even got a chance to try it out, because just as I was cutting across the viney "grass" to the door, Becky Khaim-Novello came running out of the lower apartment, screaming and screaming. She was worried because she had missed her husband at the afternoon's work detail, and when she came home to see why he was absent she found him.

Like a good Millenarist he had taken the sure escape from his condition of sin. He had done it in the approved way, with a rope around his neck.

I've never once thought seriously of committing suicide myself. But I could see how, then and there, it might have seemed like a real good idea to Jubal Khaim-Novello.

13

WE are aware that humans do sometimes end their own lives. None of us would do that, of course. How does it happen that your race survives in spite of the fact that so many of you human beings are, as you say, "crazy"?

Well, thanks a lot, but we're not all that crazy. Honestly. If you come right down to it, I bet that you people have just as many crazies as we do, only you don't notice them because of how you live.

I don't mean to be insulting. What I'm trying to say is that you live in a kind of culture where craziness just doesn't stand out. It was probably the same with us thousands of years ago, when human beings were hunter-gatherers—when our ancestors lived more or less like the way you do yourselves, I mean. In those days, if old Glaucus from the bog people was kind of slow, even stupid—what we would now call severely retarded—his condition didn't let him off his turn pulling roots. It just meant that the other people probably made fun of him and probably gave him all the dirtiest jobs. If some other guy was, well, psychotically touchy, the kind that's always starting fights, they didn't put him away. They just ganged up on him and beat the hell out of him—unless he was too big and strong—and then, who knows?— maybe they elected him their chief.

If you think about, say, the famous Greek heroes, the ones that stormed Troy and went around conquering kingdoms and so on, the way they acted would put them in a loony bin these days. Odysseus and

Hector and Priam and all those people were a hell of a lot loopier than I ever was at my worst—

Well, yes. I accept that you don't know much about any of those old Greeks. I even accept that you don't care. The point is that things are different in a more sophisticated society. I'm pretty sure we don't have more crazies than anybody else. They just show more.

I admit that Jubal Khaim-Novello's suicide shook me up. The man had not been anything you could call a personal friend, exactly, but he wasn't a stranger, either. We'd come out to Pava together and shared some work details, and he was a neighbor, after all—I felt bad that he had decided that he had to kill himself. I thought of maybe dropping in on the widow to express sympathy, ask her to call on me if she needed anything—you know, the sort of ritual thing you're supposed to do when somebody dies?

Well, no, you don't know, do you? Anyway, I didn't do it that night. Then, the next morning at the breakfast table, there was Becky, sitting next to Friar Tuck at a table raised a little higher than the others, looking pink and flushed and excited. What's more, Tuchman stood up on the table to announce that the Millenarists were going to have a special worship service that night so they could all rejoice together for their dear, departed, *fortunate* brother who had finally freed himself from the sin of existing, and Garold Tscharka was going to make a special trip down from *Corsair* to lead it.

And all the time Becky was smiling tremulously beside him, looking less like a widow than a bride. Go figure.

It seemed to me I had more or less promised Theophan I would go out with her that day. I found her sitting next to Marcus Wendt and told her I was ready. She gave me a look of surprise. "Why, thanks, Barry," she said, "but I've already arranged with Jimmy Queng for Marcus to go. I wasn't sure what your plans were going to be, you see. And Marcus is feeling a little better today, so he's going to help me out." And Marcus gave me a brave little smile to show agreement.

So I went over to Jimmy Queng and volunteered for whatever he had open.

The first thing on the list turned out to be food gathering up in the hills: eleven people in three cars, and leaving right away. It sounded as good as anything else. I jumped in one of the cars, shook hands around, and we took off.

We drove until the bumpy excuse for a road ran out, at the edge of a grove of the bamboo-like trees. It was warm and pleasant, and the air smelled fresh, and the usual bunch of lep helpers were waiting for us. We took baskets out of the cars and split up into groups of a couple of human beings and a lep. My personal lep reared up to look at me and my partner out of those immense bug-eyes. It didn't speak. It just twisted itself around and went inchworming away into the woods, leaving us to follow.

The woman who was teamed up with me was an elderly black grandmother named Madeleine Hartly, Pava-born and pushing hard on what would have been retirement age, if anybody had much of a chance to retire on Pava. Whatever her years, Madeleine was spry enough to keep a dozen steps ahead of me as we climbed after the lep through the woods. When the lep stopped, Madeleine did too. She looked around, nodded, and said, "All right, Barry, by now you probably can recognize some of the things you've been eating the last couple of weeks. Nobody's picked this area for a while, so there's plenty of ripe stuff."

She stopped for a minute, squinting up at the sky, because her voice was almost drowned out by a roar from overhead; the shuttle was sweeping past us in the sky, big, bright and noisy as it came in for a landing. "That's loud enough to be Tscharka himself," I said when the racket had dwindled.

Madeleine didn't answer that, just gave me a curious look and went on: "What we specially want to harvest are sushi and roseberries, but don't pick the sushi right away. It spoils too fast; we'll have to just mark where it is and come back for it right before we start home, okay? We want all you can find of those, but don't pass up any other fruits that look good. If you're in doubt about anything show it to me or Eleanor of Aquitaine here." She nodded to our lep. "Eleanor doesn't speak our language very well, but she'll stop you if she sees you trying to pick anything poisonous."

"Poisonous?" I said uncertainly.

Madeleine laughed. "Don't worry about it. Trust Eleanor. Pick."

All my life I have taken "Don't worry about it" as a signal to start serious worrying, but Madeleine seemed to know what she was doing. So did the lep. The first time I reached for what looked like a slightly darker-colored roseberry, deep scarlet instead of strawberry red, the lep whistled and slapped at my arm with those little hands of hers and shook her head. (Not easy to do when you don't have a neck; she twisted her whole upper body violently.) I got the idea.

The sushi fruits were easier—pear-shaped things with a spiny husk, and inside a moist, fishy-tasting pulp that I had not learned to care for but others gobbled up. I found half a dozen bushes loaded with them, several different varieties, and all looking ripe to me. I made a mental note of them, as ordered, and went on to other fruits. The lep was picking away industriously, too, with her agile little hands, and in less than an hour we'd filled our baskets and carried them down to the car to turn them in for empties.

Picking fruits in a warm, sweet-smelling wood isn't the hardest work I ever did, and it doesn't tax the intellect much. After I'd caught the rhythm I had plenty of time to think while I picked.

I thought about all kinds of things. I thought about Alma, because I thought about Alma a lot; and I thought about poor, dumb Jubal Khaim-Novello, and what a waste it had been for him to come eighteen-some light-years just to do what he could have done a lot cheaper and easier back on the Moon. And I thought about the technical problems there might be in getting the factory orbiter refueled, and in commanding it to make a copy of itself to be installed on the surface, and—well—about all the possible plans I could dream up to turn Pava into something as close as the Lederman lunar colony as I could manage.

Just thinking about those things wasn't good enough. I wanted to talk to someone who might fill in some of the gaps in my knowledge. Like Madeleine Hartly. I tried to pick closer and closer to her, in the hopes of striking up a conversation. She would have none of it. "When we pick we pick. We'll have plenty of time to talk—later. I think these baskets are full enough to take down now."

By the end of the day I had done that six times. Then Madeleine said we'd done enough; it was time to collect the sushi and go home. For the sushi-picking part of the job Madeleine stuck close beside me while I picked, examining each bush herself. "Red sushi, that's nice, blue, pearblossom—real good, Barry; we don't get pearblossom sushi much, and it's my favorite. You've got a good eye," she complimented me. "Only don't pick the fruits on the bottom branches of the blue."

"They're not sushi?"

"They are sushi, but look around the stems. See that grayish, slimy stuff growing on them? That's sort of a fungus. It's hallucinogenic. You can pick some of it for yourself if you want a high tonight—some people do—but don't put it in with the other stuff. Don't try to save it, either. If you don't eat it in twelve hours it'll make you sick as a dog, if it doesn't kill you."

I didn't pick the hallucinogens; they were never my favorite thing, even on the Moon. When we got back to the cars I took a fast look through the heaped produce in the back just to see if anybody else had, but if there were any secret dopers in our party they had hidden their stash pretty well.

In spite of the fact that I was brand-new at the game, Madeleine and I were about the first ones back. Madeleine gave me a motherly grin of satisfaction. She chose two branches of roseberries out of a basket and handed one to me. "First ones finished get to loaf while the others catch up," she told me, her mouth full of fruit. "Are you going to the rejoicing tonight?"

"The what?"

"The services for that Khaim-Novello boy. It's like a funeral, sort of, but the Millenarists call it a 'rejoicing.' I imagine most people will be there."

I said, "I hadn't really thought about it. Madeleine? Would you mind if I asked you some questions?"

"What kind of questions?"

"Well," I said, trying to juggle all the questions in my mind into some sort of order of priority. "The thing is, I keep wondering why you people haven't made a better job of being here. Obviously you need more electric power than you've got. After all this time, why don't you have it?"

She gave me a kind of good-humored, skeptical, grandmotherly look. "Oh, right, Barry. You're the one who's going to show us how to run the colony, aren't you?"

It hadn't occurred to me that I was already beginning to get a kind of a reputation. I wasn't sure I liked it, but I pressed on. "Well, why?"

She gave me a serious answer. "We knew what we needed. We weren't stupid, you know. We did have plenty of hydroelectric power, for a while. Then the dam broke. That really set us back. That was pretty discouraging, especially because we'd just about used ourselves up on getting it built; we didn't have the resources to do it over again."

"All right, I understand that. But then, why was the dam built in an earthquake area in the first place? You had a couple of trained seismologists to warn you about the risks."

"No, you're wrong about that. We didn't, at least not when it was started. The Sperlies didn't get here until we'd already got the cement plant going and the cofferdam built and most of the foundations already poured. We talked about it, but it was too far along to move it."

It was even worse to go ahead with it and then have the whole damn thing washed away, but I didn't say that. "Then what about a fossil-fuel plant? There's supposed to be oil down the river somewhere; the factory orbiter could probably make pumps and pipes to get it to Free-hold."

"Make them out of what raw materials, Barry?"

She had finished the roseberries and was sitting propped against one of the big wheels of our car. She looked sweet and kind, which she was; I tried to be tactful with my next question.

"If you'd built those ships Captain Tscharka was expecting to find here we could probably convert one to a space tug for mining the asteroids."

That made her blink at me. "Ships?"

"Short-rangers. To explore the Delta Pavonis solar system."

"First I heard of it," she said thoughtfully. "Sometimes people talk about exploring the other planets, but I never knew Garold was planning to *do* it."

That was the second time I'd heard that. I wondered if Tscharka had deliberately lied to me, and I wondered why.

"Anyway," Madeleine was saying cheerily, "now we've got all that extra fuel; maybe things will get better." She stood up, spry as ever, and ruffled my hair in a friendly way. "I guess everybody's like you, the first month they're here, full of great ideas. Well, good for you. Let's hope you can work them out. Meanwhile, excuse me for a minute, because I have to go into the bushes to pee."

By then the rest of our party was straggling in, five or six of them sitting against tree trunks or walking around in the fading sunshine, nibbling sushi and roseberries and chatting while we waited for the others. A couple of them were talking about Jubal Khaim-Novello's funeral "rejoicing," which was not a subject I cared to discuss. Two of the others were new colonists like myself, or even newer, in the sense that they hadn't had the experience of going out into the field with Theophan Sperlie. The woods were all fresh and surprising for them. One of the old-timers had shown them how to get a drink out of a water tree, and they were excitedly talking about that and all the other funny new things they'd seen, like the spiderweb plants that threw retractable nets into the air to catch bugs and spores. "But they aren't plants exactly," the old-timer was explaining. "Pava doesn't exactly have plants and animals; the spiderwebbers are warm-blooded, you know."

Well, I at least did know that, sort of, because Jacky Schottke had already explained to me what the early settler was now explaining to her audience: that on Pava the main divisions between large living organisms was between photoautotrophs (which lived largely on sunlight) and heterotrophs (which lived entirely on other living things); if you called them "plants" and "animals," he said, then you had to get used to the idea that some of the autotrophic "plants" could run faster than a human being.

"So if these, what do you call, heterotrophs eat things—" one of the greenhorns started to say.

"It's easier if you call them animals," the woman said helpfully.

"All right, if these animals eat things, are they dangerous?"

"No. Not really. The whistling snakes bite, but they'll run away if you give them a chance. The only ones that ever seriously hurt a human being are the killer ants and the dinos—dinowolves—and you aren't likely to see any of those."

Madeleine was back and listening. "What the predators mostly ate was lep larvae, but my father did get pretty badly bitten by a dino once. They worried about the children, though, so they had a bounty on the predators, as long as they lasted. We've just about wiped the dangerous ones out around here—that's why," she said, smiling down at Eleanor of Aquitaine, "there are so many leps in this area these days."

If she expected Eleanor to respond she was disappointed. The lep just "sat" there, with a couple of others, listening and not joining in. I didn't expect Eleanor to speak, since she didn't know the language, but the other leps were silent, too. One of them was a young male, I judged, third instar or so by the amount of red in his coloring. His arms and hands were well developed, which made him about the equivalent of a human teenager. Like any other teenager, he was playing. He had one of the little animals they called flying rats in his hands, tossing it into the air as he listened and catching it again. The thing was squeaking and trying to spread its bat wings.

I noticed him particularly because it had never occurred to me that leps would have pets . . . and because I saw that he was watching me, too.

I knew that three-star leps had their language skills pretty well formed and wondered if he spoke English. "Hi," I said. "I'm Barry di Hoa. What's your name?"

He looked at me with those great, weird eyes for a moment. Then he said, quite clearly, "I'm called Geronimo," and, without warning, he fired the flying rat at me.

I knew what flying rats were by then, because Jacky Schottke had shown them to me, too. They didn't have any real teeth. Their bills were soft—I guess the only Earthly things like that are platypuses—and all they ever ate was that stinking rot that collects in wet places that Jacky said was called "elephant snot." So, although I was a little startled, I caught the thing and held it in my hand for a moment. It wasn't warm—well, it wasn't a mammal—and it didn't struggle very hard, just squeaked protestingly and drooled on my hand.

"Throw it back," Geronimo shrilled. I did. Then he threw it to me again, and we had a little game of catch-the-flying-rat between us for a while, to the amusement of Madeleine and the others . . . until I missed my catch and the little thing flew away, beeping triumphantly.

"Sorry, Geronimo," I said.

"It does not matter, Barrydihoa," he told me. "I will catch another. Do you have candy?"

I looked in my pockets, though I knew the answer already. "I'm afraid not."

He stood there silently—well, leps don't *stand*, but you know what I mean; he kept the forward part of his body elevated to look at me at nearly eye level for a moment. Then he said, "Will you have candy tomorrow?"

"I could. Well, sure, I'll get some, then."

"I will see you tomorrow," he said, and turned away and stretch-slunk into the woods.

Madeleine was smiling at me. "Looks like you've made a friend," she said, and you know? I felt as though I really had.

So we'd had a nice day in the woods, and then, when we'd got back to Freehold, there was the question of what to do with the evening.

I didn't really intend to go to Jubal Khaim-Novello's "rejoicing." I certainly wasn't a Millenarist. The trouble was that, if you didn't care to go to some religious service or other, there wasn't much else to do for entertainment on Pava, once you'd got tired of playing cards or watching old vid tapes. I couldn't even take somebody aside to pump them with my questions, because it looked like the whole town was intending to go to the party.

So when dinner was over and people began to gather for the rejoicing I went, and the day that had been all cheerful sunshine turned into a very down night.

They had turned on the big floodlights so we could see each other and the platform. It was a pleasant, warm twilight to be out-of-doors in (I was grateful that Pava had never evolved mosquitoes!) which probably accounted for part of the attendance. All the same, I was astonished to see how many people had come to celebrate Jubal's passing: standing around, sitting on benches or folding chairs, or stretched out on the mossy ground. Bearing in mind that Pava's human population was less than nine hundred, any nongovernmental gathering with a turnout of what had to be four or five hundred people was a wild success.

I am sure a lot of the people were there just for the lack of something better to do, like me, but it was obvious there was a hard core of real Millenarists at work. They had decorated the platform with greenery. They had put robes on Friar Tuck and Captain Tscharka, who shared the spotlight—white with a gold cowl for the reverend, bloodred for the captain. The widow sat demurely, maybe even a little proudly, between them. They even had music—two guitars, a saxophone, and several keytones—and a choir of six people. I recognized Tscharka's first officer, Jillen Iglesias, as the lead soprano, looking earnest and virginal and pure, and when they sang their first hymn (it was "Rock of Ages"), Tscharka joined in, with a surprising, pleasant warm baritone.

Rock of Ages, cleft for me,
Let me hide myself in thee. . . .

And Tscharka came down heavy on the "hide" with a look of yearning on his face that spelled it all out: Hide yourself where? Hide yourself in death.

It was grisly, when you thought of it.

It seemed to me that most of the people there weren't thinking, though. They were feeling. I have to admit that, in a sweet-sad, wistful way, it felt good. It felt like being dirty and travel-stained and worn, and suddenly seeing the promise of a warm shower and a soft, welcoming bed. . . .

I had to remind myself that the bed the Millenarists were inviting us to share was a grave.

They didn't stress the dying-for-your-sins part of their doctrine, though, at least not at first. They took turns in preaching at us, the two of them: Tscharka dark, deep-eyed, mystical; Tuchman the loving, jolly, welcoming Santa Claus, like everybody's favorite grandpa.

* * *

Please understand that I'm doing my best to give you a fair, objective account of what went on. It isn't easy. I wasn't objective then and I'm even less so now; I was gritting my teeth and wondering just what kind of fools all these people were.

It was an impressive performance, though. They had the whole thing choreographed. After the hymn it was Tuchman who welcomed us all, beaming fondly at the crowd, as he complimented the musicians and the choir and told us how happy he was that he had found the road to salvation—the road that his dear brother Jubal had taken the night before. And he patted the widow fondly on her proud, bent head.

Then it was Tscharka who thundered at us: "What Jubal Khaim-Novello knew is what we all must learn, my brothers and sisters! We rejoice together tonight in his deliverance, but all the joys of the world are a trap. The real joy is not here, for as long as we are here we all share the certainty of sin. We did not seek to be sinners, but we cannot avoid it; we are stained with it as long as we draw breath. While we live we must do the work God has given us; but, oh, how we long to escape this vile world and enter into His holy kingdom!"

And Friar Tuck told us, grinning ruefully, apologetically, at his own weakness, how many times he had taken out his flask of sacred release— he held it up to show us, a bottle of poison pills for God's sake!— because he was weak and yearned for his own escape . . . but, he said sternly, then he had put it away again, because there were still souls to be saved.

That was when he surprised me. Two men, in different parts of the crowd, suddenly began struggling forward, reaching for the deadly little bottle. And, to my surprise, Tuchman held it high away from them, refusing them their escape into death—I'd been prepared, for one shocking second, to see a couple of additional suicides right in front of me.

Tuchman denied them their chance, sorrowfully shaking his old white mane. He stood tall and silent for a moment, the bottle of poison pills high over his head.

Then he brought his arm slowly down. Gazing reverently upon the bottle of poison pills, he said, in tones of mourning, "The time for us is not yet, my beloved ones. We must be strong awhile, so that we may carry the word to our brothers and sisters. We must rescue as many as God gives us the power to do . . . and *then* we can cleanse ourselves all at once, rejoicing. Until that blessed day, in the name of Saint Jones, be strong."

It was really astonishing how cuddly-warm the Millenarists could make the idea of mass suicide sound.

That was when I got up and left. People looked at me in disapproving surprise, but I didn't meet their eyes. I just took off. I didn't wait for the promised refreshments. I didn't have any appetite for them, and even less for listening to more of that sad, horrid preaching—maybe, I think, a little bit because it was all beginning to sound almost reasonable to me.

I still say human beings aren't basically insane, but I can see how you might think they are.

I walked around the empty streets of Freehold for a while, looking for lighted windows. There weren't many. Most of the people I knew, Millenarists or not, had been at the services; the party part had begun, and I could hear singing and laughter from it.

I wasn't really sure I wanted to talk to anybody just then anyway. When I found myself on the bank of our little branch of the river I sat down and tossed a few rocks into the water, listening to the distant chirps and hoots from the forest. Nobody was around.

It was a pleasant, warm night, and Pava's constellations were bright in the sky overhead. I wondered which star was Earth's sun, but couldn't find it. Perhaps it was on the other side of Delta Pavonis in that season, I thought. Very likely it would be too faint to pick out, at eighteen-plus light-years away.

That pleasant day in the woods had faded from my memory. I was— not depressed; certainly not in that clinical sense that came with my little genetic problem—but pretty thoroughly dejected. I had, I have to say to you, some pretty dismal feelings about my own human race.

After a while I persuaded myself that things would look better in the morning, so I stood up and headed home. When I got back to the apartment I turned on the vid without looking at it. It was some sort of musical story, out of Pava's huge library of old recorded performances. People in bright costumes were laughing and dancing on the screen, but I cannot tell you what the story was about.

I turned it off when I heard Jacky Schottke coming in. "Oh," I said. "Is the rejoicing over?"

He looked shamefaced. "I guess so. I wasn't exactly there. I was listening to most of it, though. I hid behind the toolshed."

I didn't need to ask him why—because, no doubt, as a backslider he wasn't sure of his right to be there. I didn't even ask him if he'd been tempted by Friar Tuck's little bottle of lethal joy. But I couldn't let go of the subject. "Is it possible," I asked him, as the closest available expert to help me confirm my suspicions, "that what Tuchman and the captain really want to do is convert everybody—and then try to get everybody here all to commit suicide at once?"

He looked unhappy. He didn't deny it, though.

"That's really insane," I said. "No group of normal people would do that."

"Oh, yes," he said quickly. "It's happened before. Didn't you hear what he said about Saint Jones?"

"I don't know who Saint Jones is."

"Well, you would if you'd ever been a Millenarist. Jones was one of the early prophets, a long time ago. He took his whole flock to someplace in Central America, and they all swallowed poison together. Even the babies. Saint Jones is one of the central martyrs in the church, you know."

I said, "That's bloody *sickening*."

"Only if you don't believe," he said, looking mournful. "They're not going to force anybody to do it. Only—well," he said, his voice tragic, "it would certainly be pretty lonesome for the survivors."

14

*Y*OU *have stated that the Millenarists are only one "religious" sect among many such, and not a large one at that. Why then are there so many on this planet?*

*Y*es, well, when I got here that struck me as pretty strange, too. I'd never seen so many Millenarists in one place.

The thing is, there are a hell of a lot of human beings—more than you can imagine—so even a tiny splinter cult like the Millenarists probably has hundreds of thousands of members.

No more than that, of course; their doctrines don't encourage growth. Millenarists don't want to inflict original sin on any helpless infants, so they hardly ever have children.

But a few hundred thousand are barely a pimple on the human race. We are both numerous and diverse. There are probably a hundred thousand or so of almost any kind of improbable human being you wanted to name—left-handed albinos who are more than two meters tall, for instance—and still you'd be pretty surprised if you saw very many of those people in one place.

Even so, you shouldn't exaggerate their number. Out of more than eight hundred people on Pava, less than a quarter were really Millenarists. Don't be deceived by how many showed up for the rejoicing. Everybody loves a party. You know the old saying, "Everybody's Irish on St. Patrick's Day.'' Well, you don't know it, really, I suppose, but you get the idea.

So the Millenarists were nowhere near a majority, really, and the rest of us were a sampling of all kinds of denominations. We had two or three kinds of Muslims, we had a variety of Christians. We had a clutch of about fifteen or eighteen Mormons, for instance—well, you know about them because the Mormons were about the only ones who really tried hard to convert you people to their religion. Of course they didn't succeed.

Jacky Schottke was the one who told me about that failed mission to the heathen—I guess because he'd tried his own luck at spreading his own Millenarist gospel, back when he was still a red-hot. He told me sadly that with the leps it was a major flop. He said leps had taken very well to human food and human games, and one or two of them had even tried out human liquor . . . but no lep, ever, had shown any interest at all in being converted to any human religion. Not even my little buddy Geronimo, although he struck me as about as fascinated by human ways as any lep I ever heard of—until I met you, anyway.

Geronimo was the first lep friend I made. I hadn't really expected to see him again after that day in the woods, in spite of what he had said, but the morning after Jubal's memorial service I was stuck on farm duty, running a tractor plow along what was going to be a potato field near the river. Surprise—when I broke for lunch I saw the little lep humping and hustling up from the riverbank toward me.

"Good morning, Barrydihoa," he said. "Is there candy today?"

I'd forgotten all about him and his sweet mouthpart. "I'm sorry, Geronimo. Maybe I can get some tomorrow."

He weaved his upper body back and forth for a moment in silence, watching me with those huge fly eyes. "It is okay," he said, in that hissy, whispery voice. "I will be at another place today. Good-bye, Barrydihoa." And he stretched and squirmed his way back down to the riverbank. There he scouted around for a moment until he found a good piece of deadwood. He took the chunk in his teeth—well, in whatever he had to grind things with in his mouthpart—to help him stay above water, and flopped into the stream. I watched him paddling with his little hands and wriggling his body as he swam across, holding on to the log for buoyancy. The current was strong there. It carried him a pretty long way downstream, but I saw him wriggle safely out on the far bank. He didn't look back.

The other farm workers were looking at me with curiosity. "What did he mean about the candy?" one of them asked—Pasquale Scales, it was; I remembered that he and his wife had come out on *Corsair* with me.

"I guess leps like candy." (Of course I was wrong about that; "leps" aren't all the same any more than humans are. Geronimo just happened to have acquired the taste.)

"Well," Pasquale said, "maybe we can help. Rita and I were talking about making some fudge if we could. I don't know what it's going to be like, with goat milk, but if you come by the kitchens tonight you can have some."

It was a generous offer. I thanked him, and then I told them about meeting Geronimo up in the hills, and how we'd played Frisbee with one of the flying rats. Pasquale thought that sounded like enough fun to try for ourselves, but although we'd seen some of the rats down by the grain patch we had to get back to work.

I wondered if I could catch one of the creatures for myself. It might be more interesting than playing pinochle with Jacky Schottke. I didn't expect I'd actually be tossing the thing back and forth with Geronimo again, of course. I still didn't really think I'd see him again.

But the next morning, as I was getting ready to help replace some of the shorings on the meeting hall, there he was.

"I will work with you today, Barrydihoa," he said. "Is there candy now?"

I wasn't surprised at leps helping humans; by then I'd got used to the idea. But this was special. I had no idea why Geronimo picked me out. He didn't say, and I couldn't guess. But there I was, all of a sudden, with a new lep friend and a new interest in life.

I don't want you to think that I'd given up on my plans to fix whatever was wrong with the Pava colony. I kept on bothering everybody I could find with questions. Wherever I worked—the farms, the biomass power plant, even kitchen detail a couple of times when I didn't duck fast enough—I cross-examined everybody who would talk to me. I doubt there was a person in the colony who hadn't heard that I was this new guy who was obsessed on the subject.

But Geronimo was my sidekick. Almost every day he showed up wherever I was working and worked right along with me—tending Theophan's seismological stuff when Marcus Wendt was having one of his feeling-poorly days, repairing buildings, clearing roadways after a storm—whatever I had to do, he helped. Or, if that particular task was beyond his physical powers, at least he kept me company.

When he began humping up the steps to Jacky Schottke's apartment with me after work, I wasn't sure Jacky would be happy about having him there. I mean, that grassy, earthy lep smell could get pretty strong in an enclosed space, and the place was Jacky's apartment before it was mine. Actually Jacky was delighted. He'd talked to any number of leps before, of course—that was one of the things he did as an ethnologist— but seldom, he said, one as willing to spend time conversing with a human being as my Geronimo. A third-instar lep doesn't know as much as a senior, but Geronimo easily remembered things some of the more mature ones forgot—what it was like to be second instar, for instance, basking in the sun for warmth and toddling around in a fumbling search for edible roots and fruits and the slower, softer, least aggressive bugs.

"The leps," Jacky lectured me one night after Geronimo had crept away home, "along with the goobers and the black crawlers, are a trophic species—"

"The what?"

"The goobers and the crawlers. You must have seen them in the woods. No? Well, they look like leps, but they're not intelligent. Anyway, they all eat the same things in the food chain, and I'm pretty sure they're eaten by the same predators—or were, before we wiped out most of the predators in this area. So they're a trophic species. The hard part of figuring out their relationships is that the adult leps don't eat what the young ones do, but Geronimo seems to remember every bite he ever took."

And was willing to answer all of Jacky's questions about them, too, up to a point . . . although when the questioning stretched out too long Geronimo might rear back and give him a frosty look and screech, "Play cards?"

That was the other thing Geronimo liked a lot. He liked to play games. He was willing to play indoors when it was dark or raining— he didn't mind being out in the rain, but I did—and he was quick to learn pinochle. He learned it well enough to beat Jacky and me a fair bit of the time.

He loved the vid games, too, although we didn't let him play them often. It was a drain on Schottke's computer time, and besides, Geronimo would get so wrapped up in piloting his simulated aircraft from simulated Seattle to simulated Singapore (I wondered what he made of the simulated Earthly geography along the way) that he wasn't answering any questions at all. He even tried baseball a time or two, when we could get up a scratch team. He managed surprisingly well with the bat but he couldn't really cover the outfield.

Geronimo made a big difference for me in my new life on Pava.

I didn't have that many friends in the colony. Geronimo was a welcome addition to the list—if "friend" is the right word for what Geronimo was to me. Maybe it was more like owning a particularly smart, loyal, affectionate pet . . . although it wasn't always clear to me which was the pet and which the owner.

As it happened, we had plenty of time for indoor games around then. The weather changed. For a while we were pretty much housebound as Freehold was hit by a nasty three-day storm, wave after wave of thunderboomers with spectacular lightning displays, high winds and pelting rain. Jacky Schottke and I took turns running to the kitchens to bring food back to the apartment, and the outside work of the community had to be done in two-hour snatches between waves. I used the time to work the apartment's screen to catch up on some of the colony's history and technology—not being very impressed with what I found—and to get my notions about bringing it up to speed into some coherent order. The first step, surely, was to get the factory orbiter fueled from Tscharka's antimatter store; after that I was less clear. But no less impatient.

When the clouds moved out toward the coast and Delta Pavonis beamed again, there was a lot of accumulated work to deal with. I found out that there were some jobs Geronimo didn't care to share with me when Jimmy Queng tagged me for butcher detail. Geronimo was standing right beside me at the morning show-up when I got the call, but by the time I was halfway to the little meadow where Freehold's herd of free-ranging goats grazed he wasn't there anymore. He was sloping off, as fast as he could slither, in the direction of the hills.

Friar Tuck had drawn the same detail and was just behind me. When he saw where I was looking he gave me a consoling smile. "Leps don't like to kill things," he said.

"I'm not crazy about it myself," I told him.

He said mildly, "You eat the meat, though." That was a point for him, all right. When we had stripped to the waist and begun to get into the actual nasty business of slitting throats and spilling out the guts from the body cavities of the animals, I gave serious if brief thought to becoming a vegetarian. The reverend did not appear to have any such thoughts. He waded right in, regardless of struggling animals, bad smells or gore. I suppose that when death is your dearest ambition a little extra slaughter doesn't matter much, one way or the other.

By the time we had six carcasses skinned and cleaned and cut into quarters Dabney Albright had joined us in his boat, pissing and moaning because he'd had so much trouble dodging floating debris on the way up. All the rivers had risen after the storms, and our little local stream was yellow with mud and full of storm-downed branches and even fair-sized trees.

"At least it makes it easier for the woodcutters," Tuchman said jovially as we began loading the meat into the boat. The man was determined to be cheerful about everything. He had good ideas, though; when we had all the carcasses loaded and Albright was already pushing off for the downstream run, Tuchman was the first one to get out of his clothes and into the water to get the blood off.

Although the water was cold, Delta Pavonis was hot. It seemed that Millenarists didn't suffer much from nudity taboos, and when we were reasonably clean Tuchman sprawled naked on the riverbank for a while, unconcerned with his great, pale, bare body, gazing benignly at the rest of us. One of the others, a young dark-skinned man named Phil Fass, threw a stick into the stream and said, "You know what I'd like to do? I'd like to put some trout in these rivers."

"You know we can't do that," Tuchman reminded him. Well, we all did know that. The colonists were strict about releasing the kinds of Earthly organisms that might go explosively feral in the Pavan environment; there had been too many Hawaiis and Australias in human history to make that particular mistake again. Even our free-ranging goats were all female—fertilized by sperm collected from the few closely guarded males that were allowed to grow to maturity—and kept tightly fenced in until they delivered. But Tuchman wasn't finished. He was gazing at me as he said, "There are a lot of things we'd like to do, but can't."

I took that to be a challenge. "On the other hand," I said, "there are a lot of things that we can do, and should. Like getting some use out of all that antimatter Tscharka brought."

"You're so concerned with worldly things," he said gently.

"Maybe you and Tscharka aren't concerned enough. Where's he been, anyway?"

"Shuttling cargo down from *Corsair*, of course."

"Well, what's going to happen when that's finished? We're not all Millenarists, you know."

"I do know that," he said earnestly, "and I sorrow for that fact every day of my life." He stood up and began getting dressed. "No," he said, "we're not all Millenarists, but what we are is a democracy. It isn't up to you to decide what the colony does with its resources, my friend Barry. It's up to the colony as a whole, and I have no doubt that that decision will be made in good time. Now I think we should start back to see what else needs doing."

Before dinner I decided on a social call. I hadn't seen Madeleine Hartly for several days, and I liked the woman. Her house was a one-flat at the opposite end of town from Jacky Schottke and me. I found it without trouble, but when I knocked on the door a tall, skinny young woman answered. She had a big spoon in her hand and I could smell cooking as she shook her head at me. "No, you can't see Gram right now. This weather hasn't been good for her. She's not feeling too well right now."

I asked her to please tell Madeleine that I'd stopped by and that I hoped she'd be better soon—the things you say when someone's sick. It seemed to me that she'd have to be pretty ill to have someone cooking for her in her own kitchen, and I didn't like that idea. I hadn't thought of Madeleine ever being sick. She was old; I knew that. But the way she'd loped up and down the hillside to gather fruit hadn't suggested an invalid.

On the way to the mess tables I strolled along the riverbank, enjoying the warm dusk. You could hear the river that night; it was still all yellow with mud brought down from the storm. Bits and pieces of vegetation were floating in it, and Pavans were out walking like myself.

Halfway there I heard someone calling my name, and it was Theophan. "Listen," she said when she caught up to me, "are you doing anything important tomorrow?"

I looked around for Marcus Wendt, but she was alone. "Whatever they tell me to do, I guess."

"Well, this damp is bad for Marcus's shoulder, and I need to get some stuff up to the Rockies in the morning. Want to give me a hand?"

I promised. I thought for a moment that she might suggest joining her at the meal, but she didn't; she nodded thanks and turned around and left.

Oddly, Geronimo wasn't with us when Theophan and I met the next morning. That wasn't a total surprise, because there were days when the lep had business of his own, whatever that business was, and never showed up. But I thought I'd seen him out my window, and yet when I came down he wasn't there.

He wasn't waiting at the car, either, though two other leps were. I didn't give it much of a thought, because I was looking forward to seeing the Rockies close up. Theophan wouldn't even try to do that particular jaunt when it was raining—it was going to be hard enough getting up those hills in dry weather, she promised; if it was raining we'd never make it. So I hadn't been west of the river at all.

I almost wasn't that day, either, because after we'd taken the long detour upriver to the only place where it could be forded, Theophan stopped the car and got out to stare at the water. It wasn't inviting. The river was several hundred meters broad at that point and obviously flowing fast. "It's still pretty high," she fretted. "What do you think, Barry?"

I knew my opinion wasn't worth much—what did I know about fording rivers on Pava?—but I didn't want to turn back again. "I think we can make it if we go slow," I said wisely. Theophan knew how little my opinion was worth as well as I did, but I had said what she wanted to hear. She made all the leps get out of the car and gave me a rope; I led them across, each one of them hanging gamely by its mouth-part to the rope and slithering and sliding around in the flow.

It wasn't any fun for me, either, though my only real personal problems were just the coldness of the water and the necessity for taking care in where I placed my feet. It was a good deal harder for the leps. Their bodies wanted to float. Try as they would, they couldn't keep enough of themselves below water to anchor themselves on the bottom. But we made it safely, and then it was Theophan's turn to drive the car after us.

That was tricky. There was a minute or two when I could see it beginning to slide, but she jammed on the speed and got clear.

When she finally crawled out onto the west bank I breathed easier—and, from the strained look on her face as she grinned at me, so did she.

We dried off quickly enough in the warm air as we drove back down along the river. There weren't many new sights for me to see yet. There was only one real difference between the two banks of the river and that was man-made. The colony's farm plots were scattered all along the east bank. There weren't any farms on the west—I thought—and then I began to notice that the occasional leps who raised their heads to stare at us as we passed were usually in the middle of patches of yellowish flowering plants or red-berried green ones.

That suggested something very close to agriculture to me. When I asked Theophan about them she nodded.

"Beans and berry roots, that's what they eat. They cultivate them, all right. I don't know if you'd call it real farming, though. They don't have to work very hard at it, because all they do is fling seeds into the ground and come back to collect their crops a few months later."

She looked over her shoulder at our lep assistants, whistling and snorting interestedly among themselves in the back of the car, and then added, "Now and then we've tried to show the leps how they could increase their productivity—selecting the best strains, fertilizing, and so on—but they just didn't seem to be interested in the idea. Now, with their population explosion, they may begin to pay attention."

That rang a bell. "Somebody else said something about a lep population explosion," I mentioned.

"Sure. They're hardly ever eaten by predators anymore. I'd guess there are twice as many leps around this colony now as there were when the first ship arrived," she said with satisfaction. "So they really have something to thank us for, don't they? Only they don't act that way."

"Well, but they do," I objected. "Look at the way Geronimo works with me, and he's not the only one. I mean, they're always helping out, aren't they? Seems to me that's pretty decent of them." She shrugged. She didn't look at me; we had turned west into the hills and she was concentrating on peering ahead at the rutty track we were following. I persisted. "Wouldn't you call that gratitude?"

She said shortly, "For some people, maybe. Shut up for a minute, will you? so I won't run us into some damn ditch."

I shut up, and we were both silent for half an hour or so as we climbed along the slope of one of the mountains. I was glad Theophan was doing the driving; if she seemed touchy, I put it down to the difficulty of the job. There wasn't any road. There wasn't really even the kind of primitive track we'd followed to the old hydroelectric dam; Theophan was steering us across meadows and through clearings in wooded areas that became harder and harder to penetrate. Then she put on the brakes and killed the motor.

She looked around to make sure of her bearings, then nodded. "This is as far as we can go in the car," she said. "Let's unload the gear."

And so we did, Theophan passing the bits of equipment to me from the back of the car, I handing them down to the leps outside. The leps seemed to know the drill better than I did. They took the sleds and instruments in their little hands and organized them—stringing the harnesses to the sleds, tying the sensor parts securely in place. Then they stopped, looking up at me out of those remarkable eyes.

Theophan followed me out of the car. She looked up at the hill ahead of us and sighed. "All right," she said, "let's go."

Nothing happened. The leps stayed there, silent and staring.

Theophan looked grim but not surprised. "Damn them," she said. "Barry, tell them to get going."

I wasn't quite clear what was happening, but I tried it. "Let's get going," I said . . . and each of the leps picked up its harness and began tugging the sleds up along the slippery vegetation.

It was like that all day. Theophan would tell me what the leps were supposed to do. Then I would tell the leps. Then they would do it.

I didn't have the breath to ask her what that was all about while we were lugging the equipment up the mountain. I hardly had the breath to crawl through the slick, damp undergrowth, with the pack on my back weighing about one ton more with every hundred meters we climbed. The leps didn't seem bothered by the climb. They inched smoothly along, sliding through whatever gaps presented themselves in the brush, pulling those runnered sleds after them as though they were toys. The only good part of that climb was the scenery, and the only word for that was "spectacular." We stopped to catch our breaths at the edge of a huge rock amphitheater, and although I was panting and sore I couldn't help staring at it: vertical walls of something like limestone or marble, a tiny trickle of waterfall sparkling out of a cliff top.

Theophan noticed it. "Pretty, isn't it? The Millenarists call it The Cathedral—they come up to have their retreats here sometimes."

"It's a long climb," I said. If I'd been the Millenarists I would have picked somewhere closer.

She laughed. "I guess that's what they like best about it. Nobody comes to bother them here. Let's go."

We went. It didn't get easier. When we did finally reach the top I fell flat on the ground, sweating cold sweat—it was windblown and chilly on the peak—and trying to get my heart to stop pounding. I wondered if this sort of exertion were going to accelerate my need for a booster. Then I wondered if Dr. Billygoat would have something for me next time I saw him. Then I wondered what I would do if he didn't.

Then I got up and got busy, because I didn't want to do any of that wondering anymore.

If it hadn't been for the chill and Theophan's mood, it might have been real nice to be up high in the Pavan Rockies that day. It was different from the places on the east side of the river. There weren't any traces of human activity here, no roads, no leftover debris from food-gathering parties, nothing but what we had brought with us. And correspondingly there was more wildlife; I saw a couple of jacks, the little kangaroo-like lizards that hopped like bunnies, and heard whistling snakes all around me, and saw flocks of the flyers. I even thought I saw a red-marked third-instar lep looking out from the trees at us once. It seemed to me that it might possibly be Geronimo, but it disappeared before I could call to it.

We didn't have time to look around much, because the work was hard. It took us two hours to struggle the strain gauges into place, then another hour of Theophan scowling as she tinkered the transmitter into service. It didn't go well. She kept swearing to herself as she made tiny adjustments, and then swore some more after she'd made them and the needles on her test equipment continued to wobble unsteadily. The leps silently handed over the parts needed or went off and whistled morosely among themselves. I wasn't that smart. I kept making what I thought were helpful suggestions. Theophan didn't think they were. She snapped at me until finally I just shut up, sat down, and waited.

"Shit," she said at last. "That's as good as I can get it. What I really need is a whole set of new instruments, but let's go."

Then it took us another hour to get back to the car, and when we got there all of the leps simply disappeared.

Theophan sighed. "Get in, Barry," she said. "I guess we aren't going to have any company for the trip back."

There it was again. Something between her and the leps, but what?

I hadn't forgotten any of those questions, but I didn't think that was the time to ask them. It took all her concentration to get us down the hill in one piece. I didn't want to slow her down; the sun was getting low, and I didn't want to face trying to ford that river in the dark.

Theophan didn't seem to be feeling conversational, but as we were approaching the river she said morosely, "The more I think of it, the more I'm not sure we got that gauge in right, Barry. I'll have to check it when we get home, but I bet we're going to have to come back here, okay?"

"Any time," I said, though I wouldn't have said it had been a fun trip. I cleared my throat and asked, "Mind if I ask you something? What's the matter between you and the leps?"

She glanced at me. She shrugged. "They hate me."

"I kind of suspected they did. Why?"

She thought for a moment. "You've never seen their main nesting place, have you? There's not much to see now. They had a big quake that diverted a mountain stream, and the new path took the flow right through the nests. A lot of the leps got drowned."

"Yes?"

She thought some more, then sighed and began at the beginning. "Do you remember what a fault is? It's a place where you get crustal slippage. It's usually associated with a subducting region, where the edge of one tectonic plate slides down under another. On Earth you usually find subduction along an ocean coast, like California. Oh, there are other places even on Earth—the Rift Valley in Africa for instance—but mainly they're on coasts. Here not."

"Why is that?" I asked—hoping to keep her going long enough to get to the answer to my question. Which she didn't seem in any hurry to get around to.

"What do you mean 'why'? I'm not even sure of *what*, much less *why*. I'll never know for sure until we can do a complete geodetic survey, and I don't think I'll live that long. All this crap—I'm just scratching the surface! As a minimum, I ought to be setting off acoustic blasts: dig a shallow borehole and blow up a ton or so of explosives to measure the acoustic-wave reflections. But I can't get the explosives, and—" She stopped and bit her lip. "So I theorize. The only decent theory I've got doesn't help. Besides, I've already told it to you: The tectonic activity is linked to the fact that there's just one big continent on Pava. What do you think?"

That caught me by surprise, because what I'd been mostly thinking about was that she was having a hard time getting to answering me. I fell back on the truth. "I don't know enough to have an opinion."

"Neither do I," she said gloomily. She was silent for half a kilometer or so, I guess rehearsing her worries. Then she said, still talking around the question I had asked her, "Anyway, there are faults under where we built that dam—we found that out for sure, when it collapsed—and there are also big faults under these Rockies. And now I think they're coupled."

"Yes?"

"I mean," she said, sounding as though her patience tank was running low, "when one of the faults lets go—as the one under the dam did, probably from the weight of water we impounded behind it—that may trigger the other so it lets go too. The leps' quake wasn't more than twelve hours after the dam burst. Only theirs was worse. The slippage was twice as great, at least eight meters. What I think, I think there's a much deeper fault down under the surface there somewhere that connects the two faults."

"Oh," I said.

I waited for her to go on. She didn't. Finally I prompted, "And why does that make the leps hate you?"

"They blame me for that quake," she said. "They found out that Jake and I were seismologists, and they got it into their heads that the quake that ruined their nests was our fault. That's bullshit, of course. If they want to blame anybody, they should blame the klunkhead who sited the dam there in the first place. But try to tell them that! Now, if you don't mind, I really need to get us across the river."

That was true enough; and I could see by looking at it that the river had not come down much since the morning. My heart was in my mouth as we lurched across, but practice had improved Theophan's fording skills. She goosed the car across, throwing up a big spray of river water, and we made it safely enough to the other side.

Then she stopped and hunched over the wheel for a minute before she turned and looked at me.

"I might as well tell you all of it," she said.

"Please do!"

She looked at me in a hostile way, but she said it anyway. "The thing is, most of the leps who died were *young*. That's what got them so pissed off. Leps have a funny attitude about death. When a six-star lep dies, it happens after it's laid its eggs or fertilized its female. They think that's perfectly all right. It's what a six-star lep is supposed to do. But

for a lep to die before the sixth instar is—well—you said you were
brought up Western Orthodox, didn't you? Then think back to your
early training. You'll understand what the leps believe, maybe, if you
think of somebody dying unbaptized.''

"If you die unbaptized you don't go to heaven, is that what you
mean? But I didn't think the leps believed in heaven.''

"They don't *believe* in heaven. Christ, Barry, they don't have to.
They *see* heaven all around them. It's what they get as a reward at the
end of their lives. Their sixth instar—the winged phase, when they
don't work or eat or have to think about anything anymore, just fly
around and make love and die—that's their heaven. Think about it,
Barry! Think of *angels*. The lep sixth instar is exactly what you thought
heaven was going to be like when you were a kid—plus unlimited
fucking! And so if any lep happens to die before the sixth instar, it's a
terrible tragedy. It means they've been cheated out of their final reward,
their life has lost its fruition, and when the leps think somebody has
done that to anyone, or even just been careless enough to let it happen,
it's the one thing they can't ever forgive.''

15

A QUESTION. *Explain Theophansperlie's use of term "angels" as applied to ourselves.*

And?

The significance of "and" in this context is not understood.

It signifies I'm waiting for something. Is that really all you want to say? Don't you maybe want to discuss whether you were fair to her?

No discussion is necessary. We acknowledge that the human female Theophansperlie did not in fact bring about the desolation of our nests through any act of her own. The previous assumption was an error, and the consequent behavior of many of our third-, fourth- and fifth-instar cohorts was therefore unjustified. It was not appropriate to treat her as a nonperson.

Thanks. I'm sure Theophan thanks you too.

There remains the question. Why did she refer to us as "angels"? Many of you have stated that "angels" are purely imaginary beings related to some "religious" concepts. We are not imaginary. Explain this.

Please.

Please.

Well, it's not really worth wasting time on, but what the hell.

The thing is, when she called your old ones "angels" it was just a figure of speech. It's not to be taken literally. I'm sorry you people don't ever take anything any way *but* literally, but that's actually more your problem than ours, isn't it? Anyway, since angels are considered to be a sort of idealization of all the qualities that are best in human beings, it wasn't any kind of insult to refer to you people as "angels." If anything it's really sort of flattering.

But of course you don't know anything about flattery, either, do you?

I finally got to see Madeleine Hartly a day or two later. When I knocked she called to come in, and I found her wrapped up in blankets on a couch in her living room. I handed her some flowers I'd picked on the way and said, "Your granddaughter said you were feeling a little better."

"You mean Debbie. She's my *great*-granddaughter. What pretty flowers, Barry!" She looked very small propped up on the couch, big eyes against that dark skin, but she seemed cheerful enough. She didn't want to discuss her health. She sent me to the kitchen for a glass to put the flowers in and, when I said I was hoping she could tell me what the early days of the colony were like, she showed me where to find the carrels of old pictures.

Most of the people who were laughing and talking on Madeleine's screen were her family and friends. I knew none of them. Even when I saw Madeleine herself, hand in hand with a short, slim black man on each side, all of them laughing, I didn't recognize her at first. She couldn't have been more than twenty when it was taken. In the picture, the young Madeleine Hartly winked at the camera, then turned and gave the man on her left a giant smooch.

"That's my husband I'm kissing, in case you wondered. The other one's his brother Mal. Mal didn't get along here, though; he gave up and went back to Mars a year or two later."

I wasn't greatly interested in her brother-in-law, especially since he wasn't around anymore. "What are those things back there?"

"They're tents, boy. Haven't you ever seen tents before? That's what most people had to live in; we were getting colonists coming in faster than we could build houses for them. I don't think you can tell in the picture, but I was pregnant with Matty then—she was Debbie's grandmother."

"You were very pretty," I said.

She studied the picture. "I was, wasn't I? Anyway, I guess you aren't all that interested in my family. Wait a minute; I have some other shots—"

She fiddled with the controller and the scene changed; we were looking down on Freehold from a hillside. "This is what the town looked like, oh, sixty years ago or so. We hadn't built the main meeting hall yet, but we were getting a start on housing. You can see the communications antenna just beside the creek; we moved it to the top of the hill later. Here we're unloading a parafoil from the factory. Here's the hydrogen-fuel plant down by the landing strip— What's the matter?"

I had raised my hand for attention. "What I'm really interested in is the factory," I said.

She looked regretful. "I'm afraid I don't have any pictures of the factory. I was never there—well, Barry, I guess that's the story of my life. I'm not much of a traveler; I was never off the surface of the planet at all. What do you want to know about it?"

"Anything you can tell me."

So she told me everything she could. Most of it I already knew, but she filled in a lot of details for me. Like how the computers at the factory orbiter knew what to make. "Why, we all decide that, of course. At the town meetings. Everybody makes up their wish lists, then Jimmy Queng sends the whole thing up to the orbiter to see what's possible. Then at the meeting we set priorities. That's a real mob scene, Barry, everybody fighting to try to get his requisitions approved—you'll see. There's going to have to be one pretty soon. Of course, ninety percent of the requests get turned down."

She paused, looking at me thoughtfully. "Theophan Sperlie says you think you could help get more production out of the factory for us, with the antimatter Garold brought from the Moon."

I hadn't known she was a friend of Theophan's, but it was a small community. "That's one possibility," I said.

"And you've got others in mind?"

I felt obligated to live up to my growing reputation, so I told her some of the things I'd been thinking about. She listened patiently. She even agreed that the colony certainly could have done a lot better in a lot of ways; but after a while I thought she was beginning to look tired. I stood up. "Well, thanks, Madeleine," I said, getting ready to go.

She put her hand on my arm to stop me. "Theophan's a good person," she said, out of nowhere.

"Well, I think so too."

She chose her words carefully. "It's none of my business, Barry, and I wouldn't say a word against Theophan. But I wouldn't get too serious about her right away."

From another person I might have resented intrusion into my private life. Not from Madeleine. "I'm not serious. Matter of fact, I hardly see her except when I'm helping her work. Anyway, she's got—"

I was going to say "another boyfriend," but that didn't seem fair. "She's got a lot on her mind," I said, and, since Theophan's experiences with the leps were fresh on my mind, I told Madeleine about it.

Madeleine nodded. "It's been that way," she said regretfully.

"But the leps act like they hate her, as though the whole thing were her fault."

"Ah, no. You just don't know the leps very well. Did you ever hear of 'shunning'? It's what some of the religious groups do back on Earth, when they have a member that does something wrong. The leps have the same practice. They shun. Even the leps do have a member now and then who acts in an antisocial way, and these leps are just shunned. Nobody talks to them. Nobody pays attention to them at all. Generally speaking, the shunned ones just go off into the wilderness. That's bad for them, though. When they reach sixth instar they won't breed because there won't be any other lep around to breed with. I guess that's why those genes die out in the leps." She hesitated, then said, "I know about that, because my brother-in-law got shunned."

She paused there, so I tried to be sympathetic. I said, "That's a shame."

"Actually not," she said regretfully. "Mal had it coming. He shot a lep. It was in the early days, but he should've known better. He did it, though. He lost his temper and he had a gun, and the lep was dead. And he couldn't stand being shunned, and that's why he gave up and went home. And so I have a lot of sympathy for Theophan Sperlie."

I don't really know what else to say about that particular time. By then I had settled into a routine. I was working at whatever I was given to work at, asking all my questions, spending time with Geronimo—the times with Geronimo were probably the brightest spots in a rather boring period. I know you keep telling me that I should give you the whole story, omitting nothing, but, Jesus, that's asking a lot. My life on Pava just wasn't all that interesting.

The biggest job I had every day was trying to reconcile myself to things I didn't want to be reconciled to. I was trying to figure out what I should do with this new and diminished, life I had ahead of me on

Pava. I was doing my best to learn what my options were. It was pretty tedious, if you want to know. Do you want me to tell you how many times a day I wished I had something I didn't have, or how often I wondered if I'd missed the boat with Theophan Sperlie, or how many new things I decided the Pavans were doing all wrong?

There were plenty of those. Those erratic tectonic jolts sure did screw things up, and I couldn't help thinking that there had to be something that could be done about that. Then there were the headaches with the hydrogen-fuel electrolysis plant for the shuttle. When I drew maintenance work there one day I discovered what a rat's-nest tangle of compressors and piping the plant was, and how delicate. Some essential part of the thing broke down and needed repairing about twice a year, and whenever a serious tremor came along, there were likely to be some really scary problems; now and then the hydrogen tanks would come close to rupture and you never knew if the whole thing might blow up. Or then there were those pitiful little mines. Pava *needed* mines, or at least we human parasites on it did, because you could go just so far with plastics and ceramics and wood even for the limited fabrication that was done on the surface. But Pava seemed to be a metal-poor planet—in the neighborhood of Freehold, anyway. Until they got a good source of asteroid iron for the factory orbiter, they needed to dig; and when they did manage to find a decent vein of iron ore it was not easy to persuade people to go down into the shafts. Twice a temblor had collapsed a mine tunnel already, though fortunately no one had been killed.

People did get killed on Pava, though. That was part of the price of pioneering. And yet—

And yet I don't want you to think that all my days were spent in mourning and complaining, because it all did seem sort of worthwhile.

We certainly didn't have a comfortable life. We seemed to spend most of our time just trying to keep ahead of the setbacks. But over and above all of that was the feeling that, somehow, everything we did was making history. With every day and every act we were scratching our own personal, ineradicable marks on the future of a world.

That's another sort of feeling that you leps don't ever have, isn't it? You don't have a group future to think about. The only future you have is your personal and individual one, and after you've had it you just die.

* * *

Of course, whatever optimism I could scare up about my own personal future was pretty heavily dampened by my personal state of health. I didn't tell you about going back to Dr. Billygoat.

It was the day the town meeting was scheduled. Billygoat was busy with somebody's colicky infant when I got there—even in the waiting room I could hear the howling from upstairs—so I tried to pass the time of day with his wife while I was waiting. "I saw Madeleine Hartly the other night," I told her, "and she looked kind of poorly."

Nan Goethe kept her eyes on the screen she was working on. "The doctor and I never discuss a patient's medical condition," she said primly, "especially when it's *serious*."

I didn't press further. I knew what a stop sign was when I saw one, and anyway I didn't have to. I didn't really need to have Nanny tell me just what it was that had Madeleine so housebound and frail, because I knew that at Madeleine's age "serious" meant "*damn* serious," and I didn't like having that knowledge. It's funny how fond you can get of a person on short acquaintance. I had become fond of Madeleine, and thinking about her took my mind right off worrying about what progress Dr. Billygoat had made in my case.

That turned out to be not much. When I finally got in he was waiting impatiently for me, with my whole life story spread out on his data-screens, but before he started he looked at his watch. "Are you going to the town meeting tonight?"

"I'm planning on it."

"Well, so am I. I need to try to requisition a new autoclave and a hell of a lot more pediatric medicines, so let's see if we can get through this fast, all right?" He scowled at the screens. "You know, you've made a lot of extra work for me, di Hoa."

He waved me to sit down and turned the screens around so I could see them too. I looked at them to please the doctor, but what meaning they were supposed to convey I could not say. He said, "I thought for a while there I might have a diagnosis for you that I could do something about. It didn't work out, but see this little area here? That's it. This one I could have worked with. Hartnup disease, they call it. Did you ever hear of it?"

"No." I would have remembered, I was pretty sure.

"It's an autosomal recessive defect a lot like yours—but turns out it's not a winner. With Hartnup you're supposed to be bleeding at the gums and all, too, and since you don't have any of that it can't be Hartnup.''

He sounded irritated, as though he wanted me to apologize for having the wrong disease, so I did. I said, "I'm sorry to be a disappointment to you.''

"Be serious, di Hoa. I'm trying to tell you what kind of problems I'm up against here. You don't fit any of the patterns in my database. You've got good thyroid function and no reaction-time crossover. Your glucose uptake is good, according to the brainscan. Look at the charts for yourself. You can see I did a real complete workup on you. Do you understand what I'm telling you?''

This time it looked as though he wanted a compliment, so I tried to give him one. I said, "I think you aren't a bad doctor. For a dentist, anyway.''

"Yes," he said, glaring at me. "Well, the rest of what I have to tell you isn't so good. Are you sure they said your problem was metabolic?''

"I'm sure.''

"Because if it isn't, if it's just some kind of crazy psycho stuff, then it's out of my line. I'm not qualified for psychoanalysis or anything like that.''

I didn't want to ask him what he was qualified for, exactly. I just repeated, "I'm *sure*.''

He sighed regretfully. "I guess I have to take it for granted that those other people knew what they were doing. Okay. We'll go on the assumption that it was a good diagnosis and the problem's in your body chemistry. In that case, I've got good news and I've got bad news. The good news is that I think I have a clue about what it might be that you need. The blood-assay machines tracked down a fraction that was in your blood when you came out of the freezer, but—look, you can see in this histogram here—that fraction had already become pretty scarce by the time of the last sample. I bet it's the protein you're missing.''

"And?" I said when he paused, bracing myself for the second installment.

"Well, then there's the bad news," he admitted. "In the latest blood sample that fraction's so scarce that I can't isolate enough to clone it. I tried everything, di Hoa. We aren't a fully staffed Global Health Service laboratory here, you know. Even a polymerase reaction needs a decent-sized sample to start with, with the kind of equipment I've got here, and we just don't have enough of the stuff to work on.''

He turned one of the screens back and stared at it morosely for a moment, then looked appraisingly at me. "I even wondered if it might help if I got a bigger blood sample from you."

That made me squirm, but I was game for anything that would do me any good. "How much bigger?"

"Real big. I thought for a while that we might try actually replacing all your blood. You know? Drain it all out—of course, replacing it with blood substitutes and transfusions so you wouldn't die on me—"

"Hey!"

"—but, don't worry, I gave that idea up. Even if we took all the blood, we might still not be able to separate enough of that fraction out. And then, of course, there's the other problem. While I was fooling around with your own blood, the replacement stuff you'd have left in your system wouldn't contain any of the protein at all. I don't suppose you want to spend a couple of really goofy weeks in a straitjacket while I'm experimenting, do you?"

I took a deep breath. When my temper was safely back down in its cage I managed to say, without too much gritting of the teeth, "You've got a great sense of humor, Goethe, but why don't you quit telling me all the things you can't do and cut to something you *can*."

He grinned at me. Grinned ruefully, I guess you'd say; even a little embarrassedly, because there was a touch of hangdog apology behind the grin. "I just wanted to make sure you understood how tough all this is, di Hoa. It isn't hopeless, though. We're not finished with you yet. There are some other options that are worth trying."

"Can I hear one of those now?"

"Remember we've got plenty of psychoactive pharmaceuticals on the shelf—pepper-uppers, mood elevators, tranquilizers, whatever you need to bring you back to normal, more or less. Anytime you feel you're getting into trouble, you come in and I'll give you a shot to fix that up. Temporarily, I mean; of course, you can't stay on those things forever. But maybe we can hold you while I try to figure out what I can do about long-range treatment."

"Which is what?"

"Well, maybe we can *find* something that'll work, di Hoa. What I've got to do now is start a whole series of bioassays, trying to characterize something we can get or make locally that might be close enough to what you need. Then, of course, we'll have to run a series of in vivo tests—"

"You mean experiment on *me*?"

"On who else, then? You're all I've got."

"Wonderful. It's what I've always dreamed of, being a laboratory rat."

Dr. Billygoat asked simply, "Have you got any better ideas? No? Then I'll let you know when I've got something to try—and now, if you don't mind, I'd like to try to get around to some of my other patients so I can make it to the town meeting."

16

*T*HERE *is a question to be asked concerning the purpose and putility of these "town meetings"*—

No, hold it a minute. Please?

I'd appreciate it if you didn't ask me any new questions right now. I'm getting to the important part—well, the part that's important to me, anyway. You see, I was finally beginning to wake up.

What I mean is, I guess it's pretty obvious that for the first few weeks I was on Pava I was pretty much just letting things happen to me. That's not my nature. Honest. I'm not usually so passive. I'm more the kind who makes things happen. I'm not making excuses for myself, but I did take a real mean hit when I woke up in Tscharka's freezer and discovered I had become an involuntary Pavan. It took a while to get over that.

I probably wasn't really *over* it by then, either, but Dr. Billygoat had got me mad and the town meeting was that night, and by the time I got to the supper tables I had figured out what I wanted to do.

The place was crowded. Almost every human being on Pava was there. People from the outside crews, like the woodcutters and the maintenance workers at the hydrogen-fuel plant, had been drifting into town all day for the meeting. A dozen loud little knots of people were getting a head start in arguing out their personal priorities. Theophan

Sperlie's table was the closest, and I sat down next to her. She was, naturally, with whom I expected her to be with—Marcus Wendt—and the two of them were bent head-to-head over a portable screen, hardly remembering to eat as she added up the list of tools and instruments she could not live another day without. She looked up absently as I sat, then zeroed in on me. "Oh, it's you, Barry. Hi. Listen, take a look at my requisition list, will you? I really need everything there—you know that—but the meeting isn't going to approve more than ten percent of the list. They never do, but I'll have to fight for even that much. Can I count on your vote?"

I caught a whiff of that sweet scent that hung around her, partly perfume and partly Theophan, but for once I didn't let it distract me. I went right into my pitch. "Sure, but tell me something. Why are you willing to settle for a lousy ten percent when you really need it all?"

Marcus gawked at me over Theo's shoulder, and Theophan gave me the kind of scowl you give to the willfully obtuse. Irritably she tucked a strand of red hair behind her ear and said, "What are you talking about? This isn't your damn Moon. Resources are limited, you ought to know that by now."

"They don't have to be this limited, Theo. There's plenty of fuel on *Corsair*. I'm willing to go up to the factory and see how much of a job it will be to install it."

Marcus chose to put his two cents' worth in then. He said forgivingly, "I guess you just don't grasp the problem, Barry. Fuel's one thing. Raw materials are another. We don't have them. The orbiter can't manufacture Theo's instruments out of *nothing*."

"It won't have to." I was talking to Theo, not Wendt. "There's a couple years' supply of raw materials sitting out there in orbit already. Think about it. They tell me the colony cannibalized one ship to use its materials a while ago. What's wrong with doing the same with *Corsair*?"

Marcus only looked both baffled and insulted—mostly insulted—but the stare Theophan gave me was stricken. "Oh, Jesus, Barry! You don't care whose toes you step on, do you? If we only could! But there's no way Garold Tscharka is going to agree to letting us take his ship apart."

"Well," I said, trying to sound apologetic, "I know I'm just a new boy here, but doesn't it seem to you that that ought to be up to the meeting to decide?"

She tugged that strand of hair loose again, curling it worriedly around a finger to help thought. "I don't know. Maybe, I guess. We've never voted on anything like that as long as I've been here."

"So maybe it's about time we started," I said, getting up, and at last her face lit up.

"Barry," she said, "what the hell. It's worth a try. We're with you all the way." And she caught my hand and pressed it to her cheek to show she really meant it.

That quick touch of fingers to flesh felt nice. Really nice, nice enough to derail my thoughts for a moment. Maybe that's not surprising, considering how long it had been since the Moon; I briefly considered punching Marcus Wendt in the face and dragging Theophan off to my bed.

That little aberration didn't last, though. What I actually did was to shake her hand, and Marcus's, and start looking around for other people to persuade.

The way I looked at the people there was that every one of them was a *vote*. I went after them like any politician. I table-hopped. By then I knew a fair fraction of Freehold's adult population, and I stopped for a moment to plant some seeds in the minds of as many of them as I could—Jillen Iglesias and Dabney Albright and Lou Baxto and—well, just about everybody whose name I could remember. Not quite everybody; Madeleine Hartly didn't seem to be there, though I did have a word with her great-granddaughter. And I skipped Becky Khaim-Novello. She was sitting quietly and thoughtfully by herself at the end of one table, eating as though it were a penance. I started toward her, all right, but then I turned away. She didn't *look* like a very distraught new widow, but it seemed to me that if I were in her shoes I'd really rather be left alone.

I told them all the same thing. I told them that I thought there was a good chance the orbiter could use the antimatter in *Corsair*'s hold—as an expert in the subject, I was willing to go up there and check it out—and then I told them that it probably could use *Corsair* itself, too. As I went along I got more and more creative about the kinds of things the factory could make for them: a new power plant; air-conditioners; a helicopter or two to explore more of Pava. I sketched out how it would even be possible to build a small space tug out of pieces of *Corsair* so we could go out and harvest more material from Delta Pavonis's skimpy asteroid belt, so that even after *Corsair* was used up there'd still be materials to sustain the colony indefinitely.

I got all kinds of reactions. Some were skeptical. Dabney told me flat out that I was wasting my time; he pointed out that a lot of people, mostly Millenarists, would never vote to cannibalize *Corsair* simply because Captain Tscharka would be against it, and a lot of others wouldn't because they had other plans for the ship—like using it for a ride back to Earth. Jillen looked surprisingly worried—there'd been some upsetting news from Earth, she said—but she listened to me. So did everybody else. They did more than that, too. I could see some of them talking thoughtfully to others when I left.

By that time people were beginning to leave the tables, and the cleaning party was hurrying the laggards away. I packed it in then. I considered I'd done a good evening's work. The only thing I hadn't managed to do that suppertime was actually get anything to eat for myself.

I didn't mind. I guess I was already beginning to get a little bit hyper by then, but I didn't feel particularly manic. I just felt good.

When I stopped back at the apartment to clean up before the meeting, even Jacky Schottke was playing a list of supplies from his own screen into the central processing file. "What's the matter, weren't you hungry?" I asked him.

He looked up abstractedly. "Oh, you mean about supper? I guess I forgot. I was busy."

"Busy writing your letter to Santa Claus?"

"Well, I suppose you could call it that. It's just a shame that I don't have decent preservation facilities for type specimens, at least, but they always say it isn't really high-priority stuff. . . . Uh, Barry? While I think of it, there's a favor you could do me if you wouldn't mind—"

I didn't let him finish. I said, "Sure. The answer's yes. I'll vote for everything you want. I'll vote for everything *everybody* wants." And when he gave me a look, partly hurt because I didn't seem to be taking him seriously, partly puzzled, I laid it all on him.

If I expected him to jump with joy I was disappointed. He listened quietly while I spelled the plan out, then he sighed. "Poor Garold," he said.

"The hell with Garold. He'll just have to get used to it. Everybody's got to make a few sacrifices for the common good. Anyway, there's supposed to be another ship coming along pretty soon."

"Of course. Well, perhaps we'd better get over there. I'd like to get a good seat."

*   *   *

The good feeling was still with me as we cut between buildings on the way to the meeting place. Jacky wasn't talkative. I noticed clouds building up overhead and tried some neutral conversation—"It's a good thing we're getting the meeting in now, looks like we're due for some more rain"—but he just sighed again. He was looking at a group of three or four people talking earnestly together: Captain Tscharka, Tuchman, Jimmy Queng. They glanced at me, then turned away.

"What's the matter?" I asked Jacky.

"I think it's that story from the Moon," he said.

"What story?"

Jacky shook his head. "You don't follow the news from Earth much, do you? Well, never mind. Maybe it's not important."

I let it go at that. I shouldn't have, of course, but I wanted to be up front, while Jacky's idea of a good seat was something inconspicuous in the background.

The place was all set up for the meeting. All the tables had been carted away, and most of the benches were already full. I took an open seat next to Theophan Sperlie, who gave me an encouraging wink and patted my hand. That seemed promising, too, especially because, for a wonder, Marcus wasn't with her. Out of the corner of my eye I saw him hurrying in a moment later; but then he came to a stop, looking chagrined. If Theo had been saving the seat next to her for him to occupy it wasn't saved anymore.

Things were looking up in more ways than one. I kept her hand in mine, but I had other things to deal with. I marshalled my arguments in my mind: the fuel; the plan of scrapping *Corsair* to feed the orbiter's production machines; the possibility of exploring for asteroidal metals and ending Pava's dependency on Earth once and for all. It all made sense to me. I was ready to get up in meeting and propose it for everybody.

I didn't even notice that Jimmy Queng had taken his place on the tabletop that served as a platform until he began to speak. "Quiet down, please," he said, looking somber and angry. "Reverend Tuchman has something to say to you."

That was when I began to realize that something was going wrong. So did most of the Freeholders at the same time; there was a buzz all around the audience as Friar Tuck climbed up on the table. He looked even more grim than Jimmy Queng while he waited for the noise to die down. Then he said:

"I speak particularly to our penitential brethren, but I fear this affects everyone here on Pava. As some of you know, we have had saddening news from Earth. We cannot let it pass unobserved. So, in mourning for our martyred brothers, I am declaring a retreat for three days effective at once. The congregation is asked to return here in one hour to proceed to the retreat site."

That made for some real muttering in the crowd—surprised, angry, generally upset. The only ones who seemed to know just what to do were the well-disciplined Millenarists, all of whom stood up and began to leave to get their possessions for the retreat. Jimmy Queng pounded the seat of the chair next to him for silence. "I think you'll all agree that it wouldn't be fair to continue with the meeting when so many must leave. Under the circumstances, this meeting is canceled. We will reschedule it as soon as possible."

That was that.

Five minutes later the Millenarists were all gone and most of the rest of us were just standing around trying to make sense of what had happened. "The bastards," Theo said, but without much emotion—as though she'd expected something of the kind.

Marcus nodded. "I knew it. I bet it's because of those two Millenarists on the Moon."

I blinked at him. "What two Millenarists?"

"The ones that were arrested and deported. What's the matter, Barry? It was all on the news reports; haven't you seen them?"

I hadn't, of course; I'd been too busy with my own worries and plans. Theo patted my hand again. "This whole thing is just a pretext, of course. Tscharka must have known what we were going to propose, so he wanted to stall as long as he could. 'Martyrs,' for God's sake. Nobody but Tuchman would have the nerve to call those two creeps *martyrs*."

She gave me a curious look, as though I were looking unusually stupid. As I guess I was.

"Well," she said consolingly, "we'll just have to take it up when the meeting's rescheduled. Don't worry, Barry. Our time is going to come." And she gave my arm a friendly squeeze . . . before turning away and leaving with Marcus, hand in hand. It was beginning to rain again, too.

And that's what happened that night. Now you can ask your question if you still want to.

17

*T*HE question that is still to be asked concerns the "town meetings."

Really? I thought I answered all that already. The town meetings were the place where the colonists got together to decide on their priorities and pass their laws—I hope you're not going to ask me what "laws" are now, are you? We were able to run our government that way on Pava because there were so few human beings here. If there had been more of us we probably would have had to elect people to do all that sort of thing for us, the way it's done back in the solar system, but with a total population of less than a thousand we could all get together and hash everything out. Was that your question?

No. The question is this: Is it because of such "town meetings" that so many actions of the human persons on our planet work out so poorly?

You know, you surprise me sometimes. For somebody with no measurable sense of humor, you do manage to get a zinger in every once in a while.

Anyway, the answer to your question is no. I admit that when we try to plan ahead we don't always agree on what the plan should be—that's why we have these meetings, to try to get a consensus that everybody can live with—and even when we do agree we often make mistakes. We try things, and then maybe for one reason or another they don't work out—like that big hydropower dam that was supposed to solve all the colony's energy problems, but didn't. Then we just try something else. It may take us a while to get up the will for another effort. But we never do stop *trying*.

What we're always trying to do, one way or another, is to make things better.

It's true that some of the things people do try actually wind up making things a hell of a lot worse instead—I'm talking now about wars, and terrorism, and crime, and all the other bad things that human beings have been known to try. As some famous person said long ago—maybe it was somebody like George Washington, or possibly, what was his name, Winston Churchill—every time we take two steps forward we also take one step back. Hell, that's not the half of it. Sometimes it's more like ten or twenty steps back. Over the years human beings have done some of the most catastrophically nutty things you can imagine, in the attempt to make what they think is going to be some kind of improvement.

But we never give up.

Let me repeat that: *We never give up.* Not permanently, anyway. We never stop wanting to improve the way things are. I know that's not your nature. But it's ours.

Friar Tuck's little surprise set me back, all right. It was a shocker. I'd been all juiced up for confrontation, and he cheated me of it.

But it didn't mean that the town meeting wouldn't happen, only that it would be postponed for a few days. (Well, actually for one whole calendar week. Have I mentioned that the town meetings were always on Tuesdays? That was because Tuesdays were among the very few days of the week that were not somebody's Sabbath.)

It turned out to be a tough week in Freehold for the rest of us, though. For the duration of the retreat every Millenarist was off in the hills, and there were a lot of Millenarists. When you take a quarter of the population out of a community—more than a quarter, if you only count the adults—you leave a big hole in the work force. So all the nonessential activities of the colony had to be deferred.

There was a good part to that; with all the Millenarists out of the way, the situation began to settle down as a clear case of "us against them." Most everybody left behind was in favor of change, and we did outnumber them, after all.

Workwise, though, we were stressed. Theophan had to put off one of her seismology runs so that she and half a dozen others could go out to collect a couple of new parafoils from the factory orbiter. She swore a lot about it, but she went. Without Marcus, though, because he was sent, along with Jacky Schottke and me, upriver to the biofuel generating station, to replace the firemen who had taken off on the retreat. That was hard work for me—twice as hard for Jacky. We had to fish out the rafts of brush and logs that floated down the river, as well as the random flotsam that was still coming down from the storms. Then we had to dragline them, by sweat and muscle, to stack under the canopies in the drying yards. When we got a good supply of that on hand we weren't through, we just had to switch to the other part of the job. That was taking the dry stuff, as dry as it was ever going to get, and loading it into the hoppers that would feed it into the conveyors that would dump it into the furnaces that generated the steam that turned the turbine that made the electricity for Freehold.

I'd seen the smoke from the power plant's stacks, but this was the first time I'd come close to it. I wasn't impressed. It produced about 1.8 megawatts—about one meg for domestic consumption, which meant a little over one kilowatt per colonist, and the rest for "industry." But it was a pretty primitive affair. The only energy the turbine extracted was from the primary expansion of the steam; it could have produced twice as much with a low-pressure addition, and more than that with a hotter fuel. Which I didn't fail to point out to everyone who would listen: that was just one more thing the orbiter could make for us. They listened, too. I could see that I was beginning to consolidate my reputation—as a potential leader, maybe, or maybe just as a know-it-all pain in the ass.

I didn't mind the work so much, although it was raining. What I minded was the way Jacky began to pant and turn pale after the first hour. Fortunately Geronimo was loyally there to help out, along with three or four other leps, so I took it upon myself to put Jacky in charge of the leps instead of wearing out his own old muscles. If it hadn't been for the leps we would have been in real trouble, but they pitched in.

When we all took a break I sat down next to Jacky, sharing a bottle of beer. Geronimo slithered around us, listening silently. "You all right?" I asked Jacky.

He took a swig of the beer and passed it back. There was plenty to go around; it was a liter bottle that had once held some kind of liqueur. "I'm fine," he said mournfully.

It didn't surprise me that he was unhappy. I knew that some part of him wished he had gone along on the retreat with the others.

But I had something else on my mind. "Jacky? You know that thing Friar Tuck said, about the martyrs?"

He looked vaguely apologetic. "To tell the truth, Barry, I don't think he cared that much about those guys. I suspect it was just a pretext to postpone the meeting for a while."

"I didn't doubt that for a minute. What I wondered was, have you been following the news from Earth? Do you know what he was talking about?"

He looked surprised. "Of course. It was all in the reports: their names were Bruderkind and Mallory. They were accused of bringing about the death of seven or eight people, two of them minors, and the Lederman council expelled them back to Earth."

"Bruderkind and Mallory, you say." I pondered the names. If Alma had ever told me the names of the two Millenarists who were working on her I'd forgotten them long since. A lot of time had passed since then, even allowing for the fact that any information that got here from Earth was automatically already eighteen and a half years old. There really wasn't much chance these were the same two that had tried to help Alma off herself.

But they could be.

Then I began making up some unpleasant scenarios in my mind. Alma finding out I'd been stolen away from her. Alma heartbroken. Alma seeking comfort anywhere she could find it. Alma returning to the Millenarist church. Alma finally deciding there was only one way out of her sorrow—

No. I didn't believe it. But I made up my mind to check out the newscasts from Earth first chance I got.

By the time the night shift arrived we were all bushed. The rain had stopped, which was a good thing. The other good thing was that the trip back to Freehold only required getting into the boats and letting the current carry us downstream. At the last moment Geronimo flopped himself on board for the ride. Marcus muttered a little about that, and so did one or two of the others, but Geronimo didn't pay them any attention. He was hanging half over the stern of the boat, one of his little hands on the rudder to guide us, watching the ripples that formed in our wake.

I was still concerned for Jacky Schottke, who was slumped over next to the lep with his eyes closed, but when I asked him how he was doing he stirred himself. "I'm all right. I was just thinking about the people on the retreat. I'm afraid they got wet today."

That didn't seem like the worst thing in the world to me, but I didn't say so. Geronimo spoke up, though. He twisted his face around to look at Jacky and said, in that hissy, penetrating voice, "No. Rain was outside, but retreat people were in large cloth house."

"Ah, they took the tent with them, then," Jacky said, looking happier. "It was all so fast, I wasn't sure they'd remembered. You saw them, did you?"

"First thing coming down in early day, yes. Very loud. All saying same words together."

"You mean they were praying, I suppose. They would be." Jacky looked wistful.

He closed his eyes again, and I let the subject drop. What I was thinking was that I really would have been happier if the Millenarists had got themselves good and soaked. I know that's not a very admirable way to feel. It isn't the Christian charity I was taught by the nuns; we were supposed to wish only the best, even for people we didn't like. I guess in that respect I wasn't much of a Christian, but then neither were most of the Christians I knew.

When we pulled up at the town dock most of the biofuel crew headed right for the supper tables, but there was something I wanted to do first.

When Geronimo saw that I was detouring by way of the little station under the big dish antenna he squawked a protest. "Meal time, Barrydihoa," he said reproachfully, his mouthpart working to show how hungry he was.

"In a minute. First I want to see what's been happening on Earth." He hissed reproachfully, but he climbed the hill to the station with me and stayed by my side while I tried to find what I wanted in the tapes.

Although I hadn't been watching them, I knew that Pava got regular news broadcasts from Earth. That wasn't all it got; there were daily transmissions of cultural programs, new performances, personal messages, religious programs—lots of those—and all sorts of other items that some civil servant back in the solar system had decided were worth passing on to the colony. The single channel that carried them all was crowded—especially because every nine-hour segment was repeated three times, to make sure Pava's single receiving station would get it all.

I sat down at one of the screens and selected for major news summaries of the past couple of weeks.

When I filtered out the material I didn't care about there wasn't a whole lot left. Naturally none of the news was "new" anymore by the time it crossed the eighteen and a half light-years to reach Pava, anyway. The elected councils were squabbling day and night, just like always; just like always, major projects like the re-greening of the Sahara and the cleanup of the Arctic were running behind schedule. Nothing had changed. When I selected for "Moon" and "Millenarists" I found what I was looking for. The fifth item that turned up on the screen was about William Bruderkind and Booker T. Mallory, ordained ministers in the Millenarist Penitential Church. Each of them had been arrested twice over a period of several years for improper solicitation of suicide, then finally tried and convicted when two of the suicides turned out to be young teenagers. Their status as naturalized Lunarians was canceled, and they were kicked out.

There were several stories about them, but none that gave the names of any of their victims.

On the way back to the supper tables Geronimo galumphed along beside me, looking up at me curiously with those immense eyes. He didn't speak, and neither did I. I was thinking about how long certain Millenarist ministers were willing to put off their own heavenly graduation in order to talk others into it, and mostly I was trying to persuade myself that there was really no chance that any of those unnamed victims could have been Alma Vendette.

When Geronimo went off to forage in the kitchen wastes I got into the dwindling line at the tables and helped myself to a meal, but I didn't get much chance to eat it. Everybody wanted to talk to me, it seemed. It started in the chow line and kept up on my way to a table and after, endless questions: Wouldn't the pods the antimatter came in themselves be a good source of raw materials for the factory as the fuel was used up, without the unpleasant necessity of scrapping *Corsair*? How long did I think *Corsair* would last as recyclable scrap, anyway? What did I know about asteroidal compositions—wasn't it possible that there'd still be a lot of elements we'd be short of, even if we tapped them?

I didn't forget about Alma, exactly. I never did that. But I did cheer up, because it certainly looked as though more and more of the colony was getting ready to wake up from its deep, unhappy sleep and do something serious about making Pava a decent place to spend the rest of my life.

* * *

Something else happened in those three days when all the Millenarists were out of town. I began to discover that the colonists in Freehold all had agenda of their own. They were chronically suppressed
and depressed, sure, but never without dreams. It happened when I
said something about Jacky Schottke to Dabney Albright and Dabney
said contemptuously, "What do you expect from him? He's a
mover."

"A what?"

"A mover. Or he used to be, anyway. He used to want to move
everybody down to the coast. Just piss away everything we've got here!
Start building a whole new town from scratch—can you imagine?"

That was the first time I realized that the Pavan colonists were not
the monolithic collection of lumps I'd thought them to be.

I should have expected it; that's the way it always is when you come
into some new social group. At first everybody in it looks as though he
belongs there. You're you and they're *them*, and it takes a while to see
that each individual member of the *them*s actually considers himself—
or herself—to be a more or less unique *one*.

I had learned that lesson more than once before—in the clinic, for
one; again when I first got to the Moon. Earlier than that, even: as far
back as when I was eleven years old and my father scraped up the price
of a church camp for me one summer. He couldn't afford the whole
season, though. I got there two weeks into July, and all the other
campers were well broken into their collective identity as *the campers*.
They were all tanned, had all learned the words to the songs to be sung
around the sundown campfire; all knew the daily routine, from wakeup
bugle and dawn dash to the obligatory swim in Lake de Paul to bedcheck
. . . and knew how to avoid either of those obligations when they
wanted to. It took time for me to know that some of the boys were there
for the canoeing and others for riding the broken-down race horses from
the camp's stable—and a lot of them just because their parents couldn't
stand having them around the house for another minute—and, most of
all, that none of them was exactly like any of the others.

So it was on Pava. The colony was a collection of unconsolidated
factions. There were the movers, who wanted to get out of the earthquake zone; the empire builders, who wanted to breed Pava to a billion-
strong new Earth; the industrialists, who thought everybody should live

on dry bread and hopes until the colony had dug mines and built factories and made itself self-sufficient and strong.

And there was one other group: the defeated. The ones who had put their names on the long list of Pavans who wanted nothing more out of the colony but a trip back home.

They did all have one thing in common, though—I mean the Pavans who weren't Millenarists and hadn't gone off on the retreat. They were beaten down and discouraged, yes, but they still wanted things *changed*. And I began to feel pretty sure that, when the postponed town meeting did get held, there would be some unpleasant surprises for Captain Garold Tscharka and his buddies.

After the third day of the retreat the work got easier. The Millenarists began to trickle back to their jobs, half a dozen at a time, then forty or fifty in a clump. They looked drained but happy—anyway, they did up to the time when they began getting the feel of the ferment that was building up in Freehold. Then they stopped looking so happy.

Oddly, their leaders hadn't come back with them. Tscharka, Tuchman, Queng and two or three others were still out there in the hills— "Conspiring," Theophan told me darkly at breakfast. "They'll be up to something, Barry."

"Like what? The meeting's only three days away."

She shrugged. Marcus gave me a sunny smile, and to Theophan a look of fond confidence. "We'll be ready for anything they come up with, won't we, Theo? So don't worry." And they left to get a head start on overhauling one of Theophan's cranky remote sensors. I wasn't invited.

I didn't mind. I was just as happy to stay in Freehold, where I could talk to people—especially after I found that I had drawn an easy, if unaesthetic, day's work checking the levels in the town's outhouses.

Geronimo showed up to go the rounds with me, quite curious about the whole procedure. He didn't offer to help. He didn't get in the way, either. He'd caught another of his flying-rat playthings and was tossing the little thing back and forth in his tiny hands, watching silently as I lifted the toilet seats and peered in. When the level was comfortably low there was no problem; when it had risen to anything less than a meter and a half below the seat I made a note on my screen. That meant that someone would have to fill it in and start another hole before long. I hoped it wouldn't be me.

After an hour or so of that I stopped and looked at the lep. "You could give me a hand, you know. How about lifting the lids for me?"

Geronimo turned those huge eyes on me. "Not necessary. Easy work, one person is plenty. Anyway, all humans now returning."

I puzzled out what he was saying. "You mean you leps just came to help out because we were short-handed?"

"That is exact," he agreed.

"Well, thanks," I said, thinking it over. It was true that during the retreat there had been a lot more leps in Freehold than usual, as many as a hundred, I guessed, against what was generally no more than a dozen or two.

I asked idly, "How many leps are there, anyway?"

Geronimo reared back, twisting his body to peer down the street. "Three," he reported.

"No. I don't mean just here. I mean all you leps."

He sank back, plucking a head of fern from the side of the street and nibbling it. "Many, Barrydihoa."

"*How* many?"

"Many," he insisted. "We play gin soon?"

"No, we don't play gin. We work. All day long—well, except right now it's getting about time for lunch, isn't it?" He didn't answer that. He just made an exasperated hissing noise, tossed his flying rat into the air—it wobbled as it flew away, no longer in very good shape—and went off to seek his own food elsewhere.

That was all I could get out of Geronimo on the subject of the lep population, but I was luckier with Jacky Schottke. I saw him sitting by himself, morosely eavesdropping on the conversations of a group of returned Millenarists. They must have known he was there, but they were conspicuously keeping to themselves, ignoring him.

Everybody else was sociable. Half a dozen people wanted to talk to me about the factory orbiter, but when I'd finished with them I joined Jacky. In a way, I thought it was an act of kindness. I didn't think he enjoyed his regrets.

When I asked him about the leps he seemed glad of the change. "Oh, there are lots of them, Barry—a whole continent full. Tens of millions, anyway. Maybe a lot more than that."

"But the ones we see—"

"Are only the locals. There's a lep nest up in the hills with hundreds of them; they're the ones who come down. The funny thing about the leps, if you're interested," he said, warming to his subject, "is that they're all the same species. That's surprising, when you think of the distances involved, but even the ones on the far side of the continent seem to be genetically identical with the locals.''

"We're all the same species too, and we have a lot more distance to cover."

"We're not leps, are we? Up through the fifth instar they hardly ever travel more than a few kilometers. So it has to be that some of the sixth-instar leps are wanderers. They fly long distances, so the genes get distributed."

"So they have a whole planetwide civilization?" I ventured doubtfully.

That startled him. "Good heavens, no, Barry. What gives you that idea? The six-star leps can't transmit anything but their own bodies—no customs, no information, nothing cultural. They've lost all their memories by then, you know. They're pretty much idiots—*horny* idiots."

"Are you saying that leps on the other side of the continent could have a completely different kind of society?"

He thought that over, pulling at his sparse hair. "I wouldn't think so. Most of their behavior seems to be genetically programmed . . . but we'll never know unless we start going out and exploring again," he said finally. "It's been thirty years since we had a working long-range aircraft. Barry? I really hope this idea of yours works out."

It stormed again on Saturday. I don't mean just rain, I'm talking about a real rouser of crashing thunder and fierce lightning and winds that took down trees in the hills. People stayed indoors as much as they could, and what they mostly did with their time was talk about getting the factory in high gear. There were some fierce arguments going on all that day, and I was in a lot of them.

I'd been pleased, if startled, to find out that Jacky Schottke was coming over to my side. He wasn't the only one, either. It began to look as though some of the returning Millenarists were tempted too—even my neighbor, the very recently bereaved widow lady from the downstairs apartment, Becky Khaim-Novello.

That was a real surprise, in more ways than one. I barely knew the woman. I'd hardly even seen her after her husband hung himself, and yet on Sunday morning, as I was coming back from breakfast, she caught me at the door and offered me a cup of real coffee.

I'd had it in mind to check the news broadcasts from Earth again, but she made the offer sound tempting. It would be, she promised, a better cup of coffee than anything the community kitchens could provide because it came out of their own private stock, brought all the way from Earth because Jubal loved coffee so much . . . but she actually preferred tea herself and now, with Jubal gone—

She was smiling and almost flirtatious as she invited me in. It seemed only neighborly to accept.

Well, there was more than a cup of coffee involved there, of course. For me there was the fact that Becky was reasonably nice looking and young and now wholly unattached. It was pleasant to sit in her kitchen while she put the coffee on and set out cups and a little dish of cakes she'd brought back from the breakfast. For Becky—

Maybe part of what she had in mind really was me myself, as a reasonably nice and clearly available male. I'd like to think that, anyway. However, I got the impression very quickly that she was also interested in picking my brains, because her conversation wasn't date talk, it was interrogation. Was I sure that this factory orbiter could use the antimatter from *Corsair*? Would it really be necessary to destroy Captain Tscharka's ship? What components of the ship, exactly, would be useful to the factory? And even if the ship were scrapped and salvaged, wouldn't there still be some elements that weren't in *Corsair*, so there'd still be serious supply problems?

I wasn't sure exactly what she was after, but I gave her all the answers I could, anyway. The most reliable answer to most of her questions was that the only way we could find those things out was by giving it a try. When the coffee was gone she thought that over for a moment, then stood up and thanked me politely for clearing up those matters for her. "Probably we do have to do *something*," she said, giving my hand a friendly squeeze at the door. "I guess it'll all get straightened out at the town meeting. Anyway, this has been really nice, Barry. Drop in again anytime you feel like talking. Good-bye."

Whatever her motives, widowhood seemed to sit lightly on Becky Khaim-Novello. As I headed for the receiver station—the antenna had taken some serious hits from the winds in yesterday's storm, and I was concerned about whether it was still functioning properly—I thought I probably would take her up on her invitation to come again before long. It wasn't that I particularly liked the woman; it was my glands, which were quite urgently suggesting that I ought at least to find out whether I liked her—or anyone female, for that matter.

I was thinking further along those lines when I noticed that Geronimo had joined me. He plopped himself directly in front of me and raised himself to full height. "Candy today?" he inquired.

I was prepared for him; I'd formed the habit of keeping a couple of hard sugar balls in my pocket for him. Though I urged him to suck on the one I gave him to make it last longer, I could hear it scraping against the grinding surfaces in his mouthpart. When he had it swallowed he announced, "The God person is back, Barrydihoa."

"Which one?"

"The old one. White hair on head and face. He is over by river, with children."

I decided that checking out the receiver could wait. If Jacky Schottke was leaning toward my side and Becky Khaim-Novello seemed, anyway, more or less neutral, I wondered if I couldn't try a little persuading on Friar Tuck.

I wasn't particularly confident of success. *Corsair* was more or less Tuchman's ship, too—Tscharka called him his chaplain—and he was certainly friendly with the captain. But revitalizing the factory wasn't a religious matter, as far as I could see. And, I admit, I was curious to see what Geronimo had meant about "children."

There were five or six of them gathered around him, waiting for a boat that was coming to take them downstream for some fruit gathering. The old man was doing conjuring tricks for them. They seemed to like it. So did he. They squealed with pleasure when he took pebbles out of their ears and made them vanish again, and when the boat pulled up and they got ready to board, he seemed regretful. He gave them all a good-bye hug before turning to me.

"Well, Barry," he said, cordially enough, "it's nice to see you. You look surprised. What is it?"

I tried to say it as politely as I could. "I didn't think Millenarists had much to do with children."

"Why would you think that? We love children, Barry. We're a church of love. You should come to our services someday."

I gave him a firmly noncommittal shrug for an answer, which made him smile. Then he sat down on a bench overlooking the water and beckoned me to join him. "I've been hoping we could have a chance to talk about some of the things you've been saying. Do you think it's really essential that you destroy *Corsair*?"

By then I'd had a lot of practice answering that sort of question, so I gave him the spiel. It wasn't a matter of losing the ship but of gaining more of the things we needed. More equipment. A better power supply. Maybe a space tug. Maybe, in the long run, a whole new lease on life for the Pavan colony. He listened gravely, only interrupting to ask for clarification on a point or two. Then he said, "I can see that you've got the interests of all of us at heart, Barry. I truly appreciate that. I can't help worrying about some of the dangers involved, though."

That was a new one. "What kind of dangers?"

"We're dealing with antimatter here. A lot of it. You're the closest thing we've got to an expert on the subject, and maybe you've thought it all through, but what would happen if something went wrong and it all exploded?"

"Well—" It was a fair enough question and I thought about it for a moment. "If it happened while the orbiter was overhead it would produce a lot of radiation, that's true. But it would be just as likely to happen when it's on the other side of Pava, and then we probably wouldn't feel any effects at all. Except, of course, there wouldn't be anything left of the factory. But it won't happen."

"You're sure of that?"

"Certain sure. I've done a lot of transshipping, Friar. I don't make mistakes like that."

"I'm sure you'd exercise all possible care, but still— Well, suppose it didn't explode in orbit. What if Jillen or Garold miscalculated and the whole two hundred pods fell to the surface of Pava?"

"They wouldn't!"

"We certainly hope not," he agreed, "but none of us are more than human, and human beings do sometimes make mistakes. Wouldn't it explode?"

"Well, I suppose so, sure, but—"

"And then what? Could two hundred pods of antimatter destroy the planet?"

"No. Of course not. It would certainly do a lot of damage, even as an air burst—if it were anywhere in this hemisphere it would kill a lot of organisms. But it would be a lot more likely to fall into sea, and then—" I stopped there, thinking. I was remembering some of the theoretical problems they gave us in training: what would happen if some lunatic diverted a catcherload to Earth. And then we had been talking only about a dozen pods or so.

"Well," I admitted, "an ocean impact would be serious, no doubt of that. An undersea explosion would certainly produce some giant tsunamis, at least. I suppose anything anywhere near a shore would be destroyed, and then there would be radioactive water vapor that would spread over a large area—I don't know if it would reach here. But if it did, we'd probably die."

He nodded soberly.

I thought I knew what was in his mind. I assumed he was trying to prepare arguments against using the antimatter in the factory, probably to bring up in the meeting. (I was wrong about that, of course, but I didn't find that out until a good deal later.) So I gave him truthful but cautious answers, winding up with, "Anyway, the antimatter's there in orbit now. There's a hundred pods of it sitting in *Corsair*'s hold, not counting what the next ship will bring. If it's a danger at all—and I don't think it is—those hundred pods are a danger already. All I'm suggesting is that we put it to a good use."

"Ah," he said, "but that's a question itself, isn't it? What's a 'good use,' Barry?"

"Come on, Friar. A good use is making things better for everyone on Pava."

He nodded. "So we'd be more prosperous and better fed and equipped; so the colony would increase and thrive. Is that a given, Barry? Is making it possible for more and more people to be born necessarily a good thing?"

That was when I began to get really uncomfortable. "I guess," I said, "that now we're getting into the area of religious belief, aren't we?"

"No, Barry," he said gently. "We've been there all along. It's *all* a matter of religion, and it doesn't really matter what you would like or what I would like. It's what God would like that's important."

18

THE term "factory" is not completely understood by us. What is a "factory"?

A factory is a place where we make things. Don't you people ever make things?

Of course. We make items that are needed, such as shelters for protection against storms. In the old days we made them from broad leaves; now we make them more frequently from discarded bits of your parafoil textiles. No "factory" is involved in such work; they are made by persons.

Home handicrafts, sure. We have that too.

But you also have the "factory" machine. We conceive that this machine operates like a fruit vine, producing useful things without the labor of a person, except that it can "manufacture" whatever sort of fruit you desire. Yet this cannot be correct for, if it were true, why does your "factory" not make your "medicine"?

O h, hell, you expect too much. No factory can make *everything*. The orbiters come pretty close, I admit; they tell me that this one's program stores contain the manufacturing doctrines for hundreds of thousands of different items. It has built-in instructions that tell it how to do everything from smelting and annealing the metals and just how and where to sputter dopant onto the electronic parts, to the kind of decorative finish to put on the cabinet. If you happened to need a hundred dozen pop-up toasters you just picked the model you preferred out of the catalogue and the factory would start pumping them out—taking the sheet metal from stock, winding the heating coils, fabricating the power lines; if it didn't have any of those things in stock it would make them out of raw materials. It would even make you *one* toaster if that was all you wanted; it didn't have to be mass production.

The factory orbiter isn't magic, though. It has very limited biochemical capabilities. It can't grow living tissues. Not even single cells.

There are lots of other things the factory can't do. It can't transmute elements. If an alloy calls for—I don't know, say it requires a little bit of bismuth—and if there doesn't happen to be any bismuth in stock—well, then it has to substitute some other element or try to replace it with whatever else it can find that will work. It might even cannibalize some bismuth from some other thing that it has already manufactured, but has a lower priority, if it has anything like that on hand. The factory is quite resourceful. All the same, its resources are not infinite, and if the factory can't do any of those things, it just can't fill that order.

It has other limitations. Add to what I've already said were the headaches of transporting stuff to and from orbit, add in the problem of getting raw materials to it, add in the fact that the thing was now just about a hundred years old. Even self-repairing machines don't last forever, do they?

Well, you wouldn't know whether they do or not. Take my word for it. The factory was good, but it just wasn't good enough. All I was really hoping for in the long run was that we could get enough production out of it to start making a better system somewhere else.

When the day of the postponed meeting came, it rained again. That was bad luck, and it wasn't just sprinkles. I'm talking about a steady all-day downpour that flooded the town's streets into mud and ruled out the possibility of an outdoor meeting entirely. We had to move the meeting inside somewhere. We didn't have very many options, either. The only place that was big enough—or almost big enough—was the rickety old meeting hall.

When I got inside it was really crowded. We were all damp and uncomfortable and, although crews had been working to strengthen the building all day, I looked suspiciously at the beams that had propped it up. The roof probably wouldn't fall in on us, though; with so many of us inside we could just about hold it up with our bare hands.

Naturally there weren't any seats left to speak of, but Madeleine Hartly and her great-granddaughter were occupying the end of one bench. When Madeleine saw me she nudged the girl and they managed to squeeze over enough to free eight or ten centimeters. I didn't exactly sit. I perched, one buttock on the bench and the other floating in air. I didn't mind. I was all revved up with the prospect of what was going to happen, and a little discomfort didn't bother me at all.

By then I had become a sort of local celebrity in Freehold. All around the room people were looking at me, a few with sour expressions, more nodding or waving in encouragement; a couple of rows away Theophan Sperlie had craned around to give me a thumbs-up sign. When I waved back Madeleine gave me a hooded look out of the bird's-nest of wrinkles around her bright black eyes. It seemed to me for a second that she might be going to make some remark about Theo, but all she did say was, "Are you ready for your big moment?"

"I hope so." As a matter of fact I thought I was. I'd spent most of the afternoon rehearsing the whole project in my mind. I looked around, checking the house. Nearly everybody I'd ever seen on Pava was there, all but the littlest kids—they were all installed in a temporary crèche under the care of the slightly larger kids—but at least one person I wanted there seemed to be absent. I mentioned it to Madeleine: "I don't see Tscharka here."

"You will. He'll be the last one to make his entrance," Madeleine predicted. Considering that she'd been sick she looked pretty sprightly, I thought. Which reminded me to ask how she was feeling; but when I did she dismissed the question.

"I'll be all right for a while yet," she said, "maybe. Anyway, I didn't want to miss this meeting. I think you've got the right idea, Barry. We're not getting anywhere here. You know, back on Earth they're talking again about terminating the colonies—"

She saw the look of surprise on my face; that was one more of the things I hadn't known. "You really should try to keep up with the news," she said reproachfully.

"I will," I promised, meaning it.

"Anyway, they might have the right idea. It seems to me that if we don't do something radical, maybe we should just all pack up and go home."

She startled me. "Do you mean that?"

She thought for a moment, studying my face. Then she looked away and said gently, "Some of us should, Barry. You should. You ought to go home and get married and raise babies, and I don't think you're going to find the right person to do it with here." Although she was talking to me, she was looking right at Theophan.

"Come on, Madeleine," I said, surprised, and a little nettled—I had my own mixed feelings about Theophan. "We weren't talking about *me*. I'll be fine. What I'm thinking about is the whole colony."

"All right," she said agreeably. "That's what we're here for, anyway, and I guess we can get started now, because here comes Captain Tscharka."

Tscharka didn't come in by himself. Jimmy Queng was with him, nodding and smiling to everyone they passed, making apologetic noises for their lateness. Tscharka wasn't smiling. He looked both grave and serene. The grave part I could understand—Tscharka didn't approve of secular town meetings in any case, and he must have known this one was not going to give him any joy—but I wondered what made him so serene.

Naturally the Millenarists had saved Tscharka a seat up front, next to Reverend Tuchman. When they got there Tscharka sat and Jimmy Queng hopped up to the little platform.

"Order, please," he yelled right away. "Hold it down, will you? We've got a lot of business to take care of tonight and the sooner we start the sooner we can go home." He raised his arms, making patting motions to the air, until the buzz dwindled at least to the point where we could hear the rain on the shingle roof again. Then he got started.

"Our primary job here is to allocate supplies for the next quarter. I know we've all got requests; they're all in the datastore, and I guess you've all had a chance to see them. As usual, we want a lot more than we can get—I estimate we can't hope for more than thirty percent of the total requisition list."

He was grinning as he said it. Not many people in the audience were smiling back; if he was looking for some expression of support he didn't get it, but he went gamely on. "For you people who came on *Corsair* and never took part in one of these sessions before I'll mention that that's not unusual. So that's what we have to do tonight; we need to pare the list down to what the orbiter can handle. The best way is with voluntary cuts, so I'll start. I'll waive everything on my list except for what we have to have for colony business: I need a new motor and fittings for another riverboat because the old ones are giving out. We'll just wait for everything else. Now, who'll be the next person to withdraw some requisitions?"

Theophan jumped up. "I move we approve everybody's requisitions in full," she shouted.

Jimmy Queng frowned, but he didn't get a chance to reproach her. All over the hall there were yells of "Second!" and "I second that!"

"That's out of order," he said, doing his best.

"The hell it is," she shouted. "There's a motion on the floor and it's been seconded. We can vote on it, or we can discuss it, but you can't just forget it. That's the rule; Marcus looked it up."

Somebody started clapping, and in a minute half the crowd was doing it. Next to me Madeleine was nodding approval. Jimmy hesitated for a moment, then gave in gracefully. "All right, the floor's open for discussion. Do you want to start, Theo?"

"You bet!" She dodged her way through the mob to the platform and climbed up on it. "You all know that Garold Tscharka came back with a lot of antimatter. He didn't bring us much else we could use, but he did— What's the problem now, Jimmy?"

He was shaking his head. He said, loud enough for everybody to hear, "You're supposed to limit discussion to the motion."

"I am discussing the motion! I'm saying we've got that antimatter, and more coming whenever the next ship gets here, and we've got somebody right here in Freehold who's a trained expert and can install the fuel in the factory—that's Barry di Hoa, back there—and so there's no reason we shouldn't get it in full operation and give everybody all of their essential supplies *now*."

Somebody shouted, "What about raw materials?" I couldn't see who it was, but it came from among the Millenarists clustered up front.

"We've got them, too," Theophan boasted. "There's a big chunk of raw materials right up there in orbit. It's called *Corsair*."

Well, that created a lot of noise. It annoyed me a little, too; I'd thought I'd be the one to explain the project, since I'd suggested it in the first place. Jimmy waved for order. He got a little of it, enough to be heard when he said, "We can't do that, Theo. These ships are our lifeline to Earth."

"*Corsair* isn't! What did Tscharka bring us, outside of the antimatter—that nobody had asked for—and a couple dozen more mouths to feed? He could have filled that ship with things we needed, but he didn't, and that's *unforgivable*. He should be reprimanded. Probably he should even be relieved of his command.''

That shut everybody up. Even me; I hadn't expected Theophan to go as far as a direct challenge to Tscharka's authority. Tscharka himself, I could see by craning, wasn't showing any reaction at all. He just sat there, dignified and remote, listening and not lifting a finger to protest. Next to him Reverend Tuchman was shaking his wise old head in sorrowful disagreement, but Tscharka himself never moved.

I couldn't tell by the expression on Jimmy Queng's face whether he was really startled or just angry, but he looked down at Tscharka. "Captain? Since you're personally involved here, do you want to respond?"

It wasn't Tscharka who got up and ponderously climbed to the platform, though. It was Friar Tuck. His Santa Claus face beamed forgiveness as he peered past Jimmy Queng to gaze at Theophan.

"My dear young lady," he said, "it's easy for you to criticize the captain. You weren't there. You don't know what the captain went through on the Moon. If it hadn't been for his testimony—well, and I suppose my own as well, to a lesser extent—the Tax and Budget people might very likely have terminated the colony entirely. Captain Tscharka really deserves all our thanks. He did the best he could, under worse circumstances than you know.''

Theophan was staunch. "All right, let's say you're right. Let's say that Garold was so confused and befuddled by the problems he faced on the Moon that he just couldn't remember all the things we needed. That doesn't matter anymore. What about now? We've got all that antimatter fuel, let's transship it to the factory orbiter and use it!''

Tuchman shook his head sorrowfully. "Ah, Theo, you make it all sound so easy. Do you know what you're suggesting? Do you have any idea how dangerous transshipping those pods would be? I was talking to Barry di Hoa himself about it just recently; he told me that no one could guarantee there might not be an accident. One slip and we could lose *Corsair*. Maybe we'd destroy the factory orbiter too. Even that's not the worst of it; why, an accidental antimatter explosion could even endanger us here on the surface.''

That was more than I could take. I stood up and yelled, "Not if we take precautions! I did that sort of thing every day on the Moon and never had an accident!''

Tuchman gazed out over the crowd at me, shaking his head forgivingly. "I'm sure you sincerely feel that's true, Barry," he said, "but remember on the Moon you had a whole trained support staff. Here you don't. Captain Tscharka thought of all that; that's why he left instructions for a trained team to follow on *Buccaneer*."

I felt pretty sure that was another lie—for a clergyman, Friar Tuck was pretty casual with the truth—and, judging from the growling that came out of the audience, so did a lot of others.

Theo wasn't buying it, for one. "All right," she called, "for the sake of argument, let's assume it would be sensible for us to wait to do the actual transshipping. That doesn't mean we shouldn't do anything tonight! There are still things we can decide on right now. For a starter, we should send Barry up to the orbiter immediately, just to make sure the job can be done. So let's quit stalling around, okay? I'm calling for a vote!"

That caused another noisy storm. All around the building people were shouting, "Vote! Vote!" while others were calling, "No!" or yelling things I couldn't make out.

Then Captain Tscharka moved at last. He stood up and climbed to the platform, nodding pleasantly to the others already there. He raised his hands for quiet.

When he had it—well, almost—he began to speak. "I'm sorry that some of you think I failed you. I accept responsibility for that. However, I have another responsibility. *Corsair* is my ship. On *Corsair* I am the only authority there is. So," he added pleasantly, making eye contact all around the hall, "you see, it doesn't matter what you vote here. The safety of *Corsair* is in my charge, not yours. There is nothing more that needs to be said."

And he stepped down from the platform and threaded his way to the doorway. Jillen Iglesias hesitated, then got up to follow him.

I had a sudden worrying suspicion that this had been all prearranged; maybe all two hundred or so of the Millenarists were going to take off with Tscharka, and then maybe Jimmy Queng would make that a pretext for trying to call the meeting off one more time.

That didn't happen, though. Most of the other Millenarists muttered angrily and worriedly to each other, but they stayed in their seats.

"Wait a minute! We're not through!" Theophan shouted after Tscharka.

He didn't wait. He didn't pay any attention to her at all. Jillen opened the door for him, and the two of them stepped outside into the dwindling rain.

That quieted everybody down for a moment again, until Theo shouted, "We don't need Tscharka here to vote." Then there was a roar of, mostly, agreement.

Queng bowed to the inevitable. "All right," he said, "we'll go on with the meeting, but we'll do it properly. Everybody who wants to be heard will get a chance, if it takes us all night."

It didn't. For a while there I thought it might, though, as one person after another got up to put his own two cents in. A lot of the comments were adverse—mostly from Millenarists, it seemed to me—saying, really, we ought to take advice from experts like the captain, above all we should be absolutely sure that whatever we did was *prudent*. But they were a minority. There were a lot more voices raised to say we didn't have a choice. Our needs were too great. We needed better roads, so we needed bulldozers to build the roads—and machine tools to make the bulldozers on the factory satellite. We needed instruments. We needed nursery facilities to breed new varieties of crop plants. We needed ten thousand things we didn't have, and any way we could get them was the right way, even if it meant destroying Garold Tscharka's precious *Corsair*.

As a matter of fact, even the party lines didn't hold. One or two of the Millenarists themselves got up to demand newer and better—and most of all *more*—equipment so they could do their jobs; they were as fed up with the constant shortages as anybody else.

It took another couple of hours to get all the talking done. But everything ends, if you just wait long enough, and finally Jimmy Queng raised his hand.

"Let me put it like this," he said. "Is it the sense of the meeting that, first, we send Barry di Hoa up to check the orbiter; and, second, if it turns out that it is feasible and safe to do so, then to install antimatter fuel to expedite its function; and finally, if necessary, to consider scrapping *Corsair* for raw materials?"

"Not consider! Do it!" someone yelled, but Jimmy was determined.

"We can't make that decision now," he said. "Leave it as an open option. As to the rest of it—?"

The roar that answered him was pretty nearly unanimous. "So be it," he said. "I'll talk to the captain about when the shuttle will be available for you, Barry—and meanwhile the meeting is adjourned. Let's go home."

The "go home" part was easy for him to say, and he did leave the hall then, along with about half the Millenarists. It wasn't easy for me. People crowded around me. Some wanted to shake my hand. Some asked for details about my qualifications to handle antimatter fuel. Some just wanted to wish me luck. It all took time, and Theophan, Marcus, Jacky Schottke and I were almost the last ones out of the meeting hall.

Theophan paused outside the door to give me a happy hug. "We did it, Barry," she said. "God, this stuff wears me out. Talk, talk, talk—but it was worth it."

Marcus gave a faintly disapproving cough—about the hug, I supposed. "At least the rain's stopped," he pointed out. He sounded as though he wanted to be thanked for it.

Jacky Schottke didn't speak. He was gazing up at the sky, as though he were listening for something. There was nothing up there that I could see, although the clouds were beginning to break.

"Well, good night," Theophan said, yawning. "Tomorrow I'll get on Jimmy Queng's case and make sure he sets a date for you to go up in the shuttle—"

Jacky stirred. "I don't think so," he said.

At first I didn't know what he was talking about. Then I heard the sound he had been listening for—a growing roar, loud but distant. I thought for a minute it might be thunder. Then I just hoped it was.

It wasn't. "The son of a bitch!" Theophan shouted, suddenly wide-awake again. She was staring at the sky.

Then I saw it, too—off toward the downstream horizon, a moving brightness behind the thinning clouds. "What is it? Is that the shuttle?"

She snarled, "You damn bet it's the shuttle. The bastard's taken off for his ship."

Jacky said mournfully, "I was afraid of that, when I saw he took Jillen with him when he left. He's gone, Barry. I doubt he'll be coming back to us until he figures out some way to save his ship."

19

...

*A*GAIN *there is a matter that is not understood. You have stated that the "town meeting" prescribed the actions for humans on Pava. Yet you also state that Garoldtscharka did not conform to the decisions that were taken at the meeting. How is that possible?*

Why, that's the easiest thing in the world to understand. Yes, we have laws. But, yes, we also have people who break the laws. That's why all the laws have punishments written into them for the people who break them.

Then Garoldtscharka was "punished" in some manner?

*A*h, well, no. Not exactly. In order to punish somebody you first have to catch him. Garold had taken himself out of our reach. He and Jillen flew themselves right up to *Corsair* in the shuttle, and once he was in orbit he stayed there.

He not only wouldn't come back down, he wouldn't even discuss the subject. He refused to talk on the radio to anybody but Friar Tuck, and whatever was said between them went no further. Their conversations were no one else's business, so the reverend said. All the reverend would add, benevolently smiling, was to tell us to be patient, dear ones, the captain knows what he is doing, he is acting for the best of all of us, and we just have to trust him.

I didn't, though. For that matter, it seemed that hardly anyone did but the most devoted Millenarists. Those had formed solid ranks behind Captain Tscharka after the meeting in support of his position that nobody had anything to say about *Corsair* and its cargo but himself. Very few others bought that, and so we were divided into hostile camps.

That brought a whole bunch of old problems to the fore again.

What I'm talking about now is religious problems, which are the kind I hate most. There were protest meetings in most of the churches; there were bitter arguments between Millenarists and their supposedly heretical next-door neighbors, and sometimes the arguments got violent.

Of course, not all the squabbles were serious, or at least I didn't think they were. The one that struck me as funniest was when our tiny band of Wiccas, the old witch-cult people, organized a protest demonstration against Tscharka in the square outside the meeting house.

No one really minded them demonstrating, at least in principle; that was their right. Besides, there only were about six of the Wiccas altogether, and their demonstration wasn't particularly noisy. What made a problem was that, for religious reasons, they announced they could only demonstrate effectively while they were "skyclad." What they actually meant by "skyclad" turned out to be "naked."

Even that was no particular problem for most of us—who cared if the Wiccas wanted to display their generally not-very-exciting nude bodies?—but our equally tiny group of hard-shell Baptists got really upset. The Baptists weren't defending Tscharka. They were as mad at him as anybody else, but they also firmly believed that all that bare flesh was inciting to sin. That offended them deeply. They made so much noise about it that cooler heads had to arbitrate. When the Wiccas finally agreed to confine their future skyclad activities to remote areas of the woods that one simmered down.

But the colony was still seriously divided, and that wasn't funny at all.

I didn't think so, anyway. I was frustrated and angry. I'd finally got myself started on what I thought was going to be a productive course of action. I wanted to charge ahead with it . . . and that bastard Tscharka had foreclosed it on me without warning.

Was I going through the beginning of those mood swings that meant trouble was on its way? I don't know. It didn't occur to me at the time. I knew I was in an up-and-down state, but I accounted for that by objective factors.

But there it was. I don't handle frustration very well, at least not when my medication's running thin. I found the situation depressing. And, as you know, I don't like to be depressed. It scares me.

The best antidote I know for depression is work, and I made a lot of it for myself.

The community kept finding jobs for me at its own regular chores, but when those were done I added another job of my own. If I couldn't go up to the orbiter just then I could do the next best thing. So I spent long hours over the screen in Jacky Schottke's apartment, going over and over the specs on the factory orbiter.

I know you keep saying that you want me to tell you *everything*, but that includes a lot. Should I mention that the weather stayed bad, cold, wet and windy? Or that a pack of goobers got into one of the riverside farm plots and sucked the juice out of every single tomato and green pepper on the vines? Or that we had a sudden cluster of those little quakes that I thought I had been getting used to, but hadn't? I noticed all those things, of course. You couldn't help it. But my thoughts were all on the orbiter.

The schematics told me a lot. The factory certainly had been designed to make use of any energy source that came along, including antimatter; there was an antimatter-fueled magnetohydrodynamic power generator built in, just like the ones on spaceships—at least, it *had* been built in, as part of the original plan.

But that brought up the question the screen couldn't answer for me. Was that system still there?

That was the worrisome unknown. I knew that over the years the orbiter had scrounged materials wherever it could find them. I knew it had eaten up parts of itself when its programming allowed it to make the assumption that the scrapped systems were of a lower priority than the new goods it was programmed to make.

Had some of those recycled parts been in the standby fuel system?

I could find no way of answering that question—until Madeleine Hartly offered to help me find one.

We had both been set to checking food stored in the warehouse to make sure none of it was spoiled. When I complained about my problem to her she volunteered to show me how to interrogate the factory itself, so between work and supper we went to her apartment to use her screen—she didn't want to make the trek over to mine.

Naturally Geronimo trailed along after me, but Madeleine didn't mind. She even rustled through her cupboards and found some raisins to give him—well, I don't suppose they were really raisins. I don't think they'd originally been actual grapes, anyway, but they were little dried fruits that were sweet enough to please Geronimo. Then she sat down at her screen to access the orbiter.

A moment later she looked up, frowning. "That's funny, Barry. It's asking me for a password," she said. "It never did that before. Wait a minute—"

And she tried another combination, and this time she did get a response. The legend on the screen said:

> Entrance code required. Access to operating programs is temporarily restricted, pending resolution of new manufacturing instructions.

"Whatever that means," I said. The operating system in Freehold's computers was pretty ancient, naturally enough, and one that was unfamiliar to me.

She looked annoyed. "I guess what it means is what it says. We're blocked out. Maybe Jimmy Queng was afraid somebody would sneak in a manufacturing order before we made sure you can fuel it, so he embargoed the system. Or Captain Tscharka did it from his ship."

"Can he do that?"

"I guess he can, Barry, because it looks like he—or somebody—did." She tried a couple other combinations without success, then gave up. "Well, we're not doing any good here. I'm sorry, Barry. Let's go eat." And then, as we were walking toward the mess, Geronimo loping silently along beside us, she was silent, as though she had something else on her mind. Then she looked up at me quizzically. "Mind if I ask you a question? How're you doing with your problem?"

"Which problem is that?"

"The medical one, Barry."

I stopped short. Geronimo stopped too, staring up at both of us with those immense eyes. "How did you know I had a medical problem?"

She shrugged, looking apologetic. "Everybody knows that, Barry. People have been talking about it for days. They say you're unstable, except if you have medication, and Bill Goethe doesn't have the right medication for you."

I flared up at her. "Damn the man! He's got no right to be spreading that kind of information around. Doctors are supposed to keep their mouths shut about their patients' problems!''

"Don't blame Billy. It might not be him. Anybody can access his files," she reminded me, and waited for an answer to her question.

I didn't see any way out of it, so I said unwillingly, "All right. I do have—I used to have—serious mood swings.''

"Bad ones?''

"Damn bad ones. Incapacitating ones, in fact; I did some pretty crazy things. If they were to come back I'd be in real trouble. I'm in remission right now, though, so it's not an immediate problem. I ought to be good for a couple of months, anyway, and Goethe says he's trying to work up some treatment for me before it gets critical.''

She squeezed my arm. "Let's hope, Barry," she said, and that was the end of the conversation.

It was not, of course, the end of my thinking about it. Although my head had been full of other things, I had not forgotten how little hope Goethe had offered for his "treatments.''

I wondered if the sudden flare of anger I'd felt when Madeleine told me the news meant anything. It wasn't a good sign; I was supposed to avoid losing my temper as much as possible. Then there was the unexpected new responsibility that had been thrust on me; that was a new stress, too, added to all the other stresses that were working on me.

I didn't think there was immediate danger. I was pretty sure that I wasn't going off the deep end just then. However, there was no doubt that sooner or later I certainly would . . . unless, against the odds, Goethe came through with what I needed. If he didn't—

If he didn't, I did not like to think of what my life would be like then.

Madeleine excused herself to sit with her great-granddaughter at supper. When I'd filled my tray—the cooks were serving something that resembled meat loaf that day—I looked around for a place to sit, and saw Becky Khaim-Novello waving at me.

I hadn't seen much of Becky, after that one cup of coffee in her apartment. Now and then I'd caught sight of her as our paths crossed, of course, and I'd noticed that she went about the town looking as proud and pleased as the widow of a successful Millenarist suicide should. I didn't know how deep that went. Once or twice in the still night hours I had heard, through the thin flooring, the sound of her uncontrolled weeping.

She wasn't weeping now. She seemed chipper and inviting, and there was one other thing about her just then that struck me as interesting. She wasn't alone. She was sitting next to Marcus Wendt, and the annoyed look he gave me suggested that the conversation had been personal. And what that suggested was that maybe things hadn't been going very well between him and Theophan Sperlie.

Between the time I spotted them and the time I was getting ready to sit down across from them, my active imagination went through a whole scenario: Theo and Marcus breaking up; Theo available again; Theo taking a new interest in me; Theo and me maybe making it after all. I know how foolish that sounds. Just remember how many weeks I'd had to get horny, though; I'm really a reasonably serious person, but my glands don't always know that.

"You've made yourself a stranger," Becky chided me as I started to sit down. "Don't forget that I still have some of that good coffee."

And Marcus said:

"Don't sit there. That's Theo's place."

That took swift care of my fantasies. Sure enough, a minute later Theophan came back with another helping of the something or other loaf for Marcus and a salad for herself. She was not cheerful. "Barry," she said as soon as she caught sight of me, "I'm beginning to get worried. I have to have some new equipment and I can't wait."

I shrugged, meaning *What do you want from me? I'm not responsible for Garold Tscharka.*

She went on regardless: "I've got an ugly feeling. That little cluster of tremors we've been having? I think there's a good chance that they're foreshocks for something a lot bigger. How'm I supposed to do my job? There's all kinds of data that would help. I ought to be measuring radon emissions, checking water-table levels, all that sort of thing—but I don't have the tools to do it with."

Becky said, in a superior way, "Garold says if Freehold had been established in a better place we wouldn't have that kind of worries."

Theo gave her an unfriendly look. "I wasn't consulted, was I? I wasn't even here when they picked this place. I'm just the one that gets blamed."

"So you blame me?" I said, meaning it lightly. It didn't come out that way. It came out defensive.

"Oh, not really, Barry. I'm sorry if it sounded that way," Theo said. She picked at her salad moodily. "It's just that time passes and nothing happens, and you got my hopes up. It's really Tscharka's fault."

That stung Becky Khaim-Novello. "Now, really! You mustn't say that. Garold Tscharka knows what's best for all of us. I'm sure that he'll do whatever's necessary."

"You think so? I wish I had your confidence. And what do we do if Barry here goes off the deep end before he gets around to it?"

So there it was again.

I didn't let it pass. By then I figured that it might as well all be out in the open, so I told them what I'd told Madeleine, and then I got up and started back to the apartment. I'd lost my appetite anyway.

As I left I felt as though everybody at the tables was giving me funny looks. I didn't like it. I didn't like being frustrated about the factory, either, but I was. The longer Tscharka stayed in orbit, the more unlikely it seemed that we'd ever get going on the plan to revitalize the satellite, and the more the colony seemed to revert to its torpor.

I hardly noticed when Geronimo came galumphing after me—he'd been foraging among the kitchen wastes while I ate—until I heard his whispery voice. "Candy, Barrydihoa?" he coaxed. And I fumbled in my pocket for another of those sour balls and felt a little better. There weren't many bright spots in my life those days, but there was always one, and its name was Geronimo.

I know that I keep coming back to Geronimo. I even know that I don't really have to tell you everything about him, because you know more than I do about the little guy. He was important to me, though. I never would have guessed that at a critical time in my life my best friend would turn out to be a squirmy, big-eyed caterpillar, but he was.

I didn't know what made Geronimo adopt me as a pal. He just did. It wasn't only a matter of playing games with him, and neither was it just the candy that he came for. He was there when I needed him, and he helped me. When I was sent out to hoe the garden plots, Geronimo worked right along with me. He didn't have the height or the strength for a man-sized hoe, but he did well enough humping along the muddy rows with a little spudding tool and he didn't mind the wet. When I was assigned to sort over broken tools to see what could be salvaged, he was there to tug the loads to the repair bins for me. And we talked.

Geronimo was fuller of questions than anyone else I'd ever met— well, except you, that is. The difference between the two of you was that there weren't any wrong answers to his questions. He wasn't grading me, and there wasn't any penalty if I failed.

What did Geronimo want to know? Everything. He wanted to know what spaceships were, and then what planets were—it astonished him when I told him he was living on one—and then what cities were. When I told him they were a lot like Freehold but a million times bigger he just chewed for a moment in silence on the roseberry branch we were sharing—I was eating the fruit, he was eating the leaves. Then he changed the subject. He didn't say anything directly, but he looked skeptical. I don't think he believed any rational creature would choose to live in a place as grotesquely huge as New York or Metro Mexico. Not even a human being.

Then we got into the baffling—to him—subject of human relationships. I told him about my ex-wife, Gina, and my son—you could almost call him my ex-son—Matthew, and then I tried to explain to him what "wife" and "son" meant, which was even harder for him to understand.

Our talks weren't all one-way. He answered my questions, too—well, some of them. Others just made him change the subject. He refused to talk about Theophan Sperlie, or about the recent suicide of my neighbor, Jubal Khaim-Novello. And he didn't seem to want to tell me very much about the way you people lived in your nests.

That was all right. I had plenty of other questions. There was a lot about leps that I didn't understand. Like your names, for instance.

We got to talking about that one evening, when he and I had just brought a carful of windfallen apples back to town and we were killing time while we waited to be told where to store them. It was drizzling again, though not enough to make it worthwhile to look for shelter. The apples were an unfamiliar variety to me, small and hard, but I ate one just for the sake of doing something. While we were sitting there it occurred to me to ask Geronimo why leps adopted human names.

He took a thoughtful moment to chew, the ragged, round edges of his mouthpart sawing away at the apple he had appropriated as his reward before he answered. Then he said, "I think it is because you could not say our real names."

"Try me," I said.

He vibrated his hard, slim tongue rapidly for a moment to clear it of apple pulp, then he made a queer, whistly sound. I got him to repeat it four or five times and copied it as best I could. "Is that right?"

"No."

"Is it at least close, anyway?

"Closer than I would have expected, though no one would recognize it. It is not worth your while to get it right, though. It will not matter in a few weeks."

I stopped chewing my own apple to look at him. "What's going to happen in a few weeks?"

"I will take my fourth-instar name, of course. That will be, I think, ————." And he made another of those sounds.

It was the first time I'd heard that leps changed their real names with each stage of development, and when he told me what his second-instar name had been, I thought I could detect a sort of a system.

"They get more complicated as you go along, but there are a lot of the same sounds, aren't there? What did you say your first-instar name was?"

"I did not say. There was none. We have no names in the first instar. We have none in the sixth, either, since no one in the sixth instar would be likely to recognize his name."

I tossed my apple core away, and then what he had said finally registered with me. "Hey! What do you mean it won't matter? Are you going to molt or something?"

"Indeed yes, Barrydihoa."

"Oh," I said, and stopped there, unsure of whether to follow it with "Too bad" or "Congratulations." "So then I won't be seeing you for a while?"

"I will be cocooned for about twenty days. Provided the weather is satisfactory. Provided also that there are no accidents."

"I see," I said, and just as though the word "accidents" had been her cue, which it dramatically might have been if I had been making this into a screen show instead of just telling you all the things that happened, Theophan Sperlie came around the back of the car and greeted us.

I stood up to say hello, and she shook my hand. "How are you fellows doing?" she asked politely, helping herself to a wet apple.

"Just fine," I answered, though Geronimo didn't. He had already wriggled well out of earshot and was now ignoring us, putting all his attention into a bruise spot he'd found on his apple, rooting it out with his hard, rough tongue and spitting it away.

Theophan didn't seem to notice that he was avoiding her—well, she'd had plenty of opportunity to get used to that. "Barry," she said, "can you do me a favor?" I made a non-committal noise, waiting to hear what the favor was. "I'm having more troubles with that goddamn strain gauge we set out in the Rockies. With all the other uncertainties I need its data, and it isn't reporting. You didn't drop it or anything on the way up, did you?''

"Not me.''

"Well, I need to have it working. If the weather clears tomorrow, we've got to get up there and fix it.''

She surprised me with that. I couldn't resist a small dig. "Oh, really? What 'we' are we talking about, Theo, you and me? Why not you and Marcus? Is the work getting too heavy for him again?''

She glared at me. "No, the work is not too heavy for him. Anyway, it'll be pretty easy to go up there this time, actually. All we'll have to carry up the hill is tools. But I can't ask Marcus because he has his own work.'' She hesitated, then went on: "See, he's been talking to Becky Khaim-Novello, and he got some really fine material out of her for his novel—''

I gaped at her. "His *what*?''

She sounded impatient. "Oh, why do you think he signed up to come to Pava in the first place? It wasn't because he wanted to be some kind of pioneer. Marcus has been looking for suitable material to make into a novel for a long time. He wants it to be a *big* one, you see. One that'll make his reputation when he gets home. Now he's getting what he needs from Becky, and he says he has to get it all down in store while it's fresh. I don't know, I guess that's the way authors are.''

It was the first I'd heard that Marcus Wendt was a novelist. As far as I was concerned that was just a synonym for "loafer,'' but I decided to be kind. I just shrugged. Theophan coaxed, "I need the data, Barry. It's in a critical area. Remember, I told you there's a fault segment up there that's coupled to the one by the dam? There's another segment that might be part of the same complex, and it hasn't moved for quite a while. I'm afraid it might be getting ready to pop.''

"But that fault just did pop, didn't it? When the dam broke?''

Theophan took her patience in hand. I could see her remembering that, after all, I was still a novice and she had undertaken to teach me. All she said was, "That was long ago, Barry. When you get a slip in one place it just adds to the strain in other segments. Don't you remember anything I told you? We've been getting a lot of clusters of little temblors lately; they could be foreshocks.'' She looked up at me beseechingly, her face wet in the rain. "Will you do it for me?''

I couldn't think of any reason to say no. "If the rain stops,'' I promised.

She nodded. "Thanks,'' she said, and turned and left. I was looking after her, and didn't notice that Geronimo had come back until I heard his breathy voice from behind me.

"There will be chocolate cake tonight, Barrydihoa. Will you give me a piece?"

I turned and looked at him, his fur glistening in the wet, peacefully nibbling at bits of some ornamental shrubbery someone had planted nearby.

"Why not?" I asked. "Do you want to come along if we go up in the hills tomorrow?"

He took a moment to think that over. "I will come," he said finally, but he sounded reluctant.

I thought I knew why, so I tried him again on the unanswered question. "Geronimo? Do you want to tell me why you hate Theophan?"

He said, "No." I waited, but that was all there was to it. Just no. "Please."

"No," he said again, but then he corrected himself. "Perhaps another time. First I need advice."

That sounded promising, if unexpected. "What kind of advice? Who from?"

But that one didn't even get a no. He didn't answer for a moment, while he finished mouthing and swallowing the bits of shrub. Then he reared up and looked at me. "I will come to see you when the dessert is served at supper, Barrydihoa. Good-bye." And that was that.

When supper was over Geronimo did come for his cake. He didn't stay, though. The reason for that was that as he was pulverizing the cake to swallow, Becky Khaim-Novello came up and took my arm. She squeezed it in a friendly way. "Going home now, Barry? Why don't we stop off in my place? I've got a surprise for you."

She sounded flirtatious. Whether Geronimo picked up on her tone or not I don't know, but he reared up at full height to study her, then turned and stretch-slid rapidly away without even saying good-bye.

So I let Becky lure me to her apartment, and when we were inside she produced her surprise with a wink. She'd been picking sushi fruit that afternoon. The surprise was a couple of fruits with the moldy stuff on them that Madeleine Hartly had told me about.

"I think," Becky said invitingly, slicing one of them into tiny pieces, "it's about time you and I got high together, Barry hon."

The woman was getting right to the point, I thought.

I've never been much for hallucinogenics, but the circumstances were special. Remember how long it had been since I'd had sex with anybody. It seemed clear that Becky was offering more than a little mind-expansion. The fact that I didn't even particularly like the woman just did not seem important at that moment.

So I took a nibble, and she did too, and we sat there, looking at each other and waiting for something to happen. She giggled. "God, I haven't done this since college. Do you feel anything yet?"

I explored the inside of my mind. "A little spacey, maybe," I ventured.

"Maybe we should eat a little more."

So we did. I didn't take very much. Then it occurred to me that we were sitting rather formally at her table, and that wasn't a good starting point for anything to develop. So I suggested we take the little plate of fruit and move over to her couch, and we did, and then I did begin to feel something. It wasn't a particularly pleasant feeling. It felt as though something warm and large was throbbing inside my chest. I thought it was as good a time as any to kiss her, and so I put my arm around her and did.

She eagerly kissed me back. Then she pulled away. "I've always admired you, Barry," she said.

That struck me as an irrelevant remark, not to mention that it seemed an odd time to start a conversation anyway. "That's nice," I said, playing with the lobe of her ear—she hadn't moved so far away that my arm was not around her.

"I think everybody here on Pava does," she went on. "Do you know how much we're counting on you?"

I said, "Um."

She leaned forward and took another crumb of the fruit, then nestled back against me. "The thing is," she said, letting one hand come to rest on my knee, "you shouldn't let your personal feelings about Captain Tscharka get in the way of cooperating. For the good of everybody, I mean. He's really a fine man."

"So I'm told," I said. I was a little preoccupied with engineering details. Although she was cuddling close, her head was just under my chin. That left me nothing convenient to kiss but her hair. Also, although her left hand was on my knee, her right arm was thrown across her chest and there wasn't much of Becky that was available to caress.

"So what I was thinking," she said, sounding peacefully warm and relaxed, "is that I'd like to get you and Reverend Tuchman together one of these days, so the two of you could straighten out this little difference of opinion—"

Dawn broke. I sat up straight.

"Oh, hell," I said. "He put you up to this, didn't he?"

She untangled herself. "Don't be silly, Barry. It's just that I'm fond of you both and—"

I didn't let her finish. I was suddenly furious. Maybe part of it was the drug. Not most of it, though; mostly it was one more kind of frustration, the kind a man feels when he has every reason to believe that within the next few minutes he's going to be making love, and without warning something gets in the way.

I didn't want to get up. I wanted to carry on as planned, right into her bed. But I did it. "Thanks for the party," I said. "Sorry I can't stay longer."

And I left—horny, mad, disappointed and thoroughly disgruntled.

Halfway up the stairs I thought I could hear her crying again, but I didn't stop. I really wanted to get laid . . . but not on Friar Tuck's orders. I don't know if you can understand that. I'm not sure I do myself. But I'd never wished more that I'd never been taken away from the Lederman colony, and from my comfortable life there, and from my Alma.

20

WHY do you suppose that is not understood? You are not as different from us as you believe, Barrydihoa. Leps of the sixth instar also are driven by the biological mating imperative. Although, to be sure, they are not known to regret their actions afterwards.

Maybe that's just because they don't have any intelligence left by then, do they? I did. At least I thought I did, and yet my balls kept pushing me into places where my head knew perfectly well I didn't belong.

I suppose that "biological mating imperative" of yours is why I showed up for my date with Theophan Sperlie the next morning, even though I didn't have any real expectation of making it with her anymore, and wasn't all that sure I really wanted to. I didn't feel much like making the trip. I woke up with a bad attitude, crotchety, pissed off, resentful of the way things were going; I snapped at poor Jacky Schottke for asking me if anything was the matter, when obviously *everything* was the matter.

But when I'd eaten my lousy breakfast and forced down my second cup of mess-hall coffee—the awfulness about which Becky Khaim-Novello was perfectly right—I dutifully marched over to the car where Theo was waiting.

The only bright spot was that Geronimo was there, too. I hadn't really expected him to show up. With the light loads we'd be carrying we didn't really need any help, and he knew Theophan would be there. All the same, there he was. He hopped into the backseat of the car without saying a word.

Theophan, on the other hand, was cheerfully talkative. "Morning, Barry. Morning, Geronimo. Looks like we've got a nice day for a change. What's the matter, you guys get up on the wrong side of the bed this morning?"

Neither of us answered. It didn't stop her. She didn't seem to care whether Geronimo and I felt conversational or not—well, maybe she was making allowances for the fact that she knew perfectly well Geronimo wouldn't talk to her at all. All the way down to the river and across and up into the hills on the other side she kept talking seismology to me. I was barely listening—I was replaying in my mind my scene with Becky Khaim-Novello from the night before, and not enjoying it any more the second time around—and Geronimo was in the backseat, resolutely staring at the road behind us. She kept right on with her lecture on basic principles: "The thing is, I'm pretty sure Pava's in the Pangaea phase. Do you know what that is? See, a planet like this, or like Earth, goes through a half-billion-year cycle as the land masses slosh back and forth. First there's a single giant continent like the one we're on. Then it breaks up. Then you get interior oceans developing inside the continent and they push the land masses apart until they're spread out as far as they can get. Then the mid-ocean ridges that drive the ocean growth dry up. By then the interior oceans aren't interior anymore—they're huge—but they begin to shrink again. Subduction starts. As the ocean floors get colder and denser and descend into the asthenosphere the spread-out continents are all pulled back to join together in one big one again . . . and then the whole cycle starts all over again."

She looked at me as though she was expecting a question. I took my mind off Becky long enough to oblige her. "It keeps on doing that over and over forever?"

"Close enough to forever. At least until the radioactive elements in the planet's core all wear out and there isn't enough interior heat to make it go, and it turns into a lump of solid rock." She paused there, glancing over at me. "How'd you do with the widow lady last night?"

By then I was getting used to the fact that I didn't have any secrets in this place. That didn't stop me from resenting her inquisitiveness. "Fine," I said flatly. "Why don't you keep your eyes on the road?"

She stopped talking then—for a while—but she was grinning to herself.

Although the rains had finally moved away, as promised, they had left the soil soft and slippery. After the big-wheeled car had taken us as far as it could, we walked. It was a long climb, and a real struggle to get back up that slick, wet hillside. Even with the light load I'd been carrying I was sweating. I threw my pack of tools down next to the one Geronimo had been dragging and sat, while Theo rummaged through all the packs for what she needed.

It didn't take long to help Theophan get the housing off the strain guage. After that the job was all hers. I went back to sit on my wet rock and watched, Geronimo next to me, while she pulled out one component, put in another, poked her test probes in here and there for half an hour or so and then, doubtfully, pursed her lips.

She straightened up. "Ought to do it," she said. "Let's put the cover back on, Barry." When it was all dogged down she rubbed some of the wet off another rock and sat down, resting up for the return trip.

I remembered I had some sweet trail bars in my pack. I pulled them out and passed them around. Geronimo lopped dainty segments off his with the cutting edges around his mouthpart in silence. In silence Theophan ate hers, though she was watching him carefully.

I was beginning to feel uncomfortable. I wasn't any more cheerful; the bad mood persisted; but the pregnant silences were just making me feel worse. I tried to get some kind of a conversation going. "Looks like the weather will be nice for a while, don't you think, Geronimo?"

He finished his trail bar and darted that snaky, quick tongue around his mouthpart to find crumbs before he answered, "Yes, Barrydihoa."

"I do too," Theophan said. Her tone sounded as though she were trying to be pleasant. Not very hard, though. And not very long. A moment later she stood up. "Well, hell," she said irritably. "Let's get out of here."

But as soon as we turned to start down that slippery, nasty hill again, Geronimo stretch-slid quickly between us. He planted himself in our path and put his face up close to mine, breathing his warm, wet, vegetable smells at me.

"Barrydihoa," he said, "the sun is still high. You need not go quickly back across the river."

Theophan gave me a nettled look, and I gave one to Geronimo. "Have you got some other idea?" I asked.

"Yes. I do. You have never seen our nests, Barrydihoa. I have been advised that if you wish I may take you there."

That was an unexpected offer. "Advised by who?" I asked.

He didn't answer that, just waited, swaying back and forth at full extension and watching me. I looked at Theophan to see if she had anything to say on the subject. She did, but she said it—eagerly—to Geronimo. "Does the invitation include me?"

He kept those eyes on me. "No one will prevent a conspecific coming with you, Barrydihoa," he told me, "if that is not avoidable."

It certainly was not the most openhearted invitation I'd ever heard, but Theophan settled for it.

We weren't far from the lep nests, Geronimo promised me that. I was glad of it. It was certainly far enough to suit me. It took us nearly two hours of climbing and sliding and pushing our way through heavy brush, down a slope, across an icy little stream, up another. . . . Those light backpacks were getting really heavy long before we were there.

Geronimo, of course, had no problem at all. He humped right along ahead of us, knowing exactly where he was going and singing screechily under his breath as he went. Theophan didn't sing. She swore a time or two, though, when she slipped in the mud or a branch swept back and caught her in the face. I didn't even do that much, not having the wind to spare for it.

In half an hour I was completely lost. I doubted I could find my way back to the strain gauge, much less to the car we had come in, and Theophan was looking worried herself.

Then, without warning, something big and bright came fluttering through the air toward us. It had a body the size of a collie's, and it also had lacy, bright-colored wings bigger than an eagle's. It hovered overhead for a moment, gazing benignly and emptily at the three of us.

"That is the sixth-instar person once named Marcanthony," Geronimo called over what would have been his shoulder if he'd had one. "He is newly fledged. He has left the nest just this day."

It was one of the first sixth-instar leps I had ever seen.

I had never met Marc Anthony; he had to have cocooned himself for his final transmogrification right after I landed on Pava. I found out later from Jacky Schottke that he had been a good and loyal friend of the human colony in his fourth and fifth instars, collecting biological samples for Schottke's study, tirelessly helping in whatever work was at hand. Of course, I had to find it out from someone else, since Marc Anthony was no longer able to tell me any of that himself. At his sixth instar he had passed beyond the point when he would ever tell anyone anything again—when he would ever again know anything to tell, for that matter. He fluttered around us for a moment, perhaps sniffing to see if any of us smelled like sixth-instar female lep, and then was gone. Looking, I suppose, for something that did.

Marc Anthony was the first other lep we saw, but soon there were others. I became aware that there were leps moving in the underbrush around us; they didn't approach, but they were watching. Geronimo ignored them, until some of them revealed themselves, joining our procession. They were all wingless ones, in all stages. Theophan was fascinated. "Look," she said, pointing to what looked like a giant cowflop under a moss-covered rock, "there's a first-instar baby." And when I paused to look I could hear the distant locusty chitter and screech of the whole community.

It grew louder, and then we were there.

"This is our nest," Geronimo declaimed proudly. "You are welcome, Barrydihoa. Here, they wish to offer you food."

It seemed they had expected us. Fifteen or twenty of them came crowding around us, mostly three- and four-star leps, stroking my arms with their little hands, smelling like a lawn after mowing on a rainy day. And they did offer food.

It wasn't exactly any kind of food that I wanted to eat. It wasn't lep food, though. It was worse. It was human food. At least it once had been: a soggy loaf of ancient bread, no doubt picked out of the kitchen garbage in town, and a brick of stone-hard goat cheese with bright green-and-orange mold all along one side, I assumed from the same place. I declined with thanks, for both of us, though they hadn't made the offer to Theophan. Evidently they were willing to tolerate the fact that she had come along, but just barely; she remained a nonperson. None of them said a word to her.

"I shall return with Merlin," Geronimo announced, and had slithered away before I could ask him who Merlin was. I didn't have time to worry about it; I was busy trying to take everything in.

I don't know what I had expected the lep nest to be like: A village of wattled huts? A little New England town with a church and a factory and homes with gardens around them? A hive? A giant termite mound?

I'd certainly expected a visible *community* of some sort. What I had not expected was that the "nests" were no more than an arbitrary hectare or two of groves and crops and burrows.

See, there's another big difference between us. Human beings build towns. That's because humans are used to having community projects— places to work or pray or study or to buy and sell things—and they need to cluster around those projects. The only thing leps have to cluster around is themselves. I suppose you people wouldn't bother to live in groups at all except for the fact that you like each other's company.

Well, you know all that.

You also know that that was the occasion when I met Garibaldi and Jefferson and Confucius and eight or nine other leps, fourth and fifth instars mostly—the whole English-speaking population of the community, I guess, or at least all the English-speaking ones who happened to be present in the nests at that time. Well, you know who I met as well as I do, Merlin, because I'm sure you haven't forgotten that one of the ones I met was you.

21

*I*S it then correct to state that the person of the third instar whom you call "Geronimo" did not inform you that we had proposed to him that you be brought here?

He never said a word. I don't suppose he thought it was necessary. It wasn't. Sour as I felt that day, there wasn't a chance in hell that I would have turned the invitation down, whoever it came from. I knew other human beings had visited your nests before me, Merlin, but I hadn't. I wanted to see for myself.

I hope you won't take it the wrong way, but I have to say that you didn't impress me much on that first meeting, Merlin. That wasn't Geronimo's fault. He was shrilling in my ear that you were very important to him, but all I saw was that you looked pretty funny, and a little pitiful, with your withered left arm and your one cocked eye. I didn't pay a lot of attention to you, though, and you didn't say much. You spent your time just watching—and mostly, I thought, very carefully watching Theophan, although you didn't speak to her, any more than any other lep did.

Theophan wasn't speaking, either. She just sat herself down on a nearly dry log, breaking off the moldier parts of a hunk of that cheese and nibbling at the bits underneath, both watching everything that was happening and looking forlorn and furious at being neglected.

* * *

For a while there this new experience was so exciting that I almost forgot to be sour. Not for long, though. I began to find it hard to keep interested, in spite of all your people could do to entertain me. I did my best to keep the conversation with them going—questions about all the things Geronimo had been asking me about all the time, about how I liked Pava, about what I thought the future held. It wasn't easy, though.

I suppose I was a bit of a disappointment to you people. I was to myself. I blamed it on the fact that I was physically tired from all that slippery mountain climbing, but there was more to it than that. I just felt, well, *gray*.

You'd think I would have recognized depression sooner than I did. I'd had the practice, after all.

To be fair to myself, I have to say that I didn't have the leisure to spend my time analyzing what was going on in my head. The circumstances kept me too busy. I was confused by all you odd creatures talking to me at once—"Is it true you did not intend to come here, Barrydihoa?" and "Will you mate soon, Barrydihoa?" and "Why are you not eating the food we have given you, Barrydihoa? Should we pick some fruits for you?" I was trying to answer, as much as I could answer; and I was also aware of the little distracting worries about whether Theophan and I could find our way back to the car when we wanted to go, and about how tough the hike back to it would be. I even felt a little concern, now and then, about how Theophan felt about being ignored.

Then most of the random questioning dried up, and I noticed that more and more of the leps, even more the senior fourth- and fifth-instar ones, were turning their big eyes expectantly on you.

When they were silent you studied me for a moment, scratching your withered arm with the good one. Then you said, "Is the third-instar person called Geronimo your true friend, Barrydihoa?"

That's the kind of question that I find embarrassing, especially with Geronimo shrunken down on the ground by my side, hissing softly to himself as he listened in. I tried to pull myself together to give an honest answer. I said, "I want to be Geronimo's true friend, anyway. I hope he feels the same about me."

"Do friends force friends to do things they do not wish to do, against their will?"

"Well, no. Of course not." It wasn't a question I had expected.

Besides, I hadn't really thought about that very much, and I didn't know where you were going.

But that turned out to be nowhere. That was the moment when, without warning, all you leps began to hiss and whistle softly at each other.

I could see something had gone wrong. Did you have some advance warning of what was about to happen? I didn't know. All I knew was that abruptly you shrank down to collapsed size and stretch-slipped away without another word, and all the other leps began to leave us, too.

I couldn't tell what was going on, but I had the feeling you get at a party when the hostess yawns and looks at her watch. I started to say to Theophan, "Well, I guess it's getting pretty late—"

Then it happened.

I suddenly felt as though I had tripped over something in my path. That couldn't be right. I knew that; I'd been standing still at the time and there was nothing for me to trip over. But I felt myself lurching and had to throw out a hand to grab the shoulder of Theophan, sitting on a tree trunk beside me, to keep from falling.

Then I saw that, overhead, the tree tops had all suddenly whipped over to one side. Before they came back there was a chorus of shrilling yelps from all the leps around, the ones in sight and the scores more that were hidden behind the shrubs. And Theophan, staggering to her feet to clutch at me for support, shouted, "Oh, shit, Barry! This time it's a goddamn *big* one!"

U p until that moment I had assumed that I knew what an earthquake was like. Why wouldn't I? I had had time to get used to the plentiful little temblors that came every day or so and shook dust out of the buildings and sometimes dropped a tree across a road.

I was wrong about that, though. I didn't have a *clue* what an earthquake was really like. When it happened it was immensely bigger and slower and worse than I had ever imagined. The ground rippled under me. The trees rippled overhead. I felt seasick, and then I just felt scared. There was a horrible unprecedented grinding, roaring sound from far away . . . and a horrible unexpected sudden mist of water vapor or dust or something that sprang up along invisible lines in the ground.

I had never seen anything like it before. I don't much want to again, either.

The worst part was that I couldn't stand up. I fell to my knees. Would have stayed there, too, but the leps wouldn't let me. Geronimo suddenly appeared on one side, and the lep named Saint John on the other. They grabbed me, shrilling at me, ordering me away from the bigger trees; one huge tree had already toppled over, pulling up a ragged globe of roots. Theophan crawled after me on her knees—unhelped.

Apart from making sure of my own safety, the leps didn't seem really bothered by the quake at all. I suppose earthquakes were no big news to them. Did them no particular harm, either—at least, not when they didn't get that rampaging flood that had drowned out their nests that other time—because they didn't have things like buildings to fall on them, or bridges to crash or gas mains to fracture and burn. Once they were away from under the biggest trees they could simply ride it out.

Which was all Theophan and I could do, for that matter.

The shaking and twitching seemed to go on forever—Theophan later showed me the seismograph chart and clocked it at nine minutes, a *long* one as well as a big one—7.6 on the Richter scale—and then when it stopped, it just stopped. All at once. It was over.

It might never have happened at all, except that the effects were visible. Some of the trees were bent at a funny angle. The dust was still settling. Some of the branches were still waving about. That was all. The sun was shining. A couple of leps were placidly munching thick leaves from some of their plants, and Theophan said, sounding scared and dismal, "We better get back to Freehold, Barry. If we can."

I stared at her. "What do you mean, if we can? Freehold's kilometers from here!"

"But it's a lot closer to the fault by the dam, and those are the faults that I think are coupled. Come on."

Geronimo conveyed us back to the car—a good thing; we never would have found it without him—but it was hard travel. It wasn't helped by Theophan's obvious worry about what we might find when we got back to Freehold. Her worry made me worry too.

The car was still upright when we got to it. That was one piece of luck. Even better, we found that nothing had fallen across the homebound path that the car's enormous wheels couldn't jolt right over. And when we crossed the ford, it was almost dry.

That looked like good news to me, until Theophan explained that it wasn't at all. "All that means is that a rockfall has dammed the river somewhere upstream. But it isn't going to stay dammed."

"Then what?"

She didn't answer, just shook her head. I figured it out for myself: When the dam broke through, the penned waters would come roaring down. I hoped there was nothing important that would be in their way.

The river stayed dammed long enough for us to get across almost dry, though, and then we were climbing the hill road to Freehold.

The town had taken its own hit. It appeared that Theophan had been quite right about the coupling of faults. The fault up past the old dam had let go an hour after the one in the Rockies—up in the hills we hadn't even felt it, being busy trying to slide down a mountainside at the time. Though the two epicenters were many kilometers apart, the town had been rocked by both quakes. Now the sagging roof of the town hall was rakishly down on the ground on the side facing the street, some windows had splintered, goods had been pitched off the shelves in the storehouse.

But no one had been seriously hurt. It wasn't a calamity. It was just a damn nuisance, and it all seemed very depressing to me.

See, this is where we intermittent nut-cases have a problem. It's hard for us to distinguish our perceptions from objective reality. The objective reality of the earthquake wasn't terribly bad. There was a lot of cleanup work to do around the town, yes. There were also several dozen cases of minor cuts and sprains to keep Dr. Billygoat busy. And when, two days later, that rockfall dam did finally give way again, the resulting flood of the river washed out ten hectares of riverbank crops and even did damage to the foundations of the hydrogen plant by the landing strip. Troublesome, but not really serious, although there was going to be a lot of hard repair work ahead.

But the whole thing laid me low. I didn't feel up to dealing with any of it. Depression hit hard, and what I wanted to do, most of the time, was sleep.

It took me three days before it occurred to me that things weren't really so objectively bad that I should be moping around like that, and another day before I could work up the ambition to decide that maybe all this depression had more to do with what was happening inside me than with the quake itself, and to go and see the doctor.

When I showed up, Dr. Billygoat's wife-nurse Nanny wasn't particularly happy to see me, either. Bill was really busy, she said; all those cuts and scrapes had put him way behind in his real work. When she finally admitted that I probably came under the head of real work after all and let me in, Billy seemed less happy still.

"Oh, right, yes, I know why you're here, di Hoa. I've been working on your case. But look at this place!" he grumbled. "It's just one damn thing after another! Where the hell am I going to get another titrator?" I could see what he meant. Some of his stuff had fallen, too, and he was still busily trying to figure out what all the damage was.

But when he got his mind focused on me he allowed that, well, yes, he had turned up a couple things he could try on me. No, not a long-term implant, for God's sake. We weren't anywhere near that. But he'd put together a menu of a couple of recombinants that should be some use, maybe. Worth trying, anyway.

So it was back to the needle system, and he gave me the first of a series of shots.

They hurt like hell. They didn't work, either.

The first one gave me diarrhea—not a good thing to have when you don't have indoor plumbing—and the second gave me a fever that had me bleary and confused one whole day until Dr. Billygoat decided against a second shot of that particular witches' brew and gave me something to bring the temperature down.

I could stand all that. What I couldn't stand was the conviction, slowly strengthening in my mind, that this bastardly imitation of a real doctor was shooting in the dark. He didn't know what I needed. If he did know, he didn't have it to give me. And the more I thought about it, the more furious I got.

The depression was going away; I was getting into the mild precursors of the manic state.

I was not an easy person to be around those days. I was mad all the time. I cursed Jacky Schottke for snoring when I was trying to sleep. I cursed Theophan for letting the quake hit us unwarned. I cursed the day I'd let Rannulf shanghai me; I cursed Rannulf himself; I cursed—well, almost cursed, but not quite—I came within a hairsbreadth of even cursing my lost, loved, dear Alma because she had provided the temptation that had made Rannulf do what he did. I cursed Captain Tscharka for flying the ship that took me so far away from where I needed to be, and cursed him again for taking off with the shuttle when I needed it to get something done. I cursed the factory for not working better, I cursed the whole idea of interstellar colonization—why did anybody ever start this stupid Delta Pavonis project in the first place?

I was in a conspicuously bad mood, and I didn't care who knew it.

I should have been sent to my room. Maybe I should have been sent to a room with padded walls. Any way you looked at it, I was pretty close to going really *mad*.

22

WAS this, then, the onset of your aberration?

It sure was, Merlin. Smart of you to recognize it, considering that I didn't see it myself at the time. Of course, you have a big advantage over me now. You know what came next.

If what you have previously described is understood, presumably you would then have been entering your depressive phase. Is that correct?

Well, no. Or yes and no. I wasn't a predictable textbook case anymore, you see. Maybe it had something to do with metabolic changes from being frozen. More likely all the garbage Dr. Billygoat had been pouring into my blood had screwed my cycle up.

I was more manic than depressive just then, and highly irritable. What I actually did for a day or two was snap everybody's head off, Billygoat's included. I must have been a real pain in the ass, though I didn't remember very well everything I did afterward. In self-defense Billy gave me some Dr. Feelgood pills to take.

They worked very effectively. They did more than that; they mellowed my mood so much that I must have been sickening. I went around apologizing to everybody for my previous bad attitude. I started with Jacky Schottke, who had suffered the worst of my temper because, unluckily for him, I was living in his apartment. Then I apologized to Theophan, whom I vaguely remembered giving a browbeating over the fact that Freehold was sited in a fault zone when there were low-risk areas within a few hundred kilometers. Then I even apologized to Geronimo. Yes, Geronimo. I was so full of that mixture of leftover rage and chemically induced sweetness and light that, after the lep and I had spent a sweaty hour tossing a flying rat back and forth—I was trying to make it up to him—I said remorsefully, "Oh, hell, Geronimo. I'm sorry about all that. Will you forgive me?"

He reared back to stare at me, the rat clutched in one little hand. "Have you done something improper?" he asked.

"Of course I have. I've been giving you a hard time, and I had no right do that—especially after you took us to your nests. That was kind of you. I hope I didn't disappoint you."

"No person was disappointed."

"Well, I hope not. I'd like to go back again sometime, and anyway I shouldn't have been on your case the last few days. You didn't deserve it. I was just in a hell of a foul mood."

"I do not understand 'hell of a foul mood,' Barrydihoa."

"Well—mean-tempered, don't you know? I mean, acting as though I just couldn't stand having you around. The same way you people treat Theophan."

He worked his mouthpart thoughtfully, as though chewing that over. At last he declared, "The cases are not the same. The reason we do not wish friendship with Theophansperlie is not because of 'hell of a foul mood.' It is because Theophansperlie was implicated in causing death to some and injury to many, even serious injury, as with Merlin."

I was all set to tell him all over again that nothing that Theophan did could actually *cause* earthquakes, but the last thing he said sidetracked me. "What do you mean, with Merlin?"

"You saw Merlin for yourself, did you not? His injuries were quite serious and long-lasting. He was unfortunate enough to be in transition state when the quake came, causing the floods. Merlin was not then ready to emerge. He should have remained in his cocoon for days more; but the floods made that impossible since he would have drowned. He had to be opened untimely and so did not have sufficient cocooning to complete his metamorphosis to the fifth instar."

"I didn't know," I said humbly—humility was big with me just then. I tried to make him understand. "All right. That's a pity. One person got hurt—"

"It was not one person only. Others were also harmed, some even more severely. Some died." He raised himself up, his great blotchy eyes peering into mine. "I name Merlin in particular because Merlin is my mentor. He taught me to speak your language and much else. I value Merlin very much."

"Oh," I said, and didn't know what to say after that. It had never occurred to me that there were special relationships among leps; if I had thought about it at all, which I don't suppose I ever had, I guess I would have thought that leps were all interchangeable units, like potato bugs in a field. I settled for, "Well, I'm sorry about that, but you're still all wet about Theophan."

"I do not understand 'all wet,' either. Barrydihoa? This game cannot continue, as I observe this flying rat has died through overuse. Can we not therefore go inside and play cards now?"

We didn't do that, though, in spite of the fact that after a moment he remembered to add, "Please." I was too restless to sit at a card table. I wanted action. I was hyper as hell.

I realize now that I was going into a different part of the manic phase. My mind was going all the time, churning up lists of things that really ought to be done, and I had this burning urge to see them accomplished. All the solutions to all the problems were suddenly crystal-clear to me.

If I'd been thinking clearly I would have known what was going on. I should have remembered that I'd had precisely that same churning, driving, hurry-up feeling before, way back on Earth when I first got sick.

Matthew was tiny then, but his arrival had been the one small straw that had made our old apartment too small. Even with the baby, Gina and I still considered ourselves more or less newlyweds, and so after he was born we bought ourselves a newlyweds' kind of home. It was a sixty-year-old fixer-upper condo on the thirty-first floor over an old shopping mall. The previous owners hadn't taken care of it—that's why it was cheap enough for us to afford—and I took getting it into shape as a personal challenge. The climate system was feeble, so I installed new thermostatic air pumps over all the registers, with self-contained humidifiers and filters; we could have any air we wanted in any room. The optical cables had dirt in their junctions, so I pulled them all out and replaced them with multistrand film—way more capacity than any private home ever needed; we could have run half the machines of the Census Bureau off our power system.

All of that was reasonably sensible behavior, if a little over-enthusiastic. Even Gina thought so. She cheered me on at first, because naturally she wanted our new house to be perfect, too. She began to get edgy, though, when she came home from her job one night and found Matthew cooing in his bassinet on the kitchen table, surrounded by forty liters of chili that I'd cooked up that afternoon.

It all seemed logical to me at the time, of course. I tried to explain to her that it made no sense to cook one meal's worth at a time, when we had plenty of freezer capacity. Why, I told her, we could eat chili from that batch every Thursday for the next six months.

I don't know if I convinced her. I do know what happened a couple of hours later, after she'd gone to bed. That was when I found myself standing over Matthew's crib with the butcher knife in my hand.

I don't know what I had planned to do. I only knew, from the way Gina screamed when she saw me, that something had gone wrong; and that's when I finally got taken in for medical help.

Of course, things were different now. That was Earth. This was Pava. There were big differences between them. But the biggest difference was that when I went for help on Earth the doctors there had had help to give me.

Dr. Billygoat did not. He told me that himself after I crashed.

I woke up out of a long, leaden sleep to find the doctor bent over me, looking both worried and exasperated. "What's going on now?" he asked. "Is your depressive phase starting already?"

It was, of course—brought on early by the drugs, unpredictable now because of the drugs. I didn't answer him. If I had been my normal self I would have had some smart-ass answer for him, starting with the thesis that he was the doctor, after all, so why was he asking me the questions? I didn't have those resources. I was barely able to register the fact that I was in my own bed. I was really *down*.

He was shaking his head. "Fascinating," he said, but not in any admiring way. "You go so fast from one to the other. Yesterday you were Mr. Speedy Fix-it, running around town and telling everybody how to do everything. Do you remember any of that? Do you even remember trying to call Captain Tscharka and order him to come back?"

I blinked at him. I didn't remember. Oh, I hadn't *forgotten*, exactly, either. The memories were there, if I had been willing to try to retrieve them; I had some faint recollection of a radio conversation with Jillen Iglesias, and her hanging up on me. I just didn't have the ambition to reach into the memory stores of my mind and pull out very many of those recollections.

"Making Theophan hunt through her datastore until the two of you located an earthquake-shadow place on the coast? Yelling at Jimmy Queng because that site was right on the equator, so if the first settlers had sited Freehold there, someday we could even have a skyhook in our backyard?"

I didn't answer. He sighed. "Barry," he said, "this just isn't working out. I hate to give up on some kind of a cure for you, but I don't see that I have a choice."

Then he brightened. "Fortunately now we've got the solution to your problem—oh, not a cure, but the next best thing, and it's right at hand. *Buccaneer* has called in. They're decelerating. They'll be here in a few days. So we can stick you in their freezer, and let somebody back home fix you up when you get there."

That made me—or almost made me—answer. I think all it came down to was a little beetling of my brows and a faint shake of my head, but I meant it for a "no" and Billygoat understood it that way. "What's the matter? Didn't you say you were going to go back first chance you got, anyway?"

I didn't answer that, because answering was too hard for me, but I knew what the answer would have been.

It was no.

I seemed to have changed my mind about that. Depressed as I was, I knew that much. I didn't actually want to go back anymore. Not to Earth. Not even to the Moon.

It was a definite decision, though not a particularly rational one. I hadn't come to it after careful weighing of the facts. I knew that the rational factors all pointed the other way, the biggest one being that on Earth I could get help; here I couldn't.

But I didn't want to leave Pava, and the only reason was just that, somewhere along the line, I had decided that I wanted to stay there. Forever. For better or for worse. For the rest of my life.

23

YOUR statements do not seem complete at this point, Barrydihoa. You are omitting much.

Well, sure I am. I can't help it. I already told you—I was beginning those damned mood swings; I was forgetting a lot; I was really getting pretty mixed up, and I'm afraid it'll get worse before it gets better. Is there some particular part you want to know about?

Yes: the reasons for your actions at this point. They are not clear. You would have benefited by returning to your own planet, yet you chose to stay here. Why?

I just told you that, too, Merlin. Weren't you listening? I wanted to stay on Pava because it was the only game left in town for me, and anyway I just wanted to be part of making this colony *work*. Pava had everything it needed to be a fine place for human beings to live if it were developed properly, and I saw a chance to be part of building it.

Now you have touched on a more important question, and one that concerns us greatly. In just what ways do you believe our planet should be "developed"? To be more explicit, since your language contains ambiguities, it is to be understood that the "you" we are asking about refers not simply to the singular Barrydihoa, "you" alone, but to all you human beings who have come to live on our planet. What are your collective intentions for Pava?

Well, now, that's the really tough question, isn't it?

I'm not exactly sure how to answer it. Believe me, Merlin, I would do that in a hot minute if I could. Honest to God I would.

(Don't catch me up on that "honest to God," because that's just another little peculiarity of our language. When I say "honest to God" it does not imply that I have the religious conviction that a supernatural supreme being is listening to what I say and will do me some serious harm if I then lie. The phrase is just a sort of linguistic intensifier. What it means is that I really want you to believe that what I have just said is a statement of exact truth.)

Anyway, I just can't promise what the human race will do here on Pava. I know what we did on Earth. I hope we'll have enough sense to do better here, so that you won't regret our coming.

But that's only what I *hope*. I wish I could say I was sure, but I don't want to lie to you. Honest to God.

After I crashed, I slept for a long time—a *very* long time.

It is my suspicion that that pill-pushing, incompetent dentist-doctor Billygoat helped that process along. I know he was there at my bedside sometimes, to check up on me, because I remember seeing him there. I also know that if I had been in his position I'm pretty sure I would have sneaked in a little shot of sleepytime medicine to keep me from being a nuisance, whether that was approved by the Hippocratic oath or not. I don't doubt Billy had the same idea.

I did wake up now and then, briefly and blurrily. Once Jacky Schottke was sitting there to watch over me; I remember him helping me down the stairs and out to the toilet—and back to bed after that, too, I guess, though I don't remember that part at all. Another time it was the widow lady from downstairs, Becky Khaim-Novello. She was standing by the window, glaring sullenly out at the rain. When she noticed I was awake she groaned. "I guess you've got to go to the goddamn john again," she said. (That's not a religious reference either, but never mind.) She wasn't a bit flirtatious this time. She sounded pretty glum about the whole thing, and when she'd escorted me downstairs she waited impatiently outside the door, and when I came out again she said ungraciously, "I suppose you're going to want me to dig up some food for you now. It beats me why they can't get some damn slug to do this sort of crap."

I didn't comment on the fact that she was a lot less ladylike than before. I just told her I wasn't hungry. Then, as I was getting back into bed, I remembered to ask, "Isn't Geronimo here?"

"Your pet worm? Don't ask me. You never can find the stupid things when you want them." And she kept on complaining about the work she had to do, and why the hell they had insisted she take time off from her other jobs just to keep an eye on me, for God's sake, and how nobody would give her any help. I don't know how long her monologue lasted. I fell asleep again while it was still going on, and was glad enough to do it.

When I woke up again Dr. Billygoat was beside me, holding his sensor thing against my throat. "Is Geronimo around?" I asked. I was still pretty fuzzy, and I guess I'd been dreaming about him.

"If you're talking about your lep," Billy said, "you can forget him. You won't be seeing him for a while." Billy was giving me a good deal less than half his attention, being busy studying his sensor and making notes on a pocket screen. I stretched and sat up and began to feel a little more alert. That had been a silly question. Of course Geronimo wouldn't be there, I told myself. He'd told me that it was time for his change. He was probably rolled up in his cocoon, getting ready for his next instar. Although I still hadn't got all my marbles rolling in the same direction, I definitely wished Geronimo were there. I missed his company. It was about the only thing I seemed to care much about, actually.

Maybe "care" is too strong a word. Nothing I felt then was a strong emotion, just a little colorless imitation of a real feeling. First, I felt a little pale gratitude that I had not, after all, crashed to the very bottom of my cycle—not to the sad, sick, foul-yourself-with-your-own-excrement point of despairing catatonia that I'd seen in my days at the clinic, for sure. On the other hand, second, I had a little pale foreboding that dampened any possible feeling of pleasure, because I was beginning to realize that that hopelessly terminal, all-the-way-to-the-absolute-bottom crash had become a very real possibility for me. In fact, it was surely going to happen to me, more likely sooner than later, unless something came along to change it, and nothing of that kind was in sight.

Still, I was waking up fast. Here, again, I have no doubt my speedy wake-up was helped along by something Dr. Billygoat had slipped into my bloodstream while I slept. He put the sensor away and looked at me hopefully. "How are you feeling? Do you feel up to doing a little work?"

I blinked at him. "What kind of work?"

"Any kind. All kinds. Think you could handle it?"

He was not making himself very clear, but when I thought it over I nodded. "I guess so. Sure."

"Good. We need all the help we can get. I guess you wouldn't know because you've been out of it, but the fucking leps have gone on strike."

That was startling enough to penetrate my haze. Naturally I immediately asked questions, but Billygoat didn't want to take the time to discuss it with me. "I'm too busy to chat with you now. So pay attention. What I want you to do is get yourself cleaned up and come over to my office; I've got some stuff there for you to take. I think it might help you—hope so, anyway. Nanny'll probably tell you all about the leps then. Now I've got to get out of here."

Just getting up and dressed was a harder job than I wanted, but I managed it. By the time I was on the street I could see that things had changed. It was true; not a single lep was in sight anywhere. The town seemed oddly empty, as a matter of fact. I saw a couple of teenagers resentfully dragging a cart of kitchen waste to the composting dump—the kind of work leps usually did—and when I asked them they confirmed it.

"Sure, Mr. di Hoa, the leps just went away," the older girl said. "Haven't seen any since day before yesterday. Why did they do it? I don't know why. All I know is there's no school and a lot of the grown-ups are off gathering fuel and tending the farms, and we've got to do this junk."

"The leps didn't say anything before they left?"

"Not to me, anyway. Excuse us, will you? We have to get this cart back to the kitchen before Mr. Queng gets sore at us."

When I got to the doctor's office Nanny Goethe didn't have anything useful to add to that, except that it was a damned inconvenience, having to do all this extra work when they were so busy anyway. She knocked on the wall to summon her husband and began counting pills out of two jars.

In a moment Billy appeared at the door, holding a spraydermic. "Roll up your sleeve, will you? Okay. This is just a little stimulant, to supplement—to help you out. I want you to have these pills Nan's getting ready for you. You're about as stable as I can get you right now, but who knows? So if you feel yourself getting spacey, take a red one; if you're depressed, one of the white ones. They'll pick you up."

There were three of each. As I was putting them away he said, "And if you find yourself getting *really* screwed up, come back here and let me look at you, but try not to do that unless you have to, okay? Oh, and you better go see Jimmy Queng, he'll have a work assignment for you. See you later. . . . And, Nan? Leave what you're doing for a minute; I need a little help in the office."

They left me there alone.

I thought for a moment, and then I didn't have to think anymore. I slipped quickly over behind Nanny Goethe's desk and helped myself to a couple dozen more of the white pills.

All right, maybe that wasn't the smartest thing to do. Even a doctor as marginally qualified as Bill Goethe is still the doctor, and I've always accepted the rule that you'd better do what the doctor tells you. Usually, anyway. But I wanted those uppers.

Don't think we're talking about some kind of pitiful drug addiction here. It wasn't anything like that. It was nothing more than that I just hated not being hyper anymore. I *liked* having that unbeatable vigor that came with the manic phase. When I'm going hyper I have all the energy in the world. I grasp things quickly. I see instant solutions to any problem around. I'm fast as greased lightning, and I don't get tired. It's a remarkably satisfying way to be, actually.

I'm not the only one to feel that way. People have always treasured that state. It's a historical fact that over the years many, many millions of human beings have spent all the money they could get their hands on, and all the health they had, on such ultimately destructive things as alcohol and alkaloids, just so they could get that feeling, or even just the illusion of it, even for just a moment. It's craziness, all right, but while you have it it feels so *fine*. You can't beat that feeling . . . until you crash.

Jimmy Queng wasn't around, but Dabney Albright was straw-bossing a gang unloading supplies into the kitchen storage. No, he didn't know where the leps had gone. "They got pissed off about something, I guess. Anyway, we're in the deep shit here. You up to a little work? All right, give us a hand getting this stuff stored and then you and Hillary here can go down to the landing strip for another load."

So that was the first I knew that Captain Tscharka had let the shuttle come back.

On the ride down I tried to find out more from the driver—that was

Hillary Tetsui; she'd come out with me on *Corsair*, though I'd hardly seen her since. There wasn't much to find out. Yes, because of the emergency Captain Tscharka had agreed to send down food out of the ship's supplies, but he himself was still up there. The leps? No, she didn't know any more than I did, but it was a total nuisance; she was supposed to be a *cook*, not a longshoreman. And when I tentatively asked her if she had any idea about whether I'd be able to get a ride up to the factory orbiter, seeing as the shuttle was right there on the surface now, she just shook her head.

So did Jillen Iglesias. Jillen was the one who'd brought the shuttle down, and she and two others were shifting its cargo to the ground when we got to the strip—mostly food. There was a lot of it, bags of flour, cartons of cuts of meat in their sterile pouches, concentrated soups and stews.

Jillen seemed preoccupied, as though she were worrying about something, but she managed to give me a smile—until I asked her the question. "Oh, I don't think there's time to take you to the factory right now, Barry," she said. "Nobody seems to know how long the leps will stay away, so we've all just got to pitch in to keep things going. Are you all right? I heard you've been sick."

"I'm fine," I said. I was, too, because I'd popped an extra one of the white ones on the way down.

"Well," she said, "when I get back to the ship I'll ask the captain what he thinks about getting you to the factory—when things ease up, I mean." But she didn't sound hopeful, and neither was I.

Things had changed while I was out of it. I wasn't the great white hope of the Pava colony any longer. Public opinion had shifted. The mood of the moment wasn't concerned with building for a wonderful future anymore; it was anger at the leps for deserting us without warning.

I don't suppose I'd fully realized until that time just how dependent we were on lep helpers. The leps were there; they helped out; they always had. They were a natural resource, like the rain and the sushi bushes. When they were gone it was a totally unexpected blow, and a serious one.

As I shifted cargo and pondered over this, it seemed to me that I could perhaps be of great use to the community there, too. I was thinking of Geronimo. Geronimo wasn't just my helper when there was drudge work to do, he was my *friend*. I felt that if I could just have a word with Geronimo, perhaps the whole thing could be straightened out somehow.

I didn't kid myself that that would be easy, maybe not even possible. Geronimo might well be still in his transition cocoon; I knew that, and then of course there would be no way to talk to him. But I kept thinking that maybe, if I just went up to the nest and asked around, *somebody* would talk to me.

The problem was that I had no real idea of where the nest was, in spite of having been there once, and if anyone else did they wouldn't tell me. Jimmy Queng flatly forbade me to even think about it. "We can't spare anybody for harebrained roaming around the hills. You'd better go up and help cut brush for the power plant."

I tried to be agreeable. "Then, listen, I've been thinking. As long as we've got the shuttle in service again, what about my making a quick trip up to the factory, the way we talked about?"

He groaned. "Look," he said patiently, "maybe we can start thinking about crap like that in a week or so. *Buccaneer*'s reported in; they're in full deceleration and they'll be in parking orbit by then. With any luck at all maybe they'll have brought us some extra help for the work that needs doing. Talk to me then. Now there's a boat going upstream to the woodcutters in twenty minutes or so. Be on it. You hear?"

"All right," I said—not because I was giving up on my idea—just trying to be agreeable.

At least twenty minutes meant I had time to go back to the apartment and pick up a couple of changes of clothes. I popped another pill on the way, for extra energy, and got to the boat just as they were beginning to get irritated about waiting for me.

I sat down next to Madeleine Hartly's great-granddaughter, Debbie. The weather had turned decent, and actually the boat ride up to the fuel-cutting area was pleasant enough. "At least we've got a nice day for it," I said to her sociably. "How's Madeleine bearing up?"

She looked startled. "You haven't heard?"

"Heard what?" The expression on her face was making me feel edgy. But I wasn't prepared for what she said.

"She died, Barry. She was out gathering fruit, all by herself, and she must have fallen. When they found her she had a broken ankle and pneumonia, and she died before they could get her to the doctor."

I was cutting fuel for two days before the boat came back with fresh supplies. I wasn't enjoying it, either. I kept going, with the help of some of those little white pills now and then, but they certainly weren't the best two days of my life. There were a lot of reasons for that. I was mourning Madeleine. (And blaming the leps for her death—a little, anyway—if she'd had a lep with her at least he could have gone for help.) It began to rain again, which made the work twice as miserable, but we had to keep on cutting and bundling the fuel into rafts regardless. I was physically exhausted. I wanted to talk to Geronimo. I wanted—I wanted all kinds of things, but none of them were happening. It was only the pills that kept me going—kept me in high gear, really. Sometimes I wondered if I wasn't overdoing them a bit, because once in a while I could feel myself beginning to get sort of jittery.

It wasn't just me and the pills, though. When I tried talking to the others in the fuel-cutting gang, they weren't any too cheerful, either. Or forgiving. When I ventured the opinion that, really, we shouldn't be blaming the leps so much because they weren't *obliged* to do our scut work for us, I was drowned out by a chorus of denunciations. When I very tentatively mentioned that, on the other hand, if we'd gone ahead and got the factory working properly we wouldn't need to do so much dreary manual labor, they were positively insulting.

The glory days were over for me. The kindest word I heard was "crackpot."

Well, that's the way humans are. The way they are when they're in groups, anyway. Any single human being can be quite reasonable, at least most of the time, but when they're a pack they can't seem to hold more than one thought at a time in their minds, and the big thought in everybody's head just then was angry resentment.

The person who brought the boat up was Becky Khaim-Novello. As soon as we heard the whine of the hydrogen-fueled motor, we all dropped what we were doing and gathered hopefully at the riverbank. Our hopes weren't gratified. We could see long before she landed that she was alone in the boat. "Where's our relief?" somebody shouted, but all she gave back was a look of dislike—maybe more for me than for the others, because I expect she was remembering our little disagreements, but with plenty for everybody.

She didn't waste any time trying to be conciliatory about it, either. She kicked one of the crates of food. "This is all there is," she said flatly. "If you want it, start unloading, and, no, there's nobody coming up to take over for you."

That just about doubled the complaining, and she doubled her glare at us. "You think I like this goddamn job? You've got complaints, you take them to Jimmy Queng. And, oh," she said, remembering, "he gave me a message for you. He says for Christ's sake, you guys, get your asses in gear, the power plant needs more fuel."

"Then he should send us more people!" someone called. She didn't even answer that. She was in a worse mood even than we were, I thought. She refused to talk anymore. As soon as the supplies were unloaded she cast off and putt-putted away without another word. She seemed to be brooding about something. Well, that didn't surprise me; she wasn't the only one, and if there was something special that was troubling her I didn't know what it was . . . then.

When it was too dark to work anymore we ate and climbed painfully into our sleeping bags, and I sneaked another white pill.

I know that wasn't too smart, even in itself. What I should have been doing was sleeping, and those pills wouldn't help that along. But I had other things on my mind. I lay there, wide-awake, staring up into the far hills to the general area where I thought the nest was; and after a while I couldn't stand it anymore, so I got up.

I was as quiet as I could be as I headed for the slit-trench latrine, in case anybody was wide-awake enough to ask me what I was doing. No one did, and when I got to the latrine area I just kept going.

Sure, it was a stupid idea. But it was the best idea I had, and I had to do *something*.

I don't know if I ever would have found the nest by myself. By the time I got to the slopes of those "Rockies," I was beginning to doubt it. I'd had to wade three streams and swim one. I was wet and my legs were sore, and I had about come to suspect that I might have bitten off more than I was going to be able to chew.

I thought about turning back.

The trouble with that was that I wasn't really sure how to get back to the fuel-cutting camp, either, and there wasn't anyone around to ask. I wasn't alone in the woods. I could hear distant whickerings and squeals from the local wildlife, but none I could identify, and none that sounded as if they would be of any help. I was on my own, and I was getting really tired. I reached in my pocket for another of those little white pills to start my motor spinning again.

There wasn't any. The pills were all gone. I'd taken the whole two dozen–odd.

It occurred to me that I probably hadn't been very smart about those pills. I probably wasn't being smart about this notion of going up to the lep nests by myself, either. But, since I seemed to have run out of smart ideas, I thought I might as well continue with a dumb one.

I kept on going.

I kept on for a long time—I don't know how long, but at some point along the way I happened to notice the sun was well up in the sky. What made me notice it was that the rain was over and it had become hot. I was sweating. I was beginning to feel really spacey, too. I felt as though I were being followed. I kept seeing little movements in the brush. I even thought I caught a glimpse of somebody, or something, slipping hurriedly out of sight.

What that something could have been I had no real idea. It crossed my mind that it might be something nasty, something like one of those ugly predators that were supposed to be almost, but not quite, extinct in these parts. I didn't let that stop me. I paused for a breather, leaning against a water tree, with my eyes half-closed. If something was hunting me, the best defense was a sudden attack, I told myself, and when I saw that movement again I jumped for it. Crashed into a sticky, prickly bush. Grabbed what was behind it.

It wasn't a killer snake or a dinowolf or any of the other unpleasant things I'd imagined. It was a lep.

The thing didn't want me holding on to it. It struggled energetically in my grasp. I'd never really felt what a lep was like until then—not slimy, as I'd sort of expected, and not cold either; it was like the skin of a pretty woman, kitten-soft and puppy-warm.

"Got you!" I shouted.

The lep stopped wriggling. He lay quiet for a moment, the giant, blotchy eyes turned on me. I'd seen him before somewhere, I thought, maybe around Freehold, maybe in the nests.

He made a hissing sound, as though he'd made up his mind to something. Then he said, "You are Barrydihoa. You are the friend of the person presently undergoing transformation, Geronimo."

I eased up on my grip. "I am," I agreed. "I just want to talk to you."

He stated, "I do not wish that."

"Come on, damn it! Please! I want to clear this problem up. Whatever's wrong, there must be something we can do to make it right."

He released himself from me and raised himself up, peering at me. "That is not desired."

"Do you desire that I die out here? Because I might. I'm going to keep on trying to find your nests, whether you help me or not!"

He pondered that for a moment, hissing to himself. Then he shrank down again and began to move away. "You may follow me," he said. "I will take you to our nests, where we will take advice."

And, as you know, that's what he did.

Here again, you're probably in a better position than I to remember what happened when I got there. By then I was really spaced out—with fatigue, sure, but also with the delayed effects of those two dozen little white pills. I remember seeing you, Merlin. I even remember talking to you. I remember pleading with you to call off the boycott so we could all be friends together again, and what you told me about what Becky Khaim-Novello had done, and how sadly you explained that there were things leps simply could not accept. But it's all really hazy, because I was. The last thing I remember was mentioning that I needed to lie down, please, for just a moment, and that was all I remembered at all clearly until I was back in Freehold with Dr. Billygoat bending over me.

I suppose some of you guys had somehow dragged me back to town; Billy said they'd found me snoring away in front of this office. "Jesus," he added, more wondering than angry, "you do come up with all different kinds of ways of screwing things up, don't you, Barry? Did it ever occur to you that you're a lot more trouble than you're worth?"

"But the problem was all Becky Khaim-Novello's fault," I told him. "She tried to make Saladin clean her apartment. Merlin told me so himself. That's why the leps are shunning us, because when he wouldn't do what she told him Becky picked up a stick and *hit* him."

"So what?"

"So we have to apologize to them! Make them understand we're not all like that!"

"Barry," Billy said, "listen closely to what I'm going to say to you now, okay? *I don't care.* Whatever Becky did, it's done, and we'll just have to live with it. Nobody wants you messing around with the leps and maybe just making things worse. I certainly don't want that, personally. All I really want is for you to take your problems somewhere else and get the hell out of my life for good. Please."

24

THAT is it, then, Barrydihoa. You said it for yourself. This Billygoethe person had no concern that the Beckykhaimnovello person had physically abused one of our people. This cannot be overlooked.

Oh, hell, Merlin, he didn't mean anything by it. It was me he was really pissed off at, not you guys.

It was not the Billygoethe person alone. Was it not then generally known that Beckykhaimnovello had transgressed against behavioral norms?

You bet it was. I told everybody that. I even told them about all the good things you'd done, like how some leps must have rigged up a travois or something to drag me back to Freehold, probably saving my life.

Was Beckykhaimnovello, then, in your term, "punished" for her behavior?

Well, no, I didn't say that.

I have to admit Becky wasn't exactly punished. Not then, anyway. I think she probably would have been, sooner or later. Somehow. But, as it turned out, that wasn't necessary.

Anyway, you have to realize that I was not considered a very reliable witness at the time and things were in crazy shape in Freehold. All sorts of things were going wrong. There were power cutbacks because there wasn't enough biofuel coming down to feed the generator; everybody was worried about what would happen to our crops without any lep

helpers; *Buccaneer* was coming close to its parking orbit and everybody
was excited about that; Friar Tuck was making things worse by going
around and telling all the Millenarists that he'd always known I was just
a troublemaker. People were beginning to feel a little bit ashamed that
they'd ever listened to me, and so naturally turned right to the other
side—there just was too much going on to worry about whether Becky
Khaim-Novello had lost her temper and whacked a lep.

Or to worry much about me, for that matter.

I can understand that. I must have struck most people as a thoroughly
unwanted nuisance. I don't blame them for what they did.

Billygoat may not have been much of a doctor, but he had some real
good fix-up drugs on his shelves. He gave me some shots and pills and
vitamins and tucked me in. After a good night's sleep I was ready for
action again. I thought so, anyway. Billygoat gave me a quick check
and said the same thing.

As a matter of fact, he used those exact words. "I think you're ready
for action again, Barry," he said, speaking fast and sounding rehearsed.
"And I've got good news for you. *Buccaneer*'s in full deceleration
mode. It'll be in low orbit in a couple of days. Then we'll be shipping
antimatter from both ships to the factory—as soon as it's ready to
receive—and we're going to send you up to the factory now to check
it out!"

I had no real reason to think he was lying to me, but alarm bells were
beginning to go off in my head. I said cautiously, "Really?"

"Absolutely! If you're up to it, I mean. How do you feel? Ready to
take off?"

"Ready and willing," I said, getting up. That was paying back a lie
with a lie, because by then I had no doubt that all Billygoat's good cheer
was fake.

What I didn't know yet was what was behind it, but the best way I
could see to find that out was to go along with him. I did. I observed
that Billygoat was nervous as he led me out to the waiting car, nervous
still, and uncommunicative as we drove down the hill and along the
river to the landing strip. The trip gave me plenty of time to try to guess
at what was going on, but time wasn't enough. What I needed was
facts, and I didn't have them. By the time we got to the strip I didn't
know any more than I had the minute after I woke up: Billygoat was

concealing something, I wasn't in any doubt of that, but I couldn't imagine what his secret was.

The shuttle was standing there on its stilty legs, Jillen Iglesias peering at me out of the doorway. Suspicious as I was, double-checking everything for signs of some kind of treachery, I noticed something about Jillen that also struck me as peculiar. Her face was drawn, as though she'd been crying. I was almost certain that was the case. Yet I couldn't see how that might connect with Billygoat's little deceptions.

On the other hand, what I thought did connect, Jacky Schottke, Theophan Sperlie and half a dozen other friends and acquaintances were standing around there to see me off.

Theophan was the first to come up to me. "Good luck, Barry," she said, and leaned forward to kiss me. Then the others lined up to wish me well.

That was where the connection was. I had the powerful feeling that this was not really a cheering-me-on send-off. What it felt like was a good-bye-forever, permanent farewell.

Jillen watched impatiently for a moment, but no more than that. When she had had enough of this sentimental display she leaned out of the door and yelled: "Speed it up, will you? We have to go within the next five minutes if I want to make rendezvous." And I finished saying my good-byes and climbed the little ladder to get on board, all my antennae still out and wiggling in the search for whatever was going on.

Jillen wasn't in a welcoming mood. She was businesslike and remote, but she allowed me to take the copilot seat when I asked. She didn't have any reason not to; there were only the two of us in the shuttle, after all. We strapped down and sealed up, and a moment later we were flattened against our seat backs with the initial burn.

Ten minutes later we were clear of the atmosphere and Jillen began making the burns for rendezvous as I watched the board over her shoulder . . . and then I was sure of the answer.

I waited for the current burn to stop. Then I turned to her and smiled. "Did you know I used to be a spotter-ship pilot in the Belt?" I asked her.

The startled look she gave me lasted only a fraction of a second, but it confirmed my suspicions. If she ever had known that, it had slipped her mind.

"So," I said, waving at the orbit solutions drawn on the guidance screen, "I can read a screen pretty well. We aren't really going to the factory this trip, are we? It doesn't look that way to me. Matter of fact, I kind of suspected that was the way it was all along because, you know, nobody said a word about taking tools along." I grinned at her. "I couldn't do much on the factory without tools, could I? Of course, there could be an explanation for all that. There could be plenty of tools at the factory itself, and everybody might've just assumed I'd find them when I got there—"

She had recovered herself by then. "Yes, actually that's the way it was—"

But I stopped her. "Don't bother," I said. "I told you, I can read a screen. You're not a bad pilot, and I can see that we're over a hundred degrees out of phase for a rendezvous with the factory orbiter. So that's not where we're going. On the other hand, it looks to me as though we're right on target for *Corsair*. So tell me, Jillen, is that what you've been crying about? Because this whole thing is just a trick to get me out of the way? So you can stick me back in the freezer so I'll quit being a nuisance?"

I think I must have sounded pretty smug and superior. The reason I think that is that's how I felt. I was patting myself on the back about my brilliant deductive analysis. I really thought I had it figured out.

Surprisingly, Jillen just gave me a cold look.

"Don't flatter yourself," she said. Her tone was as nasty as her expression, too. "I've got better things to cry about than you. No, you're wrong, di Hoa. I don't mean you're wrong about us going to *Corsair* first; no, that part is right enough. But the reason for that is just because Captain Tscharka wants to talk to you before you go to the factory—and, uh, make sure you know where to find those tools when you get there."

I scowled at her, trying to figure out if she was lying to me. Partly I was sure she was—if only because I was convinced Billygoat had been. But partly I thought she was telling the truth—anyway, *some* truth— and I couldn't decide which part was which.

While I was thinking it over, the cycling beep sounded, and ten seconds later the next burn came. I was a little out of practice; I let the sudden thrust distract me for a second—and so I almost missed it when, out of the corner of my eye, I saw that she was reaching down for something stuck in the seat pocket beside her.

Almost, but not quite. I was, remember, pretty fast. I had a grip on her wrist even before I recognized what the thing she was grabbing for was.

What Jillen had pulled out of its hiding place was a spraydermic. Intended, of course, to be used on me. She struggled, but I had no trouble taking it away from her.

I thought that might make her start crying again. Indeed she looked as though she might, for a moment, but then she shook her head. "Why do you want to make things worse than they are, Barry?" she asked plaintively. "I was just supposed to give you a little shot to put you to sleep for a while. They can't deal with your problems down there now. You must know that; you're a *nut*. You need to get to an Earthside clinic if you're ever going to get any real help—Dr. Goethe says so. It was his idea that we put you back in the freezer and take you home. For your own good."

That was another surprise. It sounded as though she meant what she was saying. I blinked at her, trying to figure out where I had gone wrong. "If you believe that, why were you crying?"

She gave me an angry look. "Look. I've got about a thousand things to cry about, and not one of them is any of your damn business, di Hoa."

"Maybe not, but, if I'm going into the freezer anyway, what difference does it make if you tell me a couple of them?"

"Go to hell," she said, and stared sulkily at the controls. I could see a fresh set of tears forming in the corners of her eyes and, after a moment, she crumpled.

"All right, damn you," she said. The language was still tough but the words were only words; the passion had gone out of her anger. "Since you want to know I'll tell you. Not that it's any of your business."

"Of course not, Jillen, if you say so. But please."

She glared at me, then said shakily, "The main reason I'm crying, if you must know, is because right now I just happen to be fucking *pregnant*."

25

*T*HIS *is not understood. The information that your female conspecific, Jilleniglesias, had conceived does not seem relevant. Did she not also reveal the nature of Garoldtscharka's intentions to you at that time?*

Oh, no, she certainly did not. Not then. Actually you can hardly say she ever revealed what Tscharka was up to at all; I had to figure most of it out for myself. On the way up we had nearly an hour before we finally docked with *Corsair*, but in all that time all she revealed—with some talk, and a lot of crying—was her personal problems with Captain Garold Tscharka.

Which were considerable.

It took me a while to get it all straight, but then it made sense. Jillen had simply made a tactical blunder with the man she loved. She'd deliberately got herself pregnant, in the expectation that Tscharka would come around and accept the fact—maybe even be as thrilled as she was about it—once he was aware it was a fact. She wasn't the first woman to make that mistake, and she wasn't the first to have it blow up in her face.

Tscharka hadn't clasped her lovingly in his arms when he heard the news. He had screamed at her. Sin piled on sin! How dare she add one more sinner to the sinning world? The only decent thing she could do now, he told her, was to have an abortion; and when she somehow found the strength to refuse, he got more furious still. The kindest things he said were that she was a heretic, a blasphemer and a disgrace, and physically repugnant to him for her foul sins.

I think she might have stood for anything else, but not the "physically repugnant" part.

I don't know how to harden my heart against a weeping woman, and I felt really sorry for this one. All I could think of to say was, "He isn't worth it, Jillen. Tscharka is not a good man."

That made her stiffen up and glare at me—momentarily—but then she slumped again. "Hell, di Hoa," she said, "I'm not sure I know what's good and what's bad anymore. It was all going to be good, you know. Garold promised that. Pava was going to be our sacred retreat from the evil world, where we would all be of the same faith, all repentant for our guilt in being alive. It didn't happen that way. When Garold got here and saw how the church had fallen apart while we were making the run to the Moon he was furious, but it was worse than just being mad. He was all broken up, too. I guess Pava just isn't a good place for a person to be very religious. . . ."

I didn't have any answer for that at the time except to pat her on the shoulder. But you know, now, thinking it over, I have an idea she might have been right about that. Sort of, anyway.

I don't mean that when human beings arrived on Pava they necessarily stopped believing in their gods—whoever their gods were, and assuming they had ever had any. They kept on going to their churches, no doubt of that.

But I think that was largely just a matter of habit. They had more immediately urgent things on their minds, like just staying alive. Getting into religious arguments wasn't high among their priorities . . . and, of course, there was the example of you people always before their eyes. You sowed doubt in a lot of previously unquestioning minds.

You see, you had a better deal than they did. You didn't have to take your heaven on faith. You didn't even have to earn it. For you heaven was just what inevitably happened as soon as you reached your sixth instar, whether you had done anything to deserve it or not.

I had plenty of time on the way up to decide what I had to do, and when we docked I made sure I was the first one out of the shuttle.

I kicked myself out into the open as fast as I could, ready for anything. What I was afraid of was that Tscharka would be right there waiting for me, and if he were I wanted to catch him off guard.

He wasn't. Nobody at all was in the control room. "Where's the captain?" I asked as Jillen pulled herself out after me.

She said somberly, "How would I know? At a guess, I would suppose he's down in the storage hold with Friar Tuck, shifting things around to make room for the antimatter from *Buccaneer*."

That was a brand-new surprise. I couldn't believe I'd heard her right. "Are you saying that they're going to transship all that antimatter into *Corsair* here? Why, for God's sake?"

She only shrugged. She was holding on to a clamp by a little wall locker, looking drained and miserable. I thought she still knew something she wasn't telling me, but I couldn't guess what. I looked around the control room suspiciously—

That was when I noticed that someone had taken the covers off the control panels.

That didn't make any sense, either. No one ever does that—well, except maybe when the ship's been brought in for a complete refit. Then they might do it for maintenance and inspection. Nobody has any need to do it in any other case, because there's never anything wrong with a ship's navigation programs. They are sealed in when the ship is built, with triple redundancy in the system. If anything should happen to the active circuit, which it practically never does, you would just cut in one of the standbys, and then replace the whole old one next time you were in port.

"What's going on here?" I asked, turning back to Jillen Iglesias.

She didn't answer that, because she had one more surprise for me.

This time she was holding something that, it seemed, she had just taken out of the opened locker behind her while I was looking away, and the thing she was holding was a gun.

A gun! It took me a moment to be sure that was what it was; I'd hardly ever seen one, except the harmless little toy ones they make for children to play with. Certainly I hadn't expected to see anything like it on Pava.

"Well," I said. I don't know whether Jillen noticed that my voice was unsteady, but I did. "Are you planning to shoot me?" I asked.

She frowned in concentration, pondering over the answer. She wasn't actually pointing the thing at me, I noticed. I wondered if I could get a good kicking place on the wall behind me and dive right at her, maybe, with luck, knocking the gun out of her hand before she could shoot.

Then she said, sounding faintly surprised, "No, I can't actually do that, can I? I don't want to kill you, Barry. I don't want to kill anybody—

or even help anybody kill anybody—especially a *lot* of people I've never even met. . . ."

That was when the penny dropped, and it all began to come together in my mind.

What Tscharka was planning to do, at least in general outline, was all there for me to see. Although I'd been slow to put things together, I could see that all the ingredients were there:

1. The basic dogma of the Millenarist faith.
2. Large quantities of available antimatter.
3. Setting a new course on the ship's automatic navigation controls.

When you added them up, they could only mean one thing.

"Shit, Jillen," I said, "is Tscharka crazy enough to be planning to blow something up?"

She nodded, her brow puckering in surprise that I had taken so long to figure it all out. "Of course he is, Barry. He's going to rescue the planet Earth from its sin."

I still don't know at what point Tscharka and Friar Tuck made the actual decision for genocide. Did it happen when he had ordered all that antimatter? After I had had that little talk with Tuchman about what that much antimatter could do to a planet? It could have been anytime. Tscharka could have had a dozen different plans and changed them as he went along.

I suppose I never will know all the answers, now. But I understood the important parts. Tscharka had not been willing to let himself be defeated. If the colonists on Pava were not unanimous in repentance for their original sin, maybe the next-best thing was to put an end to the world where original sin was born.

It was, of course, in his view, a kindness.

I could hardly make myself put the question into words, but I did it. "Is that what Tscharka and Tuchman want to do, wipe out life on Earth?"

She nodded slowly, as though admitting it to herself for the first time. "That's right. Oh, Barry, you wouldn't believe how happy they were when they told me about it! I guess it was what they call religious ecstasy. Bringing the Millennium to Earth—well, the next-best thing, anyway—it solved everything, they said. So he reprogrammed the navigational computer for automatic return, and when it got back it would be programmed to crash into the planet. Earth, I mean. With all those pods of antimatter aboard.'' She shook her head mournfully. ''To save all those people from the sin of being alive past the Judgment Day, you see,'' she explained.

I didn't say anything. I patted her shoulder some more, while I thought.

Would that kind of explosion really have wiped out life on Earth?

In spite of everything I'd said to Tuchman, I don't really know the answer to that. There's a hell of a lot of energy in two hundred pods of antimatter. As a minimum that would have produced, I guess, a megablast like no human being had ever seen, probably not far from the magnitude of that sixty-five-million-years-ago accident when something from out of the sky crashed into the Yucatan Peninsula—and that one did, it seems, at least kill off the dinosaurs. And, of course, with Earth gone, the habitats and the colonies would not live much longer. When the long list of things they continually needed to import from Earth ran out they would simply sooner or later die on the vine.

What I finally decided was that the exact numbers didn't really matter. The blast might or might not have killed everybody, but at a minimum it surely would have brought quite a few hundred million living sinners to a rapid state of deceased grace.

''Well,'' I said, pushing myself away from her and stretching in midair, ''I guess I need to get involved, don't I?''

She was still holding the gun, so she could have said no. She almost did, I think. She stared at me wretchedly for a moment and then, wretchedly, she nodded at last. ''Just don't hurt Garold, please,'' she whispered.

Well, you know the rest of it.

Here again, you probably know a lot of it even better than I do, I suppose, because to tell the truth I was getting pretty ballistic around that time. I knew what I had to do. I even succeeded in doing it— somehow—but it's only by the grace of God (if any) that I didn't destroy *Corsair*, and maybe *Buccaneer* and the factory orbiter as well, and possibly even a big chunk of the nearest hemisphere of Pava, because

I was playing with pretty serious stuff. All those hundred pods of antimatter fuel could have gone up at once if I'd made the wrong move, and then Pava would have had a momentary new sun in low orbit overhead.

See, crazy or not, I know how to do my job as a fuelmaster. I was a lot less skilled as a ship's engineer, though, and, unfortunately it was engineering skills that were needed.

What I did was go down into the drive centrum. I made sure the ship's internal power source was purring along the way it was supposed to be—I knew enough not to deprive those pods of external power—but then I isolated the drive itself. Disabled the safety circuits, all nine of them. Overrode the bridge controls. Opened it up full.

Naturally, the entire drive blew itself clear of the ship, the whole thing, reaction block, thrust nozzles and all.

It made a wonderful great bang, and as it went off I was laughing to myself, tickled pink because old *Corsair* not only wasn't going to be a bomb that wiped out all life on Earth, it wasn't going anywhere at all, ever again.

And, naturally, Tscharka and Friar Tuck came hurtling as fast as they could through the passages to see what the hell was going on. They didn't see, though, because I was ready. I was waiting for them, crouched at the bend of a corridor, with a crowbar in my hand.

I didn't kill them. I just caught them from behind and knocked them spinning—wondering as I did if what I was doing to Captain Tscharka was really quite keeping the promise Jillen had asked me for.

After that it all gets very confused indeed.

I don't really remember tying them up and lugging them into the shuttle, though Jillen says I did. I don't remember the trip down to the surface. I don't remember *Buccaneer* arriving in orbit, though Jillen tells me we saw it flaring its great plume of exhaust mass on the way down.

I don't, in fact, remember anything much that was real, although I do, sort of, remember a hell of a lot that probably wasn't. I remember Geronimo putting his warm little arms around me and crying—that couldn't have been happening, really; I thought that even at the time because I knew the leps were still staying away from Freehold, but mostly because leps don't cry. I remember everybody crowding around me, except that the part about them being naked and dancing can't be true. I remember screaming in pain while Dr. Billygoat was agonizingly hacking my right arm off above the elbow (he says he did nothing more than give me a shot), and I remember wondering why he was being so mean to somebody who had just been doing the best he could all along.

I even remember my dear lost Alma bending over me and kissing me.

That, of course, was the craziest delusion yet. Even in my far-out loopy state I realized that it was impossible. There was no way that Alma could be bending over me there on Pava, because I knew perfectly well that Alma was still a dozen and a half long light-years away on the Moon.

Only, of course, Alma really was there, really kissing me, really whispering my name . . . because when *Buccaneer* reached low Pava orbit it arrived there with Alma in its freezer, coming after me to tell me that, no matter what, she wanted the two of us to spend the rest of our lives together. And that was the most wonderful thing of all.

26

IT is correct to state that we do have knowledge of most of these events, but many are still not well understood. For example, there is the question of Garoldtscharka. It is clear that he was a dangerously aberrant individual, and your action in rendering him unconscious and binding him appears to conform to established norms. But what happened subsequently? It is known that the procedure by which humans customarily deal with such persons is to confine them to a small place or even to put them to death. Yet neither was done in this case. Why was it not? Why did you leave Garoldtscharka unpunished?

Well, he wasn't really unpunished, you know, not in the long run. As to what happened when I got him back to Pava, all right, he wasn't actually put in jail, but both he and Tuchman were placed under what we call "house arrest."

Maybe you think that wasn't severe enough. A lot of the colonists would have agreed with you, as a matter of fact, but what else could we do? We didn't have much choice about that, did we? We didn't happen to have a real jail in Freehold to put him in.

There was a more important reason why we didn't do more than we did, too. That was that we human beings have *laws*, Merlin. Laws are the rules we run our society by. Under our laws we don't ever punish people until they've been *convicted* of a crime. We can't convict them until they have a trial, either. There was every intention of putting

Tscharka on some kind of trial, all right, but first we had to figure out how to do it.

Practically everybody on Pava had a suggestion about that. Captain Bennetton of the *Buccaneer*, the one who had brought Alma to Pava, wanted to take Tscharka back up aboard his ship and either try Tscharka there at a captain's court-martial—if you can imagine that!—or at least stick him in the freezer, take him back to Earth, and let them figure it out. Jimmy Queng and a number of other steadfast Millenarists—they weren't all steadfast anymore; there were a lot of waverers in the faith after people found out what Tscharka had been up to—anyway, those people wanted to convene an ecclesiastical court to try Tscharka and Tuchman as heretics who had subverted the teachings of the Penitential church. What surprised me there was that so many Millenarists or fellow travelers agreed with them, Jacky Schottke among them. Dr. Billygoat had a suggestion of his own, because all the research he'd done on my own case had got him interested in psychopharmacy and related subjects. He didn't think there was any reason for a legal trial, when Tscharka's actions could just as well be considered as a mere medical problem. What Billy thought was that it might be useful to give Tscharka an experimental dose of one of the pharmaceuticals he had considered giving me (but had too much sense ever to suggest). Or, if not that, then he offered to try a little lop job on Tscharka's prefrontal lobes.

You get the idea. There were plenty of plans. Probably the closest we had to a consensus was among the fairly large number of people who simply wanted to call a town meeting and declare it a trial, but even they couldn't agree on exactly how to run it. There just wasn't any real agreement. If you talked to any ten people in the colony, you'd wind up with eleven different opinions.

While everybody was talking it over, Tscharka stayed right in his house, with no one but Reverend Tuchman for company. It wasn't exactly a jail but—now I'm finally getting around to answering your question—being under "house arrest" meant that they weren't actually free, either. They were ordered to stay in the apartment. They did— well, except for the necessary trips to the outdoor toilet. People even brought their meals in to them. That was a nuisance, but a lot better than having them turn up sitting across the dinner table from you and spoiling your meal. Nobody guarded them. Why would anyone bother? After all (we thought), they didn't have anyplace to go.

* * *

I may have been the only human being on Pava who wasn't concerning himself much about what was going to happen to Garold Tscharka. I had other things to think about.

For one splendid and overwhelming thing, Alma was there, right by my side. The love I had thought I had lost forever was wonderfully restored to me.

But there was even more than that, because Alma hadn't come to Pava with empty hands. When she had found out what the bastard Rannulf Enderman had done she had seen at once what that meant for my little medical problems. So she planned ahead. When she had boarded *Buccaneer* she took along with her a freezerful of the stuff the doctors in the Lederman clinic had prescribed for me, along with the full protocol for using it.

Even a dentist-doctor like Billygoat could handle administering the materials. He was pleased out of his head when he got his hands on the stuff and could actually treat my condition with real success—but, believe me, he was not nearly as pleased as I.

The might-have-beens scared me, though. Since I had had no idea that Alma was on her way, I could easily have screwed things up—in many ways; by maybe settling for Theophan Sperlie, when I had seemed to have that chance, or, if I'd let myself get really desperate, even for Becky Khaim-Novello. Either of those unfortunate misalliances might easily have happened, and either one could have made a mess of my reunion with Alma—not to mention what even crazier things I might have done in my even crazier moments.

When I did finally hint to Alma things might have gone more easily for me if I'd known she was coming, she was indignant. "But I wrote you to say I was going to do all that—you mean you didn't get my messages?" Alma asked reproachfully. "I sent *three* of them. One was telling you I loved you and I was never going to talk to Rannulf again, then another telling you I was coming out with your medicine on the next ship—are you saying you didn't get *any* of them?"

"Nary a one." I thought back; the messages, at light speed, would have arrived years before *Corsair* got to Pava, so I wouldn't have been there to receive them. True. But still they should have been saved for me, somehow. Then I remembered about the dam breaking. "There was a lot of trouble with the electricity for a while; maybe they came when the power was out. But that's just two; what was the third message?''

She blushed, almost. At least she looked prettily shy. "I was just telling you all the different ways I loved you and missed you, and what I wished the two of us could have been doing. It was kind of embarrassing to send that one. I put in a lot of details—and, Barry, do you have any idea what all those messages *cost*?''

"Not really," I said, rolling over and putting my arms around her— we happened to be in bed at the time. "But I do have a different idea. Why don't you show me a couple of those things so we can try them out?''

It turned out she had been working up to pretty much the same idea, so we did it. We did it a lot, in fact, Jacky Schottke having been kind enough to move out so we had the apartment to ourselves. I had several months of abstinence to catch up on, after all, and so (I was glad to find out) did Alma.

Oh, I understand that sort of thing doesn't mean much to you. I know how you leps feel about making love. You don't even think about it until your sixth instar and then, I guess, you hardly think about anything else. I'm not knocking that. It's fine, for you. I like our way better.

I don't want you to think that Alma and I concentrated on sex with full sixth-instar devotion. It wasn't like that, exactly.

We couldn't actually be out and about much, though, because neither of us was in shape for it. I'd burned up a lot of reserves over the previous week or two. I needed a lot of rest and recuperation while the new medicines began to work their repair magic, and Alma had her own problems. She'd been living in the light-gravity environment of the Lederman community even longer than I had, and maybe hadn't been as meticulous as she might have been at keeping up her stress exercises. In Pava's Earthlike gravity her Moon-adapted muscles tired easily. That is, they did when she had to be up on her feet for very long at a time, I mean, though she hardly tired at all when she could be lying down. Fortunately.

Well, that's all purely personal stuff, I guess, and maybe not all that important in the larger scheme of things. Plenty was happening all around us. Bennetton's people had decanted most of their cargo of corpsicles, and nearly fifty new immigrants had arrived in Freehold— a little surprised, I think, to find out that their new careers involved hoeing and weeding and carrying large sacks of things from one place to another instead of the more sophisticated work they had intended. But there wasn't any choice about that, either. The work had to be done, because the leps were still absent.

I fretted about that a lot. I felt that it was my fault, in a way, because I'd had a chance to make my case to you, Merlin, and to the others in the nest, and I'd failed to convince you. Now that I was coherent I explained to everyone all over again that it was Becky Khaim-Novello's fault: that she'd actually *hit* a lep to try to make him do something he didn't want to do, and so you people had all decided to shun us. That didn't make Becky popular (and it certainly didn't make me popular with Becky, who glared spitefully at me every time we passed at the door of the apartment), but it didn't solve the problem, either.

I wished for Geronimo.

I wished a whole lot for Geronimo, and not just because I thought the two of us could talk things over and maybe find a way to heal things. I missed his friendly company. I was pretty sure he was out of his cocoon by then, and I felt, well, rebuffed that he hadn't at least made one quick visit to Freehold to see how I was doing. When both Alma and I were beginning to feel a little better, I made up my mind. "I'm going to go back to the nest," I told her.

She considered that. "But you don't even know where it is," she pointed out.

"I got there twice, I can get there again. Anyway, I can try. Maybe somebody will turn up again to show me the way." I was, of course, thinking of Geronimo. "Anyway, that's what I'm going to do, as soon as I'm up to the hiking."

She said loyally, "I think you should do whatever you think best, Barry, and—oh, *hell!*" she cried, clutching at me in shock. "What's that?"

I gave her a comforting hug, but I couldn't help grinning, because Alma had just felt her first real quake.

When I had told her what it was she managed a shaky smile back. It was safe enough to smile about, because the tremor was over almost as soon as it began. It wasn't a very big one, either—under a five—but it did knock some things off shelves. And it gave me a chance to show off for Alma some of the seismic expertise I had acquired from Theophan Sperlie.

So I played back about ten minutes' worth of Theophan's lectures for Alma. I told her about faults and displacements, and how they made the earth shake. I told her that the colonists hadn't been too smart about where they located their colony, and how I hoped that sometime soon they would get around to moving Freehold to a better place. I told her how the big quake that wrecked the hydropower dam had harmed a lot of leps, and how hard they'd taken that. I told her what Theophan had explained to me about the coupled faults, and what the fact that Pava had only one big continent meant to its seismic activity. I gave her the full benefit of my wisdom on the subject, and then I waited for questions.

She had one. "This Theophan Sperlie," she said thoughtfully, "is she that kind of middle-aged woman who lives with that phony artist?"

I wondered if somebody had said something to her, or if it was just her well-oiled intuition. I temporized. "Well, Marcus is a novelist, actually," I said. "Or anyway he says he is. Yes." I did not think it was a good idea to challenge the "middle-aged" part of what she had said.

"I see," Alma said, picking up a hairbrush from the floor where it had been thrown and putting it back on the dressing table. She kept on tidying up silently for a moment, then she nodded. "That makes sense," she said.

"Well, maybe he really can write a novel, I don't know—"

"No, that's not what I mean. I wasn't talking about Sperlie's artsy-fartsy boyfriend. I was thinking about what you were saying about coupled faults."

I backtracked over the conversation, trying to see what she was getting at. I failed. I said, "Oh?"

"What I mean is that this coupled-fault thing isn't just about geology, is it? One mistake somewhere can trigger a big mistake somewhere else, like Captain Tscharka and his idea of saving everybody by wiping them out. I've been thinking about that, too."

"About wiping people out?"

"About where Tscharka got that notion. Do you know what I think? I think they just read the Bible wrong."

"Well, I wouldn't doubt that. They did everything else wrong."

"Yes, but—" She had something on her mind, though I wasn't at all sure what. Then she said, "Maybe I ought to talk to him about it. It might make him feel better."

One of the things I'd loved about Alma was her kind heart, but it seemed to me she was pushing it a whole long way too far this time. "Why would you want to make that bastard feel better?"

She flushed and shook her head, but she was obstinate. "I'd like to just meet him, anyway."

That surprised me a little—it hadn't occurred to me that there was anybody on Pava who hadn't met Garold Tscharka. But of course Alma was one. She had hardly seen the man, except when he was being dragged off the shuttle and not really in a condition for introductions.

I didn't say anything to that, and she turned around to look at me. "Would you mind, Barry?"

"Mind what?"

"Would you mind if we went over to see him? I'd like it. After all, I don't often get to meet a would-be mass murderer who thinks he's going to be doing his victims a big favor. What say we volunteer to take him his dinner tonight?"

I wasn't likely to say no to anything Alma wanted right then, but I did have one small, shadowy little concern in the back of my mind.

I knew perfectly well that Alma wasn't a Millenarist anymore. I didn't for one moment believe that exposure to a couple of red-hots like Tscharka and Tuchman would make her backslide. All the same, it made me nervous, and when we knocked on their door I kept an eye on her.

Friar Tuck was the one who answered. "Ah," he said, amiable and at ease—there was nothing in his manner to suggest that he thought of himself as an accused criminal—"you've brought our dinner. Thank you. What have we got tonight?" And he took the tray of covered dishes from my hand as though that were the end of the conversation.

"Would you mind if we come in for a minute?" Alma asked.

He hadn't expected that. He didn't object, though. He just studied her for a moment before he spoke. "Of course," he said graciously then. "Garold is at his prayers, but he'll be out in a minute and I'm sure he'll be glad to see you." And I guess he was, because when Tscharka came out he gave us what looked like a genuine smile.

"Barry di Hoa," he said, shaking my hand before I thought to take it out of reach. "And you must be Alma Vendette. It's a pleasure to meet you, Alma." And he shook her hand, too. "Won't you sit down?" he invited.

We sat, Friar Tuck setting the food on their table, the two of them looking at us hospitably. "I understand you're going to get your way and poor old *Corsair*'s going to be raw materials for the factory now," Tscharka said, making small talk.

That was a pretty self-evident fact. With no drive system anymore, *Corsair* was no longer useful for anything else so the discussion had been foreclosed. I didn't have any useful comment to make, so I just shrugged. It was Alma who remembered her duties as a good guest who had arrived in someone's house at mealtime. "Why don't you eat before it gets cold?" she said, but Tscharka shook his head humorously.

"Getting cold won't hurt it, and we'd be glad to be sociable for a bit. We don't have much company."

I cleared my throat. "I hope I didn't, ah, hurt you two. Too much, I mean."

Tscharka was politely deprecatory. "We're fine, di Hoa. I had a few stitches. Tuck didn't even need that much; he has a harder head than mine, I guess. But it's all right. You did what you thought you had to do. It's over with. If I could have completed my plan— But God did not allow it. I've been praying for forgiveness—for all of us."

"Alma thinks you were all wrong in your theology, anyway," I mentioned.

That got me a glare from Alma, and worse than that from Captain Tscharka. His face froze over. He turned those deep, dark eyes on me and then on her—not angry, just icy cold.

"It's really none of my business," Alma said, trying to chicken out. He wouldn't let her. He kept that stare on her until she went on.

"Oh, I don't mean about your religious beliefs, exactly, Captain Tscharka. Everybody has the right to believe whatever they like. Matter of fact, I was once a communicant in the Penitential church myself, you know."

"I did know," Friar Tuck put in, not reproachfully, just sadly.

"What I mean," Alma went on, "is I don't think you've read the scriptures properly."

Tscharka actually smiled at that—imagine, someone telling him he'd misunderstood his faith. Friar Tuck was less amused. He said sternly, "They are the word of God, Miss Vendette. We know what they say."

"Really? Well, I don't suppose I've read the Bible as closely as you two, but I do remember some of the verses. Like, 'For God so loved the world that he gave his only begotten son.' That verse, and a lot of others.''

"Yes?"

Alma said, "See, those same two words turn up over and over again: 'the world.' ''

"I don't think I follow you."

"It's always *the world*, Captain Tscharka. That means the world that we call the Earth, the one where Christ was crucified on Calgary. That isn't this world. It's that other one back there."

They were both looking at her with full attention now, two gazes so intent that they almost burned. Slightly flustered, Alma said, "But, you see, this world has never had that visitation from the Savior, has it? That thousand-year clock that was supposed to go from the advent to the second coming—it just never started ticking here on Pava."

She stopped to see if they would want to say anything. They didn't. They just sat there, staring laserlike at her. I began to feel tense. These were not the kind of fanatics that I wanted to set off, and they were both big, powerful men.

"All right," Alma went on, being reasonable, "I accept that you think it's a sin to be alive on Earth—I don't accept what you wanted to do about it, of course, but as you say, that's over. But the thing is, that's a different world. You're not on Earth now. There's no sin in being alive on *this* planet, is there?"

There was even more silence then. A lot of it. Especially from me. Alma had surprised me more than once, but never more than she did that time.

Finally Friar Tuck stirred. He glanced at the captain, who had not moved a muscle, and then said, "You're a kind young woman, Miss Vendette. We appreciate the fact that you're trying to give us comfort, don't we, Garold?"

And Tscharka, who had been gazing into space with that rapt, thousand-kilometer stare I'd seen on him before, shook himself. "Yes," he said. "Of course. Thank you. You're very thoughtful, but now maybe we'd better get to that food while it's edible at all."

It was as polite an invitation to get lost as I'd ever had, so we did it.

And, outside, Alma saw the expression on my face and smiled. "I haven't gone back to the Millenarists, Barry, honest. You don't have to worry. It's just that I've been thinking about those two sad, sick people a lot. Trying to figure out why they did what they did. And I remembered all the Millenarist sermons I'd listened to, and then I had this idea."

"And you thought that might make them feel better."

"They're still human beings, hon, and they're hurting. Do you blame me?"

"No," I said—truthfully, because I didn't. Not then.

27

*T*HIS *is the sort of thing that is most troubling to us, Barrydihoa.*

Oh, hell, Merlin, I wish you wouldn't keep interrupting. I was just getting up to speed for the dash to the finish line, and now you've made me break stride. All right; what's the troubling part, then?

You wish us to accept your view that you human persons are rational beings. That becomes even more difficult when you admit to us that all these nonrational traits exist. For example, how can you reconcile the human concept of "religion" with rationality?

Please, Merlin. Don't talk about things you don't know anything about. You may not understand why religion is important to most human beings, but it is. They need their religions. At least some of them do. The principal reason is that religion is comforting to them, I suppose, but it's more than that. It's their way of organizing a code of proper behavior.

It is not a rational way.

Oh, hell, what do you know about it? You don't understand what makes human beings tick in the first place. One of the most important human traits is that we want to *know* things. We're inquisitive. We want to learn everything there is to learn about everything there is.

When you keep that in mind you'll see that religious beliefs are not entirely irrational even by your own standards—well, I think so, anyway. As much as I understand what your standards are. At least, their beliefs didn't necessarily start out that way.

When religions first began they were actually more or less scientific attempts to explain the world. Those primitive people weren't stupid, Merlin. They were ignorant, yes, but they had brains. They wondered about things. They thought, quite reasonably, that there must be some reason for such phenomena as droughts and pestilences and violent storms—for all the things that threatened their lives, or even for the ones that benefited them. They wanted to understand them better, and so they formed a scientific theory to explain them.

The theory they developed was that there were supernatural beings living in every rock and river and tree, making these things happen.

All right, we know better now—about most of those things, anyway. Still, when you consider the state of human knowledge at that time, that wasn't an indefensible theory. It turned out to be wrong, sure. I'll grant you that, but so do a lot of scientific theories.

And, you know, there's still a lot out there that we don't know. We don't know exactly how the universe was born. We certainly don't know why. We don't even know if there is a why. There are a good many very logical and sensible people who still believe that there must have been some kind of god, sometime, that somehow started the whole thing going at the very beginning of time, and who's to say they're crazy?

I know none of this means much to you, because you've never troubled yourself with any of those deep questions about things like Ultimate Causes—but don't kid yourself. That doesn't make you better than we are. The way I look at it, it makes you just a little bit worse.

L et me get back to the story—we're coming pretty close to the end.

Alma and I didn't stay housebound any longer than we had to. There was work to do and we were needed. Everybody was; so we reported for duty.

The person we reported to was Byram Tanner. Jimmy Queng wasn't handing out work assignments anymore, because he had been discreetly relieved of his straw-boss job. No one actually blamed him for what Tscharka and Tuchman had done, exactly, but Jimmy had been really close to them. So now Byram was the general work coordinator.

Neither Alma nor I was quite up to a whole lot of heavy lifting yet, but Byram found us work within our capabilities; he put us to driving the big-wheeled cars down to the farm plots to pick up what was being harvested. Some of the crops were dead ripe and the pickers got to them just barely in time. That was part of our general lepless labor shortage; if the new help from *Buccaneer* hadn't arrived when it did, a lot wouldn't have been worth picking. Driving the cars there and back wasn't hard work, and we were content to go right on doing it indefinitely. Alma liked it because she got to see something of the countryside. I liked it because Alma liked it, but also for another reason.

I kept being hopeful that somehow Geronimo might show up somewhere along the way.

I didn't have any convincing evidence, but I was still optimistic enough to think it was possible that maybe, just maybe, Geronimo would have finished his phase change and just might be lurking around somewhere in my vicinity. Not willing to go so far as to pursue me into town, no. But with enough of our friendship left to—perhaps—want to get a look to see how I was doing.

I began carrying hard candies in my pockets again. I even formed the habit, when we were away from the town, of strolling off into the brush and leaving a few candies here and there, to show Geronimo—if he really was anywhere around—that I was still thinking of him.

That wasn't the total of my ambitions. Sooner or later, I was firmly determined, I would get back to the lep nest somehow and try to straighten things out, but not right then. It would have to wait awhile, because physically I still wasn't quite up to it . . . and the other people in Freehold just weren't interested.

That was a symptom of injured pride, I think.

Everybody in Freehold missed our lep helpers, sure. Nobody would have denied that. But with the new blood from *Buccaneer*, and especially now that it seemed to have been firmly decided that, yes, we would go ahead with the plan to reenergize the factory orbiter, morale in the colony was surging higher every day. People even began talking about that other scheme, of moving Freehold to some more hospitable spot on Pava, where we wouldn't have those damned earthquakes bothering us all the time.

Do you understand what I mean by "morale"? I don't know if leps have anything of that sort, but it's a fact that human beings can do wonders when they see a chance of something really good coming out of it. People were even *smiling* again.

I guess the whole colony had been through a kind of shock therapy. They say that in the old days, when some machine just obstinately refused to work, the old-timers would sometimes try a simple cure.

They would haul back and give their recalcitrant sump pump or lawn mower or Model T a good, hard kick. As often as not that would jolt the thing into working again.

I think that might be a true story. I even think something like that began happening with the Pava colony, after the shock of seeing Tscharka and Tuchman come so scarily close to genocide. There was hope again. Maybe the best news came from the factory orbiter, because about the first thing Captain Bennetton did when *Buccaneer* was in parking orbit was to send a party over to check it out, and, yes, they reported that the antimatter power systems were intact.

Well, I'd wanted to do that myself, but the important thing was that it had been done. We were in business as soon as the transfers could be arranged, and the signs were visible. Overhead in the evenings, when the light from Delta Pavonis struck them just right, we could see the glints of reflection from dead *Corsair* and its shepherd, *Buccaneer*, high in the sky as Captain Bennetton slowly towed the old ship toward the factory and its destiny as scrap.

I haven't said much about Captain Vernon Bennetton of the interstellar ship *Buccaneer*, but he was a good man. Alma assured me of that, because she owed him: He'd immediately made a place for her in his deep-freeze as soon as she told him her story. So I owed him, too.

When, one day at supper, he sat down across from us and said, "Mind if I join you?"—well, Alma almost reached over and kissed him.

After we'd shaken hands, I said, "I thought you'd be busy jockeying *Corsair* into position."

"I am—I mean we are. I'll go back up for the docking, but the ship's in good hands for now. I left Jillen Iglesias and my number two, Martine Grossman, in charge. They're both fully qualified, and I wanted to come down to talk to you."

"Ah," I said. "About Jillen, you mean." I had been wondering when her name would come up.

"Well, partly about Jillen. You know she's in *Buccaneer* now—"

"Yes." Everybody knew that. Jillen hadn't come out of the business entirely unscarred. There were a lot of people in Freehold who had wanted her locked up with Tscharka and the reverend, and when Bennetton mentioned he could use another hand on *Buccaneer* she'd jumped at the chance to get out of everybody's way.

"Well, Jillen's decided she doesn't want to stay here. She wants to go back with me and raise her baby on Earth."

"Probably that would be the best thing," I agreed.

"For her, yes. What's the best thing for the colony? You people are going to need pilots."

"For transshipping the fuel to the factory?"

Captain Bennetton shook his head. "After that. For the short-haul spaceship. It'll be a sort of a combination of explorer, and asteroid-spotter, and tug. They'll be using it to mine the asteroid belt, after the metals from salvaging *Corsair* run out."

I stared at him. "When did the colony decide to build that?"

"Well, they haven't yet, because they haven't had a meeting, but they will. It's the only thing that makes sense. The only problem is that Martine doesn't really want to stay here, either." He cleared his throat, studying me appraisingly, and added, "I understand you used to be a spotter-ship pilot in the Belt."

"Well, hell," I said, surprised that he'd even bother to ask, "of course I'll—"

Then I stopped, looking at Alma.

Staying on in Freehold wasn't entirely my decision to make anymore, I thought. I was remembering what life in the Belt had been like: getting into the suit, living in it for weeks at a time, all by yourself. That kind of existence tended to get lonesome, even there.

Here around Delta Pavonis it would be even more so. When I went out it wouldn't be for just a matter of weeks. Delta Pavonis's Belt wouldn't have any central smelter station to return to after a spotter flight, with all the (actually, fairly spartan) comforts the central station could provide. The only base for operations would be Pava itself, and if I were that ship's pilot I would be gone for months at a time.

Gone, that is to say, from the company of my lost and unbelievably restored love.

I thought about what that would mean. I would miss Alma, there was no doubt of that. Of course, missing her for a short period—even a period of months—would be a good deal easier to take than the kind of missing her that had been dampening my mood for all the months when I thought I'd never see her again.

On the other hand, how would Alma feel about that?

I felt Alma's hand closing over mine, as though she were thinking the same thoughts in parallel. Probably she was. I sighed. "Can I think it over?" I asked.

Bennetton grinned at me—he was in no doubt which way I would decide, I could see that. "Take all the time you like," he said generously, "only if you decide to do it you probably ought to get in some practice now. Take a few turns as copilot, with me or Jillen, or Martine Grossman."

I'd met Martine, Bennetton's second-in-command; she was a sharp, middle-aged lady who seemed to know what she was doing. "That makes sense," I agreed, carefully staying on the safe side of an outright promise.

"And we probably ought to try to train one or two other pilots while we're here. The way the designs look, the tug would take a crew of two, anyway."

"Ah," I said stupidly, "oh. Right." For I had been thinking in terms of the way it had been in the Belt, and the thought of a two-person spacecraft had never occurred to me.

Alma began to laugh. "Damn you, Vernon," she said, "why didn't you say that in the first place? I think I'd make a fine copilot. I volunteer. We both do."

Well, Merlin, I guess we're coming pretty close to the end now, aren't we? I've said just about everything I can say. I hope it's enough. Now it's just a matter of filling in some of the details.

Like about the town meeting, for instance. I'm sure I should tell you about that, although, speaking for myself personally, what happened at the meeting wasn't as important as what happened on the way to it. That's when Alma stopped me on the way there and looked up into my face and said, "Am I taking too much for granted, Barry?"

"Like what?"

"Well . . ." She looked a little uncomfortable. "I sort of jumped in for both of us. We haven't really talked much about plans for the future, have we? And if you wanted to back out or anything—"

"Not a bit of it," I said immediately and took a deep breath. Then it all came out at once: "I love you, Alma. I've loved you for a long time. I've been afraid to say it, but what I want to do is get married. Soon as we can. Here."

It was astonishing how easy the impossible turned out to be, once I'd made up my mind to say it. Alma didn't hesitate. She said crossly, "Well, what the hell took you so long? I accept your proposal!"

I held up my hand. "It's not that easy. I don't want to be unfair to you, Alma. What about children?"

"What about them? We'll have them." She let me hang there for a minute, before she added, "Did you forget that I've studied up on the subject? And then before I left the Moon I spent a lot of time with Helga—you remember Helga? Your doctor at Lederman? Well, she explained what we'll have to do all over again. She gave me all the datafiles and I've already turned them over to Dr. Goethe. I know," she said, "you're not too crazy about him, but all the procedures are in the files. Anybody could follow them. He says it's no problem. We can have all the babies we want, and we can be sure they won't inherit any nasties. So all we need to do," she finished, "is set a date for the wedding."

I said, "How about tonight?"

"Tonight's good," she said. "Right after the town meeting would be fine. Now, who do we get to do the job for us?"

So we had a word with Byram Tanner before the meeting began—neither of us wanted a religious ceremony, and he was just about Freehold's chief magistrate. There was no problem there. "I would be pleased and honored to perform the ceremony," he said agreeably, "especially if I get to kiss the bride. We'll do it right after the meeting, so let's get started—"

But there was a little delay there. Before Byram could call the meeting to order Jacky Schottke came fluttering up, waving his hands at us. He had news. "I just brought dinner over for Tscharka and Tuchman, and they weren't there. They've gone AWOL!"

Byram swore.

"But where in the world could they go?" Alma asked.

"That's just it," Jacky cried. "There isn't anywhere. They can probably stay alive wherever they are, I guess—there's food to be found in the woods, and if they went far enough away they could probably find leps who never heard of them, and maybe the leps would help. But they're definitely gone."

Byram thought fast. "The hell with them," he decided. "There's nothing they can do but disappear or die, and either way we're well rid of them. Let's get on with the meeting."

When he announced that the two had broken their house arrest, there were groans and catcalls from the audience, but as there was nothing to be done no one demanded we do anything. Then the meeting went really swiftly.

There wasn't really much to decide. Most of the questions had been voted on already: Recharge the factory with antimatter fuel from *Corsair* and *Buccaneer*, use what was left of *Corsair* for feedstock, start building a space tug to check out the asteroids. A few people raised objections—mostly on the grounds that we really shouldn't be making long-range plans, since we had no guarantee that Earth would continue funding us—but they were howled down by the majority, and then Captain Bennetton got up and settled it.

"Don't worry about the Budget Congress," he said. "They'll give you whatever you need."

Dabney Albright called sourly, "That's easy to say, but they never have."

"That was then," Bennetton said. "This is now. Things have changed. Barry here saved all their lives, remember, so they owe you now—they don't know that they do yet, but I give you my word they will. I'll tell them. And, trust me, I'll make sure they listen."

After that it was just a matter of voting, and then it was time for Alma and me to do our thing.

It was a nice wedding. Captain Bennetton gave the bride away. Jacky Schottke was my best man, and Madeleine Hartly's great-granddaughter stood up for Alma as maid of honor, and most of the colony joined in the extemporaneous party that formed around us afterward. The only thing we left out was going on a honeymoon. There wasn't really anyplace for honeymooners to go, and besides we'd pretty much had it already.

So the next morning Alma and I went back to hauling crops from the farm plots. Everything was just the way it had been before, except that now we were married. I think I was grinning a lot, all day long.

And at the end of the day Alma and I checked the place where I'd left a couple of hard candies.

The candies were gone.

There was no doubt in my mind about that. I'd left them in plain sight on the stump of a storm-killed tree. Now the stump was bare.

Of course, that didn't prove that Geronimo had been there. It was perfectly possible, I told myself, that some other creature with a sweet tooth had come by—

"Ugh," Alma said. "What's that thing?"

She was pointing to the ground at the base of the stump, and what she was pointing at was the crumpled corpse of a small flying rat.

* * *

That was enough for me. There was only one person on Pava who would have left that particular token for me.

I climbed up on the narrow stump and peered around. There wasn't any sign of Geronimo, but then I hadn't really expected there would be. I funneled my hands and called, "Geronimo?"

Alma stood quiet, watching; I didn't have to explain to her what was going on. I listened for an answer. There was no sound but the usual distant chirps and shrills, and an occasional unintelligible word coming up from the fields as one farm worker called to another. I tried again: "Geronimo, please talk to me."

Nothing but more nothing, but I was determined. I called, "Geronimo, I'm sure you're there. Come out, will you? I want you to meet my, uh, wife."

I stammered over that because it was almost the first time I'd said it. It felt good. And a moment later there was movement inside the hollow trunk of an old strangler tree, and a lep slid out. The colors were a little different than I remembered, and the shape was longer and slimmer, but I was in no doubt. This fourth-instar lep was Geronimo, all right.

He slid right up to Alma and raised his body to full elevation to study her. Then he said, "Hello, wife of Barrydihoa."

He was the first lep Alma had seen. I wondered for a moment if she would be able to understand what he was saying in that breathy, hissy lep voice, but she was equal to the challenge. "Hello, Geronimo," she said, unfazed. "I've been looking forward to meeting you." And she shook his tiny hand.

By then I had hopped down from the stump for my turn, but I wasn't willing to settle for a handshake. I caught him at full elevation, and I put my arms around him for a hug.

Hugging, of course, is not a lep custom. I took him by surprise. He made a little gaspy squawk and started to shrink away, but then he changed his mind. As best he could, with what his lep anatomy had provided him for arms, he actually hugged me back.

"I've missed you," I told him. "I wasn't sure I'd ever see you again."

"Yes," he said, and this time he did shrink back down. He even retreated a few steps.

I thought there might be more to come of that, but there wasn't. So

I went on: "I need to talk to you—all of you. Please? I know what Becky Khaim-Novello did. There's no excuse for it, but it shouldn't poison our relations forever. I'd like to try to straighten things out."

That didn't produce any reaction at all. Geronimo just rocked slowly back and forth, regarding me with those enormous eyes. I persevered. "You don't have to worry about Becky. She won't be here anymore. She's going back to Earth, and— Do you know who Captain Tscharka and Reverend Tuchman are?"

"The God persons. Yes."

"Well, they were just as bad as she— No. They were a hell of a lot worse than Becky ever was, but they're probably going to be sent away too. Matter of fact, they're hiding in the woods somewhere right now. So I'm asking for a favor. I'd like you to take me back to the lep nest so we can talk it over."

He rocked silently for a moment. Then, "You are human," he pointed out. "Humans have behaved in unacceptable ways."

"Not all of us!"

"Some are too many."

I couldn't argue with that. I just said, "Please, Geronimo. I'd like to try to see if we can work things out at least."

No answer to that. He just shrank back down a little farther, turned, and began to slide away. I called after him. "At least you and I can see each other now and then, can't we? Geronimo? Don't let them make you stop that."

He didn't answer that one, either. He just kept on squirming away for a couple more meters. Then he paused. "The two God persons are at the place of their retreat," he called, and was gone.

28

YOU surprise us once again, Barrydihoa. Is it possible you believed one of us would "forbid" another to do anything?

Indeed I did. Isn't that what happened?

Of course not. No one attempted to prevent Geronimo from seeing you. It is inconceivable that any one of us would ever try to prevent any other from returning to your community if he wished to.

All right, I take your word for it. We were wrong about that.

That's the whole point, isn't it? We don't understand everything about you, and you don't understand everything about us. That leaves us with one big question to answer, Merlin. Can't we try to get along anyway?

We're just about up to present time now, you know. I don't have much more to say. Then the rest is up to you—or, I guess I should say, to you-all.

At supper that night Alma and I reported that we thought we knew where our two absent felons were hiding out.

There wasn't any wild excitement over the news. No one really seemed to care. Dabney Albright cackled, "They can stay out there until they starve, far as I care," and somebody else offered, "I hope they do." But when I said that we'd heard it from Geronimo they perked up.

"I knew the leps would come around," somebody said smugly.

"Well, they haven't, really," I warned. "That was just one-on-one with my friend Geronimo. That doesn't mean they're coming back. They still don't trust us."

At the far end of the table Marcus Wendt, who hardly ever failed to talk when he should have been listening, stood up to get his own contribution into the discussion. He called, "The hell with them. Who cares who they trust? If the damn bugs are so temperamental that they're going to get their feelings hurt anytime anybody loses his temper a little we don't want them around anyway."

Theophan grabbed his elbow to pull him back to his seat. "Oh, shut up," she said, not in any kind tone. "You don't know anything about it."

Marcus looked confused. "But hell, Theo, look at the way they treated you—"

"That was stupid of them, right. They just made a mistake. This time is a whole different thing; Becky had no right to hit that lep."

Everybody else was talking, too, because everybody had an opinion, but I was paying particular attention to what was going on between Theophan and Marcus. It looked like there were strains in the relationship. I have to say that didn't displease me at all. I suspect I was smiling.

Alma was watching. "I think," she said, "that I'd like to go back to the apartment now."

She didn't put any particular stress on the words, but it seemed to me that it was a good idea to do what she said. I went. Whatever Alma had heard about me and Theophan I never did find out; maybe she just intuited that there might once have been a hint of something.

There was certainly no reason why Alma should have felt jealous of Theophan Sperlie. I surely didn't have any romantic interest in Theo anymore. The way things had worked out, I didn't in the least regret that Theo had picked Marcus Wendt over me . . . but I would be lying if I said I didn't take a little pleasure out of the thought that maybe sometimes Theo did.

You will remember what happened the next day, Merlin. Not the very first part of it, of course, but certainly the important parts—since you are the one who made that day important.

Before we got to those parts the day started out pretty nicely for us anyway. Martine Grossman had brought the shuttle back with another load of goodies from Earth, and Captain Bennetton caught us at breakfast. He had a smile for Alma and a suggestion for both of us. "How would you like to do a little pilot training today, Barry?" he asked.

"You mean you want me to fly the shuttle back to *Buccaneer*?"

"No, not that. They haven't finished unloading. Anyway, the shuttle's going to have to be refueled before it goes anywhere. What I thought was that Alma might like a dry run. Begin familiarizing herself with the controls, that sort of thing."

"Let's do it," Alma said with enthusiasm. So the three of us checked a car out, and, an hour later, Alma and I were sitting in the pilot seats of the shuttle and I was explaining the instruments to her. Bennetton hovered around for a few minutes, then announced that he and Martine were going back to town with the next load of goods from the shuttle. "I guess I can leave this part to you, Barry," he said. "See you later."

That suited me. I was pretty sure that when it came time for Alma actually to fly the thing it would be Bennetton in the seat next to her instead of me, but I was glad enough to be the one who started her out.

As I've said before of my dear Alma, she was a quick study. We didn't have power, so I couldn't activate the screens, but she learned what all the little keys were for quickly enough. I had her run through the drill half a dozen times: engine start, instrument check, main propulsion, side thrusters, landing gear up. Within an hour she was doing everything in the right order, at least. Of course, the real thing would be very different in a lot of ways. When we got up for a break we stood on the sill, catching breezes from upriver, and I tried to tell her what it was going to feel like at takeoff. That was harder than the dry run. Alma had been in shuttles before, of course—I'd taken her up to a ship in lunar orbit myself once or twice, in the old days. "It's a little different here," I said. "Pava's a lot bigger than the Moon, so it takes a lot more thrust to get into orbit. Your takeoff surge runs to three or four gees, sometimes more than that. That'll throw your reactions off if you're not ready for it. Then, the Moon doesn't have an atmosphere but Pava does. That means you have a problem with friction."

"Because it heats the shuttle up?"

"It does, yes, but the shuttle's capable of withstanding that. It isn't the heat you have to worry about. It's the turbulence. You'll be thumping and bumping in ways you never get around the Moon. You'll find out."

"Sure," she said vaguely, shading her eyes and peering out at the brush at the end of the strip. "Barry? Am I seeing things or is that your lep in the shade of those trees?"

It was. By the time we had trotted to the edge of the woods I was in no doubt. Geronimo was waiting there for us, all right. He wasn't alone. I thought I recognized the lep with him, a female fifth instar whom I'd occasionally seen around Freehold. Her human name was Semiramis.

Semiramis shook hands politely with Alma as I was getting right to the point with Geronimo. "What about it? Will Merlin talk to me now?"

He hissed reproachfully. "Some of us will talk to you, Barrydihoa."

"Not Merlin? But he's your leader—"

"I have told you before that we have no 'leader,' Barrydihoa, but Merlin will certainly be present. They are waiting. We should go."

The car we'd come down in was still there, parked right next to the stilty legs of the shuttle. I didn't ask anybody's permission. I took it, and the four of us, human and lep, went bouncing up along the riverside with Geronimo beside me to give directions.

In the seat behind us Alma was peering around in fascination. This was, after all, almost her first venture outside the well-traveled areas right around Freehold. For that matter it was her first experience ever, anywhere, of being out in a wilderness where there were no buildings or people or machines. It startled her. It didn't frighten her, though. She liked it.

I didn't have time for sightseeing. Besides doing the driving, I was trying to talk to Geronimo. With him so close beside me I noticed some of the changes that had come with his new development phase: He even had tiny little things like horns now over his great eyes, precursors of the feathery antennae that would be there later. He seemed less, well, childish, too: no requests for candy, though I had some in my pocket; no talk about games.

But in some respects he hadn't changed at all. When I asked him questions I got only highly selective answers. Yes, Merlin was willing to hear what I wanted to say, but it wouldn't be just him. Any lep who was interested would sit in; Merlin was in no sense a leader, only a lep like any other lep. Well, not exactly *only* that, Geronimo admitted. "Merlin is the person who has studied your people most carefully. It has been his main interest, since his injuries have prevented him from doing other things."

"I hope he isn't still sore about that," I offered.

Geronimo disregarded that. "For this reason," he went on, "it is Merlin who knows most about you people. It was he who taught me your language long ago, Barrydihoa. Here, we must cross the river now. Stop the car so the rest of us can get out."

Actually, I had already begun to slow down, because I recognized the ford Theo and I had taken. The crossing was no problem, though Alma and the leps got pretty wet. Then Geronimo took charge. There was a shorter way to the nests, he said, and as a matter of fact we made it in less than an hour.

I don't have to tell you about that meeting, do I, Merlin? You were there. In spite of all you people say, I still think you were the main participant, as a matter of fact. Of the dozen or so leps who were waiting for us in your nests, you were the one I saw first. Even Alma picked you out right away; I'd told her about your accident, and what it had done to your eye and your bad hand.

And you were the one who did most of the talking—as much as there was.

I had expected more. I don't mean I thought you'd welcome me with open arms, crying, "Yes, it was all a mistake, Barrydihoa, now the scales have fallen from our eyes and we will come back and be your friends forever." Actually, you were pretty hospitable, even as it was; several leps offered us food, and as we sat there two or three bright red, little second-instar infants were happily crawling over both Alma and me. What none of you offered was encouragement.

On the way up I'd rehearsed what I was going to say. You let me say it: I was sorry for what had happened, we were all sorry, we would take steps to see that nothing like it would happen again—

You did respond to that, though not in a promising way. You simply asked, "How can you be sure of that, Barrydihoa?" And I had to admit that I couldn't really *guarantee* it.

"All right," I admitted, "some of us do things we shouldn't. Even to each other, not just to you leps. Maybe especially to each other. But you have to understand that you people haven't exactly seen the best of us. The Pava colonists have had a pretty hard life—"

One of the other leps erected herself to interrupt with a question then. "The term 'hard life' is not understood," she pointed out. "Life is life. One eats and grows; that is all of it."

"Ah," I said triumphantly—it was the point I was coming to. "It isn't all of it for us. We want more than just to survive. We want to *do* things. If you understood us better you'd see that that's not a bad trait, because some of the things we do are pretty important."

Alma cut in then. "Not just 'important,' " she said. "A lot of things we do are really *good*. Barry says the colonists have actually helped you all already, by killing off predators and the like."

You were polite about that. "That is understood, Almavendettedihoa. You have also killed off some of our own people as well."

"Not as—" I think she had been going to say "Not as many," but she changed it in midstream. "Not on purpose!" she said.

You didn't answer that. You simply waited for me to go on. "So what I'd like to do," I said, "is open talks with you. Answer all your questions. Tell you everything you want to know. We can reason together, Merlin, and once we understand each other fully I'm confident we can get along."

Another lep—I didn't know his name—erected himself and shrilled, "Why do we wish to 'get along'? What is the purpose?"

I hadn't expected that kind of question. I said lamely, "Well, just because we're here, you know. It's better to be friends than not, isn't it?" Nobody responded to that one. I tried again, "Listen, there's one thing you have to be sure of. *We're staying.* The humans on Pava aren't going to fold their tents and go home. I'm sorry if you don't like the idea, but we're not going to go away."

"We can, however," the lep said. "There are many valleys, rivers and forests in other places."

I hadn't expected that, either. It had never occurred to me that you might simply move out because you didn't like what had happened to the neighborhood. I didn't have anything to say to it, but Alma did. "Please don't," she said. "Please. We'd like to be your friends."

There was a lot of talk about that—among yourselves—but not in English. Then you said, Merlin, "Is it correct to say that you believe that learning more about each other could make us all friends?"

"It's the best hope we've got," I said.

"And you wish to talk? At length? To answer all questions?"

"I do. Most of all I want to apologize for what happened to you—all of you—especially to— What was his name? Eric the Red? The one Becky hit?"

That produced a stirring and whistling among you, and you said, "That will not be possible. Ericthered has prematurely become dead."

"Oh, my God," I said. "So that was it."

I really hadn't known that. I guess nobody had. When they said Becky had "hit" the lep, I guess I was thinking of something like a slap, maybe at worst even a blow with a stick. That would have been bad enough, but it had happened before, once or twice anyway; it made a lot of trouble, but at least you hadn't all walked out.

I hadn't been aware that what she'd hit him with was the sharp blade of a shovel, and that he had then somehow managed to slither away into the woods, bleeding. No one had known that he had bled to death— well, no one but all of you. You could have said something, you know. Instead of just walking away the way you did.

Anyway, I mumbled, "I'm sorry. Really sorry."

"It is known that you are. Ericthered is nevertheless prematurely dead."

I clutched at straws. "Yes, but I know that somebody else killed a lep once; Madeleine Hartly told me what her brother-in-law did. And you forgave us for that."

"No. Not 'forgave,' Barrydihoa."

"But at least you got over it. . . ."

All the leps were clucking and cooing softly to each other by then, and I could see that you were getting impatient with me. You said, "No, we did not 'get over it,' Barrydihoa. A few of us chose to give you one more chance. Others did, too, later on; but no one has forgotten, and that second chance has been used up. Also there are other matters."

"I know there must be—"

"No, you do not know. There is more than you know about that is not understandable to us."

Naturally I asked what you were talking about, but you wouldn't listen anymore. Certainly you wouldn't let me ask any more questions. You hissed and twittered to Geronimo and Semiramis for a moment. Then you said:

"Go with them, Barrydihoa. See what they will show you. Then think how you can explain this. Then—perhaps—if you think it worthwhile, then you can come back and you will tell me all you think I should know."

And that was all you would say.

Neither Geronimo nor Semiramis would say a word to us after that. They simply stretch-slid ahead of us down the hill to the car. It was only when we were in it that Geronimo said, "You must turn upstream when we ford the river. I will show you where to go."

Then he buttoned up again too. It was a silent drive. Alma, in the seat beside me, had nothing to say, and the leps behind us were not even speaking to each other.

Then, a couple of kilometers up along the left bank of the river, I felt some movement from behind. Semiramis was leaning forward, her great head coming cheek-to-cheek with mine, her sweet, grassy breath in my face.

"Turn right," she ordered.

"Why?"

"Turn right! Go on that trail, it is not far."

She was a bossy one. I did as commanded but asked Geronimo, "Won't you tell me why we're doing this?"

"There is a reason," he said. He left it at that, and nobody said anything until Semiramis hissed in my ear again.

"Stop here."

I stopped. Before I could ask any questions Geronimo had slid out of the car, beckoning us to follow.

I looked around. "This doesn't look right. We're nowhere near Freehold, are we?"

"We are not."

"Well, look, Geronimo, they'll be worrying about us. I want to go back to town."

"We will take you there. Not yet. There is the thing you are to see first."

As usual, he wasn't interested in offering explanations. By then both leps had begun slithering away into the woods ahead of us. Alma looked at me. I looked at Alma. I shrugged. We followed.

After five minutes of hard climbing up a hillside, I began to notice things I had seen before. We were somewhere near the glen where the Millenarists had held their retreat, I was pretty sure of that . . . and then I realized I was hearing something, too.

It was a human voice.

It was distant, definitely a voice, but so hoarse and cracked, so low-pitched it hardly registered as belonging to any human being right away.

When we came around a clump of strangler trees there was Friar Tuck, knelt by the side of the trail, his head bowed. It was his voice we were hearing. He was praying aloud, and it seemed he had been doing so for a long time. He didn't bother to look up as we approached. And just beyond him—

"Oh, my sweet little Jesus," Alma whispered.

But Jesus had nothing to do with it, though the man we saw was crucified, all right. He was nailed to a big water tree. Tiny springlets of water—clear to begin with, then tinctured with threads of red blood turning pale as they mixed—were trickling from the places where his hands were pinned to branches and his feet spiked to the trunk. His head was dangling to one side, his eyes were open and unseeing, but the face above his drenched body was radiant.

It seemed the late Captain Garold Tscharka wouldn't have to face any kind of a trial after all. He had reached the state every good Millenarist longed for. He was well and truly dead.

29

*Y*OU *have said, quite properly, that there are ways in which humans
and leps do not understand each other. This is true. The incident of
Garoldtscharka is a case in point. No lep would ever kill himself. The
knowledge that humans sometimes do so—and do so in such terribly
painful ways, for purposes that cannot be understood—still fills us with
shock and repugnance.*

Is that a question, Merlin?

No.

Because if it is I have to say that I don't really share your feelings.

Oh, I think Tscharka's crucifixion was really shocking, too. If he
wanted to off himself there were certainly better ways—ways that would
have seemed better to me, anyway, though I suppose Tscharka had his
own ideas about that.

I worry a little about just what those ideas were, as a matter of fact.

But to tell the truth, I didn't give a hoot in hell about Tscharka killing
himself. If I'd known he was all that apeshit to get himself crucified, I
might have suggested other ways of doing it, but if that didn't go over
I probably would have been happy to supply him with the nails myself.
The only reason I sent Semiramis back to Freehold to get help was
because I thought people would be pleased to hear Tscharka was dead.

I'm sorry if that just makes you feel even worse about the human
race, but as I see it—in fact, as most of us see it—there are some people
who are just better off dead. That isn't for the sake of punishing them

for their crimes, at least not as far as I'm concerned. Not even because that's a good solution to the problem of crime anyway, because I totally agree it isn't. The only reason why that is acceptable at all is just because we have never been able to figure out any better way of dealing with them.

Now, does what I have just said raise a question?

No. There are no more questions, Barrydihoa. You have answered all the questions that have answers of a sort comprehensible to us— answered them in great and fatiguing detail, over this long time. There is nothing left.

Yeah, thanks, but that's not good enough, Merlin. I need to know what you intend. Does that mean you will or won't lift the boycott?

Ah, Barrydihoa, do you not even now see how puzzling this is? There is no "boycott." There has never been a "boycott." If all of our people chose to shun all of yours it was not because of a "law." It was simply because too many of your people had behaved in ways that filled us with horror and disgust. Now you have been heard, and each of us will decide for himself what to do. It appears that some will still prefer to shun you. Some will be willing to visit you, even work with you. Geronimo will certainly be one such. So, sometimes, will I. So will others among us, perhaps an increasing number as time passes. So, you see, your people will no longer be deprived of their laborers.

Ah, Merlin, let me just play your own words back to you: You don't see how puzzling this is to us, either, do you? You've just got the wrong idea about what I'm trying to do.

It isn't for slave labor that we want your friendship, you see. It never was, really—well, not entirely, anyway—and now least of all. We have more human people to do the work now than we did, and it looks as though before long we'll have a lot of new machines to do much of it for us. What we want from you is to be our friends. Or at least our reasonably amicable neighbors, on this planet that we will be sharing for a long time to come.

But I'm glad to hear what you have said. And I'm grateful to you— to all of you—for letting me come up here and try to explain it all. That was a good way to start. I hope we can keep on that same way.

I also hope this. Then there is nothing more that troubles you, Barrydihoa?

Well, no, I wouldn't say that.

There is one other worry in my mind. It's not about you, and it's certainly not an immediately urgent problem. It can't possibly make any real trouble for a good many years. But it does bother me quite a lot.

It's about *why* Tscharka had himself nailed to the wall, and about what Reverend Tuchman might do about it one day.

See, Tuchman isn't here anymore. When Captain Bennetton finally started his *Buccaneer* back to Earth, he had the Reverend Tuchman safely stowed away in his freezer.

It was the only thing that made sense. If Tuchman was going to have to face a murder charge—and there could be no doubt that he was certainly some kind of accomplice, because who else could have hammered the spikes into Garold Tscharka?—no Pavan wanted to have that trial here. No Pavan wanted Reverend Tuchman around at all anymore. We were all delighted to get rid of the sweet-talking old son of a bitch . . . but he had left some pretty hard questions behind.

I don't want you to think that I really believe in very much of this stuff. Whatever crazy notion Tscharka himself might have had, I don't believe for one minute that his self-inflicted crucifixion started that thousand-year clock ticking for Pava. Maybe he thought it would. Alma thinks he might have, and she's got a small guilty feeling that she might have put the idea in his head and thus led to his suicide. That doesn't make sense, though. That crucifixion doesn't even fit the scripture, does it?

Well, that's a rhetorical question, because you certainly wouldn't know whether it did or not, but actually, its circumstances aren't even close. Tscharka was a sort of martyr, okay, but he brought it on himself—I mean, Tuchman never could have nailed him up that way single-handed if Tscharka hadn't helped out. He certainly was no kind of a divine redeemer, except maybe in his own mind. I mean, nobody ever claimed that Garold Tscharka was the son of God, did they? And if Tscharka had ever had any revelations from on high, he had never mentioned them to me—or to anybody else, either, as far as anyone ever said. There was no Sermon on the Mount in Tscharka's résumé, no cleaning out the Temple, no miracles. No nothing that fit the biblical pattern of a savior and redeemer. You never heard of Captain Garold Tscharka raising anybody from the dead, did you? (Well, unless you count defrosting the stiffs in *Corsair*'s freezer. But I don't think even Friar Tuck could try to stretch it that much.)

The only thing is . . .

The only thing is, when you come to think of it, hardly anybody had ever heard any of those stories about Jesus himself during his lifetime.

Those stories—those scriptures—didn't get spread around until long after Jesus' death, when his disciples began roaming the world and writing all those epistles. Some of those stories didn't get told at all until long after the crucifixion, did they? Fifty years later, some of them. Maybe even later than that.

So I do have this question that lurks in the back of my mind.

It certainly isn't important right now. It probably couldn't matter to anyone until our grandchildren's time and maybe not even then.

But the feeling won't go away. I keep wondering about what will happen when, years and years from now and back on the faraway Moon, they finally defrost Friar Tuck.

He'll have a lot of legal questions to deal with, I'm pretty sure of that. But they'll take time, and while that time is passing he'll have opportunity to make his case. Whatever case he chooses to make. That's part of our constitutional guarantees, you see, and nobody would try to take that privilege away from him . . . and who can guess what kind of epistles Tuchman may be going to write then?

ABOUT THE AUTHOR

Frederik Pohl has been honored with both the Hugo and the Nebula awards for his science fiction, and he was just named Grand Master by the Science Fiction Writers of America. In his long and successful career, he has been the editor of award-winning magazines such as *Worlds of If* and *Galaxy*. His novels *Gateway* and *Man Plus* marked him as one of the all-time great SF writers. He and his wife, Elizabeth Ann Hull, live in Chicago, Illinois.